The Way It Was

By

Charles R. Castellaw

This book is my life story as I lived it. This project was much more difficult than I thought it would be, but with my wife, Betty Jo, support I was able to finish it

© 2003 by Charles R. Castellaw, All rights reserved.

No part of this book may be reproduced, stored in a retrieval system, or transmitted by any means, electronic, mechanical, photocopying, recording, or otherwise, without written permission from the author.

ISBN: 0-9748348-2-3 (e-book)
ISBN: 0-9748348-1-5 (Paperback)
ISBN: 0-9748348-0-7 (Dust Jacket)

Library of Congress Control Number: 20020096838

This book is printed on acid free paper.

Printed in the United States of America

Published by C C Publishing, 437 Crattie Drive, Springville. Tn 38256

Dedication

To the Infantry, the underdogs of World War II. They faced the rain, the mud, cold, frost, and snow. Their only protection and comfort was their foxhole. The sky was the roof over their heads. Their feet were their transportation, and their bedmate was their M-1 rifle. In front of them was only the enemy.

And

The political victims of the Great Depression.

iv

Acknowledgments

My warm and grateful thanks to Professor Squire Babcock, Murray State University, Department of English, for not only editing my manuscript but for giving me encouragement and instructions on how to write this book. I thank Quencey Harrington and Jason Bowen for their encouragement and suggestions. I thank Kathy Hillard for typing the manuscript.

To my wife and teenage sweetheart, I want to say thanks for not only encouragement and help but also for your permission to reveal our past and present relationship.

Charles R. Castellaw

vi

The Way It Was

Section 1

Today, November the 15th, the year 2000, I sit in my chair while my thoughts take me back through the past 77 years. Two very important events took place during this time span, the Great Depression of the thirties and World War ll. I want to tell my life story so younger generations can get a view of the life lived by my generation.

The Early Years

In a two-room farmhouse in the Holly Grove Community, Haywood County, Tennessee, with a warm breeze, half moon, and bright shining stars, May Rassmann Castellaw was about to have a baby. It was Tuesday the 28th day of May, 1923. Late that night, May, an 18-year-old mother of a 19-month-old son, Carl Jefferson Castellaw, woke up her 21-year-old husband, Robert Jefferson Castellaw, and said, "I am having labor pains, go get Dr. Hess, my sister Kate, and your mother Zula."

Robert dressed, saddled his horse and rode about one mile to Dr. Hess's house. Waking him, he said, "May is about to have the baby and needs you." He then rode to his mother's house and May's sister's house to give them the news. Zula and Kate both walked about a mile to May's house.

Dr. Hess dressed and jumped into his 1923 Model T Ford. About one hour after Robert, Kate, Zula and Dr. Hess arrived, I was born weighing less than seven pounds. I joined my 19-month-old brother, Carl Jefferson Castellaw, in the Robert and May Castellaw family. I was named Charles Ray Castellaw.

Justice of the Peace Mr. Thomas married Robert Jefferson Castellaw and May Rassmann on Sunday the 4th of July, 1920. Robert was eighteen, and May was fifteen. The young couple lived with his parents, Robert Edward and Zula Castellaw, until they built their own house. Their transportation for the wedding was a buggy pulled by Robert's horse, Dan.

Charles R. Castellaw

Robert And May Castellaws' Wedding Transportation

Robert was a fourth generation farmer. His forefather, James Castellaw, came to Bertie, North Carolina territory, from Scotland in the early 1700's. His grandfather migrated from North Carolina to Haywood County, Tennessee in 1834[1]. Robert dropped out of school after finishing the eighth grade. At the time of his marriage, he was working full time on his father's farm.

May's mother died from red measles seven days after giving birth to a son. May was only two years old at the time and was shifted from relative to relative. At the time of her marriage she was living with her sister Kate's family. I think the highest grade she completed in school was the seventh. May's grandfather, Christopher Ernest Rassmann, came to Ribald, Pennsylvania from Merzels, Germany, March 1852[2]. Her father, John Rassmann, was born December 31, 1859[3] at Ribald, Pennsylvania. A short time after Christopher was discharged from the Union Army, the family moved to Stewart County, Tennessee.

---

1 Family records
[2] Ibid
[3] Ibid

The Way It Was

Dr. Hess was a country doctor in the Holly Grove Community, starting his practice in 1910. At that time he rode a horse to make house calls, but later he used a horse and buggy. His first automobile was a 1923 Model T Ford. He carried a medical bag with him that contained the basic tools he used and the medicine he gave his patients. He also carried small candy pills that he gave the children when he made a house call to see Mom or Dad. Dr. Hess was one of those country doctors who believed that he was responsible for the medical needs of everyone in the community. He set broken bones, amputated crushed limbs, delivered babies and treated patients for all their medical problems. Sometimes he even pulled teeth. I know, because one time during a hot summer day, we were working in the fields and stopped for lunch. I had a severe toothache by the time we got to the house. Daddy took me to see Dr. Hess and after examining my tooth he said, "It's got to come out." Then he pulled it.

During those days health insurance did not exist in our community. Dr. Hess treated everyone. The ones that could paid him. The ones that could not pay received the same treatment as those who did. Some patients paid him in the fall with corn.

Dr. Hess dug a large lake on his farm by having patients work out their medical bill using their mules and pond scoops. My father paid our medical bill that way. This was done after the crops were laid by and the farmers had some free time. They worked a ten-hour day until they had paid their debt.

Dr. Hess's wife operated the Hess farm, while black sharecroppers worked it. It was standard practice for the landowner to furnish the sharecropper a house, a garden and sometimes a milk cow. The landowner furnished the land, mules and farming equipment. The income was divided 50-50. Mrs. Hess would ride her horse sidesaddle over the farm to supervise the operation.

Charles R. Castellaw

Holly Grove 2 Room Elementary School – Grades 1-8

Holly Grove Baptist Church (white)

The Way It Was

The Holly Grove Community is in the 5th Civil District of Haywood County, Tennessee. In 1920 the 5th Civil District had a population of 2371, 1339 blacks and 1032 whites[4]. It is estimated that 150 of the blacks were slaves before the Civil War, 61 were homeowners and 338 renters. The occupation breakdown for the 5th Civil District, including blacks and whites, among all residents was 536 farmers, 61 laborers, 1 medical doctor, 5 teachers, 2 merchants, 1 store clerk, 1 preacher-farmer, 5 timber cutters, 1 sawmill operator, 1 timber buyer, 3 blacksmith-machinists, 1 mail carrier, 3 house servants, 1 cotton ginner, and 1 insurance agent.

The Holly Grove Community had one white elementary school (grades 1-8) and one black elementary school (grades 1-8), as well as one black Baptist Church and one white Baptist Church. The white elementary school was built on land donated by my great-grandfather. His son, Robert, my grandfather, was expelled from school, and my great grandfather made a deal with the county school board that he would donate land for a new school building if the school board would permit Robert to return to school. The deal was made.

Robert And May Castellaw Build Their Home.

---

[4] U.S. Population Census 1920

Charles R. Castellaw

At the time of my birth my father and mother lived in a two-room house they built with Robert's father, Robert Edward Castellaw, known as Bob. They cut down trees on Bob's farm and hauled the logs to the sawmill to be sawed into lumber. They used this lumber to build their two-room house, outdoor toilet, chicken house, smokehouse, and a barn. The house was built with the main room to be used as both living room and bedroom. It was 16' x 16' with two doors. One door was installed in the front wall facing the dirt road and was used to enter the house from the front. The other door was used to enter the kitchen. The front room had two wooden windows. One window was in the front wall on the left side of the front door and one in the back wall. Each had two sashes with four glass panes in each sash. A fireplace was built in the center of the outside wall in the end of the room. Steps were built leading to the upstairs on the left of the fireplace. The kitchen was a 16' x 14' room built on the right side of the main room. A door entered into it from the main room and another in the back led to the back yard. It had one window in the outside wall and one in the front wall. The windows in the kitchen were made the same as those in the living room. The upstairs was one large unfinished room. With heat from the wood-burning cook stove, the fireplace heated the entire house.

The furniture in the main room consisted of two wooden beds, a small table with an oil lamp on it, a trunk for church-going clothes, four straight-back cane-bottom wooden chairs, and a wooden shipping box received from the local country store that was used to store everyday clothes. This box was kept under one of the beds and the trunk was placed at the foot. Each of the beds had a cotton mattress, a feather bed, two feather pillows, and one or two quilts depending on the time of the year. The quilts were family made. The feathers were from geese raised on the farm. The upstairs had one bed and was used for company. Along with the wood-burning cook stove, the kitchen was furnished with a wooden dining table with a bench on each side, all made by Father. An oil lamp sat in the center of the table. Wooden shelves on the wall were used for dishes and pans, and there was a small table with a water bucket and dipper on it near the cook stove.

In back of the house was an outdoor toilet with a one-hole seat and a Sears catalog for toilet paper. The chicken house had a roosting section for the chickens at night and a laying section with hen's nests

The Way It Was

made of wood and lined with straw for the hens to use to lay eggs. The smokehouse was used to cure out and store meat. The barn was used to store hay and corn and house livestock. The toilet and smokehouse had wooden floors. The chicken house and barn had dirt floors.

The structures of the house and outbuildings were made of rough sawmill lumber. 8" x 10" beams placed on white oak blocks were used for the foundation of the house and barn. Smaller beams were used for the other buildings. The frames of the buildings were made of 2 x 4's. The outside walls were made by placing wide boards vertically and using four-inch wide boards to cover the joints between the boards. The house was sealed inside using wide boards, the roofs were made of tin. Close to the smokehouse was a bored well used for water, drawn by using a long, round bucket with a rope and pulley.

When I was about two years old, my father took me out to the barn lot to talk to a neighbor. He was busy talking and not watching me. I walked up behind a mule named Bill and pulled his tail. Surprised, Bill kicked me. Contact was made just above my right eye, fracturing my skull. Daddy took me as fast as he could to Dr. Hess. The accident did not do any permanent damage, but left a dent in my skull.

One stormy night, when I was about three years old, lightening struck our house, and it burned down. My parents were able to save me, Carl, and a few things. We moved into another house on my grandfather's farm and lived there until the fall of that year. One day that fall, my parents cleaned the yard and burned the trash. That night, the wind blew some of the trash that still had fire in it against the house, setting it on fire and burning it down too. We all got out, but saved only a few things. We moved into an old log house that was built before the Civil War on a fifty-acre farm owned by my grandfather. My grandfather told my father that he could have the farm and transferred it to him in his will. He willed him lifetime rights to it and then it would go to his children. He wanted to be sure that Robert would have a home for the rest of his life. He could not sell it, and no one could take it from him.

This house was built with two large log rooms with a hall between them. Each log room had a large fireplace in the sidewall. A room

Charles R. Castellaw

was built across the back and divided into three rooms – kitchen, bedroom, and storage room that was used as a bedroom at times. Steps in the entrance room led upstairs. The upstairs was divided into three rooms, one over each of the large rooms and one over the entrance room. One of the large rooms downstairs was used for the family living and bedroom. It had two beds in it, one for my parents and one for Carl and me. The other large room and extra bedroom was usually used by one of Daddy's cousins.

When I was about four and a half years old, my Mama had a baby girl. She was named Zula Josephine after her two grandmothers. Carl and I were very proud of our new baby sister. She was nicknamed Zuline. We would ask Mama every day to put Zuline in the cradle so we could rock her. The day came when Mama put Zuline in the cradle. A short time after that Zuline started giving me a lot of problems. One that stands out in my mind is that Mama would put the baby in the cradle and make me rock her when she cried. I was about five years old and I would stand by the cradle and rock her until I got tired of standing. Then I would sit on the floor and rock her, but then she would cry. Mama would make me stand up so she could see me. The baby would laugh as if to say, "I will tell you what to do and Mama will make you do it."

On The Farm

On the farm, we raised cotton for cash income and at times we would sell cream. Corn and hay were raised for livestock feed. Corn was also used to make hominy and corn meal. We raised a large vegetable garden that we used for fresh vegetables and canning. We canned enough to last until the next garden year. We had apple, peach, pear, and cherry trees and picked blackberries from wild vines. Apples and potatoes were stored in the large room over our living room. The heat from the fireplace would keep them from freezing in cold weather. Fall apples would last through Christmas.

We raised chickens, ducks, geese, calves, goats, and hogs for meat and eggs. The geese were a source of feathers for feather beds and pillows. My Mama would make me hold the goose's head while she plucked the feathers. The goose did not enjoy this process, so if I let his head slip out of my hand he would bite Mama and me. If the

The Way It Was

goose bit Mama, I was in big trouble. At the age of five this was not a fun job.

We raised sorghum cane to be used in making molasses. Peanuts, popcorn, watermelons, and cantaloupes were raised to give us food other than what was considered essential. Broomcorn was raised to make brooms. Mama's work was never done, cooking, cleaning, making lye soap, etc. She cooked hominy in the wash pot using hardwood ashes to remove the husk from the grains of corn, washed clothes by first boiling them in the wash pot and then scrubbing them on the washboard.

One of my favorite black sharecropper families and our good friends were Murry and Tuggie Duckworth and daughter, Mable. They lived on our farm in a small house across the road from our house. Murry worked on the farm with us and Tuggie helped my Mama do the housework, cooking and other chores. They would work together gathering vegetables from the garden and preparing the noon meal. This was the big meal for the day. The white men ate first, then the black men. Mama and Tuggie would eat together last.

In those days, relationships between blacks and whites that lived and worked on the same farm, was like a big family, the land owner was the head of the family. Discipline was taught and enforced. When I was a young boy, if Tuggie told me to do something, I knew I had to do it.

I remember when I was very young and would not comb my hair, Tuggie would get on my case and make me comb it. After I got older and started combing my hair without been made to, Tuggie would say, "I know that you are looking at the girls because you are combing your hair."

9

Charles R. Castellaw

Charles Ray Castellaw At Holly Grove Elementary School.

At the age of six it came time for me to join my brother Carl at school and working in the fields. We walked about one mile carrying our lunch in a tin lunch box. We usually had a selection of the following – country ham and biscuits, fried potatoes, jelly and biscuits, sausage and biscuits, and fried dried fruit pies. It was a common practice to swap items during lunch. I would swap country ham and biscuits for bologna and crackers.

During the mid-thirties, through one of President Roosevelt's programs, a soup kitchen was started in school. We would have hot soup every day for lunch. During rabbit season (months with R in them) some of the boys would bring rabbits to school to be cooked in the soup. The boys would catch the rabbits in homemade traps. During the summer when school moms were canning vegetables, they canned some extra for the school soup kitchen.

Holly Grove Elementary School, grades 1-8, had no modern conveniences. It had two outdoor toilets, one for the boys and one for

The Way It Was

the girls. The boys' toilet was located in a low damp place that produced a strong odor most of the time and was a favorite target on Halloween night. The school was a two-room, two-teacher school. Two wood stoves heated it, one in each room. A well with a long metal bucket and a rope and pulley was used to draw drinking water from a bored well. The playground was divided into two parts, one for the boys and one for the girls, as boys and girls were not permitted to play together.

I was always small for my age. In country terms – I was a runt. During first grade, I fell in love with my teacher. I am sure one of the reasons was that she let me sit on her lap. My next love affair came when I was in the second grade. This love affair was serious until our teacher caught us with her arm around my neck. I was so embarrassed that I could not look at the girl; thus ended our love affair. My next adventure in love came several years later and was my first true love. I will tell this story later.

The classroom was furnished with a desk for each student facing the teacher's desk. Behind the teacher's desk was the recitation bench and the blackboards were on the wall. The teacher would call the class and we would go to the recitation bench and reply orally to questions asked by the teacher.

All teachers enforced a strict discipline policy. Punishment was being hit with a switch, standing in the corner, standing on one foot with your nose in a circle on the blackboard, writing off, and other things that the teacher would come up with. What seemed to be a favorite with some teachers was to have the boy go out and cut the switch that would be used on him. The switch had to meet certain specifications.

During the school year we had two special events – Valentine's Day and Christmas. We would have a Valentine party and exchange Valentines, most of which were recycled from the year before. We would erase the name on the card and write a different name on it. Our teacher would give each student a Valentine card. At Christmas we would have a Christmas party with a live Christmas tree. Three or four boys would be selected to get a cedar tree to be used for a Christmas tree. This was a big honor and the year I was selected, I felt like I had grown a foot. The Christmas program included singing Christmas carols, telling Christmas stories, and exchanging gifts. The

Charles R. Castellaw

teacher gave each student a gift. This was the only gift received by most of the students.

Christmas at home was a very enjoyable event, which we started talking about and planning for right after Thanksgiving. We would have a live cedar tree decorated with strings of popcorn, holly balls, and paper decorations. Each of us would receive a toy, candy, nuts, one orange and a banana.

In the fall, school would let out for about four weeks for cotton picking. Children were an important source of labor on the farm. This was my favorite time of the year because we had some cotton money to spend. When we caught up picking our own cotton, Daddy would let us pick cotton for a neighbor and keep the money. We bought clothes with most of our earnings but could spend some of it as we chose. A pocketknife was my favorite purchase. The income from each bale of cotton came in two checks; a seed check which was very small and a cotton check which was not very large either. The seed check money was used for recreation and store-bought food such as bologna. The cotton check money was used to pay debts and buy essentials for the farm and family.

During first and second grade I had a problem learning to read. We had no reading material in our house except our schoolbooks, and I received no help at home. My Mama had received a very limited elementary education and probably thought that I was doing okay in school. Carl was a very fast learner and did not need extra help. I was required to repeat the second grade. It was hard for me to see my classmates move on to the third grade while I stayed behind.

One summer I got sick with a fever and had a rose-colored rash on my body. Dr. Hess was also sick so Daddy took me to Bells, Tennessee to see Dr. McDonald. He diagnosed my problem as typhoid fever and gave me medication that had to be taken every three hours around the clock. Daddy paid him that fall with corn.

During seventh or eighth grade, I cannot remember which, my teacher, Cousin Grace, said that we needed a table for our water bucket. I said, "If I had some boards I could make us a table for the water bucket." She gave me permission to go across the road to her father's, Tom Castellaw's, barn and look for some boards to make the table. I found some old used boards and made a table that was used until the school was closed by consolidation in 1943. When the school was closed the table was given to my mama. I still have the table today.

Classroom water bucket table made by Charles Ray Castellaw

During our elementary school days my Daddy traded for a Shetland pony named Betty. He and his cousin's husband, Jack Stewart, made us a pony cart and painted it bright red. The pony and cart gave us social status with the other boys and girls in the community. I was able to teach Betty a few tricks and she learned some on her own, one of which was unlatching the stable door and letting out the other horses. My favorite trick for her to do was math. She could add, subtract, multiply, and divide. For her to do math I would put one hand on her neck, and when she added two and three, I would signal with my hand to start pawing. After the fifth paw I would move my hand and she would stop.

We had a good cotton crop in the fall of 1929. Daddy was able to pay off his note for money borrowed for the 1929 crop year. I believe the amount borrowed from the Bank of Crockett in Bells, Tennessee, was one hundred dollars. He used most of the remaining money to buy a new 1929 Model A Ford car, his first car at the age of twenty-seven. The family transportation had greatly improved from a horse and buggy to a new car. We were very proud of the new car and it gave us a feeling of self-respect and social standing in the Holly Grove Community.

Charles R. Castellaw

Hard Times

The Great Depression hit us hard. The demand for farm crops and livestock greatly decreased and the bottom fell out of farm crop and livestock prices. We were lucky due to the fact that we raised our own food. We bought coffee, sugar, salt, block pepper and flour. Coffee cost fifteen cents per pound or two pounds for twenty-five cents. We also bought kerosene oil for the oil lamps. In fall, after Daddy sold our cotton crop, he would buy Carl and me two pair of overalls, one jumper, and one pair of shoes each. They had to last until the next cotton crop was harvested and sold. By the following fall our overalls were patched in the seat and knees. The jumpers would have patches on the elbows. Some of our clothes were homemade. I remember one time my grandmother made me two shirts. The shirts had three buttons down the front and were closed the rest of the way down the front. I did not want to wear the shirts because I thought they looked like girl clothes, but Mama made me wear them anyway. It was said that if a girl bent over you could see "self-rising flour" printed on her drawers. Flour came in bright colored cotton sacks made from printed material. This material was used to make clothes. Fertilizer sacks were also used to make clothes.

The yard of the log house we lived in had two walnut trees, two cedar trees, and one large oak tree. The house was on large wooden beams placed on white oak blocks with the space under the house open. The dog and barnyard fowls slept under the house. The chickens and other fowls ate the crumbs that fell through the cracks in the kitchen floor. At times some of the hens would lay eggs under the house, and I would crawl under the house and collect the eggs.

Our house was on a hill, but on one side of the hill was Mud Creek Canal, a canal dug to drain the bottomland during heavy rains. In late summer and early fall the water would rise and flood the bottomland. At times you could see the tassel of the corn just above the water. Once the willows had grown up so thick on the banks and in the canal that they interfered with drainage. President Roosevelt's work project Administration (WPA) was used to cut the willows and remove them. Early that spring we could look out our window and see them working. One day when the water was up we convinced Mama

The Way It Was

and Daddy that the weather was too cold and bad for us to go to school, so they let us stay home. Daddy went to the store. Then Carl, Edward, our first cousin, and I slipped off and went down the hill to the edge of the water where it had reached the woods. Here we collected poles and tied them together with baling wire to make a raft. Floating on our raft was fun, but as usual when we did something that we shouldn't, we got caught. The price we paid was the usual punishment of a whipping by Daddy with his razor strap. Those whippings caused problems between Mama and Daddy because what Daddy called a whipping she thought was a beating. I agreed with Mama, but I did not get one that I did not deserve. Mama did not allow Daddy to whip Zuline, and Mama would not whip her either. I believe that was the reason that she was a spoiled brat, though I probably helped. Two of my favorite ways to make her angry were to call her Zula Zebra Josephine Castellaw and tell her that I had asked Mama to not adopt her. For me to tell her that she was adopted caused her to run to Mama and complain. Of course this caused me big trouble, anywhere from a tongue lashing to a whipping, usually with a peach tree limb. I think Mama kept the peach trees pruned just by breaking off limbs to use to whip me.

The outdoor toilet at the house had two holes and a Sears catalog for paper. The women used the toilet and the men and boys had to go to the barn. At times when using the toilet a chicken would peck you in the rear.

Nothing was wasted on the farm. Chickens would consume human excrement and hogs would follow the cows so they could eat their discharged waste. Table scraps were fed to the dog and hogs.

We had a shepherd dog named Jip. He would drive up the livestock, act as a guard dog, and play with us. He was like another family member. One day Carl, Edward, and I slipped off and went to Mud Creek Canal to swim. Jip went with us, but we did not notice that as soon as we pulled off our clothes and went into the water he returned to the house. He got as close to Mama as he could and gave a low growling complaint. She knew by his actions that something was wrong, so she followed him to where we were swimming. As soon as Edward saw her he got out of the water, grabbed his clothes, and ran as fast as he could to his house. Mama got a willow switch and before

Charles R. Castellaw

Carl and I were able to put on our clothes, she striped our naked rear ends with the willow switch.

At about six years of age I had to start working in the fields. One of my first jobs was chopping cotton and corn. I had this job as long as I lived on the farm. Chopping cotton in the bottom on long hot days would make me think that when I grew up, there would be no more cotton chopping for me. The next job that I was permitted to do was drag the cotton patch after planting. We used a homemade drag made out of rough sawmill planks. The drag covered two rows and was pulled by one mule or horse. I enjoyed this job and to show how important I was, one day I let Zuline ride on the drag with me. I let the horse turn too short at the end of the rows and turned the drag over, spilling both of us in the dirt. This created a big problem for me with Mama. She said that I should not have let Zuline ride on the slide. I got off with only a tongue lashing, which was unusual for her to not use the switch.

Carl and I had regular chores to do. He milked the cows and I had to bring in the cook-stove wood. As I got older, firewood was added, then feeding the livestock. In the spring Carl and I helped plant the crops by plowing the fields with horses and mules. One day I was breaking ground with a two-horse breaking plow and a young team of horses. Something spooked them and they ran, dragging me because I had the lines around my neck and shoulder. To drag me was not a problem for a team of horses because at that time I weighed less than one hundred pounds. After being dragged for about three hundred feet, I was able to remove the lines and get free. Before Daddy was able to stop the horses the plow hit the ankle of the hind leg of one of them, making a large deep cut. It took weeks for the cut to heal. At one point maggots got in the cut. This was probably a good thing because the maggots cleaned out the dead flesh.

When we were working the crops Daddy would always let Carl cultivate with a one-row cultivator pulled by a pair of mules. He made me hoe, and I say "made me" because that was the only way he could get me to hoe. I thought it would be fair for Carl and me to alternate between cultivating and hoeing. Carl and Daddy did not see it that way, so I always lost the argument.

During the summer we would have a cousin, Glover Davis, Jr. from Memphis, Tennessee, visit us and stay most of the summer. Carl

The Way It Was

and I had a problem getting him to help us work. We had to make promises such as when we got through with the job on the farm we would go horseback riding or fishing. When we got caught up with our work Daddy would let us take a team of horses and wagon, load our supplies and fishing gear, and go to the bottom to camp out, fish, and hunt. We had a rule for our food supply. We would take lard and meal for cooking, but no food for cooking or eating. The rule was if we did not catch or kill food to eat we would go without food. These trips usually lasted for two days. Sometimes when we got caught up with our work by noon on Saturday we rode our horses for six miles to Bells, Tennessee, and went to the picture show. This was a special and enjoyable trip. We had twenty-five cents each to spend—fifteen cents for the show, five cents for a Coca-Cola, and five cents for a bag of popcorn. The show was always a western and a comedy.

<u>Summer On The Farm</u>

The summer was a very busy time, spent working the crops and taking care of the livestock and garden. This was the time to make molasses, can vegetables and fruit, and make jelly and preserves. We needed to make enough to last until the next canning season. Mama would also can more than was needed to be on the safe side. It was general practice to take a team of mules and wagon to the cornfield and pick a load of fresh corn to be canned. Neighbors came in and helped. This was a big party, and I remember some of the older boys and girls doing a little courting while working. After bringing in the corn from the field we would shuck, silk, cut the corn off the cob, put it in quart jars, add one teaspoon of salt, and then fill the jars with hot water. A rubber ring was placed on the screw top of the jar to seal it. A glass lid with a spring metal fastener was placed on the jar. The spring lever was pulled down to tighten the lid so it would seal during cooking. The jars were placed in a tub, placed on the wood cook stove, and cooked in boiling water. I remember peeling red apples to can. Mama would take the red apple peelings and make jelly by placing the peelings in a pan, adding water, and cooking it to get the juice out. She would strain, add sugar, and cook until it reached the right stage. Then she would dip the jelly into jars and seal. This jelly was red and a favorite for everyone.

Charles R. Castellaw

Canning preserved vegetables and fruit

One of the following methods was used for each vegetable or fruit. The open pot method involved cooking the food completely, and while boiling hot, pouring it into sterilized jars, then sealing and storing. With the cold packed method the food would be packed cold into jars and then cooked and sterilized at the same time by boiling the jars in boiling water in a tub. We canned corn, tomatoes, peas, beans, greens, potatoes, pickles (watermelon rind was a favorite), peaches, apples, plums, cherries, pears, and blackberries.

Cheese making was one of my favorite times because this was the only time we had cheese. I remember Mama would use about six gallons of fresh milk to make about five pounds of cheese. She did not have a dairy thermometer so she had to judge the temperature based on experience. One of the standards used was body temperature. The milk would be poured into a tub and placed on the wood cook stove. The milk was heated to the desired temperature and held at that temperature until the curd had been formed, then the curd was cut lengthwise with a butcher knife, then cut cross wise into small cubes. Then the curd would be stirred gently in order to prevent the pieces from sticking together. As soon as a large amount of whey was separated from the curd, usually about fifteen minutes, heating would be started to reach a little over body temperature. During the heating process the curd would be stirred just enough to keep the small cubes from sticking together. The curd would remain in the whey at the desired temperature until the curd reached the right stage, then the whey would be removed. After the curd had settled, the whey would be dipped off. Then the curd would be placed on a rack and covered with muslin cloth to drain. The rack was placed inside a box. Stirring helped free the whey and prevent the curd particles from matting together. After the curd had drained, about one forth of a cup of salt was added and stirred through the curd. The next step was to put the curd into the cheese press. The cheese press was made by cutting both ends out of a one gallon round can and cutting two round pieces of boards to fit in each end. Small holes were drilled in the bottom board for drainage. The inside of the can was lined with cheesecloth. Two circle pieces were cut to cover the inside of the top and bottom. The

The Way It Was

curd was placed in the metal container with the bottom board in place, and then the top board was added. Bricks were placed on top for weights. After the cheese had been in the press twenty-four hours, it was removed from the press and placed on a curing shelf and turned every day for two weeks. After curing for two weeks the cheese was covered with paraffin. Then it was turned twice a week until cured. We started eating it after about six weeks.

In late summer or early fall it was time to make sorghum molasses. We stripped the leaves of the cane, cut down the stalks, cut off the heads, and then hauled the cane to the mill. The cane was fed into a press turned by a mule. This would press out the juice, which was then placed into a special pan and cooked. As the juice cooked, it moved down the pan through a series of troughs. When it reached the end of the pan, it was done and ready to be drained, put in buckets, lids placed on the bucket, and then sealed. The person doing the cooking would keep the scum skimmed off and control the flow of the syrup so that when it reached the end of the pan it would be done and ready to be drained off and put in the buckets. During the cooking process, we would put apples and pears in the pan and cook them in the syrup. The eating of this fruit was a bonus for our work.

After the crops were laid by we would go to the woods and cut wood for the fireplace and cookstove. We had to cut enough for a whole year. This was not a very pleasant job. It always seemed to be the hottest time of the year in the bottom and there were big female mosquitoes with needlelike organs that were used to puncture the skin of animals to suck their blood. I believe I was a favorite target.

In the summer, for recreation, we went swimming in the pond, broke young horses and mules, and rode horses, calves and jennies. Our grandfather traded for three jennies, one for each of us—Edward, Carl, and me. If the jennies got tired while riding, they would lie down and not get up until they had a good long rest.

Our 1929 Model A Ford car was a luxury at this time. It was used mainly in the fall when we had some cotton money. A few times during the summer we would use the car to go to Brownsville and Bells, but most of the time we used a wagon pulled by horses. Horses were faster than mules. Daddy did not have money to buy registration plates so he would borrow one from one of his brothers. At that time each car had two plates, one on the front and one on the rear. It was a

19

common practice to use one plate on one car and the other plate on a second car. Law enforcement officers understood the problem at this time and did not enforce this law.

The next big food-processing job on the farm was hog killing. The most important job in hog killing was selecting a time when the temperature was just above freezing. If the meat froze, it was likely to spoil; and if it was too warm, the meat would sour.

Daddy chose Thanksgiving if the temperature was favorable because Carl and I were out of school and could help. I am sure you have noticed that when I talk about work, I do not mention Zuline. This is because she never worked. Mama would not let Daddy make Zuline work.

Hog killing

The Way It Was

Hog killing – removing internal organs

Charles R. Castellaw

Hog killing was one of those times when neighbors came in to help, another big party. Each neighbor brought his or her own knife to use. Most of the knives were made from an old saw blade with a hickory wood handle. The hog killing was started by building a fire around two or three big wash pots filled with water. A fifty gallon metal barrel was placed at about a 45° angle to use as a scalding barrel. Boards were placed in front of the barrel to make a scraping table about four feet wide and eight feet long. The hogs were penned the day before killing, after a 24-hour fast during which time they were given all the water they would drink but no feed, so we would get a good "stick". The objective was to get a well-bled hog.

Striking them with one sharp blow with a single blade axe, midway between and slightly above the eyes, stunned the hogs. The hog would be stuck promptly after being stunned so the blood would drain out as completely as possible. After stunning, the hog was rolled over on its back and held firmly by the front feet by the helper while the sticker stuck the hog in the throat, in front of the breastbone, at the correct location to cut the artery. Then the heart would pump out the blood. Hot water from the wash pots was poured into the metal barrel then the hog was placed in the barrel by two or three men. The hog would be pulled in and out and turned to keep from cooking the skin. Occasionally, the hog would be pulled about halfway out so the hair could be tested to determine if it was loose enough to come off. If so, the hog would be pulled out on the scraping table. One man would scrape the hindquarters while another man would scrape the hair from the fore quarters, feet, and head. After the hair and scurf were scraped off, the carcass would be washed with warm water to remove dirt. After washing, the carcass would be hung up from a single tree. A single tree would be used by hooking the hooks on each end under the tendons of each hind leg. The carcass was suspended on a pole. The pole was fastened to a tree at one end; the other end was fastened to two poles forming a vertex at the horizontal pole. The pole would be long enough to hang all the hogs that were killed that day. After hanging up the carcasses, the next step was to open up the carcass and remove the internal organs. To do this a knife was inserted into the sticking place and pulled up through the full length of the breastbone. Then, from the other end of the carcass, a cut was made down between the hams to the pelvic bone allowing the intestines to fall out

The Way It Was

and hang by their natural attachments. The left hand was used to grasp the intestines and pull them out and let them fall into a washtub, also freeing the liver, heart, and lungs. Next, the head was cut off. After washing and rinsing the body cavity with cold water, Daddy would make a cut with an axe down both sides of the backbone, freeing it. The loins would be pulled out and cooked with gravy and biscuits. They would be served with butter and molasses for lunch. Each side of the carcass was hung up in the smokehouse to chill out overnight to remove the animal heat.

The next day the carcasses were blocked out and trimmed. This cutting method separated the carcass into ham, shoulder, bacon strip, and fat back, then all pieces were trimmed to the desired shape. The jowls were cut from the head, trimmed, and cured, the spareribs were removed from the bacon strip.

The trimmings were divided into two piles. One was used to make lard and one was used to make sausage. First, cutting the fat trimmings into small pieces and then cooking them in a large wash pot made lard. It was very important to stir the fat frequently and keep the fire low during the entire cooking process. The water contained in the fat tissue would evaporate. When the pieces of fat turned brown and floated, then sank to the bottom, it was an indication that the lard was rendered. The rendered lard was allowed to settle and cool slightly before the pot was empty. The lard was carefully dipped into five-gallon lard stands. The cracklings were put into a sack and placed in a press made of two boards. Placing one board on top of the second board, then boring holes through both boards, and then tying them together with baling wire, leaving about three inches between boards, pressed the lard out.

Farm-made sausage was one of the most desirable and appetizing of all pork products. It was made from trimmings that contained about 1/3 fat and 2/3 lean. The trimmings were ground with a hand-turned grinder. One person would turn the grinder and the second person would feed it, taking turns. After the trimmings were ground and put into a big tub, Mama would mix up the seasoning made from salt, home grown sage, and black pepper. Daddy would tell Mama to put some red pepper in it. She would say "No" because it would be too hot for the children. He always lost that argument. I think he said it in order to start an argument.

Charles R. Castellaw

Sausage sacks were made from clean white cotton material. It was cut into 9" x 12" pieces, folded, and sewn to form a sack that would hold 1½ to 2 pounds of sausage. The sausage would be compressed into the sacks to avoid air pockets. The tops of the sacks were tied securely with heavy cotton strips. The sausage was hung up in the smokehouse.

We canned loins, spareribs, and sausage. The meat would be cooked and placed in jars, which would be filled with boiling hot grease and sealed.

After some of our hog killings Mama would make souse. Cooking heads, tongues, hearts, lips, snouts, ears, and other pieces made souse. After cooking and removing the bones and as much hog hair as she could, she poured it into shallow pans. As soon as it set up it was sliced and served with vinegar and pepper sauce.

The dry salt process cured the hams, shoulders, and bacon. We used a wooden box made of oak planks. Daddy bought a 100-pound bag of coarse salt to cure the meat. The bottom of the box would be covered with about ½ inch of salt, and then the hams and shoulders would be placed on it with about one inch between joints. The salt would be put over the meat, filling the spaces between the joints. Then another layer would be put on top. This procedure was continued until all the meat was boxed and salted. The bacon was put on top because it finished curing first and had to be removed before the joints were cured. The time for curing was figured at 1½ days per pound of bacon, and hams and shoulders at 2 days per poundage. The minimum cure was 25 days. Days when the temperature went below freezing were not counted.

After curing, the meat was removed from the curing box, brushed to remove excess salt, placed in cold water, and soaked 15-20 minutes to remove some of the surface salt. A piece of baling wire was put through the shanks of the hams and shoulders and wire was put through one corner of the bacon and jowl pieces. Then all pieces of meat were hung up in the smokehouse to drain. After a few days the meat was smoked.

Smoking involve placing a big tub of ashes in the center of the smokehouse floor. We would build a fire of green hickory and ash wood to produce enough heat to melt the surface grease on the meat.

The Way It Was

The smoke from the green wood would color, flavor, and dry the cured parts. The smoking also had a slight preservative action.

After the meat was smoked and cooled, it was put in heavy brown bags to protect it from insects and partially exclude light and air. We would eat the shoulders and bacon first and keep the hams a year or longer, until they developed a mellow flavor and a taste that could only be found in farm cured hams.

<u>Religion in Holly Grove</u>

The Holly Grove Baptist Church for whites and the Bluff Creek Baptist Church for blacks dominated in the Holly Grove Community during that time in our history. The two Baptist Churches, their ideas and doctrines, represented a kind of "invisible government," monitoring the lives of the people of the Holly Grove Community, almost from the time they were born until their death. The churches were separate and completely distinct from the civil government; nevertheless, they were so inextricably involved in deciding crucial questions regarding moral leadership of the community that at times they became embroiled in political disputes.

When I was about eight years old, my father Carl and I were invited as special guests to attend a Thanksgiving celebration at a black church. When we arrived the usher escorted us to our seats on the front row. The program began by the choir singing two songs, then the preacher announced that the congregation would march up front and put their contributions in a container on a table in front of the pulpit. The congregation sang a chant as they came up to the front moving in a dancing motion. At that time, I thought that dancing in church was a bad thing to do. After members deposited their contributions, they would return to their seats. When members stopped making contributions the preacher stopped the singing and made a talk on why they should contribute more money to the church. Then he started the process all over. After about the third time, he said that it was time to procede with the program.

To me, the highlight of the program was when they had the hunt for the turkey leg bone. A turkey leg bone was hidden in the church and the person that found it won a prize. There was a large clock on the wall behind the pulpit. A man got a chair and placed it in front of

Charles R. Castellaw

the wall under the clock. Standing on the chair, he had to stretch to open the door to the clock, about the time he opened it, he fell to the floor. Everyone in the church laughed but him.

In 1876[5] several members of the community, traveling over four miles to Zion Baptist Church (established in 1831) in horse drawn buggies and wagons to attend religious services, met and decided to organize their own church. Thirty-eight members of the Zion Church established the Holly Grove Baptist Church. The membership met in the Holly Grove School, a one-room log building. D.H. Watridge gave a plot of land next to the school building on July 23, 1886,[6] to the deacons, co-chaired by J.B. Booth and J.W. Castellaw of the Holly Grove Baptist Church, for a church building. The members of the church cut logs, hauled them to the building site, and constructed a one-room log church building next to the one-room log school building. J.F. Castellaw and wife gave land on October 20, 1900, to the Holly Grove Church for a cemetery. The land circles around the west side and to the rear of the church.

The First Holly Grove Baptist Church and Holly Grove School were located on the north side of Poplar Corner Road about 200 feet from Dr. Hess Road. Years later the log school building was torn down and a new two-room frame building was built east of the location of the old log school, on land donated by Thomas Jefferson Castellaw, Jr. The additional land was necessary to make room for a larger school building and a larger playground. Years later the log church building was torn down and a large one-room frame building was constructed in its place. This was the church building used by my family and was replaced after WW II.

Before school integration it was common knowledge and understanding, and approved by both churches, that each race would operate and control its own church and school. The churches imposed their behavioral standards on most of the community. Religion was used to prevent social disorder, violence, bloodshed, and other undesirable, anti-social acts committed against God and the entire community.

---

[5] The Holly Grove, Jones Station and Wellwood Historiculture, Elma Ross Public Library
[6] Ibid

The Way It Was

The practical benefits of religion as preached in the community were to convert sinners to Christians, control social acts of members of the community, and keep local control of church, school, and community. The most important church event of the year was the "big meeting" revival. It was conducted during August, starting on Sunday and closing with a baptism on the following Sunday afternoon.

I was baptized in my grandfather's pond with a large group, including my father, Edward, and Carl in 1939[7]. My Mama was baptized and joined the church in 1936[8].

During revivals an old black man that lived in the community would come to church at night and stand outside of the window and listen to the sermon. This did not create a problem. The sermons were designed to teach that if you did not obey the word of God that was revealed in the Bible you were going to hell and would burn forever.

The services were as long as the wooden benches were hard. Three rows faced a plain wooden pulpit. In front of the right row of seats were benches facing the center row for the deacons. From those seats the deacons could see everyone in the church. The church was equipped with a 32-volt generator, storage battery unit, and a gasoline engine to drive the generator. This 32-volt electrical system would produce electricity for lights in the church to be used at night. This system was used in Squire Tom Castellaw's and Dr. Hess's houses, the only houses in the community that had electrical lights.

In the early 1900's Squire Baker Boren used a carbide generator to make acetylene gas that was used for lights in his house. A pipe was installed from the generator to a gaslight in the center of the ceiling in each room.

Community Values

Within the Holly Grove community a charitable loyalty existed. If any member of the community was in need, everyone responded quickly and generously, primarily on an individual basis. They believed that social concerns and welfare should be the business of the individual conscience. When a farm family got behind in working their crop or harvesting due to illness, the neighbors would take their

---

[7] Holly Grove church records
[8] Ibid

Charles R. Castellaw

teams, equipment, and whatever else was needed to their farm and help out. At times several members of the community would get together and plan the day's work, including lunch planned by the women. I remember one year when a family lost the mother and two children from an unknown disease. The day we went to work their crop it looked like all the neighbors were there.

Leadership within the community came from the Holly Grove Baptist Church. During every major crisis this power rested on a voluntary consensus of opinions in the community, more potent than any government—county, state, or national. The community accepted the social and behavioral standards imposed by the church without open opposition but without necessarily implying agreement with it. The Holly Grove Baptist Church in turn made religion and church membership accessible to everyone. The church organization operated by the democratic system, majority vote of the membership. The church fiercely defended the principle of local autonomy and the right to make decisions affecting their lives without outside pressure or influence. They also formed the largest single thread in the all-important fabric of the community—concern for the welfare of the community.

The church made decisions by a majority vote from the church membership. The preacher could be dismissed or fired at anytime. Any member, during a business meeting of the membership, could make a motion to fire the preacher. If the motion received a second, it would be discussed and voted on and by "majority rule" the preacher would stay or go. It was not unusual for the membership to have debates and sometimes heated arguments over issues such as firing the preacher, work on the church, or questions about a member's actions.

The policy of "majority rule" could be questioned because of the influence of some of the deacons. If two or three of the most influential deacons agreed, the issue was sure to pass but if they disagreed we would have an interesting debate. I remember one time Sam Castellaw and Tom Castellaw got in a debate over how to fix the front steps to the church. After a long debate the issue was settled by a vote of the membership.

After one of my father's brothers, Dan Castellaw, and his first wife divorced, he developed a close relationship with a single woman

The Way It Was

in the community. This created a church-wide discussion of the sin of having two living wives. One of his cousins, a member of the church, visited him in his home and explained to him that he was going to hell and would burn forever if he remarried. He did not marry her.

<u>Community Funerals</u>

Funerals were carried out according to long established tradition. The entire community participated in all aspects of funerals in Holly Grove. The death was announced by passing the news from neighbor to neighbor by word of mouth. At that time there were only about six telephones in the community.

Members of the community would converge at the home of the deceased and assume all the necessary household and farm chores. A few of the older women would prepare the corpse for burial. They would wash the body and place pennies over the eyelids to close them. Men were buried in their best suits; older women were buried in black. Children and infants were buried in white. After the deceased was dressed, he or she would be placed in the casket. The undertaker delivered the casket to the house.

The corpse was never left alone. Neighbors held a wake throughout the night while the deceased lay for the last time in his or her own home, usually in the living room. On the morning of the following day, the men would gather at the cemetery with their picks and shovels and dig the grave. The funeral was usually conducted in the afternoon. A large number of people would attend the funeral, and the church choir would sing several hymns. The church minister or an outside minister selected by the family would give the eulogy. The minister would take advantage of the situation to tell the congregation, in very strong terms, that they would all die someday, and if they did not want to burn in hell, they must make a confession of faith in Christ and ask for forgiveness of their sins. At the close of the service, everyone would file by the casket to gaze on the corpse one last time before the coffin lid was closed and a hymn was sung. The pallbearers would carry the coffin from the church to the graveside in back of the church. After burial, the mound of dirt would be decorated with flowers, and friends took the family home. The family would return later to view the decorated grave.

Charles R. Castellaw

I believe that Mama and Daddy carried out all the important roles in the family, transmitting religion and social values and attitudes to the next generation—Carl, Zuline, and me. In the evenings after working all day together we would gather around the fireplace to share in our social and spiritual needs. This closeness and sense of common purpose shared by us compensated for the heavy responsibility and duties that Carl and I had to assume at an early age. We did the work of full-time field workers from sunup to sundown. We would pop corn over the fireplace and roast peanuts to eat while we played cards, checkers, and dominos. During the winter Mama would do her sewing for the year. One winter, while piecing a quilt, she cut blocks to size and let the small pieces fall on the floor. Carl and I picked up the pieces and sewed them together on a piece of paper, cut to size by Mama, to make blocks for a string quilt. This was about 1931, and I still have this quilt today.

The closeness among the people of the community made it easy for an individual to be put in a class or standing among his neighbors, depending almost entirely on his or her personal behavior, attitude, and family background. The people of the community believed that qualities of character were inherited and that there were scrubs among people just as there were scrubs among cattle. A person who lived upright was not blamed for the faults of his kinfolk. An individual could lose all the advantages of descent from an honorable family by dishonest and or immoral conduct.

The Way It Was

May and Robert Castellaw (top) and Carl, Zuline, and Charles Castellaw (bottom)

Religion was a most important criterion in determining character. Men that showed loyal devotion to parents and family had far more influence among their peers than did civil or political authorities. Service to the community, combined with religion, was a second criterion of respectability. To the people of the community, religion

Charles R. Castellaw

and assisting one's neighbors could not be separated from Christian doctrine. There were many community citizens not especially religious who were always ready to aide the less fortunate. They gave their time and wealth to help the community.

Sexual promiscuity and drinking alcohol brought universal condemnation. Judgment for drinking was based on the application of a rule of social standard. If a person drank only moderately, his weakness was tolerated. Condemnation was quick and severe if a person drank excessively, abused his wife and children, neglected his work, or caused problems with his neighbors.

Preachers, schoolteachers, justices of the peace, and physicians were widely respected and trusted. They furnished community leadership. I remember one time Dr. Hess served on the County Highway Road Board.

During this time there was very little tax money for roadwork. Each physically able 21-year-old or older man was required to work a certain number of days on the roads in the civil district in which he lived, or had to pay a fixed fee. A few of the men that had money would pay the fee, while the others would stand in line to be selected to work for the money. If a farmer furnished a team of horses or mules to pull a scoop or road grader he was given credit for their use. Daddy always furnished a team.

In contrast to the spirit and social standing of the people of the community there was the alternate lifestyle of a group of families living in sub-community places. These people were outcasts, shunned by the rest of the community. These people carried instant social contamination to anyone who socialized with them. Marriage to any of these people was out of the question, and any man or woman seen visiting any of them risked the chance of losing his good reputation. A social wall was erected around them to avoid contaminating the community. They were outcasts in society because they completely rejected all the values of social order and morality endorsed by most of the community and church. With close and careful scrutiny of one's neighbors, everyone knew all behavior of members of the community.

The church revival was the number one event each year in the community. The second big event was the election for public offices. The Democratic Primary was strongly contested by two candidates for

The Way It Was

each public office. We did not have a Republican primary because there were no Republicans living in our district. At an early age I thought if you were not a Baptist and Democratic you were going to hell.

The election was conducted on the school and church grounds. The two grounds joined and the school and church used both. The election was an all-day party for the community. The church would serve stew to raise funds. Some of the men would bring their wash pots early in the morning and cook the stew in time for lunch. Usually it would be made of chicken, corn, and tomatoes, all raised on the farm and furnished by members of the church. Some of the men would go to the bottom early in the morning and kill squirrels to make squirrel stew, which was the choice of some.

The voters were made up of two groups: the ones that would not sell their vote and the ones that would. The standard price per vote was ½ pint of whiskey or one dollar. A person who sold his vote could not be trusted so the buyer would require him to get his ballot, bring it to him so he could mark it, then he would watch him put it in the ballot box before he paid him. Some of the voters after voting would load up in cars and go to another polling place and vote for the second time. Blacks did not vote and only a few women voted. The older men, like my grandfather, did not believe in women's suffrage. A large crowd would come and stay all day visiting and eating stew.

High School Years

As a result of President Roosevelt's farm program in the year 1939, we had made some progress in our income. This made it possible for us to use the car at all times as well as have better school clothes and a small amount of spending money. TVA electrical power had been installed throughout Haywood County, but we were unable to receive electrical power, as we did not live close enough to the main power line.

In the fall of 1939 my grandfather gave me a saddle and five cents per day to drive up his cattle after I got home from school. The thirty-five cents per week helped my finances and the saddle was a great improvement as I had been riding my horse bare back.

33

Charles R. Castellaw

The time came for me and my six classmates to finish elementary school. It was a large eighth grade class for Holly Grove School. Of the seven students that finished the eighth grade, only two of us went to high school. During this period in our history most country students and parents considered the eighth grade time to drop out of school and go to work full time on the family farm, as my Daddy had done. His goal for his children was to finish high school. I am sure that he did not think that college was a goal that we could achieve.

High school was a big change for me from elementary school. My high school, Haywood County High School, in Brownsville, Tennessee, was ten miles from our home. We walked about half a mile on a dirt road to catch the school bus to ride to school. The bus driver, Jessie Cobb, owned the bus and would take us back to school at night to attend school activities. My favorites were football games. Our school had a good marching band. I saw my first football game and marching band perform during my freshman year in high school.

I was surprised when I went to high school the first day to see a big two-story school building with indoor toilets, electric lights, central heat, a library, a gym, and up-to-date equipment.

There were 129 students in my freshmen class of which 61, including me, graduated four years later. This was a new life for me and it took some time for me to adjust. During my freshman year I had very few friends and did not take part in any school extra-curricular activities. I felt inferior to most of my schoolmates. Most were from nice homes in Brownsville with electrical lights, running water, and indoor plumbing, and they seemed to me to have a lot of spending money.

Meanwhile, I lived in an old log house with no electricity, running water, or modern conveniences, and I used an oil lamp for light to study by. My brother Carl dropped out of school at age seventeen and went to Memphis, Tennessee, to work for a printing company.

As I passed students in the hall, I would not speak nor would they. I thought that they would not speak to me because I was a country boy from a poor farm family. During my sophomore year I got a book, *"How to Win Friends and Influence People,"* by Dale Carnegie. I read this book several times and used it as my guide. Then when I passed students in the hall I would smile and speak and they would return my smile and speak.

The Way It Was

Both my agriculture teacher, Mr. Earnest Dumas, and one of my math teachers, Mr. Ed Thompson, had a very important influence on me. One day when I walked into math class Mr. Thompson had put a note on the chalkboard. It read, "I will not make class today, Charles Castellaw teach the class." I am sure I grew about a foot in my mind. The other students were very cooperative and we had a good class. I did my best to teach the class just like Mr. Thompson would have taught it.

My two best friends in high school, Maurice Drake and Jimmy Lee Nanney, also had a very positive influence on me. I started taking part in our FFA club and other school activities. During my junior year, I was elected secretary of FFA, and during my senior year, I was elected FFA president and vice-president of our senior class.

It was not difficult for the boys in my class to decide what to do after high school because WWII was in full progress. After graduation we would be drafted into the military service. My personal choice was to work full time on the farm.

Betty Jo and the War

One Saturday afternoon in 1943, I went to the picture show in Bells. When I walked into the lobby of the show, I saw a 4'11", 90 pound, beautiful girl for the first time. She was standing alone and I walked up to her, smiled, and said, "Hi. My name is Charles Ray Castellaw." She replied, "My name is Betty Jo Matthews." I said, "If you are alone may I sit with you?" She said, "Yes." During the show we entered into small talk. I learned that she attended Bells High School and worked part-time across the street from the show at a beauty shop owned by Mrs. Clarise McClish. She had gotten off work and walked across the street to go to the show. Walking out after the show, I asked to meet her at the show the following Saturday. She said, "Yes." The following Saturday we met as planned. I learned that she was 'sweet sixteen' and had never been kissed by a boy. It did not take me long to change that! After the show, I asked to take her home. She said she would have to ask her Daddy. Lucky for me he said "Yes." Betty Jo lived on a farm about one mile from Bells. I drove her home, and walked her to the front door. She turned to me and looked up, then I put my arms around her and kissed her good night. As I

35

Charles R. Castellaw

drove home I knew that I had met my 'true love,' my 'sweetheart,' and someday I would marry her.

We started going together regularly until I had to go into the military service. We mainly went to the movies at Bells or Brownsville. I think Betty Jo preferred going to Brownsville because her brother and sister worked at the theater in Bells. Sometimes after the movie we would park to talk and make love.

After graduating from high school the draft board lost no time classifying me as A-1. M.C., a person my age working on our farm, and I both received an A-1 draft classification in the mail on the same day. Daddy asked us if we wanted him to file a petition with the draft board requesting an essential worker classification as farm workers. M.C. said "Yes" and Daddy filed a petition for him. M.C. was deferred and worked on the farm all during WWII. I said "No." I did not want to go into military service, but my brother Carl had volunteered for the Navy. Most of my friends of military age had also volunteered for the service. I could not let my brothers and friends down. I thought it was my duty to go into the military. Most of all I thought if I did not go, I would be a coward. To me a coward was about as low as you could get in the human race.

I received greetings from the President of the United States that said, "You have been selected for training and services in the land or naval forces of the United States." There was also an order to report for induction. I reported on the departure date and met with others that had been ordered to report. As we gathered I noticed one of my young friends, Billy McCool, crying. I walked over to him and asked why he was crying. He said, "I know that I will never return home because I will be killed." Unfortunately, he was killed in action.

We had a short program before getting on the bus to go to the introduction center. A Presbyterian minister conducted the program. He read scripture from the Bible, said prayer, and gave a short speech. Most of it was about social conduct. He said that we would come in contact with bad people from whom we must protect ourselves. He said that those people, especially bad women, who may have contracted disease would give us a lot of trouble if we socialized with them. After his talk we boarded the bus for the induction center at Fort Benning, Georgia.

The Way It Was

My last night I took Betty Jo to the movies, and afterward we talked about me going into the military service. I told her that I would write to her as soon as I reached the military base. I was very sad that night because I knew that it would be several weeks before I would see her again. I told her that I would be able to get a furlough soon and come home to see her. We embraced, kissed, and said goodbye.

When we arrived at Fort Benning, Georgia, we got off the bus and a sergeant addressed us as new recruits and ordered us to line up in columns of two. He marched us to the mess hall for lunch. After lunch we were given a physical and a battery of mental tests. Later I learned that I made the upper 10% in mechanical ability. At the end of the processing line I was informed that there were openings in the Navy, Marines, and Army and that I could have my choice. I preferred the Navy but did not like the uniform so I picked the Army. Next we went to the quartermaster's and were issued our clothes. Then we were assigned to our barracks. Two days later I was shipped to Camp Fort Blanding, Florida.

I arrived at the Infantry Replacement Training Center (IRTC), Camp Blanding, Florida, weighing 127 pounds and 5'7" tall. I was assigned to Rifle Company D, Battalion 227, Regiment 69, Camp Commander Colonel Smith, IRTC Commander General Fales, Company Commander First Lieutenant Anderson, Platoon Leader Second Lieutenant Aalberts, Platoon Sergeant Williams, Squad Leader Corporal Bell and First Sergeant Bradshaw.

Lieutenant Anderson was a high school principal and Lieutenant Aalberts was a high school science teacher before they entered the military service. I thought I might have a problem with regular old Army officers because I believed that I was a civilian in uniform and would never be a soldier. So to have my officers from civilian jobs that I understood gave me a sense of confidence in them.

Camp Blanding had been developed from a land of swamps, sand, snakes, egrets, wildcats, and assorted alligators. In September, 1940, the camp began losing the jungle feel and assumed its character as a training ground for the development of tough, cagey, and alert soldiers. It mushroomed from an entirely undeveloped wasteland into a tremendous military camp spanning over 125,000 acres.

This modern metropolis of war had its own fire department, hospital, telephone and telegraph service, police force, sewage

Charles R. Castellaw

disposal plants, several huge warehouses, a water supply system, and a complete railroad organization including roundhouse.

The training facilities included well-equipped classrooms, obstacle courses, multi-acre drill and problem areas, firing ranges, modern tactical courses, and a general maneuver area that extended for miles.

In our orientation we were told that we were there as trainees because our country was engaged in a life-and-death struggle with one of the most powerful and ruthless combinations of powers the world had ever known. We were told that the enemies were tough, cruel, highly trained, and well equipped. Their defeat was essential before the world could become a decent place in which to live. During our seventeen weeks of intensive training, we would find the work hard, the hours long, and the going tough as it could be. If we concentrated our energy and determination on our work we would become alert, confident, skilled soldiers prepared to function as members of a combat division. They did not tell us that the standard training program included joining a tactical unit for additional training, but due to the critical need for combat replacement soldiers this part of the training had been discontinued in order to increase the flow of replacements to the front lines of battle.

In the serious business of training we had to strive with all our might to master every detail of the instruction each day. If you were shooting at a bull's eye and got a close-in 4, that shot only whistled by the enemy's ear and alerted him. He would then return your fire, killing you. If you were careless about tossing a grenade into a window, you left the enemy sniper in the room free to kill you and/or other GIs. We learned our lessons well during our training period to avoid having our mistakes marked by a cross on the battlefield.

After orientation, I had time to think. I set some personal objectives and plans. First I would do all I could to help win the war. Then I would return home, marry Betty Jo, and be a farmer. I had heard statements such as, "I will give my life for my country," and Patrick Henry's statement, "I regret that I have but one life to give for my country." To me this was a lot of stupid nonsense. I thought if I was going to make a statement about my country it might be, "I will live for my country." But my above statement was not exactly correct.

The Way It Was

The correct statement for me was, "I plan to live for Betty Jo and our future."

During our orientation we were informed about a program that we could use to save money by consigning it for war bonds or other programs. My pay was $50 per month, so I signed to have $30 per month sent to the Bank of Crockett, Bells, Tennessee, to be put in a savings account. The bank charged 5¢ for cashing my check so I saved $29.95 each month. I planned to save as much money as I could while I was in the military service to use when I returned home to marry Betty Jo and started farming.

By now I knew that after seventeen weeks of training I would be shipped to a combat zone and assigned to a front line combat unit. It was also clear to me that if I had a chance to live through battle it would be determined mostly by what I learned in basic training. I was determined to enter the training program with a positive attitude and carry out all my assignments to the best I could. We were informed about different punishments that trainees received for different mistakes and not doing their work. I set a goal that I would go through the seventeen weeks of training without receiving any punishment, and I did.

Basic Training—Daily Life

Our daily training was laid out as follows—wake-up call, dress, fall out, calisthenics, mess, classroom, hand-to-hand combat, drill, firing range, hiking with a full pack of 84 pounds, going through mine fields, crawling through obstacle courses with live fire overhead, and finally, going through a gas chamber wearing a gas mask.

A rifle company was made up of 193 men, broken into three rifle platoons of three squads each. Each squad had 12 men—the squad leader, assistant squad leader, automatic rifle team of three men, and seven riflemen. One weapons platoon had two sections: A Section, two squads with one 30-caliber machine gun and five men each; and B Section, three squads with one 60-mm mortar and five men each.

My specialized training was Intelligence and Reconnaissance (I and R). In this training I learned to become a competent rifle shot and to use the bayonet and all types of grenades. In addition, I learned to use the Browning Automatic Rifle (BAR), 60-millimeter rocket

Charles R. Castellaw

launcher, and the 45-caliber side arm. After learning to handle our weapons, we went on to the technical training of learning to operate and care for jeeps and light trucks. I learned to collect, study, interpret, and pass on information. I learned to read maps, make sketches, and use the compass. I learned to move quickly, quietly, and secretly, both by day and by night, to conceal myself from enemy observation, to cover myself from enemy fire, and to act as a scout in observing and reporting the activities of the enemy. I learned to operate our radios and telephones and to signal by visual means. I learned to prepare situation maps indicating the latest intelligence information concerning our own troops and those of the enemy.

When I became proficient in the use of weapons, in cover and concealment, in the use of communications, in the preparation of sketches and maps, and in scouting, then I learned to work with the other members of my squad as a team. In this phase of training I learned to coordinate my individual skills with other men in order to accomplish our mission as effectively and quickly as possible. After completing this training I was ready to be shipped overseas and assigned to a combat unit.

During my 17 weeks of basic training the thing that troubled me the most was religion. Growing up, I had learned to believe that religion and moral values went together and could not be separated. At that time I believed in my moral values, but began to question my religious belief and faith.

I grew up with a religious father and mother and attended a strong Southern Baptist Church. I had learned to believe in the Bible and trust and believe in our preachers. Camp Blanding had 23 chapels and a good supply of chaplains.

The chaplains were available for advice or consultation on any religious or moral problem and they would help in any other personal matter brought to them. We could see the chaplain without asking the permission of any superior. We could attend the church service of our choice each week, unless we had specific duties with which such attendance would interfere.

Religion on base was used to try to strengthen and help those whose lives were troubled. I am sure that the religious program was planned to try to help soldiers in a savage and brutalizing war to find peace and comfort in religion. With a foundation of religious

The Way It Was

understanding it was believed that soldiers would build a broader character out of the experiences that we would have. It was believed that this training would prepare our minds for the shocks of combat and death.

After much consideration, I reached the decision that the United States Army was only interested in the soldier's religion as a tool to use in their training program to help achieve their military objective. To do this they would enlist preachers and give them a commissioned officer's rank with a good paycheck to carry out this part of the training program.

It did not take me long to reach the conclusion that this was a hypocritical program designed for military objectives, not religious objectives. I did not attend church or talk to a chaplain during my 17 weeks of training.

One of the first things I learned was the 24-hour "Army time" system. This is a way to express time in four digits of which the first two digits refer to the hour and the last two digits to minutes; their system works on a 24-hour basis, so there is no AM nor PM.

For the first 12 hours of the day, Army time is very similar to the civilian system. For example, 1 hour after midnight is 0100; 45 minutes later, it is 0145; 10 minutes after that, it is 0155 and so on to 1200, which is noon. The first hour after noon is 1300, the next hour 1400 and so on to 2400, which is midnight. To the four-digit time system, two digits are added in front of the four digits to indicate the day of the month. For example, 051330; 05 is the 5th day of the month, 1330 is 1:30 PM.

My training program was carried out with only a few problems. On my first day on the firing range, I thought that it would be a snap because I was experienced at firing guns and could hit a small hickory nut on a hickory tree with a 22 rifle. When I got in position with my M-1 rifle and placed it on my left shoulder, the instructor informed me in Army language that I had to shoot from the right shoulder, Army regulations. I explained to him that I could not close my left eye and keep my right eye open in order to sight. He said for me to shoot from the right shoulder with both eyes open.

I could not draw a bead, so most of the time I fired I missed the target and, of course, this made the instructor unhappy. I told him if he would let me fire my M-1 my way, I would hit the bullseye every

41

Charles R. Castellaw

time. He said he did not have the authority to let me fire my M-1 from the left shoulder. After much discussing he agreed to let me put a patch over my left eye and fire from my right shoulder. Firing this way, I would hit the bullseye about every time.

The day came for us to fire our M-1 rifle for the record which was in three qualifications—marksman, sharpshooter, and expert. I knew I could qualify as an expert but the rumors were that if you qualified as an expert you would be used as a sniper. It also was rumored that snipers had the highest casualty rate of all combat soldiers. I wanted to do all I could to lower my chances of being a casualty so I made sure I did not qualify as an expert, but I did qualify as a sharpshooter.

I believe my greatest challenge during basic training was the long hikes with a full pack of 84 pounds. At 127 pounds, 5'7" tall, this was not an easy task for me, but I knew that this physical training was necessary if I was going to have a chance to survive on the battlefield.

To have a chance to win in battle, I knew I had to arrive on the battlefield in good mental and physical condition, ready to fight. Physical conditioning and handling of mind and body was essential. I knew that being able to hike all night and fight all day could be the margin between victory and defeat, or more importantly life and death. I knew how tough our enemies were and they had more training than I did. I knew that I had to be just as tough or tougher and in some way make up for their superior training.

Calisthenics, physical training, hand-to-hand combat training and long hikes were part of my training to get me into shape. After my first hike, I was tired but not worn out. I believe that my advantage was that I had come off the farm, where I had performed a lot of hard physical labor, which made it possible for me to take this physical torture.

The length of our hikes was increased as we increased our physical ability to take it. One canteen of water and a small snack was allowed. At the end of each hour, we were given a 10-minute break. On most of our hikes, some of the men could not make the distance, fell out, and were picked up by a follow-up team. I was determined that no matter how hard and long the hikes got, I would make it, and I did.

The part of the training that I did not like was formal marching and saluting. To me saluting was one of several ways that the Army

The Way It Was

used to show that officers were superior and the common soldier were inferior to officers. I believe this was the common feeling among non-career soldiers. I believe that training officers recognized this feeling among non-career soldiers because we were told that the salute was to show respect for the uniform, not the person in it. The training manual stated that saluting was a privilege; this I did not understand.

Formal marching began by the command, Fall In; we formed ranks, as directed, with the taller men to the right. On falling in, each man except the one at the extreme left of each rank extends his left arm at shoulder height with the palm of his hand down and with his fingers extended and joined. Each man except the one at the right of each rank turns his head to the right so that he can see to place himself in alignment. Each man's shoulder lightly touches the extended fingers of the man to his right. As soon as proper intervals have been established, each man drops his arm smartly to his side, turns his head to the front and automatically assumes the position of Attention. The person in charge of the group gives orders—Close Interval or Fall In. To establish Close Interval (4 inches) each man places his left hand on his hip, with the heel of his hand resting on his hip and with his fingers and thumb joined and pointing down and his elbow in the plane of his body. Then the group may be given orders—At Rest, Fall Out, Parade Rest, At Ease, or Attention. At the Command Rest you may move about as long as you keep one foot in place. At the Command at Ease you may move about as long as your right foot remains in place.

The instruction for regular marching was – Forward, March. At the preparatory Command Forward, do not lean forward. It will help you start marching smoothly if you slightly shift your weight to your right leg at this command, but do not make the movement noticeable at the Command March. Step off smartly with your left foot. Remember that all steps and marching from the Halt begin with the left foot, except Right Step, March. March at a cadence of 120 steps per minute. Take a 30-inch pace with each step. Swing your arms, without bending them at the elbows, 6 inches to the front of and 3 inches to the rear of the position where they naturally hang. There are other commands such as Right Face, Left Face, About Face, etc.

I believed that marching and saluting was okay for the regular Army with career soldiers, but for a civilian in uniform that had only

43

Charles R. Castellaw

17 weeks training before going on the battlefield to kill and be killed, this was a waste of valuable training time.

After 14 weeks of training, the climax came during the last three weeks spent in field training. In this phase of our training, we camped out or went on bivouac, in nature's great open space. This experience was certainly different from the life in the barracks or down on the farm.

Sleeping on the ground under a pup tent or in a fox hole, washing and shaving in cold water, using the ground as a mess table, and having the sun as the only light was our introduction to life in the great outdoors.

We were here to learn how to conduct ourselves in bivouac under actual field conditions. Our training was based on the assumption that the enemy was near and our actions must be such as to keep him in ignorance of our location or even our existence. That meant that we had to practice all that we had learned about camouflage and concealment and that we were constantly prepared to meet and attack our enemy whether they came by water, air, or land.

In addition to the actual practice we received based on our prior training, we were busy with many different field problems, which taught us how our unit would operate in actual engagement with the enemy. For the first time, we were able to see how all the different units in the regiment operated in unison to defeat the enemy. We learned how much each of us depended upon the other men in our unit and how it, in turn, depended on all other units. It made me realize how much real cooperation means, also how much each individual can contribute to the success of the whole group, and also how one screw up can endanger the entire unit.

When I got back to the barracks and began reflecting as I scratched chigger bites, I realized how much I had learned and how much I had to learn to accomplish the things that I had to do. I knew all future learning would be on the battlefield.

I knew that in combat, my mission was to kill or capture the enemy before he killed or captured me. I believed that all other branches of service would render indispensable support, but it would be the action of the infantry that would bring the war to a decisive and victorious conclusion.

The Way It Was

One of the high points in my 17 weeks of training was mail call. This was the time I looked forward to receiving letters from my family and Betty Jo. Betty Jo would write me and tell me what was going on at home. I would write her and tell her how I missed her and how I would like to see her.

Home From Basic Training

My training ended Saturday, May 27, 1944. After a brief ceremony, I was given my orders to report to Norfolk, Virginia, to be shipped to the European theater of operation. This order included a ten-day furlough to go home to visit Betty Jo and my family and get my personal affairs in order because the odds were that I would not return alive. It was my belief that I would go through all the pain and misery of war but some how I would return home alive.

Early Sunday morning, May 28, 1944, my birthday, I packed my duffel bag, said goodbye to my army friends and went to the bus station. I was ready to catch the bus for my trip home. I got on the bus using the ticket that had been given to me by the company clerk. I was now ready to go on my way to Norfolk, Virginia, to be shipped to the European theater of operation. My orders included a ten-day furlough to go home to visit my family, Betty Jo, and to get my personal affairs in order because the odds were that I would not return alive. It was my belief that I would go through all the pain and misery of war but somehow I would return home alive.

I had to change buses in Chattanooga, Tennessee. In Chattanooga, there was a long line of people waiting to get on the bus, more than the bus could carry. Soldiers in uniform were allowed to go to the front of the line. I did not feel bad about going ahead of the little old ladies because my time was very limited. There was a lot I wanted to do during my ten-day leave and getting to go home was most important.

When I arrived in Brownsville, Tennessee, I called my daddy to come to the bus station to pick me up. After he picked me up, the trip of ten miles home seemed longer. I was very glad to see my father, mother, and sister but all my thoughts were about seeing Betty Jo. As soon as I could, I called her and told her that I was home and would see her that night.

45

Charles R. Castellaw

After dinner I went to Bells, Tennessee, to see Betty Jo. She came to the door smiling with those beautiful green eyes sparkling, shoulder-length brown curly hair and a big smile. She was wearing a light brown skirt with a white blouse and saddle oxford shoes. I knew she was my queen, my sweetheart, and my wife to be. We embraced and kissed. The feel of her warm body against mine made me feel like this was heaven on earth.

This was a church night but we decided to go to the picture show. After the show, we parked at our favorite parking place and talked for about an hour before going back to her house. I walked her to the door, kissed her goodnight, and said, "I will see you tomorrow night."

I went to see her every night during my furlough. We did about the same thing on each visit except two. Once we went to Memphis, Tennessee, a seventy-five mile trip, and another time to Chickasaw State Park, both day trips.

The Memphis trip was with my good friend Maurice Drake and his girlfriend, later to become his wife, Verlie Mae Butler. We left home about 8:00 am for Memphis. In Memphis we visited the Pink Palace Museum, the Memphis Zoo, and Riverside Drive downtown on the bank of the Mississippi River.

The Pink Palace Museum was the Pink Palace Mansion dream home of Piggly Wiggly founder, Clarence Saunders. The beautiful 1920s palatial estate was built of pink Georgia Marble. Of all the exhibits, to me the most impressive was the exact replica of Clarence Saunders' first Piggly Wiggly grocery store.

The Memphis Zoo, located in the heart of mid-town Memphis in Overton Park, is home to more than 3,000 animals representing over 400 species. We enjoyed watching the animals and feeding them popcorn and peanuts.

The Way It Was

Charles Castellaw and Betty Jo Matthews, 1944

Betty Jo Matthews, 1945

Charles R. Castellaw

After leaving the zoo, we visited Riverside Drive, located downtown on the bank of the Mississippi River. We also visited the Jefferson Davis Park and the Confederate Park. Then it was time to go home.

When the company clerk gave me my orders, he told me that when I got home I was to take them to the local ration board. While on leave, each soldier was allotted some gas ration stamps. The first day I was home, I checked the crops and livestock. Next, I went to the ration board at Brownsville. The clerk at the ration board took my orders and filled out a form for me to sign. She then gave me some gas ration stamps. Also she stamped my orders so I could not use them to get more stamps. Then I understood why the Company Clerk gave me several copies of my orders. I went to another ration board and by using another copy of my orders I received another allotment of gas ration stamps.

On Monday, June 5, 1944, two days before I had to leave for Norfolk, Virginia, Betty Jo and I went to Chickasaw State Park. This 11,215-acre park has two lakes and is located in Southwest Tennessee about 65 miles from Bells, Tennessee. I borrowed a 1936 Buick from my friend Maurice Drake so I could have transportation.

I arrived at Betty Jo's home after 9:00 am. She came out smiling as usual, carrying a picnic lunch. When we arrived at the park, I noticed that there were no cars in the parking area and no people on the grounds. We went to the office and the park ranger told us that the park was closed on Mondays. I am sure that he could tell that this soldier boy was very much disappointed. He said, "Soldier the park is yours for today, enjoy it." We walked around in the park for quite a while until it was time to eat our picnic lunch. After lunch we put on our bathing suits, played in the water and went riding in one of the boats. We stayed in the park until late in the evening, then we started on the trip back to Betty Jo's home. Just past Jackson, Tennessee, while going up a hill, the old car quit. I got out of the car and raised the hood, then two soldiers stopped and offered us a ride to Bells. When we got to Betty Jo's home, I called Daddy and told him my problem. He came with a mechanic, Lacy Watridge, to get the old car and me.

On Tuesday, June 6, 1944, the evening before I was to leave early the next day for Norfolk, Virginia, Betty Jo and I went out for our last

The Way It Was

time before I had to leave. We went to the show and after the show, we spent a long time talking. When I got ready to go, she put her arms around my neck and started crying. I said, "What is the problem?" She said, "I know where you are going and I am afraid that you will not get back." My reply was, "Do not worry because I will be back." She said, "I will be waiting for you when you return." We kissed, hugged each other and said, "Good night and goodbye."

On Wednesday June 7, 1944, I said goodbye to my family and left for Norfolk, Virginia. After I arrived, I was assigned a bed in one of the barracks and told to check the bulletin board every morning for "shipping out" notice. In a few days the notice was on the bulletin board for us to pack our duffel bags and report for boarding on a troop ship for the European theater of operation. The ship was very crowded with the bunks three deep. The fourteen-day trip was very pleasant. At this time we did not know where we were going.

Charles R. Castellaw

Section 2

The war

When we arrived in the harbor of Naples, Italy, I saw my first display of war. In the harbor were damaged and partly sunken ships. The city of Naples had received heavy damage, delivered by the Allied Air Force. After debarking from the ship, we loaded on trucks for the trip to our bivouac area. This area was on Mussolini's son-in-law's dairy farm. On the farm were twelve large dairy barns, which we used as our camp. We spent our time getting ready to enter combat but we did not know when or where. We spent time cleaning our guns and other equipment, using new khaki pants and shirts as cleaning rags. Being a poor country boy, I could not understand this waste.

While in bivouac, we were approached by recruiters offering us the opportunity to be assigned to a special unit such as Rangers, Glider Troops, Sky Troops, Calvary (mule train), and other special forces. I thought that my chance of survival was greater as a regular foot soldier, so I did not volunteer for special service.

The day came when we were ordered to pack our gear and load on trucks. We were told that from now on, we must always carry our M-1 gun with us. We moved by trucks to Naples Harbor and we loaded onto LSTs (landing ship tanks used to land tanks and troops on beaches) for the trip to Southern France, the invasion location.

The end of the tortuous trail was not yet in sight, but the beginning of the end was. Men of the 3rd Infantry Division, doubly heartened by the victorious conclusion of the push on Rome and the successful amphibious invasion of France's Normandy coast, began to see where that trail had been leading all this time. Sometimes it had seemed there was no pattern to its crazy wanderings. There was no end—not even a remembered beginning, lost in too many endless days and sleepless nights—just the awful, eternal middle. Shells, mountain peaks, destroyed villages, and mud were the only milestones to mark the journey.

Men of the 3rd, and its brother divisions in the Mediterranean Theater, for a long time bore most of the United States' ground effort in the European war. Sometimes they took staggering casualties. They

50

The Way It Was

froze, sweated, and cursed, by turn. They fought, died, and wept without tears for dead comrades. They looked for hope when often there seemed nothing for which to hope. About the only thing left to them was faith, which was equally divided—faith in God and faith in the fighting qualities of the men on either flank.

The men who lived like rats in the ruins of Cassino and dodged death day and night were hard put to it to see the grand scale of a strategical map. The soldiers who smashed across the Rapido River, to get smashed right back, could not with a casual wave of the hand say, "Well, we took a bit of a reverse today." The men who carefully kept even the tops of their helmets from showing over the parapets of Anzio foxholes were in no position to predict the end of the war by "Oh, say, Christmas."

The beginning of the end suddenly materialized. The tentative start gradually evolved into full-scale warfare, now fitted neatly into a single picture that could be viewed from one perspective. That France, and eventually Germany, had been the ultimate objectives, everyone had known. It was the method of getting to those objectives that had sometime been obscured for the fighting soldiers.

When, with the invasion convoy in mid-journey, it was announced that the destination was Southern France, the pattern was now complete.

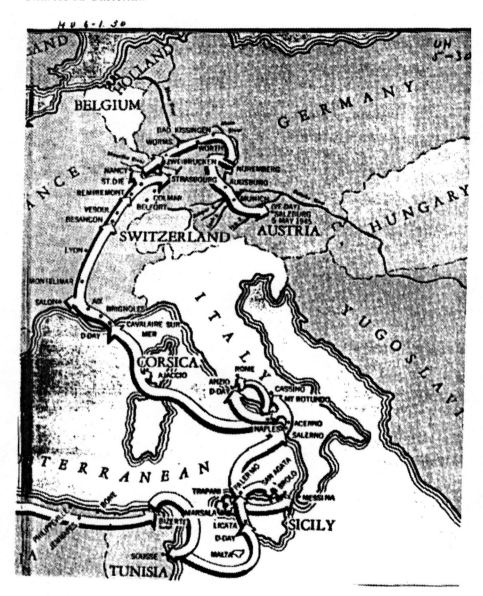

Africa, Sicily, Southern Italy, Anzio...it had taken the 3rd Infantry Division a long time to get there.

It is interesting to note how strongly events in the Mediterranean Theater exercised influence over the planned invasion of Southern France.

The Way It Was

In Vice Admiral H.K. Hewitt's report as Naval Commander, Western Task Force, on the Invasion of Southern France, there is to be found the following:

The preliminary directive[9] received from Commander-in-Chief, Mediterranean, on December 28, 1943, embodied the following mission:

Task

To establish the army firmly ashore;

To continue to maintain and support the army over beaches until all need for maintenance over beaches had ceased.

Purpose

To support the invasion of Northern France.

As a basis for planning, the preliminary directive gave the following points:

(1). Preparation for the invasion of Northern France was in progress and it was expected to take place during the first suitable day in May, 1944;

(2). Decision had been made that a beachhead would be established on the south coast of France in conjunction with the invasion of Northern France for the purpose of supporting it.

(3). Composition of the army forces for the invasion of Southern France had not been decided but would probably consist of ten divisions: three or four US divisions, and the balance French divisions.

The date *December 28, 1943* is especially important to members of the 3rd Infantry Division. It clearly indicates how far ahead Allied leaders had laid definite plans. At a time when the 3rd was nearly ready to jump off on the Anzio operation, plans were being formulated for an operation which was to place United States troops on the shores of Southern France, a program actually not put into effect until August 15, 1944, nearly eight months later. In line with

---

[9] Section 1.3, Invasion of Southern France, Report of Naval Commander, Western Task Force.

Charles R. Castellaw

this, the selection of Army forces for the operations is discussed in Admiral Hewitt's report:[10]

The question of the identity of the military forces to be made available for the operations was of great concern to the naval planners inasmuch as three major problems depended on the final assignments. In the first place, it was desired that the assault divisions each be thoroughly trained in amphibious assault with the naval attack forces until the army and navy elements were firmly welded into a finished amphibious attack unit. Secondly, the broad problem of mounting and transporting the assault and follow-up forces required considerable planning, assignment of ships, and construction in the many mounting ports. This problem was jointly considered by the Movements and Transportation Section of AFHQ, Service of Supply, North African Theater of Operations (SOS NATOUSA), the G-4 section of the Seventh Army, and the Eighth Fleet planning and logistics sections. Lastly, after having the assault divisions assigned, it was necessary for these commands to work out their tactical assault plans with respect to definite assault beaches.

During the early period of planning, since the two or possibly three US infantry divisions having the necessary qualifications were found only in the US Fifth Army, it was necessary to remove them from the Italian front. This withdrawal from the Allied Armies in Italy (AAI) raised the problem of where the divisions should be moved for training, refitting and mounting. Originally, it was proposed to train the two US infantry divisions, the 3rd and the 45th, in the Salerno area, beginning as soon as the Pisa-Rimini line was established. In order to meet the original invasion date, May 1944, promulgated in the preliminary directive issued by the Commander-in-Chief, Mediterranean, on 28 December, it was imperative that these two infantry divisions be withdrawn from combat sometime in April. At the same time, the 85th US Infantry Division was training in North Africa in the Oran area.

French divisions at this time had not yet been nominated, but they also would have to be withdrawn from the front, trained, refitted, and mounted. It was considered that training in the Salerno area might congest the port of Naples. Therefore Sicily and the "heel" ports were

---

[10] Section 1.4, Invasion of Southern France, report of Naval Commander, Western Task Force

The Way It Was

considered as suitable places for refitting some of the French divisions.

Because of the distance the 85th division would have to travel from Oran to the assault area, it was determined that that movement should be a ship-to-shore assault from combat-loaded personnel and cargo ships. The 3rd and 45th Divisions would then make the assault on a shore-to-shore basis in craft, probably staging in Ajaccio.

Army operations in Italy, south of the Pisa-Rimini line, were not stabilized in time to meet the requirements for an operation in May. Consequently, craft and ships assigned for the invasion of Southern France were withdrawn for the invasion of Northern France. By the middle of June, the 3rd and 45th Divisions were released from the Italian front and, instead of the 85th Division, the 36th US Infantry Division was withdrawn from the Italian front for participation in the invasion of Southern France.

While the amphibious operation against the Riviera coast was to be the fourth major landing against a hostile shore by the 3rd Infantry Division, and the sixth for 2nd battalion, 30th Infantry, the operation was by no means a purely routine performance. There were several important ways in which it differed from past operations.

In the past, certain elements of surprise had been major features of the success of our landings. In this case, the Normandy landing had been carried out two months previously, giving the enemy access to information on all our latest techniques and equipment. The enemy could reasonably assume that we had employed all our major new tricks in the all-important Normandy landing and had no surprises in store. In that event we had to depend solely on the surprises of time and place.

For the first time in its experience, the Division was faced with a daylight landing. This called for changes in many of the plans that had previously been successfully employed in night landings.

There was clear evidence that the enemy had constructed offshore obstacles along the Division's beaches which had never been encountered on any previous operation.

The tremendous concentration of shipping in the Naples area preceding our attack, and the shifting of the bulk of our air strength to Corsica, combined with the limited area of coast upon which we were likely to land, minimized our chance for obtaining surprise. Added to

Charles R. Castellaw

this problem was the tremendous difficulty of maintaining security on the Italian mainland, where the majority of the planning and mounting was done.

(Practice landings had been made in Nisida Harbor, within full view of hundreds of Italian bathers. Full-scale assaults had been mounted at Mondragone and Formia. For days on end quantities of material had flowed into the holds and onto decks of ships through the docks at Naples, Nisida, Pozzuoli, and Baia.)

All these factors, weighed together, meant only one thing—that we could not depend on surprising the enemy with small, scattered landings, but would have to plan on stunning him with all the firepower and concentrated mass of men and material that we could direct against a small number of closely grouped beaches. The naval gunfire and air support plans were coordinated with the Division's own attack plan to achieve this effect, and this in turn fitted into the Corps scheme of maneuver, which contemplated putting more infantry battalions ashore at H-hour than were put ashore in the Normandy landing.

Stated simply, the Division's mission in Southern France was to land on beaches in the vicinity of St. Tropez and Cavalaire, some 30 miles east of Toulon, clear the enemy from the beaches and from adjacent high ground, and advance rapidly inland, preparatory to assisting in Seventh Army's attack to the west against the ports of Toulon and Marseille. Clearing of St. Tropez peninsula, maintaining contact with the 45th Infantry Division on the right and with French troops on the left, were among subsidiary initial missions.

Personnel of the 30th Infantry were loaded aboard LSTs August 9, 1944, and the convoy sailed the same day for Pozzucli, Italy. The convoy anchored off shore at Salerno, Italy, until August 12, 1944, when it sailed for Corsico, arriving the evening of August 13th. On the evening of August 14, 1944, the convoy sailed from Corsica for Beach Red, Cavalaire, France, with H-Hour set for 0800 of August 1944.

Combat

I was in a group of replacements that was to land on the beach at a latter part of the invasion. We were to replace casualties of the

The Way It Was

invasion and the original push inland. On our way we ran into a storm. During the storm, I believe that the ship was under the water more than on top of it. Every man on ship got sick including both soldiers and sailors.

Since it was part of the Division's mission to advance inland and seize high ground in the vicinity of Cogolin at the head of the gulf of St. Tropez, it was decided to land two battalions of the 15th Infantry initially on Yellow Beach (lying between Cap de St. Tropez and Cap Camarat, on the east side of the St. Tropez peninsula) and two battalions of the 7th Infantry on Red Beach (Gulf of Cavalaire), using the 30th Infantry to land on Red Beach after it had been cleared, with a mission of exploiting to the north and seizing objectives deep in the enemy's rear to the west, north and northeast of Cogolin. The 7th and 15th Infantry Regiments were organized as combat teams, with artillery battalions, TD, tank, chemical and medical companies, mine-gapping and signal detachments attached, while the 30th Infantry had only chemical and medical companies and a signal detachment with it.

A soldier named Patelli stood up on the crowded deck. "Take it from me," he said, "the first wave onto the beach is the best one to be in. Why, you gotta choice on the first wave! If you don't like the pillbox on the right you just move over and take the pillbox on the left. But if you gotta come in later you get no choice. You gotta take the pillbox that the first wave passed!"

"The soldiers around him grinned and kept on playing cards. A little later when someone said, "Okay, you jokers, take your last look at Italy!" Only a few of the men looked up. Even when a small radio was tuned in to "Axis Sally," the Nazi propagandist, and she boasted that the Germans knew all about the coming invasion of Southern France, the soldiers kept on playing cards or talking quietly. Finally, the ship's chaplain couldn't stand it any longer. "This bunch of men is awfully unexcited," he complained. "I just had a normal crowd at services this morning. On the way across the Channel from England almost *everybody* turned out."

These men were different. They were 3rd Division men…

On the evening of August 12, a long convoy of LSTs stretched almost as far as the eye could see over a choppy sea, off the port of

Charles R. Castellaw

Naples. The sky, darkening from its midday brightness, was faultlessly blue.

A few soldiers, lining the afterdecks of each LST, stared toward the last ship in the convoy. A small speck, distinguishable as some sort of craft, was rapidly approaching. It drew closer and the soldiers could make it out to be a speedy launch. One figure was prominent in the forepart. He stood erect, disdaining to maintain his balance by a handhold.

As the boat approached to within a few hundred yards of each LST, a few soldiers stared unbelievingly. Then the cry went up: "It's Churchill!" The cry was taken up and echoed throughout the ship. Soldiers and sailors crowded to that side of the vessel.

The short, stubby figure stood straight. His thinning white hair blew awry. As the launch drew nearly abreast, he waved. Then the doughty little warrior raised his right hand to form with two fingers the V-for Victory sign—the symbol of hope and determination which, two years and more before, he had raised and flaunted at the power of the then mighty German war machine. The United States soldiers cheered and waved back.

The LST that I was on was not in this group so I did not see Churchill.

Prime Minister Winston Churchill, in Italy to confer with Italian Minister Bonomi, had been unable to resist seeing off the invasion convoy, and to wish God-speed and a quick, successful victory to the United States troops. It was a favorable omen.

Admiral Hewitt on August 9 had promulgated D-Day as August 15, and H-hour as 0800. The assault troops of the 7th and 15th Infantry Regiments debarked at Ajaccio, Corsica, for the planned staging, then once again embarked. By the morning of August 15, all the units of the 3rd Infantry Division flotilla were in place off the coast of Cavalaire and St. Tropez.

D-Day, as do all such days, began early. In the wheelhouse of each LST a naval rating kept his attention fixed on a fascinating pattern of concentric light circles. His particular LST was the constant, the hub of his own universe, the pole around which revolved the blobs of dim light which were the other ships and craft. As the vessels slowly maneuvered through the darkness into their final positions, the magic of radar kept them safe from collision.

The Way It Was

The captain stood on the bridge with the officer of the watch, and now and then spoke a few words to him, some of which the officer relayed through the speaking tube to the engine room.

Under dim blue lights in the crowded troop compartments men lay warm under a single thickness of blanket, and slept—most of them. Some, unable to overcome wakefulness, pondered at what the day might bring, tossed restlessly, and countless thoughts coursed through their minds: thoughts of the sound of bursting shells...letters from home...buddies they had known...last minute briefings...beaches... objectives...routes of advance. But most of them still slept.

In airfields on nearby Corsica, fliers were crawling from their bunks and shivering in the predawn chill. Outside, on the airstrips, ground crews already were busily warming up the motors of the bombers. The man-made thunder spoke the promise of a busy day, and of coming hell for the enemy beach defenders.

Commanders aboard the ships, awakened early, ate without much interest, and speedily turned to last-minute discussion of plans. Details, settled long before, once again cropped up for attention and reminder. Broad outlines of maneuver were reviewed. Mental estimates of time, space, and distance were checked against the opinions of others.

Soon the queues of half-asleep soldiers would move past the cans of coffee and pans of food, the men holding out mess gear as they went. The jolt of a portion of food dropped into a meat can would signal the individual to move along to the next pan and waiting mess attendant, and then down the slippery, food-splattered iron steps to the messroom.

In the supporting naval warships, gunnery officers checked the fire plans. Elsewhere, last-minute inspections of guns, ammunition, and fire tables were in process.

And in dugouts and fire emplacements ashore, a weird conglomeration of Russians, Turcomans, Poles and Slavs, their numbers spiked with a few German officers and NCOs effected reliefs, walked patrols, and turned their eyes to a still-darkened sea. There was an attitude of expectation among them. There had been stepped-up air assaults over the previous week. Many civilians had left the coastal regions between August 12-14, stating frankly that they expected an Allied landing at any hour. German radio

Charles R. Castellaw

announcements had been broadcast to the effect that an Allied invasion fleet had left Corsica for France on August 14. A rumor circulated among German soldiers and French civilians to the effect that Allied leaflets had been dropped over the St. Tropez area warning the civilian population to leave the coastal regions.

"Let the Americans come," many of the defenders probably thought. "We are foreigners to the German army. If we escape with our lives, we have nothing to lose—perhaps much to gain." But at the same time they fingered the triggers of the German machine guns and rifles, and made ready to shoot if today should prove to be the day of invasion.

It can be stated unequivocally that the D-day landings on the shores of southern France by the 3rd Infantry Division were the most successful ever undertaken by the Division in its entire history in the Mediterranean Theater. Even the landings at Nettuno, smooth as they were, did not compare with those of August 15 in smoothness of execution.

Scattered resistance on the beaches was quickly overcome. The specially-trained, reinforced, Battle Patrol which landed on the flanks of both beaches speedily smashed enemy resistance with only one of them, that of the 7th Infantry, encountering strong opposition. The mission of this Battle Patrol was to proceed about 2000 yards west from the landing point to the town of Cavalaire-sur-Mer and to clean out the town and the entire peninsula on which it is situated. The peninsula overlooks the entire beach where major portions of the landings were scheduled to be made. It was the enemy's only available position for interfering with landing operations by flanking fire; it also furnished an excellent position for directing observed artillery fire, for which the enemy was utilizing it.

"As we started inland from the water...I suddenly noticed a wire just above my head," said S/Sgt. Herman F. Nevers, leader of the 1st squad. "I looked back and ...saw...a hanging mine explode and tear the platoon leader into small pieces. The force of the explosion blew S/Sgt. James P. Connor about ten feet and knocked him flat to the ground. Sergeant Connor received a fragmentation wound on the left side of the neck...The commanding officer of the battle patrol told him to go back for aid, but Sergeant Connor refused to go."

The Way It Was

As the squad neared a bridge, a German jumped up. Connor shot him. The patrol came under a severe mortar barrage. Connor urged them forward and the group became disorganized, some of the men following another platoon, leaving only about twenty men.

At about this time a sniper shot Sergeant Connor, wounding him in the left shoulder, the bullet penetrating to his back.

Said Nevers, "I said to him, "For Christ's sake, Connor, stop and get medical attention for yourself!"

He replied, saying, "No, they can hit me but they can't stop me. I'll go until I can't go any farther." Then he said, "Nevers, get out on the right flank and get those men rolling! We've got to clean out these snipers before we can advance farther!"

Sergeant Connor told the men, "If there's only one of us left, we've got to get to that point (the objective) and clean it up, so the guys coming in after us can get in safely with no fire on them."

The platoon started forward again. Connor was in the lead again. A German rose from a hole not more than thirty feet to Sergeant Connor's front and shot him in the leg. Nevers fired over Connor as he fell, killing the German.

"Sergeant Connor called me over and told me to give him a hand to help him on his feet so he could go on with the fight. I helped him up but he couldn't stand on his leg and fell down again. I wanted to give him first aid, but he wouldn't even let me look at the wound, saying there wasn't time. He told me to take the rest of the men, about fifteen now, and to carry on, and that he hoped he would see me sometime. Sergeant Connor told me that even if I had to get down and dig the bastards out with my bare hands to go ahead and dig them out..."

Then, according to Sgt. Edward G. Collins, the group started to carry out Connor's instructions. Too many men started around the right flank and Connor called some of them back and sent them around to the left. In carrying out his orders the platoon cleaned out the entire area, killing three of four of the enemy and capturing approximately forty more.

Said 1st Lt. William K, Dieleman, Battle Patrol commander, "But for the outstanding example set by Sergeant Connor in the face of tremendous odds in fire power and men, the critically important

61

Charles R. Castellaw

mission of the whole Battle Patrol might have been delayed for a considerable time, or might even have failed entirely."

Two months later, Major John R. Darrah, Special Troops surgeon, examined the area of wounds received by Sergeant Connor and testified that the second wound must have caused him excruciating pain at the slightest movement.

Sergeant Connor received the Congressional Medal of Honor.

Establishing a Beachhead in Southern France

The 3rd Reconnaissance Troop Battle Patrol, upon landing, found twenty prisoners awaiting the pleasure of their captors. The fire delivered by BARs and rifles of the Battle Patrol, shooting from their landing craft, had converted them to the Allied cause before any United States soldier set foot in Southern France. Within a short time 115 more were added and by 1030 the Battle Patrol had returned to 3rd Reconnaissance Troop control, having completely accomplished its mission.

The 7th Infantry landed with 3rd battalion on the left, 2nd battalion on the right. There were concrete tetrahedrals offshore, and mines and wire on the beach and inland for distances up to 500 yards, yet little resistance was encountered. The naval rocket barrage that had immediately preceded the assault had apparently had good effect, as a dense, even, pattern of bursts was observed inshore, and the first prisoners taken were well shaken up. Shortly after landing, 2nd battalion, moving up the road toward La Croix, received mortar and small-arms fire from the right, and this fire continued sporadically for about two hours with little effect. By 1045, 2nd battalion had passed through La Croix and by 1430 had reached the objective.

The 2nd battalion of the 30th Infantry led the Regiment off the Beach and made first contact with the enemy North of Le Croix at 151430, however, by 151440 resistance had been overcome and battalion was on objective X. Battalion was assembled, less one platoon, at 151830 and was ordered to continue the attack to the west; passed through Cogolin and by 160300 had elements in the town of Gonfaron.

The 3rd battalion had very light opposition also, and reached its first two objectives by 1345.

The Way It Was

Both assault battalions of the 15th Infantry—3rd on the right and 1st on the left—hit Yellow Beach at 0800, reduced all beach defenses within forty minutes, and moved inland to their objectives on high ground 3000 to 5000 yards back from the beach. These objectives were occupied about noon against little enemy opposition.

Leading elements of the 30th Infantry landed behind 7th Infantry on Red Beach at H-plus-80 minutes and struck rapidly inland. Overtaking a battalion of the 7th Infantry, the 30th moved through and took objective W, and proceeded to objective D. By 1400, 2nd battalion was east of the road north of La Croix, and 3rd battalion was moving toward Cogolin, which Company K reached and entered at 1415.

Landing at H-hour in support of each assault regiment were a smoke detail from the 3rd Chemical Battalion (attached), four DD tanks (tanks made amphibious by canvas flotation aprons) from the 756th Tank Battalion, and on Yellow Beach four tank destroyers from the 601st TD Battalion.

By noon almost all units were on the Division's initial beachhead line.

During the afternoon 1st Battalion, 7th Infantry, passed through 3rd battalion on its objective, advanced to highway 98 east of La Mole, and turned west on the highway. The 2nd battalion, relieved by 30th Infantry on its objective, followed 1st Battalion. 1st Battalion was assembled, and moved west along the coast road, meeting no resistance until about 2300 when it encountered a strongpoint of six or eight machine guns, three AT guns, and several riflemen, covering a wire-and-mine roadblock. This strongpoint was still under attack at noon of the following day.

The 2nd battalion, 15th Infantry swung north through 3rd battalion, 15th Infantry, and attacked St. Tropez, reducing the last resistance there and taking nearly 100 PWs by 1945. The entire regiment then assembled and moved west through Cogolin behind the 30th Infantry.

The 1st Battalion, 30th Infantry, followed 3rd battalion, 30th, through Cogolin. Company G contacted 15th Infantry at 1500 and at 1640 the regimental Battle Patrol contacted 15th Infantry Battle Patrol on the peninsula between Red and Yellow Beaches. The 1st Battalion, 30th Infantry, entered Grimaud at 1710 against little but sniper resistance, with a reinforced platoon protecting its flank. The 3rd

Charles R. Castellaw

battalion rode on tanks west from Cogolin to Grimaud at 1755. The first enemy contacted by 3rd battalion was about one and one-half miles east of Collobriéres at 2240. This resistance was overcome and 3rd battalion had closed in Collobriéres by 0300 August 16.

By 0435 1st Battalion had passed through La Garde Freinet and was in Les Mayons reducing resistance, and taking twenty-two prisoners. An hour after that time the reinforced platoon from 1st Battalion, on flank-protection duty, was relieved by elements of the 45th Division.

By noon of August 16, D-plus-one, leading elements of the 3rd Infantry Division were twenty miles inland. Its gains were surprising, and gratifying, in comparison with its former landing operations below Nettuno.

In retrospect, here is what had happened:

A harassed German High Command was even then stretching its forces nearly to the breaking point between the long Russian front and the fluid battlefield which all of France from the Seine River to the Brittany Peninsula had become on the west. It was like a man trying to keep two determined intruders from entering a stolen house that he had taken for his home and running back and forth, alternately attempting to hold two doors shut. Suddenly he hears noises which sound like a third party about to come in through the cellar. He is powerless to do anything about this new threat.

From subsequent interrogation it was learned that the enemy had expected the main landing effort to be made in the vicinity of Toulon and Marseille. He knew that we must have in short order at least one good port through which to pour supplies to keep the advance continuous. The bulk of the enemy's force, therefore, was disposed farther west, and was in no position to intervene until after we were well ashore. But even then it was too late. The provisional airborne division, under Brig. Gen. Robert T. Frederick, which landed in the vicinity of Le Muy; the rapid advances inland of all three United States divisions; the harassment of naval gunfire along the coast; the disrupting of the enemy's lines of communications and movement of enemy reserves by well-organized and well-armed French resistance groups; the bombing "strangle"—all these prevented the enemy from making the ghost of a showing of countermeasure or even offering effective resistance.

The Way It Was

**The first French Partisans, Saint-Trapez area
Source U.S. Army in WW II**

The enemy high command issued one amazing statement about three days following the landings. "No counterattack will be launched against the invasion forces," said the enemy in an intercepted radio broadcast, "until they have driven inland far enough so as to be out of effective range of the support of their own naval gunfire." In effect, this was equivalent to a flat admission of German impotence.

"We broke a very thin crust," said one high-ranking United States officer "and behind the crust there was nothing that could stop us."

Driving Inland

So, with scarcely a pause, the 3rd Infantry Division prepared to make its longest advance in the shortest length of time that it had ever made—or ever would make—in Europe. There was no warning such as, "I want you to be in Palermo in five days." Movement and attack orders were, for the most part, to be issued verbally by the VI Corps commander, Maj. Gen. Lucian K. Truscott, to General O'Daniel;

Charles R. Castellaw

General O'Daniel's orders were usually issued the same way to his regimental commanders. The confirming orders, on paper, would be sent along later, but right now it was "to hell with written orders, let's get going." The enemy had been maneuvered back on his heels, and every man in VI Corps, weary though he might be, could not help but sense that keeping the enemy off-balance was a sure way to keep casualties to the bare minimum. The Division moved west against only scattered, unorganized resistance.

Improvisation paid dividends. It was found that an entire infantry battalion could be completely loaded on transportation within a regiment, including tanks, tank destroyers, jeeps, and other assorted vehicles without having recourse to non-organic vehicles.

It was a common sight to see a whole rifle battalion moving down a road—doughboys draped over the 3-inch guns of tank destroyers, clinging to the slippery-sided tanks of the 756th, or loaded sixes-and-sevens to trailer-hauling jeeps.

Of the 1627 prisoners taken on D-day, the overwhelming majority were from the 242nd Infantry Division, with a few hundred more from fortress and coast defense battalions, and miscellaneous numbers of them from labor, naval, air and signal organizations.

Company G, 30th Infantry, with armor, occupied Carnoules, southeast of Gonfaron, by 0530 August 16 while 2nd battalion attacked and occupied Gonfaron by 1400. Leading elements of Company E and tanks had entered town at 160300. Blocks were placed on all roads; high ground north of town was organized for defense. Company K, 30th Infantry, captured Pierrefeu by 1819, August 16, against self-propelled and small-arms fire—the westernmost advance of the 30th. The company took thirty-five prisoners.

The leading battalions, 1st and 3rd, of the 7th Infantry, overcame enemy strongpoints. By noon of August 17 our front lines ran generally from Cuers to Carnoules to Gonfaron to Le Luc, inclusive. Tanks and tank destroyers were being used with infantry to patrol and clear roads linking battalion sectors. Towns captured in twenty-four hours included Le Lavandou, Bormes, Leoube, Pierrefeu, Pignans, Carnoules, Puget Ville, Rocbaron, and Flassans.

At 1350 August 17, 2nd battalion of the 7th Infantry forward elements received small-arms fire from a road junction on the approaches to La Londe. Intense artillery and machine-gun fire also

The Way It Was

delayed the battalion's advance. The battalion engaged the enemy in an all-night firefight, during which forty to fifty Germans were killed. Patrols into La Londe during the morning of August 18 reported the town clear.

It was in this fight that S/Sgt. Stanley Bender of Company E particularly distinguished himself. The three bridges that spanned the Maravennes River just beyond the town had to be taken intact, otherwise the advance would have been slowed for hours, when every minute counted in pursuing the retreating Germans.

Said 1st Lt. George H. Franklin, "At about 1400 hours, just as we were about to round the last bend in the road...We were stopped by a Frenchman who advised us that there was a roadblock about 200 yards beyond us and that the town was full of enemy troops. We instantly dismounted from four M-10 tank destroyers and three M-4 tanks and went into a squad column on either side of the road and then went cross-country in an effort to surprise the enemy."

After going only a short distance the company was fired upon by machine guns and small arms from well-concealed positions to the left. At the same time an enemy antitank gun opened fire and destroyed one of the tanks that had left the road and was advancing with the infantry. All remaining tank destroyers and tanks moved into firing position from where they attempted to engage the antitank guns.

"We all took cover as rapidly as possible," said S/Sgt. Edward C. Havrila. "...I saw that ...Sergeant Bender...hadn't taken cover with the rest of us. The crazy guy was standing up on top of the knocked-out tank, in full view of the kraut, shading his eyes and looking around trying to pick out the source of the enemy fire. Bullets were bouncing off that tank right beside him, but he nevertheless stayed right there until he found the kraut position..."

When Bender located the position he jumped to the ground and ran to a ditch in which two squads had taken cover. He ordered them to engage the enemy while he took his squad forward in an effort to destroy the strongpoint. Then, without waiting for instructions or orders, Sergeant Bender ran forward, motioning for his squad to follow. The intrepid squad leader reached the ditch under machine-gun fire that wounded four of his men. The enemy tried to throw grenades into the ditch, but Bender did not move until his squad had joined him. Said Sgt. Forest M. Law: "The next time I saw Sergeant

Charles R. Castellaw

Bender he was in the act of crawling from the ditch at a point between seventy-five and one hundred and fifty yards beyond the Kraut strongpoint. He was all alone and making no effort to conceal himself. Walking erect...he made a fine target and one of the kraut machine gunners picked up his gun and turned it around in an effort to get him. However Sergeant Bender continued his wide end sweep in a rapid walk. He was too far away for me to see his facial expression, but his manner looked as calm and unperturbed as a soldier on pass."

Bender walked the entire forty to fifty yards, directly up to a gunner who, during Bender's entire "stroll," had had a clear field of fire. Bender shot the man with his tommy gun.

Following this, he walked another twenty-five yards to the second machine-gun emplacement and killed the gunner and his assistant. He called his squad out of the ditch and walked another thirty-five yards to kill an enemy rifleman who was in the act of firing. The squad joined him in the slaughter.

As a result of Sergeant Bender's actions, and the inspiration they caused, all bridges over the Maravennes were taken intact, a roadblock was destroyed, and the dominating high ground was seized. Sergeant Bender was later awarded the Congressional Medal of Honor.

The 2nd battalion of the 30th Infantry (less Company G) with companies E, F and H moving from Gontaron toward Flassans was halted by fire from enemy anti tank guns at 170910. The enemy guns located at (160260) were taken under fire by artillery and mortars knocking out two 75mm guns, one 88mm gun, one prime mover and one truck. The Battalion continued to move at 171130 and closed in Flassans at 171200. Company G meanwhile moved from Carnoules to Besse, south of Flassans. By 171400 the 2nd battalion was enroute to Brignoles with Company G moving on a parallel route from Besse and battalion was in contact with the 1st Battalion on the right.

The 15th Infantry regrouped during the period of 2nd battalion, 7th's action, and pushed west along the Besse-Forcalqueiret road, clearing out the hills south of the road. Opposition was light for the most part and the regiment moved swiftly. At 1900 3rd battalion pushed through St. Anastasie and across the high ground west of Besse. At the same time, 2nd battalion began a truck shuttle movement toward the regimental zone of advance after being relieved by 7th Infantry at

The Way It Was

Pierrefeu. About fifty enemy held up the 3rd battalion for a short period at Anastasie, but these were soon forced to withdraw. At 2100, 1st Battalion was south of Forcalqueiret and 2nd battalion was east of the same town.

The 30th Infantry, led by 2nd battalion, under the command of Maj. Frederick R. Armstrong, reached the vicinity of Brignoles, where it was delayed by enemy opposition from 1840 August 17, until the morning of the 18th. The enemy brought up his 1st Company, 757th Regiment, 338th Infantry Division, and other units totaling two battalions in strength, to hold the town. The forces occupied a position west of the town, covering a 300-meter front, protected by sharp terrain on both sides. At 1825 a patrol from the 3rd Reconnaissance Troop was stopped by the enemy on Highway 7 with 3rd battalion about 1000 yards behind.

The 2nd battalion, which had taken Flassans by 1200, August 17, was on its way to Brignoles two hours later. Although the 30th did not know it, the capture of Brignoles was to be the regiment's first big fight in southern France.

The plan of attack was to move astride the Flassan-Brignoles road with 1st Battalion on the right on a flanking mission, and 2nd battalion on the left. H-hour was set for 0600 August 18.

The attack got away as planned and Company B swung north to Le Val to protect the regiment's right flank, as Company G moved west from Besse to the high ground dominating Le Celle, protecting the 30th's left flank. The attack moved forward against stubborn resistance. During August 18, Company F got around south of the town and cut the road to the west. Company E drove to the center of Brignoles by 1900. The 1st Battalion ran into heavy resistance just north of the city.

The attack on Brignoles began with 1st and 2nd battalion crossing LOD at 180600, and soon running into heavy machine gun and rifle fire. Seventy-five prisoners were taken by 2nd battalion in the attack by 181200.

Company B continued to move West through VINS toward Brignoles the night of 17/18 August and after releasing armor to the 1st Battalion at RJ North of Brignoles turned North and occupied the town of VALE to protect the right flank of the sector. Company G, moving on the night of 17/18 August from Besse occupied the high

Charles R. Castellaw

ground South of Brignoles overlooking the town of Le Celle and protected the left flank of the sector.

The initial attempt to take Brignoles was not entirely successful. The 1st Battalion was engaged with the enemy throughout the day and night in an area north of town. The 2nd battalion was able to get Company F through the southern part of town to western outskirts on the 18th, however, Company E was still engaged with stubborn resistance in the center of town at dark 18 August. At 181230 3rd battalion was committed, shuttled from Flassans to detrucking point (073293), moved by marching to assembly area (013314) closing at 181640, and attacked in wide envelopment north of Brignoles, cutting road west of town at 182000 with Company I; the balance of the 3rd battalion moving toward the town of Bras. All positions of the 1st and 2nd battalions were held, and at 190600 attack was resumed with Company F attacking from south, 1st Battalion attacking from the North and Company E pushing on west. Brignoles was declared clear and 1st and 2nd battalions were assembling west of town by 191030. Enemy resistance of approximately three battalions had been killed, captured or forced to withdraw and harassed enroute by the 3rd battalion.

With no change in pace the Regiment was assigned more objectives to the West. 1st Battalion at 191415 moved from assembly area West of Brignoles toward Tourves and St. Maximin, passing through 3rd battalion, 15th Infantry at Tourves. The 1st Battalion closed in St. Maximin at 191925 and at 192005 was enroute to Aix. Battalion made contact with enemy at (6.88377) and was engaged in a firefight at 200045. 2nd battalion remained in assembly area West of Brignoles until 200500, then moved by reinforcing transportation toward Aix, detrucking at 201000 and passing through 1st Battalion.

During the night of August 18-19, 3rd battalion was committed in an envelopment to the north to cut the road west of town and continue toward Bras, as 1st Battalion (minus Company B at Le Val) and 2nd battalion (minus Company G at La Celle) worked into the town.

The attack began again at 0600, August 19. Lt. Col. Allen F. Bacon's 1st Battalion, spearheaded by Company A, came in from the north, while Company E drove from the west and Company F from the southwest, to meet in the center of the town. This coupled with the wide 3rd battalion flanking attack, broke enemy resistance and the

The Way It Was

town was completely cleared by 1030. The 3rd battalion continued toward Bras.

Elements of the 338th Infantry Division were now being counted through the cages, although the bulk of opposition, such as it was, was still being provided by 242nd Infantry Division, in addition to dozens of "spare parts" organizations, such as handfuls from the 189th Reserve Division and 244th Infantry Division.

Between noon of August 19 and noon August 20, the Division advanced nearly thirty miles, moving both on foot and by motor. Towns liberated during the 24-hour period were, besides Brignoles: Meounes, Gareoult, Neoules, La Roquebrussane, Camps, La Celle, and Le Val.

A Task Force consisting of Company C, 15th Infantry, plus four tanks, two tank destroyers, and three trucks moved from Mazauges. The 1st Battalion followed the Task Force; then on August 20, continued the advance toward Auriel. No resistance was encountered. From Tourves, 2nd battalion, 15th, continued the advance toward Trets, which was found clear, and on the morning of the 20th the battalion continued the advance toward Gardanne. The 3rd battalion had taken Tourves early in the afternoon of the 19th after a 45-minute attack, and Company L pushed on toward St. Maximin. The battalion occupied La Defenos and terrain in the vicinity. On the morning of the 20th, 3rd battalion moved by truck to Trets, thence southwest toward Peynier.

The 30th Infantry reorganized in the vicinity of Brignoles following its fight there and moved out with 1st Battalion in the lead. By 1430, August 19, 1st Battalion had gone beyond La Censies. The 2nd battalion was on high ground to the south of 1st Battalion and 3rd battalion was on high ground to the south of Bras. At 1900 3rd battalion left St. Maximin for Olliéres on foot and arrived there prior to midnight. Shortly thereafter it moved out for Pourcieux. The 2nd battalion remained in reserve near Brignoles until 0400, when it moved out along Highway 7. At noon 30th Infantry had still encountered no opposition.

During the same period (August 19-20) 1st Battalion, 7th Infantry remained in defensive positions near Pierrefeu, except for Company B, which outposted Cuers. Company A was relieved by units of the 1st French Division at 1405. By 0800 1st Battalion had begun shuttling toward La Celle, and upon arriving there prepared to move by vehicle to the regimental assembly area. The 2nd battalion, 7th Infantry, moved to a defensive position in the vicinity of Meounes and Forcalqueiret during the night of August 19-20. By noon, August 20, French troops were relieving the 2nd battalion. The 3rd battalion was completely relieved by French troops by 1405 August 19, and moved first to assembly near St. Honoré, then by vehicle to the vicinity of La Celle.

Summary of localities liberated again read like a Michelin guidebook to the area: Masaugnes, Tourves, Rougiers, Seillons, Olliéres, Pourcieux, St. Zacharie, Pourrierers, Trets, Peynier, Rousset, and Puyloubier.

The move against the most important town in the vicinity, Aix-en-Provence, began on the afternoon of August 20.

The plan of attack by the 3rd Infantry to clear town of Aix was set up and executed with 2nd battalion to hold position west and south of town to support attack by fire. 1st and 3rd battalions were to shift to north of town and attack south with battalions abreast, 1st Battalion on the right.

1st Battalion moved on the afternoon of 20 August by motor from (Point 711369) east through Pourrieres, north and northwest through St. Marc, detrucking at (Point 563434) Battalion then by marching approx. 12 miles cross country northwest to (Point 532479). 5 miles north of enemy lines a road block was established astride highway 7 at (Point 532479) and battalion after a firefight with bicyclists coming south toward Aix, closed in assembly area vicinity Celony 210045. The attack jumped off at 210600 with 2 companies abreast, one company echeloned to left rear. Enemy resistance was stiff, however two enemy self propelled guns and enemy infantry were knocked out and battalion was in the northwest outskirts of town by 211135. Enemy infantry and tanks moved southwest toward a roadblock at Celony and 1st Battalion was ordered and moved to northwest to block enemy action. Casualties were heavy with 2 officers wounded in action and 11 enlisted men killed in action and 18 Enlisted Men wounded in action.

Fire from 2nd battalion was placed on town of Aix at 210600, however, getting into position the night prior to the attack, it was necessary for battalion to knock out a road block at (Point 570386) and drive enemy infantry, mortars and a flak wagon off position to be occupied by the battalion. 2nd battalion also established a roadblock

The Way It Was

south of Aix (508390) because 15th Infantry was not in position to support the attack. Block was in position at 210855 and fires lifted from town of Aix at 210945.

3rd battalion shifted north and west at 210115 into assembly area for attack of Aix without incident. The attack started at 210600 with two companies abreast. Leading elements entered the town at 210830 and had cleared the town in its zone of action. Due to a change in orders for 1st Battalion, 3rd battalion moved to the west and then north clearing zone of action of 1st Battalion in town of Aix.

Regiment received orders to continue the attack to the west and movement was begun in two columns. The 2nd battalion entrucked at 211945 and moved to town of Ventabren, closing at 220330. The companies moved into position and patrols to the West made no contact.

3rd battalion entrucked at 211930, moved to town of Equilles and occupied defensive positions to northwest. Positions were occupied by 220330 and motorized patrols had not made contact.

In Regimental Reserve, the 1st Battalion entrucked at 220440 and moved to assembly area vicinity of Equilles, with one company and vicinity of Ventabren with two companies.

Reconnaissance to town of Salon made no contact with the enemy and the 30th Regiment was ordered to occupy that area on 22 August 1944.

The 2nd battalion, 30th Infantry, met opposition as it moved into position east of Aix. At 2215, Company G was astride Highway 7 leading into town while the entire 2nd battalion was engaged in a firefight with the enemy until 0130, when the fire died down. During the night the regiment established blocks to the west and south of town. The 3rd battalion, meanwhile, was driving northwest of Highway 7, and reached the outskirts of Aix before being fired on about dark of August 20. From this position, 1st Battalion swung north, then west, cutting across four to five "hub" roads leading into Aix, fifteen kilometers to the north of the city, in the dark, fighting bicycle-mounted Germans who came in from the north. The 1st Battalion then established blocks on roads, placing themselves to the northwest of Aix. The 3rd battalion established blocks to the north of their zone of attack.

Charles R. Castellaw

By dawn 1st Battalion, which had moved farthest, so as to be on 3rd battalion's right as it faced south, was ready to attack, and had a strong block at Celoney, astride Highway 7 (7th and 15th were not far enough west to establish these blocks as planned).

By daylight 3rd battalion, too, was poised to attack, having swung northwest inside 1st Battalion.

The coordinated attack got away at 0600. The 2nd battalion provided a base of fire as 1st Battalion attacked from the northwest and 3rd battalion pushed in from the north. The bulk of the attached armor was with 3rd battalion.

Just as the attack commenced, enemy infantry attacked 1st Battalion with strong armor support down Highway 7 from the vicinity of Celoney. The entire battalion was ordered to block to the northwest and deal with this threat while 3rd battalion continued with its mission of clearing the city. Aix-en-Provence was completely free of enemy by 1000, August 21.

The 3rd battalion, 7th Infantry, began a shuttling movement toward Chateauneuf following the fall of Aix-en-Provence.

The 1st Battalion, 15th Infantry, had overcome opposition in front of Auriel, and by 0200, August 21, entered and cleared the town. The 2nd battalion, advancing toward Gardanne, met resistance. Company G moved against it and by 1515 had a patrol into the town. An enemy pocket estimated to be from 400 to 600 men in strength generally held up the battalion, however. The battalion moved out at daylight, August 21, attacked approximately 1500 yards, and had the town by 1000.

Towns liberated were Aix-en-Provence, Gardannes, Chateauneuf, Vaubenargues, St. Mare, and Le Lollonet.

Following its capture of Aix and Gardannes, the two most important towns in the area, the Division conducted vigorous patrolling up to ten miles to the west, northwest, and southwest and established a series of roadblocks in the three directions. Reconnaissance elements entered Berre and patrolled to the lake near it.

Strategy

The broad scheme of maneuver, in which 3rd Infantry Division drove to the west, might be explained at this time. Originally, rather than make a direct assault by sea on the highly fortified area of Toulon-Marseille, VI Corps had chosen to land farther to the east. Early seizure of both of them was necessary, however, to gain a port before October's unfavorable weather set in, making maintenance over the beaches extremely difficult.

Toulon had to be reduced because the port there, in addition to being strongly fortified with big guns which could seriously interfere with shipping bound for Marseille, was a warship and submarine base whose possession by the enemy would enable him to send out damaging naval units against unprotected convoys or tie up and hinder our supply lines by forcing the Navy to convoy every LST and Liberty ship which sailed from Naples to Marseille. Marseille was the needed port since, in peacetime, it had handled the largest amount of tonnage of any harbor city on the Mediterranean.

French units which began landing over Red and Yellow beaches on D-plus-one relieved our elements along the coast—that is, 7th Infantry—narrowing the Division's then 20-mile frontage. The 3rd Division then continued the rapid advance to the west, flanking from the north both Toulon and Marseille while French units undertook the task of cleaning them out.

By this time, therefore, all roads leading north and northwest from the city had been blocked.

Over August 22-23, 1st Battalion, 7th Infantry, was sent by truck to the vicinity of Lambesc, then moved northwest of the town and set up a defense along the highway. A motorized patrol was sent into Pelissane and found the town clear of enemy. The 3rd battalion left for La Roque and relieved elements of 180th Infantry (45th Division), going into position on the road about 1000 yards east of the town. A roadblock was set up in the town.

The 15th Infantry's 1st Battalion remained in defensive positions around Gardannes and to the south and southwest. The 2nd battalion continued its blocking role also, with the command post at La Fare. At 0910, August 23, the battalion moved to its final phase line, which included Gignac, Marignane, and Martigues. An L Company patrol investigated the airport north of Marignane and found mines on the field marked with flags.

The 30th Infantry sent out a motorized patrol shortly after noon on August 22, to Lancon, which came from the south through La Fare and reported no enemy. The 3rd battalion began a motor movement toward Salon at 2030, and by 0515 had set up roadblocks in that vicinity. The 2nd battalion remained in reserve and 1st Battalion stayed in position with roadblocks covering all approaches.

Towns liberated during the period were Marignane, St. Victoret, Vitrelles, Rognac, Coudoux, La Fare, Cornillon-Confoux, Lancon, St. Cannat, Labarben, Palissanee, Salon, Vernegues, Alleins, Mullemort, and Charleval.

The swing north to parallel the Rhone River was about to begin, together with the most rapid phase of Division's most rapid advance in Europe. The German 19th Army was now almost completely disorganized. Up until noon of August 23 the Division had taken 4165 prisoners. Elsewhere in the VI Corps zone the German commander of the coastal defense area had been captured, along with most of his staff, and this early disruption of enemy communications left the 19th Army with no choice but to begin its rapid back-pedalling toward Germany.

The French Resistance

A major factor aiding the speed and success of our movement was the activity of the French resistance groups. Four years of Nazi subjugation had left many ardent French patriots with a strong urge to take to the "underground," a word loosely used in connection with resistance activities—that is to say, to go into hiding from the German Gestapo. At the time of our landing there were about seventeen of these groups which had attained a high degree of organization by consolidating, selecting common leaders, and formulating strict rules of conduct. Any man who wished to be a member of the F.F.I. (*Forces Francaise D'Interieure*—the common, but by no means only, name for the resistance groups) had to renounce completely his ties

The Way It Was

with home and family and devote his time and energies toward aiding in the liberation of France.

Strict rules of conduct did not mean that a man would be put on extra duty in the kitchen for failure to keep his shirt buttoned or his cap straight on his head, but it did mean that his comrades would put him to death if he lost his rifle. Weapons seized from ambushed German *Wehrmacht* units or dropped by parachute from British bombers were bought with blood, and were too precious to waste through carelessness. Other governing restrictions were equally as severe, although, with typical Gallic logic, applied only to things having mainly to do with life and death.

The motivating spirit was patriotism and a burning desire for freedom. The harsh conditions of service were entirely in keeping with the ascetic singleness of purpose that had dictated the groups' formation.

In certain cities, notably Grenoble, Avignon, and Lyons, and in scores of lesser localities, the F.F.I. swung into decisive action with the landings in southern France. Sometimes under the leadership of United States or British members of the O.S.S. (Office of Strategic Services), more often led by Frenchmen, whole towns were seized and held to await our coming. In addition to this sabotage activities were coordinated with our movements. If the Air Force failed to destroy a bridge, that bridge might be demolished anyway—from the ground and with hand-laid demolitions. Speeding convoys of enemy reserves ran into mysteriously laid roadblocks, and ambush. Small, isolated German pockets were sometimes wiped out to the last man, and lone enemy soldiers, if they escaped retribution at the hands of the patriots, surrendered to the first United States soldier to present himself, in preference to being the quarry in a relentless manhunt.

It is true there were a few summer patriots in the ranks of the F.F.I. These were the heroes who put on white armbands after the Germans had been cleared out, and some of them were the leading spirits in the head-shaving parties which accompanied each liberation of new territory. But these persons were in a very small minority. Most of the patriots fought behind the lines, and rendered us valuable assistance in our clean sweep from the Riviera coast north up the Rhone Valley.

Charles R. Castellaw

Further Into France

Beginning on August 23 our reconnaissance elements patrolled up to fifteen miles in front of the Division, reaching Arles on the Rhone River as a move was begun to the northern banks of the Durance River.

The 2nd battalion, 30th Infantry, relieved 7th Infantry, which was in position with its 1st Battalion near Aliens and Mallemont, 2nd battalion in Division reserve at St. Cannat, and 3rd battalion located between La Roque and Charleval. The 7th Infantry, in turn, began a relief of the 157th Infantry (45th Division) north of the Durance River. Goums began relieving 3rd battalion, 15th Infantry, was assembled in the vicinity of St. Cannat as Division reserve.

At 1710, August 23, 1st Battalion, 30th Infantry, moved north to Lamonen against no resistance, and had reached its objective by 2130.

The move across the Durance River continued. The 15th Infantry moved during the night of August 24-25, following relief by units of the 1st French Armored Division. 30th Infantry commenced its move on the morning of the 25th. Meanwhile, the 7th Infantry continued patrolling the terrain to its front and, upon finding it unoccupied, moving forward. By 1000, 2nd battalion had a patrol into Cavaillon, and during the morning of August 25, reconnaissance elements passed through the battalion to patrol the road northwest toward Avignon, which was later entered by elements of the 3rd Reconnaissance Troop.

Moves of the Division had now begun to resemble the pattern left on an ice rink by the skates of busy hockey players as successive objectives were reached, found unoccupied, and new ones assigned.

7th Infantry sent a motorized patrol on August 25th from Segonce to Montlaux, Cruix, Stetienne, and to Ongles without making contact with the enemy. The 2nd battalion sent a patrol into Caumont and picked up two straggler prisoners. The 3rd battalion sent Company L (less one platoon) to Sault and from there to Vaison. The platoon set up a roadblock at a road junction 1000 yards north of Montbrun. The remainder of the battalion remained in Division reserve near Apt. The 1st Battalion moved through Pernes and occupied the town of Orange. It remained there until all elements of the 15th Infantry had passed through it, meanwhile contacting the French to the south.

The Way It Was

The 15th Infantry moved from its assembly area in the vicinity of Apt by motor to another in the vicinity of Carpentras. At 0500, August 26, the regiment advanced to the northwest with 1st Battalion on the left and 3rd battalion on the right, making no contact with the enemy.

The 30th Infantry, after moving by truck from Salon to Vaison, was given the mission of clearing out the area northwest of Vaison and south of the Aigue River. The regimental Intelligence and Reconnaissance platoon had occupied Vaison before dark of August 25 after reconnoitering north out of Sault. The 1st Battalion trucked from Salon to an assembly area near Apt. The 2nd battalion followed the 1st, then moved by motor to Carpentras, from which point it moved to clear the area south of the Aigue River and northwest of Vaison. The 1st Battalion moved abreast, clearing between the river and the Mirabel-Vaison road.

The 1st platoon of the 3rd Reconnaissance Troop contacted elements of the 36th Infantry Division in Nyons at 1350, August 25. The 2nd Platoon had entered Carpentras unopposed at 1715. The 3rd platoon captured sixty-one prisoners in the vicinity of Orange at 1035, August 26.

The division was now moving into positions preparatory to launching an attack northwest toward Montellmar.

The 7th Infantry advanced north along Highway 7, paralleling the Rhone, to Bourg St. Andeol, 1st and 2nd battalions abreast. At Bourg the regiment was passed through by 15th Infantry, which reached Donzere after a terrific battle at a bridge 1000 yards south of the town. Several AT guns and a strong force of infantry with artillery support had to be overcome at this point. The battle lasted seven hours. On the morning of the 27th the regiment continued along Highway 7 toward Montelimar. Company L encountered enemy resistance from approximately thirty enemy on the regiment's right, armed with one machine gun and some rifles, plus an antitank gun. The enemy withdrew after a short fight. The 30th Infantry finished the job of clearing south of the Aigue River, and from Vaison to Mirabel, and continued the attack on the morning of the 27th between 15th Infantry and the 36th Infantry Division. Toward noon screening reconnaissance elements encountered an enemy strongpoint in the vicinity of Grignan. The 1st Battalion, between 1400 and 1430 of the previous day, had been bombed and strafed by four planes identified as P-47s. The 2nd battalion started at 0700, August 27, reached Valreas at 0900 and continued along its zone of advance. The 3rd platoon, 3rd Reconnaissance Troop, after engaging in a fight which netted eighty-five prisoners of war, entered Bollene.

During this period one of Mauldin's characters (from a 3rd Division newspaper cartoon) ruefully remarked something to the effect that, "We try like hell to catch the enemy and when we catch him we try like hell to get him on the run." It was at Montelimar that the 3rd Division once more caught him. By the time the brief battle was over, a considerable weight of enemy material and more than a thousand prisoners were prevented from making any further progress in their headlong rush backward.

The 15th Infantry continued to advance north along Highway 7 on the approaches to the town. On August 27, the 1st Battalion, moving on the regimental left flank, had first encountered enemy resistance in the vicinity of Donzere. The 3rd battalion advanced on the right flank, with Company L first meeting enemy opposition. The 2nd battalion, in reserve, followed 3rd battalion.

The 3rd battalion, 7th Infantry, had moved to the 30th Infantry sector at 1915, August 27, passing through Begude-de-Mazenc en route, which placed it east of Montelimar.

The 30th Infantry on August 27 had cleared the enemy out of strongpoints and rear-guard localities along the Nyons-Montelimar road and west to Grignan. The 2nd battalion, after cleaning out Grignan, moved to Salles-en-Bois during the night. At 0800 the battalion moved out in two columns to rejoin at Rochefort, where it ran into some small-arms opposition.

A coordinated attack at 0800 found 3rd battalion, 7th Infantry, on the right side of the road leading west into Montelimar, with 3rd battalion, 30th Infantry, on the left, and 1st Battalion, 30th, echeloned to the left rear. The 3rd battalion, 7th, encountered continuous rearguard resistance, but 3rd battalion, 30th, met none until 1030, when it was fired on from the vicinity of La Batie Rollande. The 1st Battalion, 7th Infantry, advanced behind 3rd battalion, while 2nd battalion remained in Division reserve near Grillon.

The 1st Battalion 15th Infantry drove relentlessly forward into the enemy resistance. The enemy force now trapped in the Montelimar

The Way It Was

area resorted to violent and incessant counterattacks to break out of the cordon. The 1st Battalion drove forward and smashed every German counterattack against it, repulsing at one time the attack of an entire regiment of infantry. It pounded the enemy force with concentrations of artillery and mortar fire.

The 15th Infantry pressed its attack during the afternoon of the 28th. The 1st Battalion encircled the town and attacked with Company A from the east, Company C from the northeast, and Company B from the north. The 2nd battalion attacked from the southeast, squeezing out 3rd battalion, which then reverted to regimental reserve. Company F, supported by Company G entered the town at 1430. During the afternoon and night, the 1st and 2nd battalions continued to clear the town of enemy sniper, and artillery fire—the last from an enemy gun located right in town. All roads leading into the city were blocked, and the area between it and the Rhone River cleared. Elements of the 3rd battalion screened to the southeast. Company C repulsed an enemy counterattack of estimated company strength from the north at 2030. The job of cleaning out Montelimar was finally completed by 1145, August 29.

During this three-day action, the 1st Battalion took 804 prisoners, killed and wounded 485 enemy, captured or destroyed at least 500 vehicles and an estimated 1,000 horses. For this action the 1st Battalion was awarded the Distinguished Unit Citation.

The 1st Battalion, 30th Infantry, had continued its attack along the south side of the east-west road into Montelimar. At 1255, August 28, the battalion moved southwest through Portes-en-Valdane, then proceeded to La Touche, where it engaged the enemy in a firefight at Hill 304. Here, forty-one prisoners were taken after a fifteen to twenty minute fight. At 1255, 3rd battalion was located on the outskirts of Puygeron and 2nd battalion was advancing toward Rochefort, which was entered by Company G by 1415.

The 7th Infantry continued attacking west and northwest, and entered Montelimar shortly before noon, August 29, as well as contacting elements of the 36th Division and occupying the important hill mass generally northeast of the town. The 3rd battalion was the unit that took La Batie Rollande; the 2nd battalion moved during the night of August 28-29 to Cardineau from which it launched its attack to the west and northwest at 0600.

Charles R. Castellaw

3rd and 1st Battalions, 7th Infantry, and 3rd battalion, 30th Infantry crossed the small river east of Montelimar during the morning of August 29.

Following clearance of the town itself, 7th and 30th Infantry Regiments took up the advance north along Highway 7, with 30th Infantry on the right.

Attacking on the left of the Division zone, 7th Infantry assaulted north along Highway 7 and the high ground to the immediate east of the highway. There was no organized resistance, but 2nd battalion met considerable sniper fire while clearing the hills, and received Flakwagon, mortar, and small-arms fire from a column of enemy vehicles which was halted along the road. The 2nd battalion relieved 3rd battalion, 143rd Infantry on high ground north of the town at 1300, August 29. At the same time, 3rd battalion was moving north of the 2nd, with 1st Battalion following to the right rear.

A Division Artillery forward observer with 2nd battalion, 7th Infantry, 1st Lt. Robert W. Metz, first spotted a huge enemy convoy moving up Highway 7 north of Montelimar. What he saw made him call for all the artillery that could be brought to bear. This was practically all of the Division's organic gunfire, plus guns of the attached 69th Armored Field Artillery Battalion. The 2nd battalion observed fire on the enemy convoy; then directed additional artillery fire on a train pulling a railroad gun, stopping the train and wrecking three or four boxcars. 2nd battalion occupied the west slope of a ridge; 3rd battalion was in position directly south, and 1st Battalion put a platoon on a hill to the east to prevent enemy from infiltrating to the rear of the regiment's leading elements.

The 1st Battalion, 7th Infantry, then started to move to the right of 2nd battalion, with its objective to cut the enemy column. This move commenced at 1700, and the battalion advanced without opposition to be on its objective by 2100. The 1st and 2nd battalions contacted each other on the highway at 0330, August 30, and at 0600 continued the attack to the north with 1st Battalion on the right and 2nd battalion on the left. All objectives were reached at 1130.

The 30th Infantry, meanwhile, had advanced abreast of 7th Infantry, over the hills north to make contact with elements of the 36th Infantry Division. Task Force Butler (Elements of VI Corps) was contacted at 1130, August 29. Then, under orders to send a battalion

The Way It Was

to protect the left flank of the 7th Infantry from infiltration, 2nd battalion was moved by motor from Sauzet to Marsanne, then advanced by foot and was on its objective before dawn of August 30. Before noon Company G had occupied Mirmande.

In 7th Infantry's initial advance, the enemy, under the mistaken impression that the road had been cut north of Montelimar by the 36th Infantry Division, surrendered in large numbers, although many of them organized small pockets which had to be cleaned out.

An outstanding feature about the area north of Montelimar, however, was the enemy motor convoy. It stretched from the northern outskirts of town for approximately 14 kilometers. It was composed of all sorts of vehicles, from German heavy cargo trucks to numerous requisitioned French sedans—about 2000 vehicles in all. For the most part traffic had been double-banked—in some places triple-banked—with vehicles facing both north and south.

The drivers and personnel had, for the most part, abandoned their vehicles and made for the Rhone River.

The 36th Division artillery had also taken the convoy under fire, and friendly fighter-bombers took several swipes at it, as well. As 3rd Infantry Division troops advanced through the debacle they saw almost unbelievable carnage. An estimated 1000 horses had been pulling carts, or trailing behind motor vehicles, tied by ropes. Many of them had been taken from the French. When the shells came down, most of them were killed. A few, some with entrails dragging or otherwise wounded, had to be put out of the way with merciful bullets. Some were unharmed, and nosed incuriously about the bodies of their dead fellows, or grazed peacefully in the pastures next to the road.

Smashed, fire-blackened trucks, halftracks, and sedans—some still burning or smouldering—clogged the road. The bodies of dead Germans, many of them also fire-blackened, lay among the ruins, or alongside the road where they had been cut down by artillery while trying to make good their escapes.

On the railroad that paralleled the highway at a distance of several hundred yards sat six giant railway guns. Four of them were the familiar 280mm monsters, sisters to the "Anzio Express." Two of them were gigantic 380mm pieces. All had been left standing, intact. Along the entire length of the scene of destruction an outrageous odor

83

Charles R. Castellaw

of burned and burning wood, scorched metal, stinking dead and singed flesh and clothing assailed the nostrils. Even the "avenues of smells" along some of the roads on the Anzio Beachhead in late April and early May, with their dead sheep and cattle, had not been such an affront to the nose.

Enemy material captured or destroyed also included 20 75mm anti tank guns, 12 88mm mortars anti aircraft guns, and 8 or 10 self-propelled guns. Prisoner total for the three days was over 1000. As it had been all the way up from the coast, the enemy order of battle, as indicated by units of PWs, was still a miscellaneous assortment from 338th Infantry Division, 198th Infantry Division, 189th Reserve Division, with the recent addition of 11th *Panzer* Division, 716th Infantry Division, 148th Reserve Division, and 244th Infantry Division. There were also other elements too numerous to mention.

The Battle of Montelimar had been costly for the German 19th Army.

French Hospitality

Thus far, nothing has been said regarding the reception of American troops by the French populace.

Veterans of Africa, Sicily, and Italy suddenly found themselves in a country in which sincere friendship and joy at liberation was expressed so vividly as to leave no doubts regarding the feelings which prompted these emotions. It was the wholehearted, warm conveyance of gladness of a proud, individualistic race once again made free.

After nearly two years of association with Italians, Sicilians, and Arabs, the genuineness displayed by Frenchmen high and low was like fresh air in a cave. Always it was tonic to morale.

When a Frenchman offered a soldier his bottle of wine there was a slight deference in his manner, but there was also apparent pride and happiness at being able to do something for his liberators. It was as if he said, "Here, m'sieu, it is about all I can offer you. I cannot give you strength when you face the enemy, although I wish I could. I cannot sustain you when you falter on the long march. That, too, I wish I could do. I can but offer you this wine, and with it try to convey the feeling of gratitude which I and my countrymen have for

The Way It Was

you." This attitude, throughout, could not but help give most soldiers some realization of why they were fighting. Freedom must be a wonderful thing. Here were those who had once had and lost it, once again to have it restored to them. The sight of their happiness was a thing to behold.

Since elements of the 45th Infantry Division had patrolled as far northeast as Voiron and found no enemy there, the 3rd Infantry Division prepared itself for an administrative move of over ninety miles.

Intelligence from the F.F.I. (which proved very accurate) at this time was as follows: "Civilians report that the enemy has pulled the bulk of his infantry out of Lyon, and that the city contains only scattered rear guard armored units. Many enemy troops were withdrawn west of the Rhone. Two civilian reports indicate the enemy is building up his forces along the Loue and Doubs Rivers, sixty miles north of Bourg. All bridges across the Doubs are guarded, and Frenchmen are not permitted to cross to the north (probably because F.F.I. forces are stronger in the south). The enemy is reported to have sizable garrisons in Dijon, Dole, Besancon, and Belfort. The last three towns are on the Doubs River and lie in the enemy's apparent escape corridor to Mühlhaus (Mulhouse).[11]

The 15th Infantry's 3rd battalion moved out at 1915, August 31, to relieve the 45th Division roadblock at St. Etienne and to screen the road net to Bourgoin. The 2nd battalion relieved 179th Infantry (45th Division) at Bourgoin, and 1st Battalion left its assembly area, but remained in regimental reserve.

The 30th Infantry entrucked and moved by motor to an assembly area northwest of Voiron. It completely assembled in the vicinity of Sauzet France on the afternoon of August 30th, and the morning of August 31 was spent by all 30th Regiment Battalions in care and cleaning of personnel and equipment. Replacements were assigned at this time. I was assigned to Company E, 2nd battalion, 30th Infantry 3rd Division.

Major General John W. (Iron Mike) O'Daniel, Commanding General of the 3rd Infantry Division, spoke to the group from a flat bed truck. From his speech, one would think that the 3rd Infantry was

---

[11] 3rd Infantry Division G-2 Periodic Reports No. 17, 2 Sept., 1944.

the best in the U.S. Army and that this division had made a greater achievement than any other in the U.S. Army. It seemed to be something magic about his speech that put young replacements in the right frame of mind for what was ahead. I believe that this was part of his job and he did it well.

Having just completed the mission of clearing the enemy from the area Northeast of MONTELIMAR, France, and providing right flank protection for the Division, the Regiment spent the morning in care and cleaning of equipment, and preparations for a motor move to the vicinity of VOIRON, France.

The 30th Regiment moved as a Regiment Combat Team and leading elements passed the Initial Point at 311300. At the end of the period approximately two thirds of the Regiment had closed and the balance were on the road enroute. The Regiment was delayed in closing due to the fact that reinforcing transportation was not available at time units were to move, and also due to road priorities given to other units of the Corps after column was in motion.

The entire unit closed in vicinity of VOIRON, France, by 010715 September without incident and preparations were underway for continuation of the attack to the North and West.

THIRTIETH INFANTRY SECTOR OF OPERATION

Summary of Enemy Operations 15-31 August 1944:

Enemy activities during the period 15-31 August inclusive were limited to rear guard actions after the initial defense. Our landing surprised him and this caused his disorganization, initially.

We overran the enemy positions in our initial assault. Because of the speed and rapidity of our advance inland he was unable to set up any type of fixed defense. His plan of action showed that he had decided to leave strong points in key positions in an effort to slow up our advance, while his main body made their hasty retreat.

At Brignoles the enemy made his first attempt at a definite stand. He held this position with three battalions and elements of two companies of Infantry. His defense consisted of Infantry on the outskirts of the town, with snipers and strong points consisting of anti tank guns and riflemen scattered throughout the town itself. The

The Way It Was

enemy reinforced this defense with at least three self-propelled guns, two or three tanks, and two artillery pieces.

During this operational period the enemy had used 88's mortars as anti tank guns in addition to his usual anti-tank weapons. At Flassans-Sur-Isole two 88's mortars and two anti-tank guns with Infantry protection were employed to impede our rapid advance. At Rochefort the enemy resisted our advance by means of three field pieces and a flak wagon.

Enemy armor had rarely been used during this period. In the vicinity of Aix, the enemy used armor to overrun one of our roadblocks. Mines had been used in conjunction with blown bridges and road barricades. All of his barricades had shown that they were hastily constructed.

At the close of the period the enemy still showed no signs of making a definite stand but continued his delaying actions protecting his escape routes.

All units had closed in by 0035, September 1. At 1130 the regiment began a move by motor to the vicinity of Cremieu, preparatory to moving west on Division order.

The 7th Infantry remained, guarding the smashed motor column until shortly after noon, September 1, when the regiment entrucked and moved first to an assembly area near Trepts, then re-entrucked and moved to a new area east of Leyment, where it closed in by 2400.

With the 15th Infantry, 3rd battalion leading, we commenced moving at 1930 to an assembly area near Lagnieu. Company I rode on tank destroyers. 1st Battalion followed and 2nd battalion commenced its move during the morning of September 2.

Meanwhile 30th Infantry already had swung back into action. The 3rd battalion engaged the enemy in a firefight at Pont de Churuy, killing seven enemy and taking two prisoners. At Janneyrieas, while 3rd platoon, 3rd Reconnaissance Troop engaged the enemy, Company L flanked the enemy position and captured ninety-nine prisoners, an anti tank gun, and three trucks. The fight lasted until about 2100, September 1. 3rd battalion protected a front from Loyettes through Charvieu, with a strong outpost at Colonbier. Contact was made with the 143rd Infantry in Catzian at 2100. The 2nd battalion, at 0600, moved out from regimental reserve to relieve 3rd battalion, 179th Infantry, on the regimental right flank.

Charles R. Castellaw

The 1st platoon, 3rd Reconnaissance Troop, after outposting Cote La Andre, moved out on the morning of September 2 to investigate the roads southwest of that town, and was recalled at 0700 to reconnoiter the road northwest of Amberieu to Chalamon, Villers, Striver, and Chatallon, during which reconnaissance it encountered some light enemy resistance.

During September 2-3, 15th and 17th Infantry Regiments remained in assembly areas with reinforcing trucks, prepared to move out on Division order. The 30th Infantry assembled during the same period. The 7th Infantry sent patrols to the north during the night but failed to make contact with the enemy. A patrol from 30th Infantry went north on a main highway through Neuville-sur-Ain and contacted a platoon of the 3rd Reconnaissance Troop and a unit of 180th Infantry. The patrol continued north and found the bridge across the Suran River blown, continued on to Villereversure, Simandre-sur-Suran and Treffort, and was told by the F.F.I. that Cruislat was also clear of enemy. A patrol from Company I crossed the bridge at Villereversure, and failed to make enemy contact. Another patrol went northwest on the road to Charlamonte with the same results. The 1st platoon, 3rd Recon, continued on its mission of September 2. It was held up at a bridge across the Ain River. The Division Battle Patrol outflanked the resistance by crossing the river south of the bridge and took and held the town of Gevrieu across the river.

The enemy apparently was still rapidly withdrawing. The 3rd Infantry Division once again entrucked and conducted a march of over seventy-five miles to contact the enemy.

At 1345, September 3, 7th Infantry led the move. The march objective was north of Lons-le-Saunier. The 3rd battalion closed into position at 2300, September 3, 1st Battalion at 0050, and 2nd battalion at 0055, all without incident and without the slightest contact with the enemy. Upon arrival the regimental Battle Patrol conducted reconnaissance to the north and northeast from Poligny to investigate reports of enemy, but failed to make contact.

15th Infantry moved in order 1st, 2nd, and 3rd battalions, crossing its initial point near Lagnieu at 2200, and closing into its new area northeast of Lons-le-Saunier at 0615. It advanced from St. Denis to Amberieu to Poncin, thence to Granges through Arinthod, Orgelet and from there to its area. During the morning of September 4, 1st

The Way It Was

Battalion established roadblocks of company strength near Montrond and on the road between Vers and Les Pasquier. The 2nd battalion put in roadblocks east of Equievillon and south of Champagnole on Highway 6.

The 30th Infantry remained in the assembly area south of Lagnieu until 1045, September 4, when it entrucked for its area in the vicinity of Lons-le-Saunier. The regiment closed in at about noon of that day.

The 3rd Reconnaissance Troop preceded the advance of 7th and 15th Infantry Regiments on their march to Lons-le-Saunier, making no contact with the enemy.

The Division continued its attack to the northeast. The 1st Battalion, 7th Infantry, moved from a defensive position near Arley at 1845, September 4, to the vicinity of Arbois. Vigorous patrols maintained contact with the Battle Patrol at Mont-sous-Vaudrey. The 2nd battalion moved to the vicinity of Arbois, with one company going to Mouchard. At 2100, 2nd battalion, reinforced, moved by vehicle to Argue, southwest of Besancon, arriving there at 0100, September 5. The battalion detrucked and began an attack toward Besancon at 0530. Company F encountered resistance at a bridge near Beure. Company E, at 0830, moved in a southeast direction to within 200 yards of Highway 73 near St. Ferjeux and fired on an enemy truck convoy. The battalion continued to fight during the September 5-6 period to secure bridges and destroy enemy motor movement along the highway southwest and south of Besancon. The 3rd battalion remained in position protecting the regiment's left flank.

The objective was now Besancon. A key communication and road net center, as well as an important industrial city of approximately 80,000 persons in peacetime, Besancon is divided by the Doubs River, with the industrial and most valuable section situated in the loop south of the river. This loop has a bottleneck opening, solidly guarded by a huge Vauban-designed fort, La Citadelle, which in turn is supported by four minor forts—Fort Tosey on the southwest, Fort des Trois Chatels on the southeast, and two other forts at a high elevation across the river: Fort Bregille on the northeast and Fort Chaudanne on the west. These forts were built in the 17th Century. La Citadelle alone took six years to complete (1667-1673). Its aspect is formidable to an attacker, presenting extremely thick walls

Charles R. Castellaw

surrounded by moats, and being situated on high ground that commands all avenues of approach.

The 15th Infantry moved from its position near Champagnole on the afternoon of September 4, 3rd battalion moving to a position south of Besancon. Company I attacked to a position south of Beure, with Company K farther south and Company L at Quingey. The 2nd battalion was disposed along the Ornans-Besancon road, and 1st Battalion remained in regimental reserve near Mouchard.

The 30th Infantry made no contact during the period.

The 1st platoon of the 3rd Recon moved ahead of 15th Infantry en route to Besancon and by noon, September 5, was standing by for 15th Infantry on the main routes south of Besancon. The 2nd platoon was attached to 7th Infantry, and reconnoitered in front of that regiment south of Besancon. At Sanitorium de la Tilleroy the platoon reported a large concentration of troops and a large convoy on the main highway. An air mission was requested, granted, and good results were reported. At 1600 many Germans were reported in the town, and an enemy roadblock one-half mile south of town was also reported. The platoon screened to the west while the artillery dug in and commenced firing at the roadblock. The 3rd platoon, 3rd Recon, screened before 7th Infantry northwest of Poligny and reported enemy in Mont-sous-Vaudrey. An F.F.I. patrol reported 700 enemy in the town. This platoon, too, spotted an enemy convoy leaving town and called down a successful air mission on it. The platoon was moving toward Dole when recalled to the Troop CP for another mission in the vicinity of Besancon.

At 1900, 1st Battalion, 7th Infantry arrived at Mouchard. The 2nd battalion was deployed south and west of Besancon in the vicinity of Beure engaged in cleaning out enemy on the high ground and along the Doubs River, and firing into Besancon. The Battalion relieved 1st Battalion, 30th Infantry at Mouchard, to patrol to the Division front and left flank. The 2nd battalion, attached to 15th Infantry, reached a position 800 yards south of a key ridge, receiving considerable enemy fire. At 2400 Company E was north of Beure with the other two rifle companies adjacent. These positions were held during the night. On the morning of September 6, 1st Battalion, 15th Infantry, relieved the battalion.

The Way It Was

Combat

During September 1-6, I entered into my first combat battle. My squad leader said, "We have received orders to take the area in front of us. We will attack at the specified time." He gave the order, "Move out." After we had moved about 1,000 yards the enemy opened fire with small arms and mortars. I thought all hell had broken loose. I panicked with a sudden fear for my life. I made about a 90-degree turn to my left and took off as fast as I could. After I had gone about a half of a mile, I realized that I had gone AWOL (Absence Without Leave).

I remembered Article 61, covering AWOL. "You are absent without leave whenever you leave your properly appointed place of duty without permission. The punishment for being AWOL may be stiff, especially in time of war."

Desertion is covered in Article 58. This is one of the most serious offenses in the Army. "If you leave your post or duty with no intention of returning, you may be sentenced to death, or at the very least to a dishonorable discharge from the army with loss of all rights to vote or hold public office and a stigma that will never wear off."

"In wartime there can be little distinction made between AWOL and desertion!"

I could hear mortars and small arms being fired by the Germans and the Americans. As I listened to the firing my thoughts were that I should have taken a farm deferment. If I had taken a farm deferment, I would be home with Betty Jo and making plans to harvest the cotton and corn and taking care of the livestock. But as I told my dad, I could not let my brother, Carl, and our friends that are in the military service down. I was not a coward but I had just committed one of the worse crimes possible against my country through a cowardly act.

I spent the rest of the day wondering about what punishment I would receive and what I should do. About dusky dark, I decided to return to my unit. When I returned, the men had dug in for the night. One of the men did not have a partner to share his foxhole, so he invited me. The squad leader or other members of the squad did not mention me being AWOL. This I could not understand.

Early the next morning just before daybreak, we were called out to get ready to continue our forward movement. The squad leader

Charles R. Castellaw

said, "Castellaw, you will be lead scout." Then I understood how punishment was handled in combat.

As we moved forward, I tried to remember everything that I had learned in basic training about being a scout. The things that stood out most in my mind wear cover, concealment and being free from noise or disturbance. As I crawled up a slight hill, I kept my 128 pounds as close to the ground as I could. After a few exchanges of small arms fire I heard Pvt. Covington, 2nd scout, cry out,—"I have been hit." We moved on, exchanging fire until the enemy withdrew. When we reached our objective we dug in and set up our defense in case of a counter attack.

The Division was continuing its attack to occupy all high ground on three sides of Besancon. The 15th Infantry continued its northerly assault. The 30th Infantry advanced on the Division right boundary, neutralizing enemy roadblocks southeast of Besancon. The 1st and 3rd battalions moved to the north by motor, starting at 1025, to cut the roads to the north and northeast and to enter the town from those directions. The 2nd battalion, 30th Infantry, followed to the rear of, and assisted, the 15th Infantry.

Company B, 15th Infantry, attacked and captured Fort Fontain during the afternoon of September 5, and Company A seized adjacent high ground, while Company C remained in battalion reserve in the vicinity of Fontain. The 2nd battalion, 7th Infantry, attached to the 15th Infantry, captured high ground to the northwest with Company G leading. Shortly after 0800 2nd battalion reverted to 7th Infantry control.

The 1st Battalion, 15th Infantry, cleared the ridge between Companies A and C and sent reconnaissance patrols to Besancon. The battalion was ordered to block the two roads in its sector leading south and southeast from the city. The 2nd battalion was attached to 30th Infantry on the right. At 2300 Company E was having a fight with a Mark VI tank and an unknown number of infantry, and drawing some self-propelled fire. Company G blocked the highway in the vicinity of Tarcenay. The 30th Infantry continued moving on the right flank against slight opposition. At 1950, September 6, 1st Battalion was located south of Salins and 2nd battalion was at Mouchard. The two battalions closed out of these positions by 0115. By 0830, 2nd battalion was located north of Tarcenay and 3rd battalion

The Way It Was

was in the vicinity of Mamirolle. The 3rd battalion then passed to regimental reserve at Lachevelotte, and 2nd battalion's leading elements were at Morre, advancing from the southeast on Besancon.

Explanation of the action was described in the G-2 report:[12] "To protect his escape route along Highway 73 through Besancon the enemy occupied the high ridge south of the Doubs River. Infantry, occasionally supported by tank fire and artillery, held the high ground. Most of the bridges across the Doubs were blown and roadblocks established on the north side of the river. Our troops began to flank the city from the west during daylight, September 5, and the enemy was driven off or withdrew from the advantageous terrain during the night 5-6 September. Roadblocks southeast of Besancon, active during the afternoon of 5 September, offered but little resistance to our attacks during the evening."

Again: "Almost continual fire was received from enemy units occupying the high ground south of Besancon. Most of the enemy positions consisted of small enemy detachments who put up stiff resistance to our attack during the afternoon and evening of 5 September, but who pulled out or were overrun during the night of 5-6 September....On the left of the Division sector the enemy occupied positions north of important bridges across the Doubs River after having blown the bridges. He had positions at Belmont, Orchamps, and Dole. The latter bridge was not blown, probably because the enemy was still using that route as an axis of withdrawal."

During the night of September 6-7 the 3rd battalion, 7th Infantry, forward Command Post, came under attack by a platoon of German infantrymen who, supported by 20mm Flak guns and machine guns, had infiltrated between the assault companies and the Battalion Command Post, virtually surrounding the latter. The Battalion Commander, Lt. Col. Lloyd B. Ramsey, and his S-3, being present in the Command Post, were in danger of being captured. Said Col. Ramsey: "Also, a rupture of communications with the assault companies, which were then meeting strong resistance, might easily have been disastrous."

The platoon advanced to within fifteen yards of the house in which the Command Post was situated. The platoon occupied an old

---

[12] 3rd Infantry Division G-2 Report No. 21, 6 Sept., 1944

Charles R. Castellaw

railroad draw, paralleling the wall that the Command Post's defenders were using for cover, and fired at everything within sight. It raked the doors and windows.

"Through all this fire," said Radio Operator Pvt. James P. Soblensky, "there was one man who just sat there calmly observing out into the darkness, taking pot shots at every kraut he saw. It was T/5 Robert D. Maxwell, one of the wire corporals. He was the coolest customer I've ever seen. Tracer bullets were just barely clearing his head, yet he didn't seem to notice it."

The Germans worked their way to within about ten yards and began throwing grenades. There was a chicken-wire extension over the wall, which saved those inside. The grenades struck it, bounced to the other side, and exploded harmlessly.

Maxwell continued calmly to take aim and fire his .45. Most of the rest of the men had "taken off," despite Maxwell's urging them to stay. One man who did stay was killed a few minutes later.

Said Wire Chief T/4 Cyril F. McCall: "The Battalion Commander saw that he would be unable to hold the Command Post with the small force available and ordered that it be moved to another location. While the evacuation was begun under cover of our fire, the enemy intensified his attack in a determined effort to overwhelm our position."

Suddenly a grenade came over the wall and landed in the group's midst. Maxwell, clutching a blanket to his body, dove upon it without a second's hesitation. An instant later there was an explosion. "I lay still for a few seconds," said Wireman Pfc. James P. Joyce, "partially stunned by the concussion; then I realized that I wasn't hurt. T/5 Maxwell had deliberately drawn the full force of the explosion on himself in order to protect us and make it possible for us to continue at our posts and fight."

Colonel Ramsey summed up: "T/5 Maxwell's zeal in the maintenance of military communications, his instantaneous acceptance of dangers which no soldier is obligated to incur, and his lofty sacrifice of self in behalf of his fellow soldiers made possible the orderly withdrawal of the Command Post personnel, contributed in high degree to the eventual capture of Besancon, and are a continuing inspiration to the officers and men of the 3rd battalion."

The Way It Was

Maxwell was severely wounded in the face and his right foot was permanently maimed, but he lived to be awarded the Congressional Medal of Honor.

The enemy indicated his strong desire to hold the city and to prevent our forces from crossing the Doubs River by moving into Besancon elements of the 159th Reserve Division that had been diverted from their route of withdrawal. Lengthy firefights with small arms, machine guns, and mortars took place in front of each of the forts and bunkers on the south and east of town. On the north side of the city scattered self-propelled and tank fire opposed the 7th Infantry.

At 1400 September 7, 1st Battalion, 7th Infantry, crossed the line of departure and attacked east. Enemy action consisted of scattered strongpoints supported by machine-gun and artillery fire. The battalion halted overnight and protected the regiment on its north flank. The 3rd battalion continued its attack and by 1530 reached la Baraque. At 2315, 3rd battalion again advanced against enemy small arms and mortar fire, until security patrols reported no enemy to the front. At 2100, contact was established with 2nd battalion. The 3rd battalion pulled out of Besancon and at 0930 the next morning attacked an enemy convoy, destroying ten vehicles.

The 30th Infantry, meanwhile, had been divided into two groups. 1st Battalion was assigned the difficult mission of neutralizing the formidable Citadelle and of clearing the southern section of Besancon, which was situated in the loop of the river, and 3rd battalion was to cross the Doubs at Avanne, circle completely behind the city and come in from the northeast.

At 0300, 1st Battalion, commanded by Captain Christopher W. Chaney, jumped off to clear the Doubs loop. On reaching the Chapelle des Bois, contact was made with 1st Battalion, 15th Infantry, and the advance continued northwest toward the Besancon goose-egg. The battalion came under fire at 0338.

As Companies C and B continuing in column reached the high ground south of the Citadelle, they came under more fire from two hitherto unknown forts guarding the right and left approaches to the Citadelle.

Aided by tanks of Company C, 756th, under 1st Lt. Rex Metcalfe, Company C, 30th battled for four hours against fanatical *Hitlerjugend* inductees and took the fort on the west side of the neck with fifty-

Charles R. Castellaw

three prisoners. While Company B attacked by fire, Company A was moved in, and after a stiff fight, took the east guard fort and about twenty-five prisoners. In a coordinated attack, using all weapons of the battalion, and even employing the direct fire of a 9th FA Battalion 155mm howitzer at a range of about 500 yards, Captain Chaney maneuvered his battalion into a final assault on the Citadelle. While Company C moved around to the northwest and rear of the fort, Company A assaulted frontally, and with the aid of close mortar fire support forced the surrender of the fort by 1830.

Troops which entered the Citadelle to handle the more than 200 prisoners (which included one battalion CO and two company CO's) reported that the massive walls had been barely more than chipped by the high explosive 155 shells, but the terrific muzzle blast combined with the terrifying sound of shell bursts had been too much for the defenders' nerves. Seventeen casualties, most of them wounded, were taken from the fort. All of these had been wounded by mortar fire.

By 2205 1st Battalion, 30th Infantry had closed on its objective, the Doubs River loop, from the south.

For its outstanding performance of duty in action during the period September 6-7 at Besancon, the 1st Battalion, 30th Infantry was awarded the Presidential Unit Citation.

During the fight for, and capture of, the Citadelle, 3rd battalion, 30th Infantry had been relieved by Company F at 1420 and moved out on trucks via the Avanne bridge to a position northeast of Besancon to join in the coordinated attack on the city. The attack was launched at 2005 that night. By 2130 Company L had met resistance near the city's railroad station. Company K was moved to assist Company L, and at daylight was in contact with the enemy while Company L was engaged in clearing enemy from the city. Both companies continued to work on this strong pocket of enemy resistance throughout the day of September 8 while Company I moved to establish a roadblock. By 1220 resistance was broken and over 100 prisoners taken. By 1645 the battalion was assembled and moved to a regimental assembly area, where it closed in at 1900 and prepared to push to the north.

The 2nd battalion had been in reserve during most of the fight. At 0810 that morning the battalion crossed the Doubs River Bailey Bridge into the city and at 1050 was held up by continuing fighting within the city. Company F held the high ground overlooking the city

The Way It Was

and was committed to assist 3rd battalion in its street-fighting assignment. Company F took 196 prisoners in this work and in the later afternoon moved to the regimental assembly area, closing there with the rest of 2nd battalion at 1900.

Cost to enemy in the Battle of Besancon had been about 653 prisoners, not including wounded (and taken prisoner) and killed. Numbered among the latter was a Brig. Gen. Schmidt, who was killed at a roadblock of Company A, 7th Infantry, on the afternoon of September 6. His orderly, who was taken prisoner, said that the general was 56 years old, had fought in Russia, and had been commanding an artillery school at Autun from April 26, 1943, to September 2, 1944. He supposedly had been en route to take command of a division (probably the 159th) in the Besancon area when the four cars in his party took the wrong road and the general stopped an M-1 bullet.

Following the axis of two main roads to the north, the Division continued its attack in the direction of Vesoul. The 7th Infantry advanced to the northeast to Rigney, then turned west toward Rioz. It moved against slight resistance until enemy were encountered at Traitie Fontaine. The 2nd battalion led this advance, followed by 3rd battalion.

The 15th Infantry continued to advance north toward Rioz against strong resistance in the form of organized defenses as well as a number of by-passed pockets of enemy forces. The 1st Battalion reached Tallenay without resistance. After fighting all through the night of September 8-9, Company F captured Ecole and Company E captured Miserey-Salines. By noon, September 9, Company G had reached a point just south of the Ornan River. The 3rd battalion continued its advance against strong resistance to the vicinity of Chatillon-le-Duc. By 1005, September 9, Companies I and L were abreast near Devecey, continuing the attack.

In Besancon, 30th Infantry made a thorough sweep of the town until, by 1400, September 8, it had been determined that the last enemy soldier was rounded up. The regiment moved out during the night of September 8-9. The 1st Battalion encountered considerable resistance during the morning of September 9, but overcame it. The 3rd battalion followed the 1st Battalion.

Charles R. Castellaw

At 2000, September 9, Company G moved to the northeast side of Rioz and was 2000 yards from its outskirts. Three hours later the company was 800 yards from a road north of the town and 500 yards from the town itself. During the fight it captured prisoners from the 634th Guard Regiment which had been moved into the sector to assist in the disengagement of elements of the 198th and 338th Divisions and to reinforce the positions. The 2nd battalion did not enter Rioz in force, but early in the morning of September 10 contacted elements of 15th Infantry in town. The 3rd battalion, 7th Infantry, sent a platoon of Company I to Loulans, then reinforced the position with the entire company. The remainder of the battalion was located in the vicinity of Cirey during the night, then assembled at Loulans, and at noon, September 10, was moving northeast against light resistance. The 1st Battalion was located at Regney, with Companies A and C on the outskirts of Vandeland to screen the Division's right flank. The 2nd battalion assembled in the vicinity of Cirey and at 1000 crossed the line of departure moving northeast.

The 1st Battalion, 15th Infantry, moved by truck to Neuville-de-Cromary, then moved by foot to Sorans-le-Breury on September 9. On the morning of the 10th, the battalion estimated a platoon of enemy, reinforced by a tank and self propelled gun, but soon took care of the trouble. The 2nd battalion moved against a series of enemy roadblocks near Voray, and at *1545,* September 9, was at Sorans-les-Breury after destroying three strong roadblocks and capturing three 88mm guns. The battalion moved on toward Rioz, aided in clearing the town, and set up roadblocks. The 3rd battalion, 15th Infantry moved by truck through Traitie Fontaine and assisted 2nd battalion in clearing Rioz, and also set up roadblocks.

The 30th Infantry was originally on the Division's left flank in contact with the 36th Division. One company of the Battalion crossed the Ornan River between Cussey and Boulot to protect the crossing of the rest of the battalions. Company B forded the river and at 2000, September 9, was on the outskirts of the Boulot. The 3rd battalion, at 1940, had a platoon in Bussieres, and 2nd battalion closed in an area near Voray on the north side of the Ornan River. At 0600, 3rd battalion led the regiment in a move to the north. Company K headed the battalion, moving to the left of Voray. The 2nd battalion pushed through Rioz on trucks while 3rd battalion moved cross-country to

The Way It Was

Boult on the Division left flank. At 1115, 3rd battalion was moving north against scattered small arms and machine-gun fire.

Enemy rear guard and delaying forces south of Vesoul made our advance difficult during September 10-11. The 1st Battalion, 15th Infantry, advancing toward Vesoul, was held up by strong enemy resistance in Quenoche, encountering small arms, machine-gun, antitank, Flakwagon, tank, and artillery fire. By 1500, September 10, the battalion was on the outskirts of the town, and by 1900 the town of Quenoche was in our hands, although some mopping-up remained to be done. The 2nd battalion, following the first, was on the left flank at 1335. The battalion moved to Hyet and contacted the enemy. By 2000, Hyet was completely in our hands and the battalion moved north to Pennesieres. On the morning of September 11, 2nd battalion continued the advance through Courboux without resistance, while 1st Battalion advanced until it received enemy Flakwagon fire, which it eliminated.

The 2nd battalion, 30th Infantry, detrucked northwest of Rioz and advanced toward Tresilley over the September 10-11 period. Slight opposition was encountered and at 1730 artillery fire was directed on enemy personnel and vehicles. The 1st and 2nd battalions continued to advance against slight resistance.

At 0600, September 11, 1st Battalion, 7th Infantry attacked north toward Filain. The battalion encountered enemy resistance toward noon and engaged in a firefight southwest of Vy-le-Aubertans. The 2nd battalion, during the afternoon of September 10, had encountered strong enemy resistance south of Aubertans. The resistance was overcome during the night of September 10-11 and at 0630, Company G moved out toward Authoison against heavy machine-gun fire. Toward noon, however, the battalion was advancing without opposition.

During the same 24-hour period, 3rd battalion overcame strong enemy resistance at Ormemans to encounter an enemy strongpoint at Roche-sur-Linotte at about 2000. At 0730 the battalion attacked north, encountered strong resistance, and pushed on into it.

The objectives of Vesoul and the road nets east of the city were being stubbornly defended.

The 1st Battalion, 7th Infantry, advanced through Filain, while 2nd battalion left Authoison, and 3rd battalion engaged in a firefight

Charles R. Castellaw

outside Dampierre. The 7th Infantry finally occupied Hills 418 and 405 after attacking through the Bois de Dampierre.

The 30th Infantry advanced northeast toward Presle, meeting strong enemy resistance all the way. The wooded, hilly terrain necessarily made advances slow.

The 3rd battalion moved by motor from its assembly area near Mariox to its line of departure for the attack on Presle. At 2000, the battalion, having cleared out machine-gun and rifle outpost positions on the way, prepared to attack Presle at daylight September 12.

During September 12, the 3rd battalion continued the attack on Presle. Because of the dogged resistance and heavy enemy fire, it became necessary to commit the 1st and 2nd battalions on a flanking movement to encircle the town.

The 3rd battalion jumped off at daylight as planned, but was immediately met with fire from three sides, and the attack was halted. A combat group of infantry, tanks, and tank destroyers was sent to clear the enemy from a ridge on the left flank. This was accomplished, but heavy fire from Presle as well as observed artillery fire from Mt. Jesus, and machine-gun and sniper fire from the Bois de Petit Pas continued to halt the attack. Company I moved to Thieffrans at 2130.

The Battalion was committed at 1715 with the mission of outflanking and cutting off the determined enemy from the north. The battalion entrucked and advance elements met and fired on about seventy-five enemy at a crossroad. At 2000, the balance of the battalion jumped off in the attack on Esprels. The battalion moved forward without opposition but met many unmanned roadblocks that the 10th Engineers cleared to permit the advance of attached armor.

The 2nd battalion was committed at 1645, September 12. Company E was sent by truck with the mission of clearing the roadblock on the main highway by attacking it from the rear. The balance of the battalion moved down the main highway through Dampierre to assault Presle via Trevey. Trevey was occupied by 2010.

In the face of pressure exerted by this three-battalion attack, the enemy withdrew on September 13. Presle, Vallerois-le-Bois, Les Patey, Chassey-les-Montboxon, and Esprels were all occupied.

The 3rd battalion, 15th Infantry was committed on the regiment's left flank, bypassing 2nd battalion, and advancing to the southern

The Way It Was

outskirts of Vesoul. By noon of September 12, it was in the first few buildings there. The 1st Battalion advanced against constant enemy resistance with a mission of advancing north and flanking the town from the east. The 2nd battalion advanced through La Demie with a mission of blocking a road in that vicinity.

Vesoul finally fell during the afternoon of September 12 to elements of the 15th Infantry and two battalions of the 36th Division.

<u>Individual Heroics</u>

Two heroic actions especially marked the September 12-13 period.

Second Lt. Raymond Zussman of Company A, 756th Tank Battalion, was a platoon leader. As his tank and another of his platoon were approaching Noroy-le-Bourg at about 1900, they were in front of 3rd battalion, 7th Infantry. The intercommunication system was out between tanks and throughout the subsequent action, Lieutenant Zussman directed the tank from outside, either verbally or by signals.

Zussman went forward on foot to reconnoiter the highway. He disappeared from sight; there was the sound of small-arms fire and the lieutenant reappeared, to motion the tank to the highway. Several infantrymen proceeded forward with the group.

After directing the tank through a boobytrapped roadblock, the group was fired upon by an enemy machine gun and some riflemen about forty yards to the right front. Lieutenant Zussman stood on the right of the tank, directing fire on the enemy positions, and in a matter of seconds, three of the enemy were killed and eight had surrendered. After collecting these prisoners, Zussman again directed fire, this time on a German *Volkswagen* at a road junction; three more enemy were killed and seven or eight surrendered.

Lieutenant Zussman then obtained a tommy gun, being out of carbine ammunition, and started toward town, across a field paralleling the road to town. The tank followed. Again he was fired upon. Again he returned under intense fire to direct the tank in neutralizing the opposition. Standing up straight, he pointed out the enemy, and within a few minutes twenty more had surrendered.

"Lieutenant Zussman had the infantrymen collect these prisoners while he went ahead alone to investigate some houses on our side of

Charles R. Castellaw

the road about fifty yards in front of us," said Cpl. Theodore Coller, a crew member of the tank.

Added Pvt. Calvin E. Eaton: "...1 saw Lieutenant Zussman approach the back of the house, running and firing his tommy gun en-route. A few wild small-arms shots were taken at him, and as he neared the far corner several hand grenades were thrown in his direction, but he was unharmed and beckoned us forward. He directed our fire through a back door of the house and into a small shed nearby, and twelve more Jerries who were in and around the house hastily surrendered."

Reconnoitering for a route for the tank out to the highway, a storm of fire and a grenade came Zussman's way. He returned fire and the enemy ceased. He called the tank up again; by the time the tank had neared the house he had gone to the front again, and by the time the tank had rounded the corner, Lieutenant Zussman had returned with fifteen more prisoners.

He directed the tank's fire on a house across the road, toward which a number of the enemy were scurrying in an attempt to escape. At least two or three were killed and several wounded.

The miniature armored force continued down the main street of Noroy, Zussman still leading. A wagon started across an intersection to the front; the tank fired on it and killed eight or ten enemy. "Lieutenant Zussman figured the intersection might be zeroed in for antitank fire, so he had us wait while he went around the corner to investigate," said T/5 Espiridion Guillen. "We heard Lieutenant Zussman repeatedly yelling, *'Hände hoch! 'Hände hoch!'* and heard frequent bursts from his tommy gun. In a few minutes he stepped out in the intersection where we could see him, and a string of about thirty prisoners filed around the corner and were taken into custody by the infantrymen. Lieutenant Zussman said he routed them out of a basement."

As night fell, Zussman again went forward alone to a truck. There was another hand-grenade explosion, but when the smoke cleared away, he returned with another prisoner.

The results of his actions were seventeen enemy killed, ninety-two captured, and two antitank guns, one 20mm Flak gun, two machine guns, and two trucks captured.

The Way It Was

Lieutenant Zussman was killed in a subsequent action, but was awarded the Congressional Medal of Honor Posthumously.

Another officer, 1ˢᵗ Lt. John J. Tominac, of Company I, 15ᵗʰ Infantry, also especially distinguished himself during this same time.

The 3ʳᵈ battalion, having captured the hill mass south of Saulx-de-Vesoul, drove down the hillsides toward the city in the face of stubborn resistance. Forces in the hills north of Saulx-de-Vesoul hammered the German positions with artillery, mortar and machine-gun fire. In this operation the other forces were the anvil, the 3ʳᵈ battalion, the hammer.

As Tominac's platoon neared a bend in the road down which they were proceeding, an enemy machine gun opened fire, raking the highway with bursts of knee-high fire.

Lieutenant Tominac sized up the situation and shouted back to bring up tank support. Within a matter of minutes, an M-4 came up and halted just ahead of the platoon's leading elements.

Under heavy fire Tominac ran forward ten yards to direct fire on the enemy machine-gun nest, as two squads of his platoon worked their way forward into firing positions on the road, protected from the enemy by the tank's hull.

A second enemy machine-gun nest remained, following the neutralization of the first. Working his left squad to within fifty yards of the weapon, Tominac halted the men and rushed headlong into the weapon, firing his tommy gun. He killed the three men manning it.

This action alerted the main enemy defensive force. The occupants of this position were about 200 yards to the left front. Tominac led a squad against the enemy strongpoint. Although the area was swept by infantry fire of every type, Tominac rushed back and forth from one squad to the other, supervising and directing the one he led personally, and one which he had directed to clean out any enemy who might be in a group of nearby houses.

He and his men overran the hostile strongpoint, killing about thirty of the enemy. The squad resumed the advance. After proceeding a few yards, Tominac spotted a concealed 77mm self-propelled gun in a "V" intersection of the road, about 200 yards to the front.

Charles R. Castellaw

He ordered his men to halt and went ahead, alone and on foot, followed by the tank. The self-propelled opened fire on the tank and neutralized it. The tank caught fire and the crew bailed out.

Driverless and burning, it began to roll down the road toward the German position. Tominac ran and jumped on it, stood boldly upright, silhouetted against the sky, grasping the M-4's .50-caliber machine gun. As he opened fire on the 77's crew, a rain of bullets from hostile machine guns, machine pistols and snipers ricocheted off the turret and hull of the tank, with the 77 also still firing at it.

Tominac fired burst after burst at the self-propelled gun and the infantry foxholes around it. After raking the area with fire, he jumped down from the steadily accelerating tank.

S/Sgt. John B. Shirley, one of his squad leaders, noted that Tominac was painfully wounded in the shoulder. Shirley took out his penknife and removed a dollar-sized fragment from the shoulder. At about the same time the tank crashed in the midst of a group of German gun pits, bursting into flames as its gasoline and ammunition exploded.

Again Tominac led his men forward. The enemy had been forced to abandon his roadblock. The self-propelled gun withdrew into Saulx-de-Vesoul. Refusing medical aid, Lieutenant Tominac sent Shirley's squad to clean out a group of houses in the city, while he led the remainder of the platoon against a strongly fortified group of buildings which contained about a company of Germans. Despite his painful wound, he took his men to within pointblank range of a wall that surrounded the buildings from which the enemy was firing. Hurling hand grenades into the enemy's midst and simultaneously deploying a portion of his force around to the rear of the buildings, Tominac compelled thirty-one enemy soldiers and one officer to surrender and captured at least half a dozen enemy vehicles, together with machine guns and a quantity of other material.

At the cost of only four casualties, he had led his men in overcoming four successive enemy strongpoints, killing at least thirty of the enemy, taking thirty-two prisoners and capturing the platoon's sector of Saulx-de-Vesoul. For this he later received the Congressional Medal of Honor.

The Way It Was

Rapid Progress

By straight-line distance, it is more than 400 miles from Cavalaire and St. Tropez to Vesoul. The American VI Corps, advancing not in a straight line, but tacking first to the west, then north, then northeast, back to the northwest and finally north and northeast, as the tactical situation required, had covered the distance in less than a month— truly an amazing feat. In a war of movement, this accomplishment stood out as an example of speed and mobility. The 3rd Infantry Division had played a prominent part in making that feat possible.

French forces, coming up from the rear, reinforced and emphasized the rapid cleavage, but the spearhead was always VI Corps.

There were immediate and telling results of the avalanche that rolled north from the Riviera beaches. Somewhere south of the Loire River, in western France, 20,000 enemy soldiers surrendered to a United States platoon. Four United States correspondents drove a jeep through supposedly enemy-infested territory, from south to north, and did not encounter a single German soldier. Isolated enemy pockets were swiftly wiped out by avenging F.F.I. bands. When French forces joined those of Lt. Gen. George S. Patton's Third Army near Dijon in early September, all of Central and Western France, with the exception of a few western ports, was automatically freed. Instead of a slow slugging-match to liberate France, the United States armies were now free to concentrate on the western approaches to Germany. The ultimate end of the war in Europe was probably speeded many months, and in the zone of VI Corps, the German 19th Army received a blow from which it never recovered.

Probably the outstanding difficulty of the rapid move had been the ever-present bugaboo of supply, magnified many times over. Even the most optimistic planners had not foreseen moving so far, so fast.

Initially, while pre-invasion beach reconnaissance had indicated that Red Beach at St. Tropez would be excellent for beaching craft, only one section was good enough to beach LCIs, and this was so heavily protected with underwater mines that it could not be used until H-plus-8 hours. These unexpected difficulties would have been extremely serious had more than slight resistance been met by the infantry, as supporting tanks and artillery were not ashore and

105

Charles R. Castellaw

assembled until late on D-day. The Group became better organized, and by H-plus-20 hours all small craft except the five supply LCTs were completely discharged.

Unloading of the ocean-type ships lagged far behind schedule, primarily because all Liberty ships arrived at the transport area behind schedule. Due in the transport area at noon of D-day, seven of the ten Liberties arrived at noon of D-plus-one and the other three not until the forenoon of D-plus-two.

While the delay in unloading caused considerable difficulty due to lack of transportation, its most serious implication was the almost complete lack of supply. Through unforeseen difficulties, a critical gasoline shortage existed by H-plus-30 hours when supply LCTs were finally beached.

Normally, Army supply bases keep within twenty miles of Division rear. Initially Division transportation was used exclusively to move supplies from the beaches to supply dumps, reaching a round trip of 400 miles before Army was able to establish forward dumps at St. Maximin. This relief was short-lived, as Division was called upon to furnish forty trucks to Corps for special missions, and 3rd Infantry Division began a 150-mile move from Aix to Montelimar, which again eventually put Army dumps 150 miles behind the troops. That the supply problem was whipped is a credit to the men who worked 24-hour days for days on end to keep the supplies flowing.

Some measure of what it takes to make a move of the proportions of VI Corps' move north is furnished by a look at the wire summaries of the Division Signal Officer. During the sixteen days from August 15 to 31 alone, 2207 miles of wire were laid, and only 190 recovered. Communications, at that, were often solely by radio.

Fighting in the Vosges Mountains

The 3rd Infantry Division continued its push, and found itself at the approaches to the Vosges Mountains. It was still mid-autumn on the calendar, but the cold winds already had begun to blow, and the weather had turned rainy. It seemed only a short time ago that the Anzio sun came out to stay and ended the long, cold, wet Italian winter. Now the seasons had once more rolled around, and with the annual change came winter fighting in France's Vosges Mountains.

The Way It Was

The Vosges Mountains had never been crossed by a military force. That solid fact stood out as the divisions of VI Corps set out to commence the fight. Miles ahead lay the Rhine River and the frontier of Germany.

Dense clouds hung between the mountains of the lower Vosges. The roads glistened with rain and the wind swept cold over the plains. The soldiers who bathed for a long time in the warming sun of the Riviera coast froze in the unaccustomed climate. The shelter halves over their shoulders are wet because they had no chance to dry them out at any of the roadside farmhouses. There had hardly been a pause during the arduous march of the last two or three weeks, during those disengaging movements which brought so much grief in their various phases.

"Now the Army which used to stand guard in the sunny south, many hundreds of miles away, stands at the frontier of the Reich and the thunder of the guns echoes in the peaceful dales and the villages beyond.

"The conversation of the soldiers these days centers around the question: 'When shall we hold a definite line again?' They talk about it frankly without false hopes, without defeatism, with the clear perception and the straight opinion of soldiers who see things as they are and will not be influenced by the black prophets who are present in any situation, who form their own honest opinions which it is their right to do. For whoever has experienced the ordeal of the withdrawal through the Rhone Valley, the withdrawal which often turned into a veritable hell, has proved that he knows no fear and no despair..."[13]

Those words were written by the enemy.

The 3rd Infantry Division, without perceptible pause, found itself in its second winter campaign. There seemed to be no dividing line. One week we were racing through Southern and Central France in the middle of a temperate autumn; the next, fighting in difficult, wooded terrain in rain and cold. The local inhabitants, as local inhabitants will the world over, said, "This is very unusual weather for this time of year," whatever that means.

During September, enemy action passed through three definite phases. The first phase was his rapid withdrawal, leaving only small,

---

[13] *Die Wacht,* German Nineteenth Army Newspaper "On the Threshold of the Reich," September 13, 1944.

Charles R. Castellaw

disorganized forces to attempt delaying action. As this phase reached its climax, he turned and attempted the stand at Besancon. Our troops attacked Besancon on September 6, and two days later all enemy resistance in the city ceased.

From Besancon to the Moselle River the enemy put up definite resistance, although in the main it was delaying action, and each day's fighting usually ended with the enemy's falling back to prepared positions in the rear. There was a gradual build-up of enemy artillery during this phase. The first counterattack was launched September 15 at Longevelle, east of Lure. As the enemy fell back toward the Moselle River his daily withdrawals became shorter and his positions gave an indication of considerable work prior to occupation. As artillery fire increased, so did the employment of mines, boobytraps and log roadblocks.

The Division was about to enter this final phase, which was to prevail until the crossing of the Meurthe River. On the high ground east of the Moselle River the enemy finally occupied a definite line of resistance, ceased his withdrawals and held on tenaciously, counterattacking when overrun. He resorted to jungle tactics in the heavily-wooded terrain between the Moselle and Mosellette Rivers and frequently infiltrated behind our lines, ambushing supply trains. When the Moselle River line was taken, the enemy occupied a second, definite, well-organized position northeast of St. Ame' and in the vicinity of Cleurie. Here the enemy resisted fiercely, counterattacking and infiltrating to retake ground lost to our attacks and bringing in both reinforcements and replacements.

The granite massif of the Vosges rises steeply from the Plain of Alsace, lies northeast-southwest, and blocks easy entrance to the Rhine Valley from the west. The Vosges consist of low, generally rounded mountains from 1000 to 4000 feet in height, arranged in parallel ridges which individually tend more to the northeast than does the range as a whole.

This is an area of forested mountains forming the southern part of the Vosges chain which lies along the Franco-German frontier and reaches from Belfort in the south to Kaiserslautern in the north. The Saverne Gap divides the High Vosges from its northern extension, the Low Vosges. To the south, the High Vosges terminate abruptly in a series of summits towering above the Belfort Gap.

The Way It Was

The average height of the Vosges eastern ridgeline is about 3000 feet, but many summits rise about 4000 feet, with elevation increasing southward where the highest point is the Grand Ballon (over 4600), lying northeast of Belfort. The Hohneck, the highest point on the main watershed, rises 4400 feet just north of Grand Ballon. The long ridgelines are usually flat-topped, fairly level, and carry stretches of moor, coarse pasture, and peat bog, as well as large amounts of rock debris. Many granite tors rise above the level surface. The ground drops sharply to the east but slopes more gradually to the west, falling in a series of plateaus toward the Lorraine Plain.

A feature of the Vosges is its number of valleys. Main valleys stand at right angles to the main ridges and tend to lie northwest on the western side and east or east-northeast on the eastern side. Tributary valleys parallel the ridges, lead far into the range, and terminate in a series of headstreams on the slopes of the main ridges. Valley bottoms within the Vosges itself are sometimes poorly drained and long narrow lakes and swampland areas often result.

In autumn, the evergreens are in sharp contrast with the changing colors of the deciduous trees and the yellow and brown of the stubble fields. In winter, the reds of the sandstone rocks and some of the granite become more noticeable after the forest leaves have fallen. Forests remain green at higher levels, but on the lower slopes browns and russets predominate.

The road net in the Vosges is somewhat constricted by terrain. Main routes often bottleneck in narrow village streets. Sharp turns and steep gradients are common in the Vosges and very winding roads are found in the lake areas near Belfort. Secondary and local roads tend to be narrow and sometimes muddy. In wet weather, they are generally unsuited to military traffic. They are often bordered by ditches or embankments and the crown on old cobbled roads is often so great that vehicles are required to travel at reduced speeds.

Above moderate heights, winters, particularly in the Vosges, may be long and hard, with drastic and sudden changes in temperatures. At all seasons bad weather is more persistent over the mountains than in areas 300-400 miles north because there is a decided tendency for "fronts" to slow up as they approach the Alps barrier; frequently a "front" becomes stationary along the line of the Alps, creating a broad belt of rain and cloud over the foothills which lasts for a day or two.

Charles R. Castellaw

The 3rd Infantry Division was on the western foothill approaches to the Vosges Mountains when Vesoul fell on September 12.

The 2nd battalion, 15th Infantry, which was one element of the forces which took the town, did not pause but continued through, and by 1645 September 12, was on Hill 349, a dominating feature northeast of the town in the direction of Velleminfroy. Movement of the Division at this time was pivoting to the northeast on 30th Infantry, the hub of which was generally at the town of Vallerois le Bois.

Shortly after noon September 12, 1st Battalion, 15th Infantry, moved to Hill 360, with two companies occupying the position at 1325. Company A, leading, encountered enemy machine-gun and small-arms fire at 1446, but outflanked the enemy and was near Quincy at 1640 with roadblocks to the southeast, northeast and northwest. At 1720, 1st Battalion was prepared to continue the advance to the north, and at 1930 moved out, shortly to encounter small-arms fire. The 1st Battalion continued to advance during the night and at 0345 reported the town of Calmoultier clear of enemy.

The 30th Infantry, which attacked initially in a north and northeast direction on the Division's right flank, later moved to the southeast toward Esprels, maintaining contact with the 45th Infantry Division. Shortly after noon of September 12, 3rd battalion captured thirty-six enlisted enemy soldiers and one officer, obtaining information on other enemy locations that aided in a successful advance. During the afternoon of September 12, 1st Battalion went to Dampierre, flanked to the left, then began a movement to the southeast against Hill 309. Late in the night of September 12-13, 1st Battalion began encountering enemy opposition, plus log barriers placed at intervals of twenty-five yards along the road to slow 1st Battalion's armor. Despite this, the advance continued.

The 2nd battalion, 15th Infantry, moved from Hill 349, which it had captured previously, and continued to advance against scattered enemy opposition through Comberjon to Moncey. Moncey was cleared at 0645, September 13, and the battalion moved on through Colombotte toward Velleminfroy, toward noon meeting about a platoon of enemy armed with small arms and machine guns.

During the same period, the 7th Infantry, in the center of the Division sector, occupied high ground past Noroy-le-Bourg, which it cleaned out en route. The 3rd battalion performed this task during the

The Way It Was

night of September 12-13, taking 100 to 150 prisoners and killing and wounding an unknown number. At 1830, 2nd battalion had been ordered into Division reserve, and 1st and 3rd battalion had advanced toward Hill 452 past Noroy-le-Bourg. By 2030, the 1st Battalion had captured the hill, with 3rd battalion almost directly to the north. At 1000, September 13, 3rd battalion attacked toward Hill 410 and Montjustin. Company C attacked from Hill 459 at 1030 and pushed toward Hill 430. There was scattered, unorganized small arms and machine-gun fire in opposition to the morning attacks of 1st and 3rd battalions.

The 2nd battalion, 30th Infantry, attacked Presle and by 2115, September 12 was in the corner of the woods near Trevey. At 2300, 2nd battalion began its move toward Presle and at 2400, Company F entered the town, with Company E generally to the northeast and Company G to the southeast. There was little resistance at the town, but there were indications that the enemy had just pulled out. Companies F and G remained in Presle while Company E blocked to the northeast until 0700, when the battalion moved out toward Vallerois-le-Bois. The 3rd battalion's Company I, which had been on a flank-protection mission at Thieffrans, was relieved by a company of the 180th Infantry and at 0850 attacked to the northeast toward Montbozon. The remainder of the 3rd battalion prepared for an attack on Mt. Jesus, moving in from the west.

During the foregoing period, 1st Platoon, Company B, 601st TD Battalion, scored a notable success by catching a column of enemy foot troops and killing seventy-five to a hundred enemy.

During the afternoon of September 13 the entire Division advance continued against strong enemy opposition, but the Division occupied all immediate objectives before dark. The 3rd battalion, 7th Infantry, sent one company on to Hill 410 while the remainder of the battalion moved to the east flank. The 1st Battalion advanced through Cerre-les-Noroy and started up the slopes of Hill 430. The 2nd battalion was released from Division control at 1445 and returned to regimental control. The 3rd battalion's remaining two rifle companies moved southeast to Autrey-les-Cerre. The 1st Battalion encountered considerable opposition and at 1915 some enemy still held on Hill 430. The 3rd battalion, meanwhile, continued pushing until its leading company ran into heavy artillery, small-arms and mortar fire. The 2nd

111

Charles R. Castellaw

battalion rested during the latter part of darkness and resumed its advance at 0400, toward Borey and Arpenans. The battalion moved against light opposition. The 1st and 3rd battalions moved out at 0830 and by noon 3rd battalion had occupied Montjustin without making contact with the enemy and was sending a company toward Arpenans. The 1st Battalion moved ahead steadily on 3rd battalion's flank.

Company A, 15th Infantry, occupied Lievans during the evening of September 13 and one platoon was left in the town until relieved by the 7th Infantry. On the morning of September 14, Company B, followed by Company A, moved to Mollans without resistance. Company C moved northwest toward Pomoy and Company B moved toward Genevreuville toward noon September 14. The 2nd battalion, Companies F and G leading, entered Velleminfroy at 0920, September 14 and upon occupation of the town went into regimental reserve.

The 3rd battalion's Company L occupied Hill 289 and on the morning of September 14 followed Company I into reserve. Company K attacked Saulx-de-Vesoul, meeting enemy small-arms and machine-gun fire, but had the town cleared at 1855, September 13. Elements of the 141st Infantry relieved Company K, which then moved to Creveny and Chateney. Toward noon Company K was advancing toward Colombe-le-Bithaine. Company I moved from Chatenois and occupied La Creuse at 0945 September 14 against practically no resistance. Toward noon 3rd battalion was continuing the advance toward Adelans.

The 1st and 2nd battalions, 30th Infantry, began their attack at 1530 September 13, with 1st Battalion located about 1000 yards beyond Esprels and 2nd battalion on the left (northeast) flank. The 3rd battalion moved up to Les Patey. Both battalions advanced against small-arms fire. The 3rd battalion sent a platoon to Autrey-le-Vay in conjunction with a platoon from the 45th Division to protect the sector between divisions. At 0630, September 14, 2nd battalion, from its position reached the night before, resumed its attack due east toward Oppenans and advanced without meeting enemy resistance. 1st Battalion fired interdictory machine-gun fire into Marast during the night, and on the morning of September 14 moved into the town against no opposition.

During September 14-15, the Division continued its steady pace toward Lure, swinging to the north and east against enemy resistance

The Way It Was

that became increasingly stronger during the afternoon of September 14 and which continued strong. The 15th Infantry, on the Division left flank, occupied Pomoy, Genevreuille and Mollans against strong resistance and moved toward Lure from the northwest. The 7th Infantry had contact with the enemy throughout the period, receiving small-arms, machine-gun, and mortar and artillery fire as it advanced to Arpenans, Les Aynans, and headed toward Vy-les-Lure.

Company C, 15th Infantry, entered Pomoy at 1200, September 14, then moved on toward Genevreuille. At 1315 a patrol encountered enemy artillery, mortar, machine-gun and small-arms fire, but the company continued its advance against well-prepared enemy positions and dug-in enemy and at 1830 reached the outskirts of Genevreuille in spite of heavy casualties. The company was pulled back from the town and an artillery barrage laid down. Company B was relieved at Mollans by a company from 30th Infantry at 2245 and moved to rejoin the battalion at Pomoy.

At 1245, 3rd battalion was located at Colombe-le-Bithaine, from where it moved to Danbenoit. Company K occupied Citers and patrolled to Quers.

Company A, 30th Infantry, entered the town of Aillevans at 1310 against no opposition, then moved to the east, Company B moving to the northeast. Company A crossed L'Oignan River and reached Hill 324 at 1600. Company C cleared the town of Longeville after overcoming considerable sniper fire. Patrols were sent north of Longeville and to the northeast up to 1000 yards, making negligible contact.

At 2125, the 2nd battalion, 15th Infantry, was ordered to move to Bithaine and to send a reinforced company to Hill 412. Company F reached the hill at 0925, September 15.

After continuous fighting over September 14 and during the night, 1st and 2nd battalions, 7th Infantry, continued to advance on the morning of September 15. At 0840, 2nd battalion was in contact at Les Aynans, our troops on the west side of L'Oignan River, the enemy on the other side. The 1st Battalion by noon had sent patrols toward Vy-les-Lure, ready to attack the town from the northwest.

The 3rd battalion, 15th Infantry, assembled during the morning in the vicinity of Citers. Company K attacked Quers in the face of considerable enemy fire and occupied the town by 1750 that evening.

Charles R. Castellaw

The remainder of the battalion moved toward Lure from the northwest. The 1st Battalion, 15th Infantry, moved on Genevreuille and at 1210 Company B entered against little opposition. The battalion continued toward Amblans, which was occupied in the face of moderate resistance.

The 2nd battalion, 30th Infantry, was assembled at Aillevans. At 0115, September 15, the battalion moved by truck to Lievans, closing in at 0345.

The 3rd battalion moved from Les Patey to Mollans, its last company closing in at 0200, and remained in regimental reserve. The 2nd battalion was in Division reserve.

The 1st Battalion, 7th Infantry, entered La Grange du Veau shortly after noon, September 15, and prepared a defensive position around the town. Strong enemy harassing fire was received, and at 2015 the battalion launched an attack toward high ground to the east. Enemy resistance was strong and the Germans had to be routed from their holes with bayonets and grenades. The battalion dug in for the night about halfway between La Grange du Veau and its objective.

The 2nd battalion, 7th Infantry, secured two bridges near Les Aynans at 1310. One platoon of Company E, assisted by fire from Company G, attacked Hill 383. Patrols were sent into Gouchenans during the night and reported enemy in the town, which Company G took the next morning.

At 1410, 3rd battalion, 7th Infantry, attacked Vy-les-Lure and at 1500, Company L was almost in the outskirts with Company I on its right flank. Determined enemy resistance, supported by considerable machine-gun, artillery and mortar fire prevented I and K companies from entering the town.

Company L, led by Capt. Ralph J. Yates, advanced through heavy artillery and mortar concentration, to seize a cluster of houses on the outskirts of the town. The company was swiftly surrounded by an enemy that outnumbered the men three to one. For seven hours the company beat off savage counterattacks one after another, as artillery and mortar fire scored eight direct hits on the company Command Post, tearing down a corner of the house and demolishing an adjacent shed.

The Way It Was

At the cost of 37 casualties, the company repulsed all counterattacks and inflicted heavy casualties—18 dead, 70 wounded—on the enemy.

At 0150 a patrol from Company K entered Vy-les-Lure and contacted elements of Company L. The 3rd battalion entered the town in strength at 0900, September 16.

For the foregoing action, Company L was later awarded the Distinguished Unit Citation.

The 1st Battalion, meanwhile, resumed its attack toward the high ground east of La Grange du Veau at 0710 and reached its objective at 0945. Toward noon the battalion was moving toward Lure.

The 2nd battalion, 15th Infantry, in its attack on Adelans during the afternoon of September 15, met considerable resistance. Patrols were sent into the town during the night and the attack was resumed the morning of September 16. The town fell before noon. Company K, 15th Infantry, moved to Francheville during this time and protected the regiment's left flank while the remainder of 3rd battalion moved toward Lure from the northwest.

The 1st Battalion, 30th Infantry, sent a patrol toward Gouchenans, which engaged approximately forty enemy in a firefight on the afternoon of September 15. At 0015 four enemy infiltrated into Company B lines, killing one man, but losing one captured, and two killed. The other escaped. Later, Company B patrols captured nine enemy who were asleep and at 0804, September 16, patrols captured six more. The 2nd and 3rd battalions remained in Division and regimental reserve, respectively.

Lure was entered first by 1st Battalion, 15th Infantry shortly after noon, September 16; 1st Battalion, 7th Infantry, following shortly after.

The capture of Lure ended the toughest battle that the Division had had for some time and the series of coordinated attacks over a wide front that was required in the operation was an indication that the Germans were stiffening their defense.

The actual occupation of Lure was unopposed insofar as enemy infantry was concerned but considerable artillery fell in the city all day September 16, coming from positions north of the town.

At this point, the Division's right zone was taken over by the 1st French Armored Division and the 3rd veered almost straight north in the direction of Faucogney.

Charles R. Castellaw

The 15th Infantry had just moved out of Lure when the 2nd battalion was hit by artillery fire and then by five machine guns at a strongly defended roadblock in a dense woods just northeast of the city.

Hand grenades bounced from tree to tree and the clash of bayonets rang through the forests as the two forces met in this eerie setting, shrouded in pitch darkness. Maj. John O'Connell's men never fought more savagely as the enemy fell, one by one, in individual fights. The Germans retreated after about an hour and the battalion moved on toward St. Germain shortly before midnight.

The 30th moved generally in the same direction as the 15th but the advance was slowed by an increasing number of mines along the roads. The 1st Battalion attacked and occupied the villages of Linexert and Lantenot by noon the following day, repulsing a strong enemy counterattack in the vicinity of Lantenot.

The 7th Infantry occupied Lure and the vicinity south and east of the village, and spent the next three days in patrolling and establishing roadblocks in that area.

The 1st Battalion of the 15th, attacking east from Francheville, had many fights before it finally gained the next objectives on September 18, when St. Germain, Froideterre and Lemont were taken without opposition. The 2nd battalion encountered heavy resistance including Flak, mortar and artillery fire just south of Froideterre but, as in the battle for the roadblock on the previous day, the enemy was decisively defeated, after which the battalion went into regimental reserve near Lure.

The 30th, after taking Lantenot, met a strong defense when the 3rd battalion, commanded by Lt. Col. Richard H. Neddersen, attempted to take Raddon, a small village about three miles west of Faucogney.

Attacking north, Company L, under Capt. Robert B. Pridgen, reached a ridge and began defensive preparations along a low, rock wall overlooking Raddon. Shortly after noon, heavy enemy tank and 20mm fire swept over the ridge and the concentration was immediately followed by an assault by some 200 frenzied, shouting Germans, many of whom yelled in English that "they wanted to die for Hitler."

The Way It Was

Captain Pridgen, later describing the counterattack, said, "They rushed into our fire in an insane manner, as if they had been given liquor or drugs before the assault."

The right flank squad of Company L, led by Sgt. Harold 0. Messerschmidt, bore the brunt of the charge and was subjected to a hail of fire from machine guns, machine pistols, rifles and grenades. Firing his submachine gun as he went (180 rounds in all), Sergeant Messerschmidt passed from man to man, encouraging and instructing them as he went.

Sgt. Bob J. Tucker, one of the squad members, stated that Messerschmidt was struck down by automatic fire early in the battle, shot through the chest and shoulder.

"Although badly wounded, he laid burst after burst of fire on everything moving up that slope," Tucker said, continuing, "I saw him grab his tommy gun by the barrel when he ran out of ammunition and kill a kraut by crashing the stock on his head. He sure killed a lot of Germans that day."

First Lt. Glenn Shuler, who brought a squad to relieve the beleaguered men, said that Messerschmidt was fighting alone when he arrived, all other members of the squad having been killed or wounded.

"I saw the sergeant run to the rescue of a wounded comrade who was being overpowered," the Lieutenant said. "Messerschmidt got the kraut and then I saw him disappear down the slope, flailing his empty gun at another fleeing German. The sergeant's body was later found at the bottom of the hill."

Colonel Neddersen said that the Nazi group which attacked our numerically inferior force was "the most determined and fanatical that we encountered." True, these SS Panzer troops, wearing long black overcoats, gave an excellent account of themselves.

Sergeant Messerschmidt was awarded the Congressional Medal of Honor posthumously.

Captain Pridgen's men fought off the enemy for several hours before they received reinforcements from Company K, commanded by Capt. Thomas A. Dawson.

The Distinguished Unit Citation which was later awarded to Company L for its gallant stand stated: "For six hours, the heavily outnumbered company fought on without respite, repulsing the

Charles R. Castellaw

German assault forces time and again with heavy loss despite the enemy's immense superiority in firepower... When the last wave of counterattack was rolled back, the men of Company L, their ammunition almost entirely expended, their ranks reduced by casualties and their situation apparently hopeless, prepared to assault and break through the German lines, although they had but four rifle squads with which to do it. But the enemy had already withdrawn, battered and beaten, abandoning his broken line to attempt a new stand at the Moselle."

By 2000, the enemy counterattacking force, which comprised Flakwagons, armor, an antitank gun and several bazooka teams in addition to the large infantry group, was driven from the Slopes and at daylight of September 18, Company K, commanded by Capt. M.B. Etheredge, Jr., moved into Raddon, which the badly-mauled Germans elected not to defend.

The retreating enemy fell back rapidly after the fight at Raddon and the next two days were spent in setting up a series of roadblocks in the Division zone and in maintaining vigorous patrols.

The 3rd was now only a short distance from the headwaters of the Moselle River, which rises on the north face of Ballon d'Alsace. The Moselle is the most important river in this area and it captures all other streams in the vicinity as it courses northeast toward the Lorraine Plain.

While awaiting relief by French units, the Division on September 20 launched an early morning attack northeast toward the Moselle, guided along the main road out of Faucogney, which the Germans had deserted in their flight.

The route of advance was through a semi-valley edged on both sides by hills, which the enemy employed to good advantage in slowing our movement. Snipers, defended roadblocks, concealed machine guns, and mortars lined the route.

With the 7th Infantry on the left, the 30th on the right and two battalions of the 15th in reserve, the Division moved steadily forward, overcoming continuous resistance from the hills.

Company I of the 30th felt the brunt of a counterattack in the vicinity of Melay, where the 3rd Reconnaissance Troop, commanded by 1st Lt. Allen R. Kenyon, also suffered heavily when it ran into a minefield just as the enemy opened fire on the troop from a hill near

The Way It Was

Melay. Company K withdrew and our artillery then laid a terrific concentration on the area.

During the period September 20-26, the 30th Infantry engaged in some of the most bitter and exhausting fighting in its entire history and contributed materially to the 3rd Division's outstanding role in the Seventh Army's flanking attack on the Belfort gap.

In the past three weeks of combat, I had come to believe that lead scout was the best position in my squad. When we were advancing, mortar and artillery fire would go over me. My problem was mines and small arms fire. While advancing in one of our attacks, I tripped over a wire leading to an explosive charge that was used by the enemy as a signal. Their mortars were zeroed on a point several yards behind me. I was lucky again. I had accepted lead scout as my position in the squad.

Jumping off in the attack to the northeast at 0630, September 20, the 2nd battalion, in fog and rain, moved forward with Company F in the lead, followed by Company E, with C Company in reserve. The objective was the village of Voleaux, eight miles distant and north of Faucogney. The route of the battalion led through a valley with rugged wooded high ground on either side. At 1145, elements of the enemy defense system outside the village began a harassing action and by 1400 had built up sufficient resistance, using small arms, machine guns, and mortars, to force the battalion to deploy and bring up artillery and mortars to soften enemy positions preliminary to frontal assault.

As Company E attacked under this fire, it almost reached the ridge, only to be forced back by a violent counterattack. Company F launched an attack directly up the south slope of the high ground, but was cut in half by a German thrust from the flanks and forced to pull back. At 1600, G Company, in reserve, was sent one mile to the north, across a waist-deep stream, through heavily wooded, mountainous country to a point 500 yards southeast of the objective to prepare for an attack early in the morning.

At 0700, September 21, Company G attacked forward, northeast along the ridge, meeting intense opposition including much close-range grenade fighting, but the company succeeded in capturing its objective.

Charles R. Castellaw

Bitterly counterattacked without rest, the company and a reinforcing platoon from Company F beat off no less than nine counterattacks in as many hours in one period. Numerous counterattacks were launched by fanatical Nazis who yelled allegiance to Hitler as they attacked.

Relief reached the company late on September 21 when Company F finally broke through the enemy positions which had been established across the rear of Company C. In the bitter action, the Germans lost an estimated 140 men killed or wounded and twelve as prisoners. Company G lost twenty-nine killed, wounded and missing. For this action Company G received the Distinguished Unit Citation.

Throughout the September 20-21 period, the 1st and 3rd battalions, 30th Infantry, were engaged in bitter fighting with the enemy in the vicinity of Melay and La Mer. Mined roads prevented extensive use of armor, and heavy mortar and artillery fire caused numerous casualties. Heavy rains made the poor roads impassable.

The advance of the 7th, which was generally north, met only harassing fire as it moved forward to occupy Hill 753 after silencing several machine guns on the hill which overlooked the Moselle River.

Turning its attack to the southeast, the Division advanced steadily against decreasing opposition, then turned sharply northeast. This sudden shift took the Germans by surprise and the badly disorganized enemy abandoned trucks, field pieces and other material as they broke and fled by whatever transportation they could jump onto, and by foot, across the bridge at Rupt-sur-Moselle.

The bridges had been prepared for demolition with nineteen cases of TNT but the 1st Battalion of the 7th Infantry, commanded by Lt. Col. Jesse F. Thomas, struck so quickly that the baffled Germans who remained to fight were killed or captured and the others retreated across the river. Company B, under 1st Lt. William K. Dieleman, effected the bridge capture and repulsed numerous attempts of the enemy to infiltrate back to detonate the explosives during the night. The company also beat off several efforts to recapture the bridge and by daylight of September 24, the entire 1st Battalion had crossed the bridge and was engaging the enemy in a firefight in Rupt-sur-Moselle, which lay just east of the Moselle.

A platoon of the 3rd battalion, 7th Infantry, made another crossing of the river at Maxonchamp, about one mile north of Rupt-sur-

The Way It Was

Moselle, at noon. The 3rd battalion of the 15th was attached to the 7th to protect its flank during the river-crossing operation.

Meanwhile the 1st and 3rd battalions, 30th Infantry, following relief by the 117th Reconnaissance Squadron, assembled in Faucogney the morning of September 22 and at 1200 jumped off in a coordinated attack, the 3rd on the left and 1st on the right—the 2nd holding the line of departure. The objective of the attack, which was straight northeast on the east side of the Faucogney-Remiremont highway, was the high ground east of Corravillers-lePlain.

Opposition was immediate. All roads in the rugged regimental sector were mined and blocked by trees. Fog and rain added to the difficulties. Every type of enemy fire was encountered. When the 1st Battalion reached the vicinity of Evouhey and encountered a well-prepared enemy line, the advance was halted for coordination purposes, preparatory to a renewal of the attack. The 2nd battalion, meanwhile, cleared the roads to Esmoulieres.

Throughout September 23 the advance continued, with the two assault battalions jumping off at 0645, the 1st Battalion securing Evouhey at 0717 and the 3rd battalion moving up on the left only to encounter stiff resistance from by-passed enemy positions in the 7th Infantry sector. The 3rd battalion continued its blocking mission to the right flank and east of the regiment.

At 1400, September 24, a strongly held enemy roadblock on the main road, manned by enemy infantry, with a Flak gun in the woods behind, prevented a further advance by the 3rd battalion. When it appeared that a battalion from the 7th Infantry could not clear this area before dark, the 3rd battalion, 30th Infantry, bypassed the resistance, leaving K Company as a blocking force, and proceeded to clear out the enemy in its assigned sector. Company F meanwhile was attached to the battalion, abreast of the left flank positions on the Le Chene road.

At 0630, September 25, the 30th Infantry jumped off in an attack to the southeast to secure high ground overlooking Le Thillot, which was to serve as a springboard for French armor to attack that important city and continue on toward Belfort.

The 3rd battalion advanced on the left and the 1st Battalion on the right of the Corravillers-Chateau Lambert road. The 3rd battalion, whose left flank on the Moselle River was exposed to enemy fire, found the going through dense woods and over the rough terrain very slow, enemy small-arms fire being extremely persistent. Company F attacked and found the Le Chene road almost entirely blocked by fallen trees and heavily mined. By 1620, however, the company had reached the outskirts of Le Chene.

The 1st Battalion, although making no contact initially, ran into well-defended positions at 1305, with mortar, self-propelled artillery and Flak guns composing the opposition. The assault companies forced their way slowly through pouring rain, dense woods, and numerous roadblocks, with visibility very low, to reach the final objective at 1910. The battalion barely missed capturing an enemy divisional commander, but took a German battalion command post with telephones intact that was in communication with the German division command post. More than 150 prisoners, including three officers, were taken in this outstanding action.

At 1845, Company L was sent to assist Company F in the attack on Le Chene, which had proved in early efforts to be too large a job for one company.

The 3rd battalion, having continued throughout the night of September 25-26, reached its objective at 0930, September 26, after killing, wounding, or capturing fifty-two more enemy soldiers.

On the same day 2nd battalion, less Company G, captured Le Chene after a 40-minute fight, taking twenty more prisoners.

That afternoon the 30th Infantry was relieved by French troops and closed in assembly areas at La Longine and Corravillers. During the afternoon of September 27, the regiment moved by motor to Remiremont, and spent the following day in preparation for the attack toward Le Tholy.

Rupt-sur-Moselle was cleared of all resistance by noon, September 25, and Hill 867, which rose directly behind the village and served as a vantage point from which the enemy fired on traffic crossing the bridge, was occupied. The high ground east of Maxonchamp likewise served the enemy well until it was cleared by the 7th, which had expanded its area by fanning out north to Dommartin and south to La Roche.

The 15th Infantry, meanwhile, had moved out from positions in the vicinity of Remiremont and attacked northeast from St. Ame', with

The Way It Was

the 7th Infantry protecting its right flank south of the Moselette, from a high wooded area containing many enemy gun positions.

With nature as the greatest obstacle to progress, the 15th moved steadily forward after the attack began early September 27, but on the next day the enemy, in well dug-in and previously prepared positions between Le Syndicat and Cremanvillers, put up a terrific fight.

Two night counterattacks, coupled with constant infiltrations after dark, taxed the15[th]'s strength to the utmost and on September 28 the 30th joined in the attack, going into position between the 15th and the 36th Infantry Division on the 3rd's left flank.

The 7th continued to clean out the Germans between the Moselle and Mosellette Rivers and occupied Ferdrupt, east of the Moselle and a little north of Le Thillot, shortly after noon.

It was at Ferdrupt that Company F of the 7th Infantry particularly distinguished itself. For six consecutive days, it had advanced in chilling rain up the precipitous slopes of a 2,500-foot hill mass against determined opposition to seize its objective. Fighting at hand-to-hand range raged for days in the densely wooded terrain. German infiltration attempts through the wooded area and enemy counterattacks were repulsed time and time again. Having secured the top of the hill mass the weary, thinned-out ranks of the company continued to drive off German attacking forces to hold the terrain feature they had so dearly won in the fog and cold. For this grim battle and victory the Distinguished Unit Citation was later awarded the doughty warriors of Company F.

The 15th Infantry approached one of its greatest battles in the Vosges (and the entire war) as it neared the Cleurie Quarry. During the afternoon of September 26, the 1st Battalion relieved elements of the 36th Infantry Division in the vicinity of St. Ame'. The enemy still held a roadblock on the bridge crossing the stream south of the town, which was covered by fire from positions a mere 300 yards from the bridge. The battalion immediately seized it and the crossroads there in the face of heavy enemy fire, just in time to prevent the enemy from detonating 250 pounds of dynamite laid to demolish the bridge. The 1st Battalion had thus secured the southern extremity of the line of departure for the following day's attack, and seized an important bridge.

Charles R. Castellaw

The same afternoon, 2nd and 3rd battalions moved into positions in preparation for the attack; 2nd battalion to an area just west of St. Ame', and 3rd battalion farther to the north.

At daylight, September 27, the 2nd battalion attacked east through the densely wooded sector following a 15-minute artillery concentration. The battalion pushed through the gloomy, rain-soaked foothills and almost at once, the leading elements drew enemy mortar fire. The first group of enemy was contacted immediately north of St. Ame' and was protecting the secondary road leading north from the town from the woods west of the road. Elements of the 2nd battalion surprised the enemy from the rear and there was a brief skirmish, during which thirty-two prisoners were captured.

The battalion continued to the northeast through small arms, machine-gun, and mortar fire, and booby-trapped roadblocks. By 1400, it had reached the secondary road running southeast from Bemont. Resistance then slacked off and the 2nd battalion pushed rapidly to its objective on the high ground northeast of St. Ame'.

The 3rd battalion, which had held back initially to support the 2nd's advance with fire, attacked at midmorning toward Cleurie, from the vicinity of Putieres, and moved along the ridge to the northeast without opposition. In the afternoon, the advance was punctuated by bitter hand-to-hand fighting, but the battalion battered its way to positions on the high ground south of Cleune.

At dusk about 150 Germans launched a counterattack against Company K. This attack was preceded by a short, intense artillery barrage, but was repulsed within three hours.

The fight for the Cleurie Quarry was in the mold. Company I attacked all night and secured Bemont. Company G continued toward Cremanvillers, held up in the woods, and sent patrols to the town. At 0230, the enemy hit Company G with a heavy counterattack, which was beaten off. Daylight found the company again heavily engaged just northeast of Cremanvillers. Company C was attached to the 2nd battalion to aid G Company, and pushed east from St. Ame', where it was counterattacked by the enemy in the wooded areas.

The enemy was now completely aroused. He struck again at K Company and again was beaten off. The constant, driving rains, the fog and mist, cut visibility almost to the zero point and the Germans

The Way It Was

used this to advantage to move between our elements in attempts to disorganize our lines and demoralize the men.

Company F, moving south from the 2nd battalion hill position toward G, again was heavily attacked, and fought throughout the day. Other enemy groups pushed through the gaps between the companies of the 2nd and 3rd battalions, one group even penetrating almost to the 3rd battalion command post.

By dawn, September 28, the entire effective strength of the 15th Infantry was committed. Elements of the 1st Battalion were pushing toward Cremanvillers and Bemont to assist the other two battalions, moving out to attack north through the woods in the zone east of the road leading north out of St. Ame'. As the 1st moved north into the clearing east of Bemont, it drew heavy fire of all descriptions from the woods to the east, and consequently it attacked northeast through the woods to outflank the enemy positions from which the fire was coming. 1st Battalion remained heavily engaged throughout the day.

Enemy tanks were encountered for the first time in several days. One moved south almost to Bemont, where it was beaten off by artillery. Two others fired on the houses east of Bemont.

Ration details were forced to run a gantlet of roving enemy tanks and snipers while hard-carrying their heavy loads up slippery, wet slopes. Even litter teams were not exempt. Many a wounded doughboy had to be carried through small-arms and mortar fire.

The ferocious fighting continued throughout the day and through the night of September 28-29. In the early morning hours five enemy tanks moved in to shoot up F Company positions in a group of houses, and before the armor could be turned away with artillery the company had become badly scattered, the Commanding Officer and much of company headquarters either killed, wounded, or captured. Only seventy men could be accounted for by the time the attack was beaten off.

Company E was counterattacked and forced to fight for four hours to hold its positions. The attack was finally broken.

Company L, fighting south toward K Company, was hit by 250 enemy and engaged in a furious battle to hold its hill. Two platoons of the company were split and scattered and it was daylight before about seventy or eighty men could be rounded up, organized and moved up to the original hill positions.

Charles R. Castellaw

The 1st Battalion continued its drive as the remainder of the regiment cleaned out the enemy who had infiltrated everywhere into the regimental sector. Company I was attached to the battalion. From the area east of Bemont the 1st drove up the main road, against small-arms and mortar fire. Our artillery raked enemy strongpoints near Cleurie and in the buildings south of town. The battalion made good progress and turned east along the edge of the woods. Late on September 29, the forward elements were hit with fire from about forty enemy who were lodged in the vicinity of Cleurie Quarry. It was then that the great battle began.

Company B held up—then pushed on. A few hours later the enemy launched a light counterattack. At midnight, a full-force counterattack hit the tired company. Capt. Paul Harris and his men groped their way toward the top of "Great Rock," to reach the crest and hole up, but under the thick night fog the enemy once more slammed back. Closing in, feeling their way along like blind men, the enemy approached behind a heavy artillery preparation to within fifty yards. Slinging potato-masher grenades and blasting away with machine pistols, the enemy hit B Company's right flank. Fanatical young Nazis pressed the attack for five hours. The attack mounted in fury. Then, just before the dawn of September 30, the enemy withdrew. Although the right flank platoon of B Company, which had borne the brunt of the savage battle, had been forced to pull back, the bulk of the company was still holding firm.

In the remainder of the 15th Infantry zone, the constant attempts at infiltration had continued. One group of enemy had probed its way between G and C Companies; another counterattacked E Company, and still another struck at G Company twice during the day, and the night of September 29-30. All attempts finally were repulsed with the help of prepared concentrations from mortar batteries and the regimental Cannon Company. But the battle was not yet over.

On September 29, the 30th Infantry assumed offensive action, with the objective of seizing Hill 781, high ground overlooking Le Tholy. The 3rd battalion led the attack, crossing the line of departure at 0700 and continuing without resistance until 0835, when strong resistance in the form of small-arms and artillery fire was met from well-defended all-around positions, which blocked maneuvering elements at every point. The 2nd battalion, following to the right rear, found it

The Way It Was

could not pass through 3rd battalion without becoming engaged in a firefight, and 1st Battalion was then committed. The 2nd battalion became the reserve battalion and established roadblocks.

Company A relieved Company K, 15th Infantry. Later A Company was relieved by E Company. It took part in a cross-country march with 1st Battalion which began at 1500 September 29 and continued until 0020 September 30, when the entire battalion relieved 3rd battalion, 141st Infantry (36th Division).

At 0715 that morning, 1st Battalion jumped off in the attack again, and began receiving heavy fire at 0810, initially from machine guns, mortars, and small arms, but which was intensified with the addition of heavy artillery concentrations at 0945. Severe casualties, numbering up to 150, were received. Company B, under 1st Lt. Lyle Standish, attempted to maneuver and flank enemy positions, and was met with heavy automatic-weapons fire, which slowed the advance. The 3rd battalion resumed its attack at 0915, September 30, but strongly entrenched enemy in commanding positions held up the advance. Another attack at 1815 secured a line and gained strategic ground, while the 2nd battalion remained in regimental reserve.

As the month of September closed, the Division was embroiled in heavy fighting. Enemy counterattacks were characterized by a ferocity hitherto encountered only in Italy the previous winter. Increased artillery fire from 75s, 88s, and 105s was evidence that the German commander had received reinforcements in this all-important branch as October came and actual winter began to set in.

THIRTIETH INFANTRY SECTOR OF OPERATION

Summary of Enemy Operations 1-30 September, 1944

Enemy activities during the period 1 to 30 of September may be classified as intensive delaying actions. To accomplish this mission the enemy employed flak wagons, both anti tank and anti-personal mines, mortars, artillery and well organized defensive positions.

At the beginning of the period the enemy was catching stragglers at Belfort, organizing them into separate battalions and sending them to the front to fight.

At Besancon the enemy opposed our advance with a well organized unit and attempted to deny us the important road nets leading therefrom by occupying and defending the tactically employed ancient fortifications surrounding the town. The enemy held these fortifications until the tactical situation or the lack of ammunition forced his surrender. The enemy within the city of Besancon itself held out with determined resistance. Bitter street and house to house fighting finally resulted in the clearing of the city itself. All prisoners of war said their orders were to hold out to the last. The enemy blew all bridges over the Doubs River in an attempt to prohibit our crossing the river into the city itself.

The enemy established his first defensive line in the area of Ecromagny-La Voivre-Faucogney. He took full advantage of the terrain, mined the main roads as well as the numerous side roads and trails. The enemy used Teller, S and box mines in his defense in this area in a larger quantity than heretofore. His defense was in depth, supported by artillery and self-propelled fire as well as the Infantry, mortars and automatic weapons. The enemy had no intention of giving up the aforesaid sector as was shown by his dogged resistance and fanatical counterattacks. During a period of two days the enemy made a total of 12 counterattacks against our positions ranging from squad to company in size. His artillery was registered and prepared concentrations of 24 to 48 rounds in small areas were not unusual.

The enemy again resisted our advance up the main road from Faucogney to La Longine and Corravillers with extensive use of mines and tree blocks covered by automatic weapons fire and artillery and mortar concentrations. The enemy defended only strategic roadblocks but stayed on these until they were killed, captured, or wounded.

Enemy resistance in the Hazintray-Cleurie sector was the most determined during the period. The enemy used the terrain to the greatest advantage. Artillery fire was used to its utmost. The enemy occupied defensive positions on the heavily wooded high ground overlooking the valley between Hazintray and Le Tholy. Each clearing in the woods was occupied by the enemy. Prisoner of war reports indicate that this sector was held by an estimated 600 enemy. The enemy used the "S" mine in this area for the first time. The mines were laid in streambeds, woods, and along the roads. Trip wires were attached to a great many of the mines and some teller mines were also used. There was a noted increase in artillery fire in this sector.

The Way It Was

At the close of the period indications were that the enemy planned to continue his resistance and deny us the Le Tholy-Gerardmer road.

The Division was well into the first phase of October, with the three regiments battling for important ground in its over-all attack northeast toward Le Tholy in conjunction with the move east to overrun Vagney and Sapois. The second phase was to come following the capture of these important centers, and consisted of an attack through elements of the 45th Infantry Division that carried across the Mortagne River and to the high ground overlooking the important enemy communications center of St. Die'. The latter attack was to begin at noon, October 20, and result in a breakthrough of the enemy's strong defensive line based on the Mortagne River. But much fighting remained before this could be achieved.

By September 30, the 7th Infantry had taken Ferdrupt and was pushing on toward Vagney to come up on the 15th Infantry's right flank. While the remainder of the 15th was forced to halt and clean out its zone of infiltrating Germans, the 1st Battalion continued to batter away against the quarry positions.

The quarry was a major thorn in our side and had to be cleaned out, although it was proving a tough obstacle. It controlled the main route of advance, the Le Tholy-Gerardmer road, which itself had to be cleared before the Division could continue on the over-all mission of penetrating the Vosges proper. The quarry was the anchor point of the enemy main line defending the important St. Ame' hill mass, and the largest hill in the area which controlled the entire situation all the way back to Remiremont.

There were several reasons for the difficult mission that the quarry proved to be. First, it was situated on the slopes of the large, thickly wooded hill mass. The only approaches to it were up the steep, almost cliff-like sides of this mountain. On the north and south sides of the quarry were steep cliffs covered by machine guns. In order to gain entrance to the interior, our men had to charge up the sides in the face of furious fire. East and west ends were blocked by huge, stonewall roadblocks constructed by the Germans. The steep cliffs on either side made it impossible to by-pass these, and thus the only way left open was to go over the top of them which again was covered by terrific concentrations of small-arms fire.

Charles R. Castellaw

The quarry was honeycombed with passageways, tunnels and walls, rendering the defenders virtually safe from mortar fire. Another difficulty was that it was impossible for us to use artillery after the companies had closed in around the position, since our guns in position in the flat lands near St. Ame' had to fire over the top of the hill mass, and with our troops so close to the enemy, tree bursts often fell within our own lines.

As October came, prisoners reported that there were two companies, approximately 100 men each in strength, with orders to fight to the death for the position. The regimental plan now was to coordinate with the drive of the 30th Infantry in a house-to-house push down the valley toward Gerardmer, the VI Corps objective, where the enemy was known to be entrenched in strength.

All three battalions of the 30th Infantry during the period October 1-8 continued an unrelenting pressure toward the northeast. On October 1, the 3rd battalion, 30th Infantry, resumed its attack at 0700, and the 1st Battalion jumped off at 0800. The 2nd battalion patrolled into the valley, encountering and charting minefields, and taking and occupying fifteen houses. Despite enemy artillery concentrations and counterattacks the 1st and 3rd battalions continued to advance.

After a day of driving the Germans out of a small village, we were spending the night in the basements of houses with some local civilians that had returned after the battle. All activities had ceased for the night. I was planning to get some sleep when I heard a soldier tell a teenage girl that he would strike a match so he could see a picture that she wanted to show him. I called out, "Do not strike a match." He replied, "It will not matter." As he struck the match, I dove out the door. The Germans fired a mortar shell through an air vent that exploded inside. Because I was outside, I did not get a scratch.

I am sure that matches and cigarettes led to the death of several soldiers. They made a good target at night.

While in combat our food was K rations, consisting of a paraffin coated box of food that was made up of one small can of eggs and bacon for breakfast, one small can of cheese for one meal and one small can of meat for another, which had such an odor it was impossible for me to eat it. We had dry biscuits, graham crackers and powdered coffee. This was the ration for one day.

The Way It Was

On October 2, the 2nd battalion was moved by motor to the extreme left of the regimental sector, behind Hill 769, to outflank enemy positions on the high ground and open the route across the Tendon-La Tholy highway to the high ground beyond. The 1st Battalion, meanwhile, continued a yard-by-yard advance against well dug-in and held enemy positions, sustaining heavy casualties and overrunning one enemy mortar platoon. The battalion also captured four mortars, two antitank guns, two Flak guns, and fifteen soldiers plus an artillery observer. Throughout the day the 2nd battalion continued the slow advance through heavily mined areas, and was relieved by 15th Infantry and 10th Engineer Battalion elements at 2010, following which the battalion entrucked and moved to an assembly area, prepared to attack on October 3.

In the 15th zone, virtual stalemate had set in by the morning of October 2. In some places the lines were barely seventy-five yards apart. It was jungle warfare, with thick nests of enemy snipers and infiltrating German parties. At the mouth of the quarry the enemy now had constructed a rock wall squarely across both entrances, then covered it with fire from positions in the rock piles. During the night of October 2-3, Companies C and I were returned to their battalions, and took up positions in their respective zones.

The all-out drive got underway October 3. At first light two tank destroyers and two tanks mounting 105mm assault guns were moved into position across the valley from the quarry, from where they pumped 500 rounds of high explosive into the tunnels and main part of the quarry. At the same time, 1st Battalion mortars laid in a terrific concentration. When the fire lifted, patrols from all three rifle companies of the 1st Battalion ranged out to probe the quarry. Opposition still remained, and brisk fighting raged throughout the day. Company B patrols were hit by an enemy machine gun immediately in front of its lines short of the quarry, and captured a sniper. Other prisoners indicated that a complete company of sharpshooters, eighty men strong, had been brought into the area, each man carrying a rifle equipped with telescopic sight. One squad of marksmen was attached to each regular rifle platoon of the 601st *Schnelle* Battalion, defending the quarry, for employment as snipers.

Contact with the enemy was constant throughout the day. Plans to launch the cleanup attack the following day were made. While on his

Charles R. Castellaw

way to an observation post, Col. Richard G. Thomas, regimental commander, was stricken with a heart attack, and command of the 15th Infantry passed to Regimental Executive Lt. Col. Hallett D. Edson. In the 3rd battalion, Lt. Col. Frederick Boye, commanding, left for the United States on temporary duty and his executive officer, Maj. Russell Comrie, replaced him.

At 0530, October 4, the 3rd battalion launched an outflanking attack. In conjunction with the 30th Infantry, the battalion drove northeast down the valley from positions just northwest of L'Omet, and sent Company I around west of the quarry to cut the road. The other two battalions remained in blocking positions.

Despite the fact that the enemy had poured strong reinforcements into the quarry and prepared for a bitter stand, Company I surprised the first positions short of the quarry and the enemy here withdrew.

Behind the supporting fire of three battalions of artillery, the 3rd battalion drove on. In less than two hours L Company had destroyed two machine guns, captured a crew of six, and driven two other machine-gun crews back. By noon, Company I was halfway around the quarry on the west side and was meeting heavy sniper fire, while L Company was overrunning the houses in the valley and bringing up tanks to blast them.

All afternoon and during most of the night the fight went on. By dark, I Company had cleared the enemy from the western approaches to the quarry, after bringing up tanks to blast down the stone-wall roadblock at that entrance with their guns.

The 3rd battalion had now established a line from the main road just west of Razintray, bending around almost to the western edges of the quarry. Before midnight one platoon-sized patrol from I Company pushed into the eastern end of the quarry after men of the 10th Engineer Battalion had been committed to blast the stone wall blocking the road at that end.

The fight was at a climax and the job completed on October 5. Mortars of the Battalion opened up with a 1100-round continuous creeping barrage. Then combat patrols from the battalion, plus the 3rd battalion Battle Patrol, and a platoon of Company I pushed out to destroy the last positions. By midafternoon, the Battle Patrol, under Sgt. John J. Shermetta, came up to the quarry from the west and met S/Sgt. John D. Shirley's I Company platoon coming from the east.

The Way It Was

The quarry had now fallen after a grueling six-day fight.

The Medal of Honor was awarded to 1st Lt. (then 2nd Lt.) Victor L. Kandle for his action performed during the last days of the fight for the quarry. While leading a reconnaissance patrol in the vicinity of La Forge in enemy territory, Lieutenant Kandle engaged in a daylight duel at point-blank range with a German field officer and killed him. Having taken five enemy prisoners during the morning, he led his skeleton platoon of sixteen men, reinforced by a light machine-gun squad, through fog and over precipitous mountain terrain to fall on the rear of the approach positions of the German quarry stronghold, which had checked the advance of the 1st Battalion. The citation of Lieutenant Kandle reads in part:

"... Rushing forward several yards ahead of his assault elements, Lieutenant Kandle forced his way into the heart of the enemy strongpoint and by his boldness and audacity forced the Germans to surrender. Harassed by machine-gun fire from a position which he had by-passed in the dense fog, he moved to within fifteen yards of the enemy, killed a German machine gunner with accurate rifle fire, and led his men in the destruction of another machine-gun crew and its rifle security elements. Finally, he led his small force against a fortified house held by two German officers and thirty enlisted men. After establishing a base of fire, he rushed forward alone through an open clearing in full view of the enemy, smashed through a barricaded door, and forced all thirty-two Germans to surrender. His intrepidity and bold leadership resulted in the capture or killing of three enemy officers and fifty-four enlisted men, the destruction of three enemy strongpoints and the seizure of...."

Meanwhile the 30th Infantry had jumped off on October 3, with the 2nd battalion now committed in a new attack on the regiment's extreme left with the final objective of seizing Hill 781, north of Le Tholy. At 0700 the attack was well under way, with the 2nd battalion coordinating with the 1st Battalion on the right. Throughout the bright moonlight night of October 3-4, the regiment continued its determined attack. At 0500 the 1st Battalion was counterattacked on its exposed right flank. Company B beat off the attack and at 1320 the enemy counterattacked this battalion again, but failed to dent it. The 2nd battalion's attack met equally fierce resistance, but the 3rd battalion reached its objective by 1230, taking eight prisoners and a mortar

Charles R. Castellaw

position, using the mortars to fire back at the enemy. Casualties for the period October 1-3 totaled more than 400.

Throughout October 4, the enemy continued to make limited attacks against the 1st Battalion's right flank. Both the 1st and 2nd battalions continued to press the attack, but enemy resistance was determined and progress was slow. During this period enemy artillery increased considerably with several three-gun batteries firing simultaneously at 30th Infantry troops.

The 1st Battalion maintained its pressure on the enemy, and advanced slowly toward the objective. The 2nd battalion, by late afternoon of the 6th, placed fire on enemy positions astride the main Tendon-Le Tholy highway, driving the Germans out. During the night this position was occupied by 2nd battalion troops.

At 0730, October 7, the 1st Battalion jumped off in an attack which gained the crest of the objective by 0930, while the 3rd battalion moved Company I to reinforce the 1st Battalion's sector.

On the 8th, the 1st Battalion launched a concerted cleanup attack at 1515, coordinated with tanks and TDs to drive all the enemy from the ridge by dark, despite heavy enemy 150mm artillery opposition.

Remaining in opposition on the 9th, and consolidating its positions, the regiment took its final objectives on October 10, with the 2nd battalion pushing Companies E and F across the Tendon-Le Tholy road under cover of darkness and seizing the objectives by 0700. The entire battalion was consolidated on the high ground north of Le Tholy that night and the 3rd battalion moved up to occupy positions left by the 2nd battalion.

The 7th Infantry, in this tedious fight for control of the Vosges, entered Vagney after overcoming stubborn resistance. The 1st Battalion, which had borne the brunt of the fighting, established its Command Post approximately in the center of town. The regimental command post was set up just north of Vagney, and the 3rd battalion command post was also moved into town. A dense fog covered the area on October 7, and small, by-passed groups of enemy still held out in the hills and pine forests that flanked the narrow valley floor on which Vagney was located.

The decision to displace 7th Infantry headquarters units forward while Vagney was still receiving strong shell fire involved a deliberate sacrifice of security, but the necessity of establishing and

The Way It Was

maintaining control over the combat elements required it. Vagney was still under observation from high ground in the direction of Sapois.

Terrain, the weather conditions and the progress of the offensive all conspired to create perfect conditions for a hostile counterattack and the Germans took advantage of one of the darkest and foggiest nights of the early winter to conduct a raid on the 3rd battalion command post.

T/Sgt. Gerald T. Hennings, the battalion sergeant-major, later described the action.

"I heard a terrific roar as a tank came down the road and stopped in front of the house next to the command post," Hennings said. "I knew that some of our tanks were expected to return to the rear areas for a short rest and naturally thought that this was one of them. I heard the sound of a grenade as it exploded in the next house. Then another came through our own window in the command post!"

A supporting tank platoon, under command of 2nd Lt. James L. Harris, was in the town square at the time. The noise brought immediate action from the lieutenant's crew.

"There was confusion as to the identity of the tank at first," Hennings continued, "and Lieutenant Harris elected to go forward afoot in an effort to identify it. The first burst of machine-gun fire from the enemy tank caught the Lieutenant squarely, knocking him to the ground. The next burst killed a man beside me. We were really in a bad spot.

"Lieutenant Harris didn't forget his mission and despite his painful wounds, he crawled thirty yards through a hell of machine-gun fire to his tank, where he ordered the tank into a covered archway, but it burst into flames, struck by five direct hits, while still in the center of the street."

Pvt. Burton B. Roberts, a medic attached to the Battalion, said that Lieutenant Harris refused medical aid until the sole survivor of his tank had been cared for.

"After I had evacuated the enlisted men I returned to help Lieutenant Harris," Roberts stated. "He asked me if I had taken care of his men and I told him I had. He seemed relieved. He told me he was done for and I saw that his right leg had been cut off at the crotch, apparently by the flying pieces of armor plate from his tank. He was in bad shape. I don't see how he lived as long as he did."

Charles R. Castellaw

Col. Ben Harrell, commanding officer of the 7th, commented, "The Germans had struck at the heart of a vital command area. As a result of Lieutenant Harris' heroism and single-minded devotion, the force of their blow was warded off; the battalion command post was saved from possible destruction and an interruption of offensive operations in that sector of the Vosges was averted."

The posthumous award of the Congressional Medal of Honor that followed Lieutenant Harris' act was the recognition of many similar deeds performed by the *756* Tank Battalion during the battle for the Vosges and Lieutenant Harris' heroism was typical of many other officers and enlisted men during the bitter winter warfare.

The 1st Battalion of the 7th repulsed a strong tank-supported counterattack at Vagney while another that isolated Companies E and I from the rest of the regiment for a short time was beaten off after a bitter fight in the same vicinity.

The 7th Infantry occupied Sapois and completed the occupation of Zainvillers, clearing out many sniper nests in the process. The regiment was taken out of the line October II and began a five-day training schedule in the vicinity of Eloyes. On the same day, Peck Force (elements of the 15th Infantry) took LaForge and the rest of the regiment continued its march to the northeast while the 30 remained in the vicinity of Le Tholy where the Germans were firmly dug in.

During one of our battles, my squad leader became a casualty and I was appointed acting squad leader. I explained to my squad that the procedure would be the same. When we went into battle, I would lead the squad as lead scout. (I believed that my chances of survival were better as lead scout). One member of our squad, K.O. (not his real name) had a habit of disappearing during the fighting and showing up as soon as the fighting was over. I informed him that if I caught him disappearing during battle, I would kill him. This method of punishment was not specified in the Articles of War or approved by Senior Officers, but they did not have this problem. We called it "Combat Justice."

Later one of the men told me that K.O. had tried to get them to refuse to take orders from me. They told him that their chance of survival was slim, but with my leadership, it was better. It may have been because I would always take the lead. He said that I should

The Way It Was

watch K.O., because he thought if he got a chance, he would shoot me in the back.

Shortly after I was promoted to acting squad leader, my platoon leader sent for me about dusk one evening. He told me that he had received orders to send out a reconnaissance patrol and that he had selected me for the assignment. We went over a sketch that he had of the area and how to reach our designated point. My assignment was to determine if the enemy was still in this location. The purpose of a reconnaissance patrol was to collect information. You never fired your gun unless you are fired upon. He gave me permission to select from the platoon the men that I wanted and the number I needed. I selected a BAR team of two men, one man with a sub-machine gun, one man with a M-1 and I carried a M-1. This gave us a team of five men. I gave a lot of thought to this mission because I knew if we were able to return it would not be our last mission.

At the set time, we moved out and proceeded in formation. I was in front, the BAR Team to the right about fifteen feet behind me, the sub-machine gunman to the left about fifteen feet behind me. There was a distance of about twenty feet between the BAR Team and the submachine gunman. The M-1 rifleman was ten feet directly behind me with orders that if we received fire, he was to move right or left of me and start firing. The others were ordered to fire from their location. We proceeded until we reached a point close to the specified position, then I signaled to halt and seek cover. We remained in position for about thirty minutes, and then I signaled to withdraw. I had decided that I was not going to get killed just so headquarters would know that the enemy was at this point. When we got back to our unit, I reported that the enemy was at the designated point.

After that night, I was assigned Reconnaissance Patrol about once a week. I used my same team and made the decision of what to do based on my gut feeling.

Charles R. Castellaw

Army WACs on break

One of the two 380 MM German railway guns abandoned by the enemy in the Battle of Montelimar

The Way It Was

President Franklin D. Roosevelt during the "Casablanca" conference

American troops meet Russian troops

Charles R. Castellaw

Riflemen moving through snow-covered wooded terrain

The Way It Was

Charles Castellaw's sister Zuline and her husband Warren Blackburn

Cannons in Fort at Mutzig

Charles Ray Castellaw on his horse with his sister Zuline

The Way It Was

Carl Castellaw with two farm hands

Charles R. Castellaw

May Castellaw's sister Kate's husband Dallis Stubblefield and his mules, Jug and Nug

The Way It Was

Charles Castellaw's brother Carl and his wife Elise

Charles R. Castellaw

On one patrol, we were looking for a house that we believed the enemy was using for an outpost. I had veered to the left and by-passed the house. I realized that I had gone too far. I then turned back. As we returned, I kept to the left and after going a short distance we reached a rock fence. We stopped to observe and listen. It was very dark and we could not see the outline of any buildings. Then we saw an enemy soldier light a cigarette. We were able to see the outline of the house. The men wanted to open fire. I told them that we were ordered not to fire unless we were fired upon. Orders meant about as much to them as they did to me. We lined up against the rock fence.

They were to fire only when I gave the order and after firing to take off as fast as they could. That was exactly what we did. The enemy did not return fire.

When we returned to our unit, I made my report to the Captain. I reported that we were fired upon and had to return fire.

Regimental raider platoons and reinforced combat patrols raided enemy positions frequently during the next few days and although no major gains were made during the period, the Division maintained a continuous pressure that was slowly pushing the enemy back.

The Porter Force of the 30th, led by 1st Lt. Morris C. Porter, commander of the regimental raider platoon, and including a platoon of the division battle patrol led by 2nd Lt. Walter Gill, who was captured in the action, engaged in a torrid fight in the early morning hours of October 16 when another raid was conducted against Le Tholy. Lieutenant Porter's men suffered heavily when they were caught from the front and flanks upon entering the town. The battle lasted for several hours and the force withdrew at daylight.

The 15th was relieved by French units on October 17, leaving only the 30th in the line. The latter regiment maintained contact with the enemy through vigorous patrolling until October 20, when the Division renewed the attack northeast toward Vervezelle and Brouveheures.

The setting for this action was generally as follows:

VI US Corps was still fighting with the same divisions which had landed on the Riviera two months before—the 3rd, 36th, and 45th. All had been continuously engaged. Now, with winter approaching and the rugged terrain adding to the difficulties imposed by the weather, our tired troops were finding it increasingly difficult to keep up their

The Way It Was

day-to-day advances. Meanwhile the enemy's lines of supply had shortened, his replacements were becoming more numerous and frequent, and above all he now had time to place and employ his artillery.

Against this, the Allies had in their favor the slow but steady buildup of troops and supplies, which everyone knew spelled eventual victory, but which was powerless to offset the temporary enemy advantages. It was part of the Allied build-up that the French were to come into the line opposite Belfort, and relieve United States troops as far north as Le Tholy; the slowness of the Allied build-up was emphasized by the fact that our troops could not be relieved fast enough to build up a really large striking force, strong enough, say, to break through and reach the Rhine.

Thus the 7th and the 15th Infantry Regiments, relieved by the French in the Vagney and St. Ame' areas, were able to effect a breakthrough at Brouveheures, and the 30th, relieved around Le Tholy, was able to exploit the breakthrough nearly as far as St. Die'. But there the advance momentarily stopped, while our forces regrouped and our build-up continued, augmented next by the 100th and 103rd Infantry Divisions, recently arrived from the United States.

F Company in an old position was relieved by 15th Infantry at 280330A and moved out to join the remainder of the battalion. At 131 SA, G Company moved to area vacated by Company 1(348662). F (365643) with mission of driving enemy from ridge and preventing further flanking of E Company and the roadblock. Resistance was met at 1400. The attack continued making slight gains. About dusk the enemy threw an artillery supported counterattack and company consolidated and dug in for the night at (363650).

It was quiet and all the men were in their foxholes. I heard a loud voice and as I looked outside, I saw Lt. Col. Frederick R. Armstrong 2nd battalion Commander and my Captain coming toward me. They stopped about 30 feet from my foxhole. The Colonel was chewing out the Captain with old-fashioned Army language. When my Captain would try to explain, the Colonel would make him shut up and then he would continue chewing him out. The enemy observer saw them and fired two mortar shells at them but missed. They then used trees as shields. I believe that the problem was the Colonel had ordered him to take the hill before he stopped. Colonel Armstrong came over to

Charles R. Castellaw

my foxhole and said, "Soldier, what should we do?" I believe that he did this to humiliate the Captain. I said, "Colonel, the enemy knows that we are here and they think that we plan to attack early in the morning. I think we should attack now." He said, "That is what we will do!" I believe that the Colonel had made the decision to attack as soon as possible before he asked me. He turned to the Captain and said, "Attack as soon as possible," then they both left.

The mortar section started firing to soften up the enemy before our attack. We climbed out of our foxholes and started up the hill. After going about 500 yards, we received word that the observer and director of fire had been hit and that they did not have another man they could use to replace him. This was one of the most frightening times that I had experienced. The enemy had started responding with rapid heavy fire. It seemed that they had set up and zerocd in on a certain location in the hill and when we reached that point they started firing. I knew that if something was not done very quickly, our casualties would probably be 100%. I was frightened to the extent that I thought that the only chance I had to live was to reach the observation post and direct the mortar fire so I said, "I will go and direct the firing." I crawled up the hill following the phone wire and finally reached the dugout that was used for observation. After crawling in the foxhole and making phone contact with the mortar section, I began coming down. I observed the enemy in a wide formation, moving in our direction about 300 yards from me. I requested that they fire one round so I could determine their target. When they fired, I observed that they were firing over the enemy. I requested that they reduce their range 250 yards. He replied, "If I do, I will put it in your lap." I said, "Do not worry about me, just do what I tell you to do." He fired one round that hit the troops moving in front. I said, "That is it. Open up with all you got," and he did. After a time the enemy withdrew and we moved to the top of the hill and dug in. What I did was not through bravery, it was through fear.

As I sat in my foxhole, I thought about how lucky I was because we lost almost fifty percent of our men and I was not one of them. I thought about home, Betty Jo and family. The big question, "Will I be this lucky the next time?"

The shape of the battle was roughly as follows:

The Way It Was

The 7th and 15th Infantry regiments attacked abreast at noon, October 20, the 7th on the right heading due east for Vervezelle, the 15th on the left swinging to the northeast toward Brouveheures. The enemy had previously stabilized his positions on the high ground west of Brouveheures, where the 45th Infantry Division, strung out as far as Rambervillers on the north, had been unable to concentrate enough force to penetrate the enemy line. (As a matter of fact, a strong enemy counterattack with armored support had hurt the 45th badly in this very area the previous week).

Now, with the 36th Infantry Division engaged in a successful attack on Bruye'res, and the 45th continuing to attack farther north, the added kick provided by the 3rd caused the enemy line to give way completely, and by the end of the second day a definite breakthrough had been accomplished.

The 3rd battalion of the 15th Infantry, commanded by Maj. Russell Comrie, helped the campaign tremendously by seizing a bridge over the Mortagne River just north of Brouveheures before the enemy could demolish it. The regiment crossed as rapidly as possible at this point, and began an attack to the east along the ridge on which the town of Mortagne was situated. The 15th met many strong detachments of enemy trying to escape over the few roads leading away from this ridge-top to the east and northeast, and fought a series of spirited engagements during this advance.

The 7th meanwhile had captured Vervezelle and Domfaing in two powerful attacks, and had then swung east up the south side of the valley leading to Les Rouges Eaux. In night marches over the heavily forested hills the 7th secured valuable ground, although control was so difficult that the 1st Battalion on one occasion had a hard time locating itself on the map when daylight came. On the high ridge southeast of Etival, and south of Les Rouges Eaux, the regiment first made contact with the 201st Mountain Battalion, a fresh formation of well equipped Austrian mountaineers, some 600 men strong. Fortunately the 7th hit this unit before it had a chance to get well dug-in, and smashed it so badly the first day of contact that it never gained its full fighting efficiency.

It was in this vicinity north of Les Rouges Eaux, on October 25, that S/Sgt. Clyde L. Choate, Company C, 601st Tank Destroyer Battalion, engaged a German Mark W tank in a one-man battle, with

Charles R. Castellaw

Choate stalking the tank until he finally destroyed it just as it was about to break through to an infantry battalion command post area.

"The Germans had launched a surprise attack on densely wooded positions on a hilltop occupied by our forces," related Lt. Col. Walter E. Tardy, Commanding Officer of the 601st, "and the enemy struck with force and decision.

"The only tank destroyer available in this sector was knocked out before it could open fire. The German tank proceeded straight down a wagon road, slashing through the infantry positions and shooting the soldiers in their foxholes."

"Sergeant Choate couldn't find all of our crew and he believed the driver was trapped in the burning tank destroyer. Choate ran through a rain of enemy fire to the M-10, which was empty. Kraut infantry followed the Mark IV as it headed toward the infantry battalion command post about 400 yards to our rear,' added Sgt. Thomas L. Langan, who was a gunner in the ill-fated tank destroyer.

"The German tank cruised through the woods, firing down into the foxholes of the doughboys and crushing soldiers to death under its tracks. Grabbing a bazooka from one of the foxholes, Choate immobilized the enemy tank, which the Germans then converted into an armored pillbox."

"Choate ran back to our infantrymen again, got another rocket and closed in on the tank to within ten yards, always under heavy enemy fire. The shot was a bull's eye and Germans began piling out of it, with Choate shooting them with his revolver."

T/4 Jay W. Shively, who also witnessed the event, said that Choate "winged" at least two Krauts and threw a hand grenade into the tank to be certain there were no more live ones in it.

Losing their tank, the German infantry became disorganized and the melee ended with thirty Germans killed, wounded or captured.

How Sergeant Choate "got his man" and stopped enemy armor without a tank destroyer is legend in the 601st Tank Destroyer Battalion.

For this action, Sergeant Choate was awarded the Medal of Honor.

The determination displayed by Choate was characteristic of the Battalion's efforts ever since it was first attached to the 3rd Infantry Division at Monte Corvino, Italy, on September 20, 1943. Lt. Col.

The Way It Was

Tardy was commanding throughout the period of the attachment, except for short periods.

The Commanding General at this time decided to commit the 30th Infantry, with the mission of attacking through the 7th Infantry and driving east. Col. Lionel C. McGarr, regimental commander, directed patrols be sent between the 7th on the south and 15th Infantry on the north, which got through the lines to a depth of 600 yards. Colonel McGarr then recommended that the regiment not battle against the strong resistance which was holding up the other two regiments, but drive through what apparently was a soft spot. The Commanding General approved the suggestion.

The 1st Battalion led off, followed by the 2nd, which swing from a road "spiderweb" north to a mill near the south side of the Nompatelize Valley. It was there that armor attached to the 2nd battalion encountered enemy armor and shot it up.

Lt. Col. Eugene Salet's 2nd battalion of the 15th followed the 30th here, swung in behind and took a hill to the northeast of the crossroads at which the 15th Infantry had been held up for several days. This maneuver allowed the 15th to flank and clear a strongly-held road junction halfway between Les Rouges Eaux and La Bourgonce for which it had been battling fiercely. On the last day of this road-junction battle, Company I of the 15th, attacking from the east destroyed nine enemy machine guns in a few hours, and provided the flanking punch that drove the enemy clear out of the position.

Both the 1st and the 2nd battalions of the 30th were committed along the ridge-top to support the 3rd, the 1st taking over the left half of the zone in the area dominated by Les Jumeaux, or twin peaks, which jutted into the plain south of Nompatelize, and the 2nd going into the right half of the zone, holding a long east-west line north of Le Haut Jacques.

The type of battle that was being waged during these days resulted in a situation on October 28 that brought the 3rd Infantry Division another Congressional Medal of Honor.

The 30th Infantry was pressing through the Mortagne Forest toward the heights overlooking St. Die' when elements of the German 201st Mountain Infantry Battalion, which had been by-passed, succeeded in cutting the supply line of the 3rd battalion, disrupting the flow of ammunition and food to the unit.

Charles R. Castellaw

The 2nd battalion pushed two reinforced platoons of Company E and F Company across Tendon-Le Tholy road under cover of darkness. E Company platoon occupied (V-252448) at 0515. Company F Platoon occupied (V-246448) at 0700. At 0955A a reinforced platoon of Company E received a counterattack but this was beaten off, as the balance of E and F Companies took up positions to reinforce their two platoons. During the afternoon G Company passed through enemy artillery to take up positions between Companies E and F. At 1530A, the enemy launched an artillery supported counterattack with about 60 men hitting Company E from the East. The attack was beaten off by artillery and chemical mortars. By the end of this period the battalion was firmly established along line (V-243447 - V-252448).

The 3rd battalion moved at 1100A to occupy positions left by 2nd battalion. L Company took over the position of Company G (V-241438) at 1325A and Company K took over the position of Company F (V-241445) at 1400A. During the remaining hours of daylight positions were consolidated and organized and patrols briefed for night operations.

During the period 11, October to 21 October, the 30th Regiment held the positions gained during Phase I. Excellent outposts were established and every target in and around vicinity of Le Tholy and the gap to Gerardmer as well as the Northern entrance of the St. Ame-Le Tholy valley was covered by artillery, chemical mortar, and 50-caliber machine-gun fire. Patrols were operated continuously during the hours of darkness, increasing in intensity during the latter part of the period as a part of the cover plan for the Third Division's proposed attack toward St. Die. Patrols maintained contact with enemy. A good many of the patrols were given combat missions and engaged the enemy in numerous firefights. The largest of these was an attempt by the Regimental Battle Patrol with the Division Battle Patrol attached to knock out enemy strongpoints in Le Tholy and seize the high ground to the north-northwest. The enemy, however, proved to be too firmly entrenched across the Le Tholy gap, and aided by concealed SP guns and numerous MG's he was able to keep our penetrations from completely piercing his line. This action took place on the nights of 14-15 and 15-16 October during the hours of darkness. While the attack proved unsuccessful, numerous enemy

152

The Way It Was

positions were identified and heavily covered by observed mortar and cannon fire.

With the relief of the 15th Infantry by the French 4th RTA on October 17th, the 30th Infantry occupied the entire Division sector, while the other two Regiments rested, reconsolidated, and trained for the St. DIE operation. The Regimental Staff a[nd] battalion Staffs completed preparations and outlined a program for a similar proposed seven-day rest and training period for the 30th Infantry.

Company I, commanded by 1st Lt. Maurice Rothseid, was in reserve position when it was called on to drive the enemy out. Going into the attack at 1400 that afternoon, the company was immediately subjected to intense fire from automatic weapons and small arms coming from an enemy that was well concealed in the dense undergrowth and woods.

At this point, S/Sgt. Lucian Adams, a squad leader of the 2nd platoon under 2nd Lt. Frank H. Harrell, took charge of the situation and began a one-man assault that ended after he had killed nine Germans and captured two singlehanded. The number that he wounded as he dashed from tree to tree with his BAR was not determined.

He engaged an enemy machine gun at twenty yards and succeeded in killing the gunner.

Lieutenant Harrell described Adams' action, saying, "Sergeant Adams moved so fast and had such a head start on the rest of us that he killed a great number of them before we could maneuver to shoot at the enemy without endangering him by our fire."

Adams' charge disorganized the enemy in their strong defensive positions and was mainly responsible for the quick manner in which Company I cleared the supply line to the assault companies of the 3rd battalion.

For this action Sergeant Adams was awarded the Medal of Honor.

By this time the exploitation phase had ended, and during the closing days of October the Division fought a bitter, costly action against a constantly-reinforced, infiltrating foe. The 2nd platoon of the 3rd Reconnaissance Troop, commanded by 2nd Lt. John Begovich, holding a hillside position just north of Le Haut Jacques, fought almost nightly actions against enemy who came up draws both from the east and west. All three battalions of the 30th had "hot corners" where two enemy seemed to spring up for every one shot down. This was almost literally true, as the enemy, sensing the threat posed by the 3rd Division to St. Die', robbed other sectors of the front to throw in the 291st and 292nd Special Employment Battalions, the 737th Infantry Regiment, the 726th Infantry Regiment, and finally introduced another fresh mountain battalion, the 202nd. By this time the German 16th Infantry Division, whose 221st, 223rd and 225th Infantry Regiments had opposed our initial attack west of Brouveheures, had virtually disappeared from the picture, although the division's General Haeckel still commanded the sector opposite the 3rd.

The fighting in the western Vosges was weirder than any engaged in before or since by the Division. Crushing concentrations of 120mm mortar fire smashed into the wooded ridges without warning, sometimes wiping out half a company in a comparatively few minutes. Casualties mounted rapidly, largely because of these tree-bursts of artillery and mortars. The nights, chilly before, suddenly turned cold, and frost gave way to snow on the ridge-tops. The artillery airstrip had to be corduroyed because of the deep mud. Logging trails that ran the ridges had to be rebuilt by the engineers in order to support the supply traffic which ran nightly to the farthest units. There was only one area practicable for gun positions, the plateau south of Mortagne, and it was constantly lit by flashes from scores of artillery pieces.

With a bit of improvisation, Maj. Norman C. Tanner, Division Artillery Air Officer, provided his spotter planes a landing field during the difficult weather which characterized the Vosges throughout the whole campaign there. It took the form of a 250-by 15-yard wooden runway, and at the time it was built it 6000 yards from the enemy front lines. To camouflage it, Major Tanner had it painted olive drab.

Capt. Alfred W. Schultz, Assistant Air Officer, commented after his first landing, "I checked my map twice to make sure that I had the correct coordinates, for that little strip looked like a ribbon up there," to which Pilot 1st Lt. Warren T. Ries rejoined, "Yes, a very tiny ribbon."

Meanwhile the Division faced the enemy on three sides-the north, east, and south. Enemy armor showed up in unexpected places—one Mark IV tank was destroyed by one of the enemy's own mines

The Way It Was

several hundred yards north of Le Haut Jacques, on the crest of a wooded ridge. Friendly supply parties were ambushed. Small groups of enemy, cut off by our rapid advance, showed up in our rear and fought with command post groups and wire crews. One whole company of the enemy, cut off by the 7th Infantry, surrendered after negotiations that covered an entire night.

October 25 saw the first issue of the Division weekly newspaper, the *Front Line*. In an opening statement written for the paper, Commanding General O'Daniel declared: "It is fitting that this paper is being published today for the first time. It is the mouthpiece of a fighting Division, and as we are now in the midst of a great attack, we can say that the 3rd Division *Front Line* was born in battle."

"We shall therefore be able to submit very soon additional reports on more deeds of valor as performed by our fighting men. This paper is one way we can let them know what we think of them. Therefore, the names of all men who are cited in orders of this division will be published in this paper. We salute them all."

At first crude in form, the paper rapidly acquired polish, and by June, 1945 was able to announce proudly that it had been adjudged by Camp Newspaper Service the second best overseas letter-press organizational paper.

November began with fights for Hill 256, near Les Jumeaux, and for the crossroads town of Le Haut Jacques.

Survivors of the battle for the crossroads at Le Haut Jacques were later to refer to it as "The Crossroads of Hell." Anzio veterans said that at times the fighting was worse than any they had seen all during the beachhead siege and the drive to Rome.

To advance a few hundred yards took the 7th Infantry five days. The enemy had—and used—every weapon in the book: 120mm mortars, Flakwagons, mines and booby-traps, machine guns, artillery, and small arms.

The hot spot was first encountered on October 31st. All three battalions were on line: 1st, under Capt. Kenneth W. Wallace, on the north (left) flank; 2nd, commanded by Lt. Colonel Clayton C. Thobro, to the right (slightly back); and Maj. Glenn E. Rathbun's 3rd battalion on the regimental right and echeloned somewhat to the rear.

On the 31st, 1st Battalion moved slowly along the St. Dié road. Company A moved north behind a mortar preparation, with the

Charles R. Castellaw

intention of flanking the town from that direction, Company B was in reserve, and Company C attacked due east. Companies E and G of the 2nd battalion took Hill 652, which they had fought for the entire previous twenty-four hours, and continued east slowly. The 3rd battalion, which was attacking southeast, had been stopped the day before by heavy fire in the vicinity of an enemy roadblock. The area, in addition, was found to be heavily mined. On the morning of the 31st the attack was resumed, but initially only Company K made any progress, due to slightly lighter resistance than that encountered by L Company. Hill 499 was taken by K—its second objective. In the afternoon, however, some slight progress was made as Company K engaged the enemy in a moving firefight. Company L found itself, likewise, in a strong exchange of fire.

The 2nd battalion, under extremely heavy mortar and artillery fine on its company areas and outpost, nevertheless shoved forwards, but it was slow, painful going.

The following day, November 1, this same inching forward continued. Every bit of firepower available to the 7th was called down on Le Haut Jacques and the vital crossroads, but the enemy more than matched it with the combined fire of every emplaced weapon. That afternoon the enemy fired a heavy artillery concentration at the 2nd battalion at 1500, and followed up with a counterattack at Company G which was repulsed. Company C was forced to beat off a counterattack at 1615. During this time mines were encountered throughout the zone of both 1st and 2nd battalions.

The 3rd battalion continued the attempt to push to the southwest. Company L destroyed an enemy machine-gun nest during the morning of November 2.

The 2nd battalion was counterattacked about noon of the same day and repulsed it. Company F was relieved by the 7th Infantry Battle Patrol at 1230 and in turn relieved Company C, which moved further north toward the remainder of 1st Battalion. Relief of the 3rd battalion was started during the afternoon by 2nd battalion, 141st Infantry.

Meanwhile, 1st and 2nd battalions had launched an all-out attack at 1415, but failed to make any appreciable gains. The enemy fire was of an intensity rarely encountered before in the entire war by the 7th Infantry. The 3rd battalion joined this attack on November 3, and worked further toward the achievement of getting to the east of the

The Way It Was

village for the final assault. The 2nd battalion would have to attack directly east as 1st Battalion pushed in from the north.

As the attack went into its fifth day, the bloody battle reached its climax. The entire regiment (less one company) moved out at 0615, determined to smash the enemy at Le Haut Jacques. The enemy, aggressive in the defense, almost immediately made a counterattack at Company A and 1st Battalion was held up. Company I encountered withering fire from four well-emplaced machine guns and also stopped, but K Company continued moving on against strong resistance.

To Companies E and F—commanded by 1st Lt. James F. Powell and 2nd Lt. Earl E. Swanson, respectively—and especially to E Company, fell the task of moving in directly from the west. By 0940 Company F had control of one house in the village and F was taking prisoners.

By 1150, after weathering murderous mortar and artillery, 2nd battalion had cleared the village. Companies I and K still had a fight on their hands, but the back of the enemy resistance was broken. Over a hundred prisoners were taken. The regiment had suffered 125 casualties in the final push. Le Haut Jacques was a costly objective.

"It seemed to me that we were just a handful of men trying desperately to push the whole top away from that mountain," said Pvt. Alfonso Pesko of E Company, later. "It was worse than Anzio, because we were steadily going up hill and were in such a confined area."

Although the entire regiment had experienced grim fighting E Company had been especially outstanding and those members who survived were later awarded the Distinguished Unit Citation.

With the village occupied, the 7th moved east and north.

During the attack by the 7th Infantry on Le Haut Jacques, the 30th Infantry helped greatly by flanking the town from the north—with Task Force Kenyon and Task Force Greer, and without this help 7th Infantry might never have taken Le Haut Jacques.

On October 30, while the bulk of the 30th Infantry was passing through the Mortagne Forest, Company G, 30th Infantry, passed through Company F to press the battle on Hill 616, north of and part of the Le Haut Jacques position which the 7th Infantry had been attacking form the west. The attack of Company G was made through

Charles R. Castellaw

cross machine-gun fire against enemy established in deep dugouts and bunkers along the forward slope of the hill. The attack progressed to within two hundred yards of the company's objective where it was halted because of the frightful number of casualties exacted by the defending enemy. The company dug in under harassing enemy fire. Private Wilburn K. Ross had placed his light machine gun in a position ten yards in advance of the foremost supporting riflemen. Shortly thereafter the enemy counterattacked. Thirty-three men remained in the company, fifty-five having been lost in the attack. Private Ross, exposed to machine-gun and small-arms fire of the attacking force, fired with deadly effect upon the assaulting enemy troops and repelled the counterattack. Despite the hail of automatic-weapons fire and the explosions of rifle grenades within a stone's throw of this position, he continued to man his machine gun alone, repulsing six more German attacks. The citation of the award of the Medal of Honor to Private Ross is quoted here in part:

"...When the eighth assault was launched, most of his supporting riflemen were out of ammunition. They took position in echelon behind Private Ross and crawled up during the attack, to extract a few rounds of ammunition from his machine-gun ammunition belt. Private Ross fought on virtually without assistance, and, despite the fact that enemy grenadiers crawled to within four yards of his position in an attempt to kill him with hand grenades, he again directed accurate and deadly fire on the hostile force. After expending his last round, Private Ross was advised to withdraw to the company command post, together with the eight surviving riflemen, but as more ammunition was expected, he declined to do so. As his supporting riflemen fixed bayonets for a last-ditch stand, fresh ammunition arrived. Having killed and wounded at least fifty-eight Germans in more than five hours of continuous combat and saved the remnant of his company from destruction, Private Ross remained at his post..."

Such was the fury of the battles fought at the hellhole, Le Haut Jacques.

The 15th, which had a tough day in attacking Hill 526, occupied its objective the next morning with no resistance as the Germans had evacuated their positions during the night. Les Faignes and Nompatelize, villages in the path of the 15th's advance, were also

The Way It Was

yielded without a fight but definite resistance was met in the attack on La Salle.

THIRTIETH INFANTRY SECTOR OF OPERATION

Summary of Enemy Operations 1-31 October 1944:

Enemy activities for the period 1-31 October consisted of a stubborn defense and counter-offensive action designed to stop our advance to the East and the flanking of Belfort. In attempting to carry out his defensive mission the enemy not only employed his usual weapons such as artillery, self-propelled, flak wagons, anti tank and AP mines, mortars and well organized defensive positions, but also delved into his bag of tricks for such harassing agents as wire tapping, agents, false radio messages and false messages supposedly from civilians.

At the beginning of the period the enemy was withdrawing to his positions along a hill mass that dominated the Tendon-Le Tholy road from the East, these positions extending to include the town of Le Tholy. He attempted to slow our approach by roadblocks of felled trees and mines that were usually covered by small arms or machine gun fire. The enemy cleverly utilized the dominant terrain of his heavily wooded sector by placing a series of strongpoints from which he sent strong outposts at night to block the Tendon-Le Tholy road, Le Tholy and avenues of approach to his position.

Our numerous patrols carefully felt out the enemy positions each night and found that while his main line remained constant, his outposts varied. The town of Le Tholy was, at first, lightly held and our reconn patrols were able to pass through the town completely. However, when our strong combat patrols attempted to occupy Le Tholy, they encountered as many as seven machine gun positions and at least one company holding the town. Our patrols heard sounds of wire being laid by the enemy but this wire was never actually encountered.

The enemy had frequent recon patrols attempting to enter our sector. Most of these hastily withdrew when fired upon by our outposts.

That the enemy was nervous and alert to any possibility of an attack by us, was evidenced by the number of times sounds of frantic

Charles R. Castellaw

firing, for no apparent reason, could be heard from his sector. On one occasion, we simulated an attack with artillery, mortar and machine gun fire. The enemy retaliated with intense s/a, automatic weapons and defensive artillery fires although he had no target outside of his own imagination.

The Le Tholy phase of this period was characterized by a strong enemy defensive action, supported by moderate amounts of artillery, SP, tank and mortar fire.

After we were relieved in the Le Tholy sector we moved North to St Die sector where the enemy had a strong line designed to deny us possession of the high wooded ground that overlooks St Die, St. Michel, that sector of the Meurthe River and it's valley, Nompatelize and La Salle. By a swift night attack we put our 3rd battalion through a weak spot in the enemy line. The next day this penetration was exploited by pushing the other two battalions through the gap and quickly taking possession of key terrain features and the best outposts, all this against moderate resistance. From our new positions we had observation of enemy rear areas in the vicinity of La Salle, St. Michel, the River Meurthe and St. Die. As the enemy did not seem to be aware of our occupation of such outposts and continued with his normal functions, our observers had a field day directing fire, knocking out some 9 flak wagons, 2 tanks, numerous vehicles, horse-drawn carts and pieces, several gun positions and many troop concentrations not to mention one troop train. While the outposts were busy, others of our element were clearing the sector of pockets of resistance and picking up stragglers lost from their units.

The enemy soon realized that we held this ground and started to probe out our positions with a great many small recon patrols. Many of these patrols carried communication wire with them, evidently planning to work into points of observation and report back to their headquarters information thus gathered. Since we were responsible for such a large sector of woods and mountainous terrain, it was not possible to stop all infiltration, especially by small patrols. This period of active enemy reconnaissance was followed by a series of counterattacks of company size with which the enemy desperately strove to drive us from our positions. With each failure to overrun our units the enemy made more frantic counterattacks, rushing units to this sector and committing them to the attack without delay.

The Way It Was

Indicative of the enemy's frantic efforts to regain this sector is the manner in which he committed any possible unit against us, even platoons and companies that had to operate without support of higher headquarters or other units. He was able to commit two ATHQ mountain battalions consisting of first class troops. These proved to be the most effective fighters but even they were unable to drive us from our positions. His pattern of attack was heavy mortar and artillery barrage followed by a company sized attack accompanied by intensive bazooka rifle grenade, and machine gun fire. As soon as one attack slowed down, he launched another from the flank or rear, these counterattacks continuing for hours, usually until darkness.

The enemy had employed moderate amounts of artillery, SP and some Nebelwerfer fire against us but his primary fire support was from mortar, bazookas and rifle grenades of which he had plenty.

At the close of the period, the enemy was still trying to retake this tactically valuable terrain feature and bitter, close-in, forest fighting continued throughout the area.

At the close of the operations period 1-31 October, the Regiment was the spearhead of the 3rd Division attack toward St. DIE, France. A salient into the enemy lines 3500 meters deep and 4000 meters wide at the broadest point was the extent of the area assigned to the Regiment. Much of this area still had to be cleared of the enemy and his patrols were active, sometimes approaching within 200 yards of our supply line. This salient packed with numerous high points enabled artillery observers with the Regiment to fire into enemy rear areas. The roads of the Meurthe Valley were heavily shelled and accurately observed fire was causing considerable damage and casualties to enemy equipment and personnel.

The Regiment was continuously engaged in patrolling between strong points held and in attacking and throwing out of enemy infiltration and penetration between these points. In the meantime, limited objective attacks were being planned to drive all enemy from the Foret de Montagne and to secure the road net around its northern, eastern and southern perimeter.

The 2nd battalion, commanded by Maj. Eugene A. Salet, hit La Salle from three directions. Company F, under 1st Lt. Charles F. Adams, closed in from the south, Company F, commanded by Capt.

Charles R. Castellaw

Hugh H. Bruner, advanced from the northwest and Company G, under Capt. Richard B. Dorrough, assaulted the village from the west.

We had pulled back to receive new replacements and change sectors. My platoon leader had become a casualty and I was acting platoon leader. From our replacements, I received a platoon leader fresh from the States.

When I met the new Lieutenant he said, "I have heard a lot about you and I want you to continue acting as platoon leader until I learn the ropes and for the present time consider me one of your men and tell me what to do." I looked at him and the carbine that he had on his shoulder and said, "Throw that carbine away and get you a M-1 rifle." To my surprise, he did. He may have been told that he was my third platoon leader.

We were ordered to enter a village and clear it of the enemy. Shortly after arriving at the village, we were pinned down by a machine gun nest. The gunner would fire a short burst and then stop firing, then repeat. By using this procedure it was hard to locate his position. Also, the enemy used smokeless powder. We used the old black kind. When we fired, it was like sending a signal that said, "Here we are!" My Lieutenant was sticking close to me and after some time, he spotted the location of the machine gun nest, which was well camouflaged, and pointed it out to me. I knew that I had to take it out before we could advance.

The machine gun nest was located on a fence row that ran past our location. I crawled up the fence row until I got in range and then I fired a white phosphorous grenade with my M-1 launcher. I hit the target but the grenade was a dud and did not explode. I knew if they located me before I could fire again it would be the end for me. Fortunately for me, I reloaded and fired before they saw me. This time the grenade hit the target and exploded, knocking out the machine gun nest. I had four white phosphorous grenades left. I used one to set fire to the first house that had enemy soldiers in it, a second one to set fire to the next house. My Lieutenant said, "Do we have to burn the houses?" My reply, "One American soldier's life is worth more than all the houses in this town." I used the two remaining grenades to burn two more houses. It was my personal policy to never try to enter a house occupied by the enemy if I could burn it. I did not plan to be a dead hero by being stupid. The enemy withdrew.

The Way It Was

By now, I had learned that the German Army was enjoying every initial advantage because of their superiority. The 88mm mortar was a triple-threat rifle that could be used to fire several rounds of armor-piercing shells at our tanks, then suddenly begin firing airbusting fragmentation shells at our infantry following their tanks, and a few minutes later throw up anti-aircraft fire at planes supporting the ground operation. Our 90-mm rifle had no such flexibility. It could not be depressed low enough for effective anti-tank fire.

A second marked German advantage was in gunpowder. German ammunition was charged with smokeless, flashless powder, which in both night and day fighting helped the enemy tremendously in concealing his firing position. Our riflemen, machine gunners, and gunners of all type had to expose their positions with telltale muzzle flashes or puffs of black powder smoke.

Another example of German superiority was the heavy tank. From the summer of 1943 to the spring of 1945, the German Tiger and Panther tanks were superior to our Sherman tanks in direct combat.

The German infantry rocket, the *"Panzerfaust,"* had greater hitting power than the U.S. Army bazooka.

The German troops were better trained and disciplined than the American troops.

What was our advantage? "Numbers." Total Allied mobilization exceeded 62,000,000; total enemy mobilization, 30,000,000. The figures show how greatly we outnumbered the enemy.

All companies were halted at well dug-in positions that surrounded the village and after these were overrun, a house-to-house fight ensued as the Germans were occupying every building in the settlement. Heavy artillery and mortar fire was laid down on the attackers but Company G finally broke through and entered the town at noon on the second day of the battle. By 1200 hours, November 3, the town was cleared.

The 1st Battalion of the 30th Infantry, commanded by Maj. Mackenzie E. Porter, attacked the town of Sauceray. In a perfectly coordinated attack, employing machine guns, mortars, and artillery, the battalion closed in from south and west. There was a sharp 30-minute fight, but the pre-battle conception had been excellent and the town fell. This attack was the first of a series of battalion attacks in which the regiment had to pull a battalion from a defensive position

163

Charles R. Castellaw

and extend it over the other two battalion fronts in order to close up a large gap and make an attack.

During the days of the 7th Infantry's fight for Le Haut Jacques, the 30th Infantry's 2nd battalion, under Lt. Col. Frederick R. Armstrong, launched and completed a successful coordinated attack on Hill 616, a key terrain feature for the defense of St. Die'. The regiment had been battling for this hill even before the 7th Infantry encountered the defenses of Le Haut Jacques, but previous attacks met with furious fire and fanatical resistance. The final attack the enemy also resisted fiercely, and with reinforcements. Enemy artillery fire caused a number of casualties when the command post of Company C, commanded by 1st Lt. Rex Metcalfe, was struck on the third day of the attack. Much air activity, both friendly and enemy, was present during the days that the Division fought on the hills in front of the Meurthe River and our forces were strafed many times by enemy planes. Hill 616 was occupied by the 2nd battalion on November 5 when elements of the 7th Infantry entered the attack.

The day witnessed also the seizure of Biarville by the 15th Infantry. This attack was short lived but it demonstrated great determination.

Biarville was fairly covered by fire when it was attacked by a force comprising Company A of the 15th, one platoon of light tanks, a platoon of mediums, one platoon of tank destroyers and a platoon of engineers. The withering fire brought quick results and the town fell in a short time.

The Germans by now had started a real flight rearward and although the Division was still subjected to heavy artillery and mortar fire during its continued advance, the resistance became more scattered and sporadic as the 3rd battalion neared the Meurthe River.

The towns of Brehimont and La Vacherie, overlooking St. Michel, were weakly defended and most of the defenders were taken prisoner when the 3rd Division occupied them. The prisoner of war total mounted rapidly as scattered pockets of left-behinds were cleared.

One by one, the towns fronting on the hills along the Meurthe were occupied with the chief action in the Division zone being waged in the 15th and 30th Infantry sectors. Enemy troops in a draw and in the woods to the north opposed the 15th's advance toward Le Menil, while at the same time the 30th Infantry was clearing the St. Die' hill

The Way It Was

mass by battalion attacks around its entire perimeter which, in addition, helped the 15th Infantry by covering its right flank. The 2nd battalion, 30th Infantry, took Chalet on the morning of November 10, and the 3rd battalion took La Bolle after an afternoon and all-night fight on November 10-11, with Companies I and K in the assault. Fighting ended the morning of November 11 when the bridge across the Taintrux River was taken and the Chalet-Saucerey highway was completely cleared.

2nd battalion continued to drive to clear the slopes South and East of hill 622 of enemy. The enemy force, however, was well dug in and resisted stubbornly our attack. At 081545 Company F had advanced down slope to make contact with its platoon on Company E's left at (379646). However, an estimated enemy company with 3 MG's still remained in a strong position between F and C Company. Meanwhile the right flank of the battalion was advanced to put a reinforced platoon of Company E in Chalet (378641) at 090400A. At 091015, Company F again jumped off against the enemy pocket but enemy fire, apparently reinforced during the night and hitting Company F on the left flank, temporarily halted the attack.

Because of the slow progress of Company F in cleaning the slopes of hill 621, G Company came into position on hill 621 and passing through AT Company lines attacked South and East at 091400. By 091620 they had secured the tree line at (380647). Contact was made with C Company. At 092130 a patrol to the position of E Company platoon in Chalet met enemy fire. No contact with this platoon could be secured during the night. At 100800 both E and F Companies attacked to clear the pocket in front of their positions. By 100845 both E and F Companies reached the tree line a[nd] battalion positions consolidated along line (381646 to 373643). Patrols got through to Chalet at 100900 and found E Company platoon missing, presumably captured.

I received orders from my Captain to report to his foxhole. When I reached him, he told me that we had lost one platoon the evening before. This platoon was trying to take the Chalet. The Captain appeared to be upset about the loss. He said, "Castellaw, if you will take the Chalet, you can spend the night in it." It was very cold and wet and I thought how nice it would be to spend the night inside a building. I said, "We will take it." My problem was how. By looking

165

Charles R. Castellaw

at the area as the face of a clock with the Chalet in the center, we were located at nine o'clock. The enemy's rear was at twelve o'clock. We could move to our left and circle to twelve o'clock with plans to cut the enemy off and kill and/or capture them. I had one big problem with this approach. There was the chance that they would fire on us with their mortar. This we could not handle, so I ruled out this approach.

We could attack at nine o'clock but the enemy knew our location and was probably prepared for us to attack them from that direction. If so, this would almost be like suicide. I decided that we would circle to the right and attack at six o'clock, the same way that the last platoon had attacked. My platoon attacked and after a short battle the enemy withdrew, leaving one of their men dead. We moved in and secured the Chalet. After the battle was over, the Captain crawled out of his foxhole and came in the Chalet and took charge. He came up to me and said, "Castellaw take a couple of men and set up an outpost." I looked him in the eye and said, "You told me if I took the Chalet that I could spend the night in it. Well, I took it and I am going to spend the night in it." He said, "Okay, okay." He assigned the outpost to three other men. After they set up the outpost in an old dug-out, the enemy dropped a mortar shell in it, killing all three men. Cost of taking the Chalet-loss of one platoon; three killed, and one man with a minor wound. To our knowledge, the enemy lost only one man.

When the weather turned cold and wet with scattered snow, we were wearing the same clothes that we wore in August.

The enemy was "winterized". One day I captured a German soldier and he looked at me and said "cold" as he laughed. We finally received heavy rough wool underwear from England. I thought it might be better to freeze than to itch to death from wearing the wool underwear.

On the afternoon of November 8, Companies E and F of the 15th attacked Le Menil, supported by tanks of the 756th Tank Battalion, commanded by Lt. Col. Glenn F. Rogers. There were four light tanks from Company D under Capt. Robert F. Kremer, and two mediums from Company B, commanded by Capt. David D. Redle with the 2nd battalion, when it launched its drive. As at Biarville, the attack was well-planned and vicious and lasted but a short time since the Germans withdrew in the face of the onslaught.

166

The Way It Was

While the 2nd battalion was entering Le Menil, the 3rd attacked Deyfosse, a short distance to the south. A wooded area outside Deyfosse gave the enemy convenient emplacement positions but Company K, commanded by 1st Lt. John J. Tominac, wore down the resistance after Companies I and L had made a house-to-house clearance of the south part of the village. Company K completed clearing the village late that night.

The 15th continued the Division advance while elements of the 7th were being relieved by the 103rd Infantry Division. Etival, a small village located on the edge of the Meurthe, was taken by the 15th with little resistance.

At a conference conducted at VI Corps headquarters at Grandvillers on the afternoon of November 10, Corps Commander General Brooks outlined to his division commanders the operations incident to the Corps mission of proceeding east through the Vosges from the St. Die' area, capturing Strasbourg, and destroying the enemy west of the Rhine River in its zone. He presented three plans, all of which involved crossings of the Meurthe River by the 3rd Infantry Division.

Plans "A" and "B" called for the 3rd to cross the Meurthe in the vicinity of St. Michel, and to establish an initial bridgehead on the east bank. In plan "A" the 3rd proceeded due east on the axis Saales-Schirmeck-Strasbourg, with the 100th Infantry Division operating on its left, and the 103rd Infantry Division on its right, following an administrative crossing behind the 3rd and subsequent passage through its right to the south and southeast. In plan "B" the missions of the 3rd and 103rd Divisions were interchanged after the establishment of the initial bridgehead by the 3rd. Plan "C" called for the 3rd Infantry Division and the 103rd Infantry Division to cross the Meurthe River abreast, with the 3rd on the left. The action of each division following establishment of the initial bridgehead conformed to the maneuver outlined for plan "A", which was favored.

General Brooks indicated that the probable date for the 3rd Division crossing would be November 20. This date was contingent upon the progress of the 100th Infantry Division in its action southeast from Baccarat, and of the progress of the 103rd on the right of the 3rd in seizing the high ground southwest of St. Die'. Successful consummation of these operations would serve to draw enemy

Charles R. Castellaw

reserves from the front of the 3rd, thereby weakening the enemy in the zone of crossing.

At the time of the issuance of the Corps Commander's plans, the 3rd was in the process of undergoing relief by the 103rd Division of its center and right regiments (30th and 7th Infantry Regiments). At the same time the 15th Infantry was carrying out an operation to the northeast to clear the enemy from the west bank of the Meurthe as far north as Clairfontaine. Necessarily, then, the 7th and 30th were earmarked for the assault, whereas 15th Infantry was to hold the west bank of the Meurthe in the Division zone and to cover all preparations incident to the river crossing, then assemble in Division reserve following the crossing.

One day the 2nd battalion was moved into a bivouac area in the outskirts of a town to spend the rest of the day and move out early the next day to reengage in combat. We were assembled and given the old canned speech about being confined to the area and what would happen to us if we left the area. As soon as we were dismissed, I told one of my buddies to get his M-1 because we were leaving. He asked, "Where are we going?" I said, "To town." He replied, "Did you hear what was said?" I said, "Yes, but if they catch us and lock us up, they will turn us out before our unit pulls out in the morning. Also if we spend the night in the bivouac area we will sleep on the ground. If we spend the night in the lock-up we will sleep on cots."

We walked around town and found that it was almost deserted. We found a nice looking small restaurant and decided to go in for a meal. We went in, walked to a back corner so we would be facing the door. We placed our M-1's against the wall within easy reach. The waitress came over and explained to us what they could fix for us. We placed our orders. Shortly after our orders were placed, two MPs entered the door and one of them barked out, "The town is off lirnits for you two soldiers and you must go back to your post, now!" I looked at them in their fresh clean dress uniforms, fresh shave and haircut. I thought about the nice clean cot in a comfortable building that they slept on and three good hot meals each day. I reached for my Ml and said, "We have ordered meals and we are going to eat them." The one doing the talking changed his voice to a regular civilized tone and said, "Okay, but as soon as you are finished, return to your post." I said, "We will." They left and we did not see them again. We took

The Way It Was

our time and enjoyed our meal. As soon as we finished, we returned to our post.

Men of the Division heard many explosions during the next few days as the Germans methodically began destroying St. Die'. This town, seat of the Congress which named America in honor of the Italian, Amerigo Vespucci, had been shelled to some extent but was not nearly as thoroughly battered as Bruye'res, for example. But now reports were received at the Division headquarters from front-line infantrymen and artillery forward observers that "St. Die' is in flames."

It was revealed later that the enemy, without reasons justifiable even on the grounds of military necessity, had ordered St. Die' destroyed. Giving scant notice to the occupants of the town's houses and business structures, the Germans reduced the greater part of the town to ashes; the wall skeletons which were left standing intact testified that high explosives played little part in the needless destruction of St. Die', but rather that it was gutted by German-started fires. General Haeckel, German 16th Infantry Division CG, was responsible for the destruction of St. Die' and surrounding villages.

Crossing the Meurthe

"Powerhouse I" was the name given the Meurthe crossing operation. On the face of it, this was an extremely difficult job.

Division engineers had made careful map, photo and ground reconnaissance, but had failed to locate good bridge sites except where hard-surfaced approaches reached the river at points where bridges had been demolished. The Meurthe twisted northwest across a flat bottomland several hundred yards wide which was flooded north of Etival, and boggy everywhere else.

The river itself, swollen by fall rains, was everywhere too deep and swift to be forded by foot troops. Worst of all, the "winter line," a solid chain of prepared enemy defenses, ran all the way from Fraize Raon L'Etape, especially strong in the sector opposite the 3rd. These defenses consisted of trenches, barbed wire, weapons pits, anti-tank gun positions, anti-tank ditches, and lines, and had been under construction since early fall. Our machine gunners on the west bank could see many of these defenses clearly.

Charles R. Castellaw

Rather than make a frontal assault against these defenses behind an artillery heavy barrage, General O'Daniel decided to try to gain surprise by infiltration force under cover of darkness. Plans were made therefore to throw footbridges across the river at last light, move the foot elements of the 7th and 30th regiments across during the night, and attack from the west bank at daylight with strong preparatory fire. Caliber .50 machine guns, Flakwagons, tanks, tank destroyers and all available weapons were to provide fire support from the west bank.

The 15th Infantry held the line of departure (the west bank of the river) for several days prior to the attack, and patrolled vigorously to determine the conditions of the river and the nature of enemy opposition on the far bank. The patrols confirmed the fact that fording for any large body of troops was out of the question, and that employment of boats and rafts would be difficult because of the current. It was then that the use of prefabricated footbridges was decided upon.

Enemy reaction to the patrolling, however, was surprisingly weak, and although no prisoners were taken, it was fairly clear that (1) the enemy held the east bank very thinly, and (2) enemy troops who were present were neither aggressive nor alert. The enemy was compelled to keep his line thin by continuing attacks on the part of the 103rd Infantry Division in the Taintrux area, on the 3rd's right, and the 100th Infantry Division's attack southeast through Raon L'Etape, on the 3rd's left.

Then, for two or three days prior to the attack, friendly planes strafed and dropped fire bombs all along the enemy's line of prepared positions, to further lower the already low morale of the German soldiers holding those positions.

While plans went forward for the crossing, 7th and 30th Infantry regiments were engaged in training with their respective combat-team engineer companies. Since the crossing plan had been communicated to the appropriate commanders at the outset of the five-day period, it was possible to make all training objective in nature. To this end full emphasis was placed on engineer training in assault-boat operation and in construction of footbridges of the prefabricated type. Infantry received training in assault boats and in crossing over footbridges. This training was conducted on a battalion basis. Half of the training

The Way It Was

was conducted at night with a view to developing speed, coordination, and control. Directional aids such as luminous markers, telephone wire, engineer tape, ropes, and markings on the rear of helmets were stressed. Finally, special exercises were conducted for the assault platoons earmarked for covering footbridge construction.

Late that evening after every thing was quiet, the Captain's runner came to me and said, "The Captain wants to see you." I went to the Captain's post and as soon as I walked up, he said, "I see you are not drunk. It was reported to me that you were drunk." I knew that K.O. was still trying to get rid of me.

In order to deceive the enemy as to the date and time of our crossing, the Commanding General directed the artillery commander, Brig. Gen. William T. Sexton, to increase harassing fire on the Division front during the three days prior to the crossing. In addition, he prescribed for these three days a 15-minute pre-daylight shoot plus a 15-minute after-darkness shoot. It developed later from prisoner accounts that this program served as an effective cover plan for the main preparation which was fired from H-minus-30 to H-hour, since the enemy had become accustomed to heavy firing at this time.

On November 18 notification was received from Corps to the effect that the splendid progress of the 100th Infantry Division southeast of Baccarat warranted cancellation of crossing plans for the 3rd Infantry Division in the interest of passing the 3rd through the 100th to exploit its progress. Immediately upon receipt of these instructions, the concentration plan for the crossing which had been underway for two days was cancelled, and the assault regiments were directed to reconnoiter forward assembly areas in the zone of the 100th Division in the vicinity of Raon L'Etape. A movement order was issued covering concentration in forward assembly areas preliminary to passage through the 100th Infantry Division. Movement was to be initiated on Corps order during the night of November 19-20.

At a meeting on the 18th, originally intended to be a final review of crossing plans, General O'Daniel made the announcement of the new plan and initiated discussion on it.

The original plan was destined to carry through, however. For, on the morning of November 19, word was received from General Brooks that the progress of the 100th Division for the preceding twenty-four hours had been considerably retarded, and that instead of

Charles R. Castellaw

passing the 3rd through the 100th in the face of increasing resistance, the 3rd would effect its crossing of the Meurthe as originally planned.

Fortunately, the thorough preparation pertaining to both the concentration and crossing plans enabled the Division to resume its concentration and complete all preparations without incident. It was impossible, however, due to the loss in time, to emplace all tanks, TDs and smoke generators originally scheduled to move into position during the three nights prior to D-Day. The tanks and TDs were instead tied in with artillery fire-direction centers and used in an indirect fire role to support the crossing.

The Division drew a damp, moonless night for the crossing—the night of November 19-20. A platoon of Company I, 15th Infantry, had crossed two nights before by boat in the 7th Infantry's zone and occupied a house immediately in front of the enemy's main position without being detected. This platoon had radioed back several reports on the 19th, all of which indicated that the enemy was holding his main position with light forces, who appeared entirely to be occupying buildings along the Raon L'Etape-St. Die' highway.

To observers not actually on the river line, it seemed unbelievable that a large-scale river crossing was in progress. There was hardly as much shooting as on any quiet night of ordinary patrol activity. Division artillery dropped its normal quota of harassing shells along the enemy's supply routes with studied haphazardness; rifles cracked occasionally, but there was nothing approaching a genuine firefight. Obviously, the enemy was totally unaware that two of United States' finest regiments were moving onto his doorstep on a narrow front.

By 2400 the footbridge assault platoons, which had been ferried across by Company A, 10th Engineers, under the command of Capt. Albert Cook, were in possession of a line of departure approximately 300 yards from the Raon L'Etape-St. Die' highway. Footbridges were installed with exceptional speed, being completed by approximately 2359. Foot troops of the main assault forces proceeded from detrucking areas to the footbridges without incident. Immediately they started over—riflemen, BAR men, machine gunners, mortar squads, communication men, aid men—everybody who walks in the infantry team.

Meanwhile the bridge trains of the 36th Combat Engineer Regiment were moving toward St. Michel and Clairefontaine, to be in

The Way It Was

position for beginning construction of the Bailey and treadway vehicle bridges as soon as the far bank had been cleared to sufficient depth. Company B of the 10th Engineers, under Capt. Daniel A. Raymond, and Company C, under Capt. Homer M. Lefler, also ferried advance troops and took part in the bridge construction. The treadway and Bailey bridges at St. Michel drew intermittent enemy artillery fire all during the first day, but this did not prevent the construction and continuous use of the bridges until the approaches of the treadway bridge finally became unusable.

At 0600 hours, five battalions of United States doughboys stood on the east bank of the river, having won a solid victory by their quiet crossing before even beginning the attack.

It was now time for Division artillery, with Corps artillery and several other battalions in support, to raise the mask of secrecy and fire an all-out preparation. Tanks, tank destroyers and Flakwagons stationed on the west bank of the river opened direct fire on houses and strongpoints known to be in the enemy main line of resistance. Under cover of this fire, infantrymen of the Division struck, and in less than an hour the 7th had seized Le Voivre while the 30th had captured La Hollande and Himbaumont, preparatory to springing a trap on Clairefontaine.

It was one of the smoothest operations ever conducted by the 3rd Division. It was easily the quickest and most successful large-scale river crossing we had ever made.

The Winter War of Movement was under way.

The 36th Engineer Combat Regiment, together with certain personnel of the 10th Engineer Combat Battalion, initiated reconnaissance of the four heavy bridge sites at daylight of November 20. Reconnaissance of the two Clairefontaine sites was rendered impossible by small-arms, mortar and self-propelled fire from the town. At the two St. Michel sites, however, reconnaissance proceeded satisfactorily and by mid-morning engineer material had been moved to the vicinity of the bridge sites. Work was initially concentrated on construction of a wide-track armored force treadway bridge in the vicinity of St. Michel. After initial progress the work was suspended for several hours due to accurate enemy mortar and self-propelled fire on the bridge site. Although efforts were made to smoke the sites by means of generators, smoke pots, and chemical mortars, shifting

Charles R. Castellaw

winds and the fact that the enemy had registered on the bridge sites minimized the effect of the smoke.

At approximately noon, orders were received from Corps that two regimental combat teams of the 103rd Infantry Division were to be crossed over 3rd Division footbridges at the earliest possible moment and, following assembly on the far bank, were to pass through the right of the 3rd and continue the attack to the southeast. Immediate contact was made with the 103rd, and it was ascertained that the two regimental combat teams (409 and 410) were in assembly areas on our right rear in the vicinity of the town of La Bourgonce. The 103rd was requested to send its reconnaissance forward to the footbridges and to the command posts of the assault regiments of the 3rd. Brig. Gen. Robert N. Young, Assistant Division Commander, was designated as coordinator of crossing and was stationed at the footbridge sites.

Quickly exploiting the crossing, 7th and 30th Infantry Regiments moved to the east. The 1st Battalion, 7th Infantry, shoved on toward Hurbache. The second battalion, 30th Infantry, entered the town at 1635 in conjunction with Company C, 7th Infantry, and the village was shortly cleared. The 2nd battalion 7th, leaving Company G to block on the right flank, continued to advance without opposition. The 1st Battalion, 30th Infantry, cleared Clairefontaine on the afternoon of the 20th.

The 15th Infantry moved from its defensive positions on the west bank of the Meurthe River to the vicinity of La Hollande commencing with the 3rd battalion at 1530 and followed by 1st Battalion at 1600. Both battalions crossed on the northern footbridges in 30th Infantry sector.

The 3rd battalion, 7th Infantry, had seized Denipaire by 2100.

Meanwhile on the "engineer front" the progress of front-line troops was such that by late afternoon the enemy was unable to bring fire to bear upon the bridge sites. At darkness, therefore, work progressed in earnest and continued steadily through the night. The light assault bridge at the footbridge crossing area, which had been completed prior to daylight of the 20th, had passed approximately seventy-five ¼ ton loads prior to 2300, at which time the approaches to the bridge were rendered impassable by rising water and mud. Had

The Way It Was

it not been for this bridge, the Division resupply and emergency evacuation at the most critical time would have been imperiled.

With daylight on November 21, work on all four heavy bridge sites was intensified. By 0645 the wide-track armored force treadway bridge at the St. Michel site was completed and promptly passed seventeen armored vehicles and about twenty other tactical vehicles. At this time a tank bogged down at the exit of the bridge because of flooding of the approach by rising water, and the bridge was inoperative from this time on.

During the night the two combat teams of the 103rd Infantry Division had crossed the Meurthe over 3rd Division footbridges, and during the morning of the 21st had passed through Company G, 7th Infantry, to the south.

On the morning of the 21st Denipaire became the assembly area for the 1st Battalion, 7th Infantry, and 2nd battalion, 30th Infantry. The 3rd battalion, 30th Infantry, which had been pushing steadily, despite Company I's meeting small-arms fire a good part of the way, was still moving. Company I cleared La Paire. Companies I and K followed Company L toward La Chapelle. The 3rd battalion, 7th Infantry, which had captured Denipaire the night before, shoved on toward St. Jean d'Ormont.

We pulled back in a reserve area to pick up replacements and reorganize. Up to this time I had been acting Squad Leader and Acting Platoon Leader with only a PFC rating in between officers. I thought that this time I would receive a noncommissioned officer's rank. The day that we were to go back in combat one of the men in my platoon (I will call him Bill, not his real name) was promoted to Staff Sergeant and I was told that I could not receive a promotion because the Company had received several noncommissioned officers from the States in our replacements, but I would be the next man to be promoted. Several of the men in my platoon got upset because they knew that I had been given a dirty deal.

We went back to the front that evening and dug in for the night. It was quiet that night but early the next morning one of the men came to me and said that Bill had been killed during the night. I did not ask how because I did not want to know. I thought that he had undermined me to get my promotion. I thought he got what he deserved.

Charles R. Castellaw

The 2nd battalion, 15th Infantry, was the last of that regiment to cross the Meurthe, which it did at Etival at 0715, after which it closed in its assembly area at La Hollande before noon.

The 3rd battalion, 7th Infantry, seized St. Jean d' Ormont on the afternoon of the 21st.

Task Force Whirlwind

Task Force Whirlwind was activated on that same afternoon. This consisted of the 1st Battalion, 15th Infantry; Company C (minus one platoon) of the 756th Tank Battalion; a platoon of Company C, 601st TD Battalion; 3rd Recon Troop minus one platoon; B Battery of the 93rd Armored FA Battalion; a platoon of Company B, 10th Engineers, with an armored bulldozer; and the 2nd platoon of Company D, 756th Tank Battalion. Division provided twenty-five 2 ½ ton trucks to motorize the battalion of infantry.

The 1st Battalion, 7th Infantry scarcely paused in its rapid move as it seized La Fontanelle, Launois, and Maire. Its fight carried over to November 22, when it encountered strong resistance at Nayemont.

The 3rd battalion, 30th Infantry, pushing east, sent its Company I into La Chapelle without opposition, at 1230, November 21. At 1300, Companies K and L moved from La Chapelle and headed for Menil which they entered at 1500, meeting no opposition. The 1st Battalion moved by marching from Clairefontaine to La Paire, with Company C moving on to La Chapelle. The remainder of the battalion closed into La Chapelle during the afternoon, reverting to regimental reserve. The 2nd battalion continued its attack, attaining successive objectives before Laitre, which fell at 1700.

By late afternoon of November 21, the attack of the 103rd Division on our right (south) flank, which had commenced at 0900 that morning and moved out to the southeast through elements of 2nd battalion, 7th Infantry, had progressed from two to four kilometers on its entire front. At 1430 the 103rd was given traffic priority over the St. Michel bridge. Upon completion of the crossing of the 103rd Infantry Division tactical transportation, the 103rd's passage phase as applied to the 3rd Division was complete.

During the night of November 21-22 3rd battalion, 7th Infantry, occupied Baltant de Bourras.

The Way It Was

Task Force Whirlwind moved out of its assembly area at 0730, November 22, and passed through 7th Infantry along the route La Hollande-Hurbache-Denipaire, north to a road junction, and then southeast toward Launois. The 3rd battalion of the 15th moved from the vicinity of La Hollande at 0800 and followed the Task Force by shuttling. Task Force Whirlwind had reached Launois (which had fallen to 1st Battalion, 7th) by noon and was prepared to continue the advance.

The 3rd battalion, 7th Infantry during the morning seized Hill 619 and drew enemy fire from a nearby crossroad.

The 1st Battalion, 7th Infantry, had run into a definitely tough battle at Nayemont. Here the enemy "Winter Line" positions were first encountered by 7th Infantry elements. These consisted of elaborately constructed zigzag fire trenches, machine-gun emplacements, and partially finished concrete bunkers. These positions had been under construction for several months preceding, and it was here that the enemy had planned on spending the rest of the winter. The VI Corps attack, spearheaded by 3rd Infantry Division in its surprise crossing of the Meurthe and rapid advance eastward, gave the Germans no opportunity to utilize fully the well-built positions. The 103rd and 100th Divisions (the latter attacking on our left) had helped draw enemy strength from our zone and stretch his reserves to the breaking point.

The positions were so formidable, however, that 1st Battalion was engaged in a harrowing fight that lasted several hours before the line was cracked and the German remnants forced to withdraw. Nayemont was occupied at 1650.

The 2nd battalion, 30th Infantry, took Le Roaux in its stride, reaching the town by 0820, November 22, and continuing to Chatas, which was cleared at 0945. By 1010 the battalion had reached a further phase line and was still pushing.

The 3rd battalion's Company I reached Grandrupt and was still clearing the town at noon.

The 2nd battalion, 7th Infantry engaged an enemy roadblock force in the village of La Fraiteux during the afternoon and, after reducing it, continued east on the Saales road, but was passed through by the 3rd battalion at 1600. The 7th Infantry Battle Patrol advanced east on

Charles R. Castellaw

the Saales road after Nayemont was taken and encountered a mined enemy roadblock.

Task Force Whirlwind had shoved off from Launois at 1200, and made good progress until it encountered enemy resistance in the early morning hours of November 23, when it halted for the night.

The 2nd battalion, 15th assembled in La Fontanelle and moved to Grandrupt at 1625, establishing roadblocks on main roads leading into town upon arrival.

At 1645 2nd battalion, 30th Infantry continued its advance and seized the high ground overlooking Saales.

The Division advance scarcely paused during the night of November 22-23. The 3rd battalion, 7th Infantry, by-passed the roadblock on the Saales road which the regiment's Battle Patrol had encountered during the afternoon of the 22nd and at 0100 Company I seized the town of La Grande Fosse. While 2nd battalion, 30th Infantry sent patrols into Saales which destroyed an 88mm gun and actually cleared the northwest corner of town, Company K, 7th Infantry spearheaded its battalion's attack on the town, entering at dawn and promptly becoming engaged in a firefight. The 3rd battalion was engaged in this mission all the morning of November 23 and into the afternoon. Capture of the town symbolized entrance of the Division into Alsatian territory, but still more important was the fact that one of the two principal hinges of the Winter Line (the other being Saulxures) had been taken and that now the enemy could not hope to stop us short of the Rhine River.

My company (E) working to the North cleared the Sanatorium at 231540, after about a three hour rifleman fight. I entered the Sanatorium with one of my men and was met by a man in a dark suit. He asked, "Who is in charge?" The other soldier pointed at me. The man started talking in German because of his lack of English skills. I could not understand him and he could not understand me, so he motioned for me to follow him. The other soldier said, "This may be a trick, do you want me to go with you?" I said, "No, I want you to stay by the door and if this is a trick, I will blow him to hell." We had been warned that we had entered into an area that had German sympathizers in it. I motioned for him to lead and that I would follow. He led me down steps to a basement. The basement was full of women, children and old men.

The Way It Was

They looked at me with a fear of fright on their faces. I said, "I am an American soldier." There was a young lady in the group that translated what I said. The group started laughing, rejoicing, hugging and kissing me. Later I learned why they were so happy. The day before, they had received word from the German authorities that all young boys and old men of a certain age group should get ready to go into Germany to work in the factories. They understood that after the arrival of the Americans this would not happen.

As soon as things settled down, I talked to the young lady that had translated my statement. She invited me to have dinner with her that evening. I accepted the invitation. This practice was against standard orders. I followed the practice of obeying orders that I believed in and disobeying the ones that I did not agree with.

After establishing an outpost, which was a problem because one of the men that was in line to go out on the outpost had found some whiskey and gotten drunk, I then ordered the next man in line, who was K.O., to take his place. K.O. said, "I will not go!" I removed the safety on my M-1 and said, "You have a choice, you go or you die." He said, "I will go but I will get you." I told one of my men where I was going and if I was needed, he should come for me.

I arrived at the girl's house at the designated time. She invited me in and said, "Dinner is on the table and we will eat." She served Welsh Rabbit. She was living with her father and mother and had thirteen-month old twin girls.

After dinner she said, "We will go in the living room and talk while Mother and Daddy clean up the kitchen." I followed her into the living room and sat down on the couch. As I looked up at the mantle, which was in front of the couch, I saw a picture of a young German soldier in dress uniform. She saw me looking at the picture and said, "He is my husband." I gave the twins some GI candy and talked about thirty minutes, then returned to my post.

Charles R. Castellaw

Mr. and Mrs. Schlapach with twins Elsie and Edith

That night I thought about what a nice family I had met and I was sure that her husband was the same kind of a person. The reality of war was, that if I got a chance, I would kill her husband and if he got a chance he would kill me. The truth is, war is hell on earth.

The Saales, France area is a beautiful and old city with a strong German and French history. It is surrounded by beautiful hills and covered with trees and other vegation.

The roads leading into the city has entrance gates that were built during the early years. Most of the buildings are old but beautiful and well maintained. One of the outstanding characteristic of the city is the tremendous amount of flowers throughout the city.

The citizens of the city are like a strong knit big family. They are very friendly with outsiders as well as citizens of the city.

This information is based on my visit to the city in 1997, which was quiet a contrast from my visit in November, 1944.

I went back to this town in 1993 to visit the sanitarium and met the twin girls again after all that time. The town rolled out the red carpet for me and articles were written in the local newspaper.

The Way It Was

The 2nd battalion, 7th, eliminated the roadblock in the wake of 3rd battalion. The 1st Battalion entrucked at Nayemont and moved to a point near St. Barbe, north of Saales, where the men detrucked and marched to the heights of St. Barbe, from which point the battalion moved south to assist 3rd battalion in clearing Saales. Upon entry into the town the afternoon of November 23, 1st Battalion found that Saales had been cleared by 3rd battalion at 1535. The 1st Battalion thereupon headed east again, toward Bourg-Bruche.

Task Force Whirlwind had been held up by an enemy roadblock and small-arms fire from the vicinity of Saulxures. At 1400, in conjunction with 3rd battalion, 30th Infantry, it attacked Saulxures. Companies I and L, 30th Infantry, attacked the town while Company K went over the high ground east of town and there seized Hill 512. Companies I and L entered town, along with elements of Whirlwind, at 1400, and had cleared the town at approximately 1630 against stubborn enemy resistance. The Winter Line was now completely broken. The condition of prisoners captured both in Saales and Saulxures indicated that they had been expecting a protracted stay behind what their superiors fondly imagined to be a secure line. Many of the rear-echelon personnel had acquired such appurtenances as skis and snowshoes, in anticipation of moments of relaxation. The skis found new owners and the dispossessed would-be skiers found exercise in marching back to the prisoner of war cages, hands clasped firmly and resting lightly on top of the head.

Only disconnected battles along the route to Strasbourg now remained. One of the toughest of these was encountered by 1st Battalion, 7th Infantry, at Bourg-Bruche. It was here that the Germans had marshaled a striking force and were on the verge of counterattacking the 3rd battalion in an attempt to recapture Saales. At 1730, November 23, 1st Battalion moved out to attack Bourg-Bruche.

Approximately 150 yards beyond Saales, elements of Company B encountered heavy machine-gun and rifle fire from both sides of the road. S/Sgt. James P. Wils, a squad leader, immediately rushed an S-shaped communications trench from which a storm of enemy fire was issuing, jumped inside it and fired eight clips of M-1 ammunition, coming out with twenty prisoners. The company's 3rd platoon on the other side of the road wounded and killed another sizable number of enemy, putting the rest to flight.

Charles R. Castellaw

At 1930 the battalion resumed its advance along the highway. A mile ahead, machine-gun and rifle-grenade fire flayed the assault company. Reconnaissance disclosed that a strong German force was defending a railroad overpass which had been partially demolished by explosives.

Riflemen of Company B worked their way forward, firing at enemy muzzle blasts in the gloom. Soldiers of an enemy platoon attempting to strike at the company's left flank silhouetted themselves on the embankment and were decimated by a prompt fusillade of M- I fire.

After tough fighting, the enemy was gradually driven from the embankment. At 2300, the 1st Battalion resumed the advance toward Bourg-Bruche. Spearhead elements of Company B worked their way from building to building upon reaching the town, toward a crossroads in the center of town. A pair of building strongpoints held up the advance. Flakwagon and 88mm gun fire deluged the intersection.

A tank was brought forward by 1st Lt. Wendell D. Leavitt, who rode it up to direct cannon fire on the enemy 88mm guns and Flakwagons. The assault platoons then charged forward into the building strongpoints to destroy or put to flight the German occupants.

Company C drove up the right side of the highway and penetrated into the eastern section of Bourg-Bruche. The 3rd platoon, with a strength of nine men, held its gains against strong enemy pressure for five hours. A squad of Germans assaulted the house in which the platoon had taken cover and demanded that the platoon surrender, only to be greeted and repulsed by fragmentation hand grenades.

Another group similarly held out in a nearby house throughout the night.

In the morning, Company C's 1st and 3rd platoons joined forces and proceeded to clean out the houses on the right side of the east-west road through Bourg-Bruche, leaving the 2nd platoon in support. This attack took place under strong enemy artillery emplaced on a ridge running north-south and masking the eastern portion of the town. The ridge contained a long communications trench and heavily fortified emplacements.

The Way It Was

The two platoons pressed their attack and reached a tavern near the railroad overpass, where they remained under concentrated fire and from which they directed artillery on the German gun emplacements, destroying an 88mm gun, blowing up an ammunition dump, and destroying a dug-in 20mm Flak gun.

During this time the Battalion CO, Lt. Col. Kenneth W. Wallace, committed Company A in an attack on the eastern section of town. As the company advanced it came under fire from two machine guns and a 20mm gun emplaced on a ridge, but these weapons were silenced by tanks and a tank destroyer after a duel which lasted several minutes.

Rounding a curve in the road, the company resumed the advance. The men drew furious blasts of Flak and machine-gun fire from the right. The enemy opened fire with an intensive mortar concentration. The company halted, having had five casualties. An unsuccessful assault on the enemy positions in which a platoon leader was killed and two men wounded followed; then a bazooka team crept forward and placed three rockets on the position, killing two Germans and crippling the position. The 3rd platoon assaulted and destroyed it.

Companies B and C occupied positions in a cluster of buildings and rained fire on the Germans emplaced on the ridge. By mid-afternoon of the 24th they had killed between forty and fifty of the enemy and silenced two machine guns.

At about 1500 the third platoon of Company C assaulted the communications trench that was dug into the ridge. As the platoon surged up the hill slope, the effect of the M-1, machine-gun, and intense artillery fire, added to the assault, convinced the Germans of the uselessness of the struggle. Approximately eighty-five prisoners were taken. Remnants of the battered German garrison fled from Bourg-Bruche only to be captured in large numbers by the 3rd battalion, which had maneuvered into position beyond the town. By 1630, BourgBruche was firmly in our hands, lacking only the clearance of isolated snipers. Approximately 200 prisoners had been taken and seventy-five of the enemy killed.

The 2nd battalion, 15th Infantry, had moved from St. Stail to Chateau St. Louis. Company G remained in St. Stail and sent patrols north to Le Vermont, contacting the 398th Infantry of the 100th

Charles R. Castellaw

Division. The 3rd battalion, 15th Infantry remained in assembly in the vicinity of La Fontelle, alerted to move.

The 1st Battalion, 30th Infantry was in flank-blocking positions along the regiment's route of advance over the 24-hour period from noon to noon of November 23-24. The 2nd battalion's Company E reported Sanatorium clear at 1540, November 23, after a brief firefight, while Companies G, F, and H were assembled and moved toward the town. At 0700 of the 24th the battalion moved out toward St. Blaise, sweeping the edge of the woods en route.

The 3rd battalion, 7th, passed through 1st Battalion in Bourg-Bruche and encountered enemy north of the town on the afternoon of the 24th. This resistance was taken care of and the battalion had pushed on to an assigned phase line by 1840. The 2nd battalion moved north from Lehan and cut the Bourg-Bruche-La Saales Road, leaving Company F there to block. The remainder of the battalion pushed north and assembled.

On November 25, 1944, I received word to report to Company Headquarters. When I reported, I was told that General O'Daniel, Commander of the 3rd Infantry Division, had set up a Division Rest Center where front line soldiers would be sent for four days on a rotation system. The Center would have hot showers, clean clothes, hot food, motion pictures, stage shows and a dry place to sleep. I was one of two soldiers that had been selected to go. I will call the other man Joe (not his real name).

Joe (about age 35) and I were transported to the Rest Center at Bourbonne-les-Bains. As we entered we were greeted by a big sign, "A KING FOR 4 DAYS." As soon as we entered the hotel, we were given clean clothes (I had been wearing the same uniform for four months) and directed to the showers. After showering and dressing, we were served a hot meal. We went to the recreation room where I sat at a table in the back of the room with my back against the wall. A USO girl came over, sat down at my table and asked me if I wanted to write letters home. I said, "No." Then she asked me if I wanted her to write some letters for me and I said, "No." Then she asked me if I wanted to play cards or checkers and I said, "No." She got up and said, "If I can do anything for you, let me know." I was exhausted and wanted a bed. After a night's sleep, I felt a lot better.

The Way It Was

The next day when I met Joe, he told me about an Army-operated whorehouse in a small hotel across the street from us. He said that the Army had two MPs on the front door and permitted only soldiers from the Rest Camp to enter. He said they had pretty whores in the hotel lobby and if you chose one of them, they gave you a condom to use. The girl would take you to a room. Afterward you would give her two dollars, and one of the MPs would give you a chemical prophylactic. This was all new to me, and I did not have the stomach for it. The third day in camp, Joe came to me and said that he had spent all his money and wanted to borrow four dollars to go back to the whorehouse two more times before we had to return to our unit. He said that when he received his paycheck at the first of the month, he would pay me. I gave him the four dollars, but he was killed before the first of the month.

The second night in camp we saw a good stage show of all French girls. I did write letters home to Betty Jo and my family the second day that I was in Rest Camp. After four days, we were returned to our unit.

Task Force Whirlwind continued to push east until 0550 the next morning when it made contact with an isolated group of enemy. By 0830, this group had been cleared up and the Task Force, its mission accomplished, was dissolved and its elements returned to control of parent units.

Charles R. Castellaw

3rd Infantry Division Rest Center at Bourboune - les - Bains

The Way It Was

Approaching the Rhine

The last phase in the Meurthe-Rhine River push was a sweep out onto the Alsatian plain, clearing scores of towns enroute. There were only brief firefights with bewildered, isolated enemy groups. At the town of Mollkirch there were nearly a hundred Germans who wanted neither to fight nor surrender. They finally decided to fight a little, then surrendered almost wholly. Taken prisoner, most of them stated that their only hope had been to make their way back across the Rhine.

The 30th Infantry took Grendelbruch. The 2nd battalion, commanded by Lt. Col. Frederick R. Armstrong, had an all-night house-to-house fight at Grendelbruch. Shortly before midnight, Company E, under Capt. Ralph R. Carpenter, moved around to the right of the town, sweeping out the woods as it went. The company then attacked from the east as Company F, commanded by Capt. Marshall T. Hunt, struck simultaneously from the west. By 1000, November 26, the battalion headquarters was doing business at a command post situated in the center of the town.

The 3rd battalion, 15th Infantry had advanced from La Broque to Schirmeck, Wisches, Schwartzbach, Urmatt, and Dinsheim, to west of Mutzig along the main road to Strasbourg by noon of the 26th. On the afternoon of November 26, 3rd battalion cleared Mutzig.

Combat Command A, 14th Armored Division passed through the 3rd Infantry Division, moving from Schirmeck at 0700, following two routes. One column followed the route Schirmeck-Mutzig-south to Obernai east in the direction of Erstein. The second column followed the route Schirmeck-east to Russ-Grendelbruch-Obernai south to Coxwiller.

On the night of November 26-27, 1st and 2nd battalion, 7th Infantry assembled and moved by truck to an assembly area in the vicinity of Strasbourg, to which patrols had gone and met elements of the French 2nd Armored Division which reached the town ahead of the 3rd Division, having come in from the northwest. The 1st Battalion, 15th Infantry, also moved by motor to take up defensive positions along the Rhine River south of Strasbourg that same night, and 2nd battalion prepared to join it.

Charles R. Castellaw

The 1st Battalion, 30th Infantry cleared Rosheim, and moved on to establish defensive positions in the vicinity of Dorlisheim by 0330 on November 27. The 2nd battalion established roadblocks during the same period to protect 1st Battalion's flank. Company G patrols cleared Laubenheim and Mollkirch.

The 3rd battalion, 30th Infantry captured Boersch, Klingenthal, and Obernai. Roadblocks were established on all roads leading out of Obernai.

On our north flank, the 117th Cavalry Reconnaissance Squadron, attached, screened the last move into Strasbourg. Isolated enemy elements occasionally offered resistance, but the squadron encountered no real fight until it approached the vicinity of Gambsheim, where determined SS troops made a stand. After much tentative probing of the strong positions here, the 117th settled down and awaited stronger forces to attack the town.

Strasbourg is the great communications and market center and capital of the Bas-Rhin Department, located on the Rhine River. The 7th prepared to relieve General Jacques Le Clerc's famed 2nd French Armored Division which had taken Strasbourg and held positions in the city in the vicinity of the Kehl Bridge, which crosses the Rhine east of Strasbourg.

The port of Strasbourg, third largest in all France, stretches east to northeast between the Rhine and Kleiner Rhine (small Rhine) opposite the Kehl Bridge and has a peacetime annual capacity of ten million tons.

Strasbourg's peacetime population was nearly 200,000 persons. The Ill River crosses the city in two branches, one along the northeast edge and the other along the southwest. Upstream, the Ill joins the Rhone-Rhine Canal and the Breusch River whereas downstream, the river receives the waters of the Rhone-Rhine Canal.

The 7th Infantry took up defensive positions on the western outskirts of Strasbourg, 15th occupied positions south of the city along the Rhine River, and the 30th continued to scour the rear sector of the Division for straggler groups of enemy that had been by-passed in the rush to the Rhine and that had taken refuge in some old forts near Mutzig.

In one of them some 200 Germans, armed with bazookas, machine guns and small arms, offered stubborn resistance to all

The Way It Was

efforts to dislodge them. Benko Force of the 2nd battalion, 30th Infantry, commanded by 1st Lt. John F. Benko, spent several days searching caverns and hammering the strongpoints with fire from our tank destroyers which had little effect on the occupants.

These forts had been a part of the Maginot Line. This one had been built in the late 1800s and later modernized, completely equipped with generators, water supply, and ample ammunition. In its location and structure the fort posed a perplexing problem to the 30th Infantry, artillery, and 10th Engineer Battalion. Special interest was manifested in it owing to the fact that the VI Corps command post wished to move into Mutzig, but thought it inadvisable to locate with such proximity to the enemy.

The fort was built below ground level on the crest of the highest terrain in the area and was enclosed by a moat thirty feet wide and thirty feet deep. Any attempt to enter the fort could be frustrated by fire covering all angles of the moat. Direct fire could be brought to bear only on the steel turrets housing ISOmm guns and the entrance, which was set at an angle to the fort proper. Tanks could not approach the edge of the moat to pound the walls because of extremely accurate *Panzerfaust* fire from slits in the walls.

Construction on the fort began in April 1893 and finished in 1914. It had an area of 40,000 square meters and could house 6500 men in time of war. It had 4 electric generators, 4 wells, 6 bakeries, 8 Howitzers of 15Omm and 30 cannons sizes 53mm to l05mm. It was built as a self-contained fort.

The 30th Regiment in Division Reserve started assembling in an assigned area just west of Strasbourg. Regimental Command Post and Headquarters Company moved to Holtzheim (932956), closing at 291630A. 3rd battalion moved to Entzheim (925925), closing at 291830. 2nd battalion was alerted to move on the morning of the 30th around daylight, however battalion was halted at Rosheim to wait the outcome of enemy counterattack against the 103rd Division on the southern flank. Company E was sent to an abandoned Maginot line fort at (802940) where an estimated 100 enemy were holding out and repulsing efforts of one platoon of Company E to occupy the fort. Tanks, Tank Destroyers and assault 105's were being used to batter in the entrance without success.

Charles R. Castellaw

1st Battalion was attached to Task Force REMY of the 2nd French Armored Division and entrucked at 300700A, moving to Valiff and detrucking at 301030, vicinity (832804). Battalion started movement to blocking and screening positions to South and East.

1st Battalion continued on its mission for 2nd French Armored Division. At 301600, 2nd battalion (less Company E still engaged at the fort) left Rosheim and closed in on Oberhausbergen at 301715A. All units organized anti-paratroop defenses with alert companies and continuous patrols of the areas of responsibility.

The 30th Regiment during the latter part of the month of November completed its drive to the Rhine. Technically the 30th Regiment was in reserve, assembled just west of Strasbourg. The 1st Battalion, however, had been attached to the French 2nd Armored Division and had reinforced their Infantry to screen and block for them to enable them to attack to the south and form a junction with other French troops, who had broken through at Belfort. All enemy resistance within the sector had collapsed and was overcome with the excepfion of one old Maginot Line fortress in the vicinity of Mutzig, which still held out, refusing to surrender. The balance of Regiment was set to meet any enemy attempt to penetrate the Strasbourg salient while all organizations performed anti-paratroop alert missions.

THIRTIETH INFANTRY SECTOR OF OPERATION

Summary of Enemy Operations 1-30 November

As this period opened, the enemy counterattacks were raging at the height of their fanatical fury. Realizing that our positions on the high ground overlooking St. Die' and the Meurthe River valley constituted a serious threat to his plans to defend on the East bank of the Meurthe, the enemy was throwing against us every attacking force he could muster. These units, including two new, well-equipped mountain battalions continued to counterattack our positions for several days without success and with heavy loss to themselves. After he was forcibly impressed with the impossibility of dislodging us from the high ground, the enemy organized defensive positions in an attempt to contain us. These positions, in heavy woods, were well dug in and carefully overheaded, and camouflaged, making them very difficult to reduce. Another interesting feature of these positions was

190

The Way It Was

that all dugouts were connected by a thin wire. Apparently this wire was used as an alert warning. The first man to observe any activity gave the wire a tug, thus alerting others. The success of this system was demonstrated by the fact that the enemy was very sensitive to our patrol actions, responding to any activity with prompt machine gun, small arms, and mortar defensive fires. As our determined attacks pushed the enemy back, he took up reverse slope defenses at the base of the high ground and continued to resist with all force at his command. This stubborn resistance continued even after he had been driven from the wooded high ground to the flat valley sector.

It is interesting to note that from the time we first entered the St Die' sector until we were relieved there, the enemy was apparently unable to correctly evaluate our threats against him. When we first entered the sector his troops sometimes walked right into our lines, and afterwards as we continued our attack, the enemy's defensive main line was seldom placed to meet our threat effectively.

Generally, artillery in the St. Die' sector was light but mortar fire was heavy, especially of the large calibers. The enemy placed roadblocks of felled trees on all roads entering his sector and usually reinforced these blocks with R-Mines. He used antipersonnel mines sparingly in this sector. Enemy use of armor, after unsuccessful attempts to penetrate our positions with tanks, was confined to employing tanks as mobile artillery. The enemy reached a new low in vicious warfare in the St. Die sector. When he saw that St. Die could be of no further value to him, the enemy systematically looted this and nearby towns and then burned public buildings and private homes.

After being relieved in the St. Die' sector we started preparations for a crossing of the Meurthe River North of St. Die. Although our patrols made contact with the enemy on both sides of the river and there was an unavoidable increase in activity on our side of the Meurthe, the enemy gave no indication that he had guessed our intentions. The actual crossing was made without event—a few rounds of mortar and artillery were laid on the West of the river but this was probably at the sound of movement.

Enemy security measures were so inadequate that we were able to put three battalions across the Meurthe without his knowledge. These battalions moved out to attack at dawn under cover of a very heavy

Charles R. Castellaw

artillery preparation. Enemy resistance was stubborn in some sectors, especially around the bridge site at Clairefontaine, where pockets of resistance held out until the following day. There was very little coordination of the enemy positions and individuals had very little knowledge of other sectors.

After our initial assault across the Meurthe River, the enemy was able to offer only scattered resistance to our advance. This resistance was in the nature of rear-guard actions, but not too well planned or executed as bridges were not blown and only a few mines laid. The enemy continued to withdraw towards the Rhine while losing heavily in men and material. There were several "Winter Lines" established but they were quickly overrun by our troops. The most formidable of these was in the Saulxures-Saales area where dug-in positions of the most elaborate sort were met. These consisted of a series of trenches, overheaded dug-outs, tank traps, obstacles and wire entanglements, but they were lightly held.

Reports from prisoners of war indicated that the enemy had planned to hold a winter line in the Vosges, but on finding himself outflanked and in a precarious position, he continued his withdrawal toward the Rhine. It seems that the enemy left his units on the West of the Rhine to delay our advance as much as possible. These units had little hope of being able to escape from our advance and were written off the books by the German High Command.

Artillery was light during the advance, consisting of isolated guns placed to delay us as long as possible. These guns were not withdrawn as we approached but were overrun by our troops. Mines were not laid in abundance.

After we had passed the Maginot line by about twenty kilometers, a group of the enemy gathered together and occupied one fort North of Mutzig. Civilian reports placed the size of the group as high as 200 including some high-ranking officers and party officials. At the close of the period, this fort was still holding out against our efforts to clear it, however they were securely contained and offered no great threat to our rear areas.

Lt. Col. John A. Heintges, 30th Infantry executive officer, was in charge of operations, and Company E was charged with maintaining a cordon around the fort. A 155mm Long Tom was first employed in an attempt to batter down the entrance, only to find that entrance to the

The Way It Was

fort proper was still blocked by a series of steel doors and compartments, each of which could be sealed off from other sections. The second measure taken was to call on the Air Corps, and two missions with dive bombers, using heavy, delayed-action and fire-bombs, were flown, but with scant success because of the planes' inability to register successive direct hits. Company E maintained its vigil and Company H pounded the fort steadily with mortar fire.

Company E kept the fort in the vicinity of Mutzig encircled while tanks, tank destroyers, assault guns, and dive-bombers vainly endeavored to smash in the concrete and steel bastion. Finally at 041415 a captured personnel carrier loaded with 8000 pounds of TNT was maneuvered into position against the inner wall and detonated, causing a large breach in the fortification. During the night the garrison endeavored to break out through Company E's fire but after making three unsuccessful attempts, the detachment of 84 men and officers surrendered at 050900. Company E guarded the fort until it could be sealed up by the Engineers and rendered useless. Company E assembled at 071730 and rejoined the rest of the battalion in Oberhausbergen (964006), closing at 071905.

While the 84 prisoners were being searched, one of them told me that they had only raw horse meat and dry hard kernels to eat for several days. He said that they had been starved out.

Colonel Heintges finally devised a plan. First, he announced in German to the garrison over a loudspeaker that the men had one-half hour in which to surrender, or else to be subjected to something new in secret weapons. This failed to budge them. At the end of the elapsed time, Company H resumed it 88mm mortar fire to cover the work of a tank-dozer which was cutting a driveway to the edge of the moat. When the driveway was completed a captured halftrack personnel carrier loaded with four tons of explosive was started by Company C, 10th Engineer Battalion, and sent driverless toward the driveway. The vehicle toppled over and fell into the moat with its load of explosive resting against the wall.

The electrical detonator was disconnected by the plunge, so mortars fired on the vehicle. There was an explosion that rattled windows in Strasbourg, thirty miles away, and when the dust had settled a fifteen-foot hole marred the side of the fort.

During the night of December 4-5, the garrison endeavored to break out through the fire of Company E. After three unsuccessful attempts the detachment of eighty-four men and officers surrendered at 0900, December 5. Only the commander, a major, escaped and he was rounded up at a roadblock a few days later.

Company E guarded the fort until it could be sealed by the 10th Engineers and rendered useless. On December 7, Company E rejoined its battalion at Oberhausbergen.

As November ended, the 79th Infantry Division was on the 3rd's left flank and the 103rd was on the right.

84 prisoners from Fort Mutzig

Watch on the Rhine

The 3rd Infantry Division of World War II now began its "Watch on the Rhine." The first day of December found the 7th Infantry launching an attack to reduce the German bridgehead at the eastern outskirts of Strasbourg, opposite the town of Kehl, while other elements of the Division began police and guard duty in Strasbourg.

The 7th met stubborn resistance when it attacked on the morning of December 1. Small-arms, automatic-weapon, machine-gun and

The Way It Was

rocket-launcher fire from dug-in positions on the west side of the river and mortar and artillery fire from the east side comprised the enemy defense.

The 2nd battalion, commanded by Lt. Col. Clayton C. Thobro, took up the "Battle of the Apartment Houses" in the eastern section of the city while Company C, commanded by Capt. Beverly G. Hays, continued the street fight which it started shortly after midnight. Members of Company C will long remember the hand-to-hand battles that were staged in the vicinity of the Hippodrome and in the railroad yards on the edge of town. Sniper fire from across the river also added to the misery.

Organized resistance began to dwindle with daylight of December 2 after the 2nd battalion had cleared the peninsula between the Bassin De L'Industrie and the Rhine River. The entire area rocked late that afternoon as demolitions set off by the Germans destroyed all three bridges across the river. The last Germans to leave the bridgehead escaped by boat.

While the 7th was chasing the Germans from the west bank of the Rhine, the 1st Battalion of the 30th, attached to the 2nd French Armored Division, veered suddenly south and crossed the southern branch of the Ill River between Sermersheim and Kogenheim. The mission was to secure a site for the French to build an armor-carrying span.

At about midnight, Colonel Porter's battalion crossed in boats and came under a concentration of heavy mortar and artillery fire. Company B, commanded by 1st Lt. Lysle E. Standish, made the crossing at Kogenheim and Company C, under 1st Lt. Charles H. Skeahan, Jr., landed at Sermersheim, about a half mile upstream. The two companies came under more artillery fire in the towns, where an estimated 600 rounds of heavy enemy shells fell the next morning. Supported by French artillery and tanks, the attackers pushed the Germans out of the villages and carried the assault into the woods east while Company A, commanded by 1st Lt. Willard C. Johnson, took over blocking positions to the southeast.

Action described by a veteran doughboy as the "toughest three days I have ever spent" came to a close when a French colonel announced that the battalion attached to him by the 30th Infantry "is the finest outfit of its kind I have ever seen.

Charles R. Castellaw

So satisfied were the French forces with the job that they awarded twenty-three Croix de Guerre to members of the 30th, 1st Battalion from CO Major Mackenzie E. Porter down to the privates of the front ranks, who received most of the decorations.

In the same way the French 2nd Armored Division's plaudits were passed out to Company C. At Company C, 1st Lt. Rex Metcalfe accepted the tribute by passing credit on to his doughfeet, who ended their 48-plus hours of fighting by sitting on the division objective for fourteen hours alone.

The 15th Infantry continued to maintain defensive positions, check the numerous pillboxes that the enemy had evacuated, and provide anti-parachute alert units. Our troops occupied many of the pillboxes as outposts.

Marnemen will recall the guard duty in the old Alsatian capital— the Physics Building, Adolf Kosmier, Matford Factory, Hotel De Ville, the Pioneer Gasno, the laboratories at Fort Ney, and the interminable strings of railroad cars that filled the yards.

Many will remember the worship services that were held in the world-famous Strasbourg Cathedral, the first since the Germans came in 1940. Others will recall the burial given Pfc. Simon Quiroz of the 15th Infantry, who was the only 3rd Division man to die in the liberation of the little village of Mutzig. M. Haller Eugene, mayor of St. Maurice, was given permission to conduct the services, which were attended by a guard of honor from VI Corps artillery. After eulogizing Quiroz and paying high tribute to the 3rd Division, the mayor announced that a plaque would be erected in honor of the fallen soldier.

Strasbourg, as the largest and most important city occupied by the 3rd Division in France, called for special attention from the occupying forces. The 1st Battalion, 7th Infantry, for instance, guarded intelligence targets prescribed by Sixth Army Group's T-Force, which had the mission of protecting and exploiting anything that might yield information of the enemy's army or war industry. Included in the targets were an amphibious-motor-vehicle plant and the notorious laboratory at the University of Strasbourg, whose doctors were accused of performing experiments with poison gas and disease cultures on living humans.

The Way It Was

Before reaching Strasbourg, the Division also liberated one of the most brutal of the Nazi concentration camps—that at Natzwiller, northeast of Schirmeck.

The Division established a supervisory city administration (G-5) under the A C of S, G-2, Lt. Col. Grover Wilson. Until the arrival of the French 10th Military District headquarters under the French General Schwartz, the Division was responsible for guarding food dumps, utilities and warehouses, arranging for transportation and distribution of food, and other functions performed by military government personnel.

The prize prisoner of war of the Strasbourg episode was General Major (equivalent: Brig. Gen.) Vaterrodt, the town commandant, who was described by interrogators as cringing, totally opportunistic, and only too willing to give information if it might improve his position with his captors.

On December 8, the Division started a program of deception, designed to assist the VI Corps in its attack in the north toward Germany.

Artillery registration on points east of the Rhine River, apparently "careless" revealing of rubber assault boats on the banks of the river with an occasional boat being sent downstream on the loose, and many other measures were perpetrated, designed to make the Germans believe that the 3rd was going to cross the Rhine in the Strasbourg sector.

Once the restoration of some degree of order, if not normality, was well under way in Strasbourg, the 3rd had some chance to reflect upon its recent accomplishments. The effect of the sullenly-bitter Vosges battle manifested itself in several ways.

LeClerc's 2nd Armored Division, the outfit which had been first to enter Paris the previous autumn, and which had moved on Strasbourg from a general northwest direction in the recent drive with characteristic celerity, had spearheaded that effort to crack German defenses before the Rhine River. Enemy elements west of the river were already partially frustrated in their efforts to hold a sizable salient when elements of the French First Army reached the Rhine just above Basle, Switzerland, and moved up to liberate a section of territory which included Mulhouse. This occurred a short time before our own all-out push from the Meurthe.

197

Charles R. Castellaw

The 3rd Infantry Division had broken through the enemy's intended winter line, spearheading Seventh Army's push through the central Vosges in the latter stages of the drive, to widen the breach made by the first breakthrough to Strasbourg, and to help reduce German forces west of the Rhine in our sector and split them into two groups: a large pocket which included Colmar on the south and a German foothold on Alsatian soil to the north which was rapidly dwindling under continued Seventh Army pressure.

The recent drive had been record-making in several ways. In a congratulatory message, VI Corps Commander Major General Edward H. Brooks made note of one precedent-shattering fact:

"Since the beginning of the military history of Europe, to force a successful passage of the Vosges Mountains has been considered by military experts as an operation offering such small opportunity for success as to forestall consideration of such effort. [No military force had ever before crossed the Vosges against organized resistance.]

"To march, supply and maintain a large body of troops through these natural obstacles, without hostile opposition, is a major problem in itself.

"To fight cross-country, in the face of unreasoning, stubborn Nazi resistance, at times supplying over snow-covered mountain roads and trails, through this region and at this season of the year, is a military achievement of which all who participated can be justly proud.

"To those men of the 100th and 36th Divisions who battered the flanks, to those of the 3rd and 103rd Divisions and of the 14th Armored Division who poured onto the Alsatian Plain, to those supporting combat troops of the Corps, and to those indispensable elements of supply, maintenance, and evacuation, I extend my thanks and congratulations. Teamwork, throughout, to a superlative degree.

"It is with pride and humility that I realize the pinnacle and the magnitude of this concerted achievement of American soldiery—your achievement. I have every confidence that the future of the VI Corps rests secure and bright in your capable hands."

Bare statistics pointed up another important feat. From the beginning of the attack on the morning of November 21 to the time leading elements of the 7th Infantry entered Strasbourg on the night of the 26th, the distance covered was at least fifty miles, measured by

The Way It Was

road. The troops who ended the long march in the vicinity of Strasbourg were very near exhaustion.

They were not particularly articulate about their great success. The trail was too rocky. Even at the finish, when the Rhine forced a temporary halt, the job was not done. There had been the grinding, nerve-wracking "Battle of the Apartment Houses" under small-arms, machine-gun, and *Panzerfaust* fire, and heavy caliber artillery from Germany for the 2nd and 3rd battalions, 7th Infantry. There was the temporary attachment of 1st Battalion, 30th Infantry to LeClerc, and Company E's battle to reduce the Mutzig fort.

There was to be no sustained period of rest in Strasbourg. On the north the bulk of the Seventh Army was continuing to force the issue with the enemy remaining in Alsace in that sector. The 36th and 103rd (the latter very shortly relieved and sent to rejoin the Seventh) were still in strong contact with the Germans to the south. The French 2nd Armored slowed down in its attack toward Colmar as the enemy, anticipating a pincers between I French Corps on the south and II French Corps on the north flank, demolished bridges along every possible route of approach and offered tenacious resistance to the attackers. The 36th Division was attached to II French Corps.

There was much speculation in regard to 3rd Division's next assignment. Cross the Rhine? Go north and into Germany through the old Maginot Line? Or south, to join the French...?

Charles R. Castellaw

Table of Casualties[14]
Vosges Mountains and Early Colmar
(September 15, 1944 through January 21, 1945)

Killed in Action	1277
Wounded in Action	4852
Missing in Action	108
Total Battle Casualties	6237
Non-Battle Casualties	7895
Reinforcements Officers	195
Reinforcements E M	5667
Hospital Returned-to-Unit Off	196
Hospital Returned-to-Unit E M	6563
Known Enemy Casualties	
Killed in Action	1151
Wounded in Action	655
Captured	7258

Although many units of the 3rd Division seized the opportunities offered them to rest and rehabilitate in and near Strasbourg, at no time was the Division off the front lines or out of contact with the enemy.

Following elimination of the Kehl bridgehead (with the weird "Battle of the Apartments," and the end, by German surrender, of the publicized Mutzig *"Ostfort"),* nightly contacts in the form of vicious exchanges of fire across the Rhine punctuated the 7th and 15th Infantry Regiments' otherwise almost monotonous vigil along the banks of the river.

The Colmar Pocket

The 3rd Infantry Division was on the defensive for the second time in the war, but despite the lack of face-to-face contact it was an uneasy period. Through no direct connection with our activities, stalemate had overcome the Division as a whole. A crossing in strength of the Rhine River was not then feasible nor contemplated;

---

[14] Figures from AC or S, G-1, 3rd Infantry Division.

The Way It Was

consequently a good deal of wonderment was in store as to the immediate future.

To the north, other units of the Seventh Army were pushing into southern Germany. To the south, the First French Army, with the U.S. 36th Infantry Division attached, found with a growing realization that it still had on its hands an embarrassing German bulge west of the Rhine, and that temporarily it was unable to do anything about it. As the Germans, to preserve Colmar, pushed back some French units and elements of the 36th Division around Selestat, the fact emerged that here was no mere line on the situation map to be wiped out at leisure, but a stubbornly-fighting pocket of enemy who were becoming fortified more strongly daily, and that a full-scale coordinated army-sized attack was going to be required to eliminate them.

At first it was called "the bridgehead around Colmar," but as it persisted, a name was given it which stuck: "Colmar Pocket." The 3rd Infantry Division was to learn that it was a pocket bulging with fortifications and sudden death; and an area whose elimination was to develop into our second greatest fight of the entire war—some said the greatest—in the same degree of ferocity as the attack to break the Anzio "iron ring." Yet, even following the elimination of the Colmar Pocket, comparatively few persons on the outside knew Colmar, if they knew of it at all, as anything more than the name of an upper Alsatian city whose liberation came only after a lengthy period of waiting.

Following receipt of the Seventh Army order that 3rd Infantry Division would relieve 36th Infantry Division, 30th Infantry was designated as the vanguard, and commenced moving south on the afternoon of December 13, to be attached to the 36th.

The complete force was dubbed "Task Force McGarr"—so named because Col. Lionel C. McGarr (then acting Assistant Division Commander) was ordered to lead it into the Colmar Pocket action. Lt. Col. Richard H. Neddersen commanded the 30th Infantry. Initially the force was composed of the complete 30th Infantry; 41st Field Artillery Battalion; Company C of the 10th Engineers; Battery D, 441st Antiaircraft Battalion; a section of tanks from Company B, 753rd Tank Battalion; and a platoon of tanks and a section of tank destroyers from Combat Command IV, 5th French Armored Division *(Cinquie'me Division Blindee)*.

Charles R. Castellaw

The attack, which was coordinated with that of a regiment of the 36th Division, commenced one day before the enemy in the north launched the tremendous counteroffensive in the Ardennes-Schnee Eiffel area, although this was not known until two days later.

The 30th Infantry, of all the 3rd Division units, had had the least rest. During its 15-day stay in Strasbourg the 1st Battalion had been attached to the 2 DB (LeClerc's famed 2nd Armored) for the five-day engagement near Kogenheim for which twenty-three officers and men had been awarded the Croix de Guerre. Company E, in addition, had been assigned the mission of neutralizing the Mutzig fort, which it accomplished successfully.

The regiment's attack, following its commitment in the Colmar Pocket, got off between 0700 and 0800, December 15, the three battalions attacking simultaneously from assembly areas in the vicinity of Aubure and Freland. The 2nd and 3rd battalions moved through the mountainous forest of Sigolsheim into firing positions near Ursprung. The first opposition was encountered by Company I, which received intense enemy machine-gun fire at 1300 from a force emplaced on Hill 651, an irregular mountainous mass which dominated the then critically important Toggenbach-Alspach area. After a 25-minute firefight, Company I destroyed three machine guns, and killed several enemy riflemen.

The two assault battalions moved across the twin hill masses flanking Toggenbach. At 1417, approximately fifty Germans, manning concrete and earthwork emplacements of World War I type on Hill 672, opened fire on Company E with machine-guns, machine pistols, and rifles. Company E accepted the challenge. In a swift flanking movement it overwhelmed this segment of the German outpost line of resistance and swept southwest along the rugged wooded ridge toward Hill 621. The movement of the battalion along the ridge line which pointed like an arrow at Kaysersberg directly to the south was harassed by continuing small-arms and automatic fire, but the advance was uninterrupted.

We were in our foxholes in a holding position against what might be a counterattack by the enemy. We received word that one of our platoons had been destroyed by the enemy and for our platoon to counterattack. We walked over dead bodies and body parts, but to me the worst thing was the dying men that had turned blue and their eyes

The Way It Was

looking at you as if to say, "Help me." When you are in an attack in combat, you keep moving. You cannot stop to help a wounded soldier. The medic comes behind to take care of the dead and wounded. We were in a wooded area, moving from tree to tree. One of the men got my attention and pointed to a camouflaged pillbox that was almost impossible to see. The enemy was picking off our men one by one, using smokeless gun powder which made it almost impossible to locate them. I worked my way, moving from tree to tree, until I got within range and then I fired a white phosphorous grenade into the pillbox, destroying it. My thoughts were, not only do the Germans have good equipment, they are well-trained, intelligent soldiers.

My platoon leader was a very good man and had served his country well for quite some time, but he was falling apart. He had tolerated all the combat duty that he could take and was having a breakdown in combat effectiveness and had to be relieved of duty. I was appointed active platoon leader, to be in charge of the platoon until we received another platoon leader.

The 3rd battalion meanwhile advanced on Toggenbach, a cluster of houses between Aubure and Kaysersberg. A roadblock, manned by a determined German force, was reported 1300 meters north of the village, and a combat patrol was dispatched to demolish it. Sgt. William A. Nagowski was instrumental in clearing this roadblock. Another 3rd battalion patrol sliced the highway south of Toggenbach at 1500 after a brisk firefight.

While Company G was pounded by heavy howitzer fire along the high ground north of Hill 666, Company E organized night positions to the east of the Toggenbach road and plans were completed for the final assault on the village. One platoon of Company K guided on the ridgeline for the attack, but encountered a large force of determined enemy on the hillside due west of the village. Fighting in dim light in deep weeds at almost hand-to-hand range, the platoon took eighteen prisoners and killed or wounded the remainder of the German force.

Company G moved through a tempest of howitzer fire to establish night positions at the north base of Hill 666. Companies E and G were deluged by heavy artillery concentrations during the night, in one of which 2nd battalion CO Lt. Col. Frederick R. Armstrong was killed

Charles R. Castellaw

while personally assisting his most advanced assault unit—Company G—in its forward drive. Maj. James L. Osgard succeeded him.

At 2200, Company M headquarters repulsed a 10-man enemy patrol, wounding six of the attackers.

As engineers cleared the Toggenbach-Kaysersberg road of mines, tanks thrust their way through Toggenbach. At 1835, patrols of Company B established contact with Company I inside the village. Tanks and engineers with bridging materials moved up to await patrol reports on suitable crossing sites over the Weiss River. The report came back at 2250 that the stream could be crossed without difficulty near the Kaysersberg road, although the stream was swift and elsewhere and the banks steep.

Two separate reconnaissance patrols, one from Company I, the other from the 1st Battalion I & R Platoon, thrust into Kaysersberg, the heart of the enemy defensive position, and engaged an antitank strongpoint and drew withering fire from the buildings.

In the first day's action, Toggenbach had been captured, the Toggenbach-Alspach road cleared, a vital bridge site over the Weiss seized, and the first five houses in Kaysersberg taken. In addition, 2nd battalion had taken Hill 672, establishing a line of departure to attack Hills 666 and 621.

On December 16, the Task Force was strengthened by the addition of Companies C of 756th Tank Battalion 601st Tank Destroyer Battalion, and 3rd Medical Battalion, all normal attachments to the 30th.

The three battalions of the 30th were now ready to join in the assault on Kaysersberg, located on the rim of the Rhine plain where the Weiss River flows through a narrow channel between rugged, forested mountain masses, which flank the town to the north and south. East was the flatland of the Rhine; west the valley winds upward through the hills toward the La Bonhomme pass, one of the main corridors through the Vosges.

The 1st Battalion drew the assignment of crossing the Weiss and ascending the steep slopes of Hill 512, south of the town. The 2nd battalion was to thrust its way down the precipitous, oblong mountain mass to the north of Kaysersberg, consisting of Hills 616 and 612. The 3rd battalion had the assignment of driving into Kaysersberg itself to clear the town.

The Way It Was

There were confused clashes between patrols and isolated enemy groups as the 30th Infantry moved silently forward to join the battle in the early morning hours of December 16.

By 0630, Company B had moved through the factory area of Kaysersberg and found no enemy. The battalion attack on Hill 512 commenced. The main force was preceded by a screen of scouts, especially coached by Maj. Mackenzie E. Porter to be on the alert to report all evidences of enemy activity. The aim of the battalion commander was to gain his objective by stealth, avoiding all fighting until the troops were established on the crest of the hill.

Using circuitous routes, the 1st Battalion reached the trail net on Hill 512, which constituted the point agreed upon with French Goums. By 0930, the entire hill was cleared with no contact other than overrunning a five-man enemy observation post. The enemy began pounding the hill with mortar fire. The 1st Battalion sent out patrols to guard its positions and repel all counterattacks.

Meanwhile Company I had thrust aggressively into Kaysersberg from the southeast, followed by Company K and supporting armor. The hard, bloody work of house clearing began. Withering small-arms fire whipped up and back the narrow streets as our troops advanced. Company I changed commanders twice during the battle for the town.

By 1300, footholds had been gained in the heart of the town, at heavy cost. The 3rd battalion command post set up in Kaysersberg, and the work of clearing snipers continued. Suddenly, the enemy launched an all-out counterattack to regain his principal stronghold. Tanks opened fire on 3rd battalion troops in the town, while at the same time Companies I and L were hit from the east by a force of 300 Germans. Heavy artillery, mortar, tank, and machine-gun fire poured in on the troops in the town.

The counterattack continued for two hours, during which numerous separate acts of heroism stood out. The attack was repulsed, but the powerful German force, still determined to regain Kaysersberg, established and entrenched itself around the city, gathering its strength for new counterblows.

Meanwhile, 2nd battalion had commenced its attack on the hill mass north of Kaysersberg and east of the Toggenbach-Kaysersberg road. At 1300, Company E's 1st platoon moved to the nose of the long hill which ended at Kaysersberg while Companies F and G continued

205

Charles R. Castellaw

their slow advance along the wooded slopes of Hill 666 against heavy opposition.

The enemy held the oval hill mass with a determined force of crack troops, abundantly supplied with all types of weapons, and greatly aided by the concrete and earthwork strongpoints originally built by the French in the early part of the war.

The way was prepared by Cannon Company fire on Ammerschwihr and systematic pounding of the hostile hill positions with mortar rounds and machine-gun fire. The battalion then moved toward the crest. By mid-afternoon Company G was halted by fire from three concrete machine-gun emplacements, which were difficult to locate due to the dense vegetation in which they were sited. At approximately the same time Company F found its attack interrupted by intense fire from six enemy machine guns.

The 2nd battalion decided to postpone its attack and made preparations for a full-scale assault the following day. The engineers began to clear roads to the hill positions so that three tanks, assigned to the battalion from the 756th, could be brought into action. While diversionary fire was laid on the west side of the hill, Company E was to attack from the east. Clearing of these two hills was considered the key to the position and the central objective of Col. McGarr was in command of the Task Force.

The 1st Battalion, which had seized its objective swiftly and without strong opposition, rained artillery, mortar, and small-arms fire from Hill 512 on the Germans fleeing from Kaysersberg. A decision was made to strike southward from the hillcrest, setting up a roadblock at Bridge 267, commanding an important east-west highway leading from Ammerschwihr. First Lt. Charles P. Murray, Jr., Command Officer of Company C, led the two platoons which performed this mission and in accomplishing it performed an outstanding deed of gallantry and intrepidity to the successful accomplishment of the mission.

Unwilling to risk his men in the attack, Murray went forward with an SCR 536 to a suitable vantage point. Here he attempted to place artillery on the withdrawing enemy, but found his radio out of commission. Returning to his platoon, he borrowed an M-1 with grenade-launcher attachment, returned to his exposed position, and opened fire on the enemy. The German force of 200 replied with

The Way It Was

intense fire, but Lieutenant Murray stayed at his post until all of his ten grenades had been thrown. He withdrew to secure a BAR and returned to his hazardous position to engage the enemy in a half-hour attack. Fighting alone, he compelled the Germans to withdraw, leaving three 120mm mortars, then directed mortar fire on the withdrawing enemy with devastating effect; he led his men forward in an assault from foxhole to foxhole although wounded in eight places by an exploding grenade. He personally killed twenty and captured eleven of the enemy, for which he later received the Nation's highest award—the Congressional Medal of Honor.

On December 17, fighting in the Kaysersberg salient reached a climax. The 2nd battalion continued its difficult drive to seize the hill masses north of the city, and 1st Battalion weathered a furious German counterattack that was delivered with great power and determination. The 3rd battalion drove deeper into Kaysersberg under accelerated enemy artillery and mortar fire. Company I directed tank-destroyer fire on a medieval tower north of Kaysersberg which the enemy was employing as an observation post. Companies K and L advanced to the south and southwest of town and toward the base of Hill 512. Tank and bazooka fire was received from the northwest edge of the city, but the battalion directed artillery on the tanks, destroying one.

The fighting still continued unabated at noon. Heavy fighting also occurred at the Weiss River bridge. The enemy jabbed at 3rd battalion's positions with small-scale tank and infantry attacks. Attack and counterattack continued throughout the day with unflagging violence. By midnight, the enemy was definitely losing his hold.

The 2nd battalion jumped off on its all-out attack at 0645, December 17. Three tanks from the 756th Tank Battalion supported Company F in its attack on Hill 621 as Companies E and G drove on Hill 666, making such rapid progress that the section from Battery D, 441st AAA ("anti-anything, anytime") Battalion, which had fired sixty-three rounds of 37mm high-explosive shells and 2660 rounds of cal. 50 ammunition, was obliged to lift fire. Company E scaled the precipitous slope, losing eight men killed and seventeen wounded, but reaching the summit and killing, wounding, or capturing all Germans there. Simultaneously Company G made its frontal assault on the hill through a screen of enemy howitzer, mortar, machine-gun, and *Panzerfaust* fire.

Charles R. Castellaw

Hills 666 and 621 were cleared by 1130, with at least fifty Germans killed and a hundred wounded, plus thirty prisoners. Twenty machine guns were destroyed, and three mortars captured, as well as a vast quantity of small arms and ammunition.

Companies E and G regrouped and drove southeast toward Company F on Hill 621, encountering strong enemy opposition. In the fierce fight to make this linkup, troops of the battalion destroyed five more machine guns. They also killed thirty and captured forty-five more Germans in the all-afternoon fight, and themselves took heavy casualties. Contact was made with Company F at 1545 by Company G. The companies immediately began to organize night defensive positions. Despite incessant German infiltration and savage patrol combat in the forests, the battalion succeeded in maintaining its grip on the high ground.

The 1st Battalion's daylong fight had commenced with a German counterattack, delivered by an entire regiment, driving from three directions at once. The enemy swarmed toward Hill 512 from Ammerschwihr and Kaysersberg, hitting Company B's line at 0811.

The battalion had not had time to consolidate its hill positions and tie in closely with the remainder of the Task Force. There was but one mountain trail to the summit of Hill 512. No armor had been able to get to the summit and the battalion requirements of ammunition, food, and water had to be hand-carried up the trail, necessitating a four-hour trip each time.

At 0825, approximately a hundred enemy advanced from the southeast to drive a wedge between Companies B and C on the high ground designated Objective "X". By 0840, the three prongs of the enemy counterattack had overrun the eastern nose of the battalion position.

The Battalion CO, Major Porter, placed artillery fire on the enemy's rear to prevent reinforcement of the counterattack and pounded the Germans with a mortar concentration. The enemy, however, continued to gain ground, overrunning the eastern end of Company C's position.

Major Porter consolidated his forces and ordered the battalion to hold the high ridge line at all costs. The nose of the hill had been temporarily lost, but the crucial ridge line and the road net junction were firmly in our hands. The reinforced platoon at Bridge 267,

The Way It Was

finding itself isolated by the sudden counterattack, now fought its way back through hostile lines, finally reaching the ridge to join the defense.

The battalion engaged the Germans from its high ground position in a firefight that lasted all day and all night. The enemy forces were composed of German officer candidates, who had been promised that once they regained Kayserberg and the surrounding hills they would be returned to Germany to complete their courses. Fresh, fanatical, and more intelligent than the average *Landser,* these men fought with skill and determination. By the end of the day an estimated fifty had been killed and twice that number wounded.

The German recapture of Bridge 267 was disastrous for the enemy. Mortar and artillery fire placed on the bridge and roadblock was so intense that the enemy retreated, leaving behind twenty-five dead.

On December 18, Task Force McGarr was further strengthened by the addition of Company B, 99th Chemical Battalion, but the battalion's tank and tank-destroyer support from the French CC4 and 753rd Tank Battalion was withdrawn.

At daybreak, the 1st Battalion was still weathering furious counterattacks. It was noticed by Major Porter that the enemy chose the same avenues of assault; accordingly, he regrouped his forces so that they could effectively control with small-arms and machine-gun fire and mortars the draws and pathways along which the enemy so persistently advanced.

The supply problem grew more acute. The battalion rear echelon was mobilized, almost entirely, to carry ammunition. Supplies were thus assured for the rest of the day.

Patrols were sent from the beleaguered hill position. First Sgt. Nicholas F. Kiwatisky of Company B reflected the temper of several valorous actions by leading his small patrol deep into enemy territory, killing a machine gunner and assistant with M-1 fire at 200-yard range, and moving straight into the core of the German position to silence a second machine gun and kill seven enemy soldiers singlehandedly.

By 1300 the battalion had repulsed three counterattacks from the east, from Ammerschwihr, and from the southeast, each of them consisting of from 200 to 300 men supported by tank and self-

Charles R. Castellaw

propelled-gun fires. Three more counterattacks were hurled against the battalion during the afternoon and all were repelled. By 1845, after bringing the combined weight of all fires on the enemy, the counterattacks ceased. At 2055 a check revealed that 1st Battalion had not lost an inch of ground during the day's counterattacks.

During the morning of the 18th, the 2nd battalion expelled the Germans from their last remaining positions around Hill 621, then continued its drive to the southwest to link up with the Task Force positions in Kaysersberg. Company F remained behind to eliminate a small German pocket.

The 3rd battalion received counterattacks during the day but pressed forward, tightening its control over Kaysersberg and establishing patrol contact with the French CCV at approximately 1300. Company L, having cleared its sector of Kaysersberg, was ordered to move up the hill south of town to join 1st Battalion and reinforce its west flank. Preparations were made for the final attack to eliminate the enemy from his remaining positions on and around Hill 512.

The primary task of December 19 was to smash the German positions in the 1st Battalion sector. Tremendous preliminary fires deluged the enemy line. At 0815 1st Battalion, with Companies B and C in the assault, fell on the German force. By 0920 the enemy was driven in confusion from the nose of the hill which he had fought so desperately to retain. Dazed by the furious fire, the Germans put up little more than token resistance. Then, at 1115, Company C reported the establishment of contact with the French in Ammerschwihr and set up and manned a roadblock at Bridge 267.

Company F eliminated the pocket in its zone after a fierce firefight, destroying eight machine guns and three mortars and taking eleven prisoners, then continued over Hill 21 and entered Kayserberg at 1100.

At 1845 two battalions of enemy were sighted approaching Task Force positions from the west. Company C set up a roadblock on the Alspach-Kaysersberg road to thwart this move and brought a section of Flakwagons up for its defense.

At daybreak on December 20, the 441st Flakwagons fired 4,900 rounds of 50 caliber ammunition and 170 rounds of 37mm HE ammunition, saturating the woods where the Germans were preparing

The Way It Was

their counterattack. The 30th Infantry, with the aid of this fire, shattered this counterattack before it got under way.

At 1030 another and final enemy blow was reported in preparation, this time from the south in the vicinity of Bridge 267. Again the Task Force deluged the assembly areas of the Germans with artillery, mortar, and cannon fire. Results of the entire mission, now completed, were striking. A 5,000-meter German penetration between the 3rd French DIA *(Division Infanterie Algerienne)* and the 36th U.S. Infantry Division had been sealed off and smashed, opening a vital supply artery from St. Dié to the Rhine Valley for the passage of troops and material. A preliminary battle to the major offensive that was to obliterate the Colmar Pocket had been waged and won.

The accomplishment of this task involved the most exacting type of mountain warfare in icy weather. Scaling steep slopes, their passage was barred by a tangled undergrowth and a maze of forest. Subjected to harrowing fire from German casemates of lumber, earthwork, and concrete, the men of Task Force McGarr had fought with determination and quiet heroism.

Prisoner interrogation revealed that nine battalions of German infantry, two of engineers, a specialized support battalion and a minimum of four artillery battalions had been shattered. The victory was accomplished at a cost to the Task Force of fifty-eight killed, eighteen missing, and 190 wounded. In comparison, known enemy losses were 298 killed, 327 prisoners, and an estimated 1185 wounded. In addition, the enemy lost four tanks, twelve mortars, two Flakwagons, forty machine guns, and a large number of artillery pieces.

The 41st Field Artillery Battalion fired 7226 rounds of 105mm Howitzer ammunition in seventy-four concentrations and ten TOTs (time on target, a system whereby the fire of all guns of a given number of artillery units is brought to bear simultaneously). Cannon Company fired 5864 rounds of 105 and 75mm ammunition, and a total of ninety-nine rounds of 4.2 mortar ammunition were expended by Company B, 99th Chemical Battalion.

Charles R. Castellaw

Bennwihr and Sigolsheim

Beginning December 16, the Fifth and Sixth *Panzer* Armies of Field Marshal Von Rundstedt lashed out in a counteroffensive in Belgium and Luxembourg which stunned the entire Allied camp. Known later as "Battle of the Bulge," German elements achieved a maximum penetration of approximately fifty-five miles before the tide of battle turned and the Third and Ninth Armies to either flank of the attacked United States First Army began slashing at the sides of the Bulge. Colmar Pocket, in the big picture, was an irritating little red grease-penciled twist on the lower end of the situation map, only a minor battle—unless one was there.

On December 17, the 3rd Infantry Division began moving south for the continuance of the relief of 36th Infantry Division. The 2nd battalion, 15th Infantry, was first relieved to commence its move to the vicinity of Riquewihr, where it closed in on the following day. The 3rd and 1st Battalions followed it on December 19. The 1st and 2nd battalions, 7th Infantry were completely relieved on defensive positions in Strasbourg by other elements of the 36th Division, and command of the former 36th sector passed to Brigadier General Robert N. Young (commanding the Division in the absence of General O'Daniel, on temporary duty in the United States) at 1430, December 21.

Two days later, December 23, the 15th Infantry launched an attack against the two towns of Bennwihr and Sigolsheim, as the first step in securing a more stable line of defense. Defense was the keynote at this time. The Seventh Army had received a sizable German counterattack against its barely won positions in southern Germany and was forced to withdraw to a more tenable line in lower Alsace. It was known that the Germans had announced their intentions of retaking Strasbourg, if possible, as a "Christmas present" for *der Fuhrer*. A pincers between the forces opposing Seventh Army forces and those opposing French First Army, of which the 3rd Infantry Division was now a part, was considered a definite possibility. Our first step, therefore, was to secure Bennwihr and Sigolsheim, the last two towns of any size between that part of our line and the key city of

The Way It Was

Colmar, and to drive the Germans from all high ground north of a line Sigolsheim-Kayersberg.

Sigolsheim and Bennwihr are located at the extreme western edge of the Alsace Plain and just east of the last high slopes of the Vosges. Advance reconnaissance indicated that Sigoisheim in particular was strongly occupied by the enemy, and later events proved this to be entirely true.

Besides drawing the assignment to take the two towns, 15th Infantry also had the mission of clearing Hill 351, a high mass that lies between them.

The 15th's drive was directed east from positions in the vicinity of Kientzheim, which was held by the 2nd battalion, 30th Infantry. The 1st Battalion, commanded by Lt. Col. Keith L. Ware, was to capture Sigolsheim; the 3rd battalion, under Maj. John O'Connell, to attack Bennwihr, and the 2nd battalion, under Lt. Col. Eugene A. Salet, was to block and support the attack of the other battalions from positions on the northern slope of Hill 351.

At H-hour, 0730, Companies A and C attacked. Particularly stiff resistance was encountered just before reaching the town when a convent just north of it was found to be an enemy stronghold, with enemy manning machine guns, mortars, and small arms. After a stiff two-hour fight, Company A succeeded in pressing through and past this opposition to reach the edge of town at noon.

The entrance of Company A into the town of Sigolsheim was only a forerunner to a terrific fight that lasted five days. The small village was a shambles, having been reduced by our bombers and artillery and by tank and tank-destroyer fire provided by the 601st and 756th attachments to 1st Battalion, 15th Infantry, under command of Lt. Colonel Ware.

The 3rd battalion, meanwhile, had marched south from Mittelwihr in the morning and attacked Bennwihr from the north and west. Companies I and K under command of Captains Warren M. Stuart and Robert W. Hahn, respectively, moved into the town at 0800, and it seemed as if resistance would be light until Company K suddenly came under terrific fire from a school near the center of the village.

Accepting the challenge, Company K stormed the school. The enemy was entrenched in the rubble of houses and cellars, and resisted bitterly. Finally Company K drove the enemy from the school

213

Charles R. Castellaw

and established the buildings as a temporary prisoner of war cage. The conquest, however, was short-lived. A desperate enemy counterattack was launched that afternoon and the Germans retook the school and some sixty prisoners who were being held in it. Enemy armor figured strongly in this attack; a Mark IV tank was reported to have withstood several bazooka and rifle-grenade shots which apparently struck it squarely. As darkness came, the 3rd battalion withdrew slightly to prepare for another attack the following morning.

In Sigolsheim, too, there was a bitter fight. Several armored vehicles of the 756th Tank Battalion, under command of Lt. Col. Glenn F. Rogers, bogged down in the muddy terrain, thus reducing the striking power of our force.

Complete penetration into the village had not been accomplished. The battalion was still attempting to gain a good toehold in Sigolsheim when the enemy counterattacked from the center of town with infantry and armor late that night, and from the direction of Hill 351 to the north, with mortar and artillery fire. The position became untenable and 1st Battalion relinquished its slender hold on Sigolsheim and, under orders, withdrew to Kientzheim and Riquewihr for the night.

It was now apparent that before any position in Sigolsheim could be held, the enemy must be driven completely from Hill 351 or else the same thing would happen again.

During darkness Companies K and L, the latter commanded by 1st Lt. Earl B. Hobbs, struck Bennwihr again in an early morning thrust, this time from the east. Each company destroyed an enemy tank shortly after the attack got underway and this seemed to help demoralize the enemy, who always had placed a gook deal of faith in his supporting armor. Moving in, the 3rd battalion again commenced the grinding, dangerous, and physically exhausting work of eliminating the enemy form the basements and house-fragments of Bennwihr. By 12:25, a major portion of the town had been cleared.

Intent on eliminating the harassing interference from Hill 351, 1st Battalion attacked up the northwestern slope of the hill on the morning of December 24, from the direction of Riquewihr. Company B, commanded by 1st Lt. George W. Mohr, encountered a heavy firefight en route, coming under machine-gun and small-arms fire from well dug-in and concealed positions. This pocket was eliminated

The Way It Was

and the company proceeded. Company A, under Capt. Elmo F. Tefanelli, reached the top of the hill twice, but was badly disorganized on the barren slopes by heavy flanking fire and concentrations of mortar and artillery, and was forced to withdraw. Company C, commanded by Capt. Samuel H. Roberts, took up the fight and, with Company B, succeeded in reaching the northeast slope of the hill at noon.

At this point Lt. Col. Keith L. Ware, 1st Battalion commander, reviewed the situation and decided that a vigorous display of personal leadership was necessary to invigorate the troops with an offensive spirit that had been dampened by the extremely heavy losses that had been sustained, the icy-cold weather, and the continuous fighting.

After a two-hour personal reconnaissance, he led a handful of men and a tank in a daring assault on the enemy positions on top of the hill, which was crowned with six enemy machine guns.

In describing Colonel Ware's action, Capt. Merlin C. Stoker, S-3 of the 1st Battalion and himself a member of the group that went with the Colonel, said: "It is my opinion that Colonel Ware's display of icy courage was an act not only of heroism but of necessity. It was essential that the deadlock in the Sigolsheim sector be broken and that the discouraged troops be given a new injection of the offensive spirit."

Capt. Vernon L. Rankin, commanding Company D, who directed mortar fire on the hill during the assault, said that Colonel Ware personally killed five Germans and captured about twenty others. Tank fire, which the Colonel directed, accounted for four of the six machine guns that comprised the hard core of the German hill position. At the end of the assault, twenty German dead were counted, thirty captured, and about 150 crack troop, were put to flight.

Colonel Ware was awarded the Congressional Medal of Honor for this feat.

The 2nd battalion coordinated its fires with the attack of the 1st in the final clearing of all-important Hill 351.

The 3rd battalion, having cleared all but a few houses on the south edge of Bennwihr, proposed to turn southeast out of the city but again struck a stronghold at a road junction on the edge of town. A platoon of Company K, which had been deployed in the vicinity of the junction, was attacked from two directions, from the southern edge of

Hill 351 and from the basements of houses that lined the roads at the intersection. As the Germans closed in from Hill 351, the others, apparently in a prearranged plan, jumped yelling from the basement windows. The remainder of Company K, with a tank destroyer, took up the fight, but the enemy also brought in reinforcements and forced the company back. Captain Stuart then reorganized his men, launched them into a fierce counterattack, and by 16:00 the company had killed a great number of Germans and retaken control of the road junction.

This terrific fight over a mere road junction was typical of the entire fight over the small area. Bennwihr and Hill 351 were still the scenes of great violence as night came on—the eve of the birth of the Prince of Peace.

The roast turkey, creamed potatoes, and other supplementary items which the Division Quartermaster had received for the Yule dinner were not to be consumed on Christmas Day by the 15th Infantry. On the contrary, the day was to be only another fierce episode that saw the Germans resisting with a fanaticism generated partly by the exaggerated version of the Rundstedt drive to the north given them by their superiors.

Statements from prisoners indicated that the enemy morale, especially that of the younger and more fanatical soldiers, had been greatly raised by such statements as, "The U.S. First Army has been completely destroyed," which led them to believe that help from northern Germany would soon be on the way.

West of Echternach the Germans had been engaged at two points near the frontier. The columns of the enemy had been halted some thirty miles from Namur, Liége, and Sedan Gap.

On the north flank, the enemy had failed to take his objectives. The shoulder of the salient above Stavelot was beaten back some six miles. In Belgium, the advance was not halted but was being well canalized. Elements of the 1st SS Division were cut off with the loss of fifteen tanks and 200 prisoners taken. The two regimental combat teams of the U.S. 106th Infantry Division that had been cut off during the initial phases of the counteroffensive had made contact and were still fighting. They were being supplied from the air.

The 84th Infantry Division had just been committed south of Maffe. The 2nd Armored and 75th Infantry Divisions were assembled just to the north. Some 7,000 Allied air sorties were flown on

The Way It Was

December 24. Ten thousand tons of bombs were dropped. One hundred and sixteen enemy aircraft were destroyed. Enemy movements were limited to darkness. One spectacular raid blew up a hundred vehicles loaded with gasoline.

Goebbels told the Germans that it was the worst Christmas of the war. He also told them not to worry, that the Fuhrer was filled with plans and visions for the future.

On the main street of Bennwihr, a small figure was implanted in the ground in front of a ruined church. It was a reproduction of Christ crucified. The head was missing.

Although Company K held the road junction at the dawn of Christmas Day, enemy snipers and machine gunners in the houses near the junction wrought death and injury on a number of our men in that area. At 1700, flame-throwers were brought into use and several houses were fired. In a little more than an hour, over fifty Germans had surrendered and the other occupants were either casualties or had retreated to a safer place to spend the rest of the holiday.

Hill 351, Bennwihr, the little road junction outside Bennwihr, and a large number of prisoners constituted the holiday gift that Brig. Gen. Robert N. Young, acting division commander, received from the 15th Infantry.

Sigolsheim remained as the only uncaptured objective of the regiment's offensive, and it was attacked from the east on December 26-27.

The 1st Battalion, after clearing out some of the diehards on Hill 351, tied in with 2nd battalion on the left. Company G moved to the road east of the town and joined with Companies K and L, which had been driven back after attacking the east side of the village Christmas night.

The coordinated attack began at 0930, December 26, with Company K advancing along the north road into town from the east, Company L moving along the center road and Company G taking the south road. Air-support missions were also being flown.

The enemy put up a suicidal defense as he fell back from house to house in the streets of Sigolsheim. It was not unusual to see a German standing completely exposed in the center of the street, firing a bazooka or sometimes only a rifle at our tanks as the armor relentlessly mowed him down or the doughboys took pot shots at him.

Charles R. Castellaw

The fighting continued unabated all day, throughout the night and into the next day. Company K was the first unit to report its zone "all clear." When the company finished mopping up the northern part of the town at 1450, it swung north toward the convent, which, like Hill 351, had been a thorn in the side of the regiment's operations ever since the attack began.

Company L found opposition stiffest in the center of town but continually kept pounding at strongpoints behind rubble, stone fences and pillboxes until the enemy finally began disintegrating and retreating from the city in small groups.

During Company I's bitter fight to clear the enemy from the houses they held in the fire-swept streets of Sigolsheim, 1st Lt. Eli Whiteley particularly distinguished himself and earned the Medal of Honor. In the midst of the savage street fighting, he was hit and badly wounded in the arm and shoulder. Despite this, he attacked alone a house on the street, fire from which was delaying the advance of the company. He killed its two defenders. Hurling smoke and fragmentation grenades, he charged a second house, killed two and captured eleven enemy soldiers. He continued to lead his platoon down the battle-crazy street, eliminating house after house. Finally, he reached a building held by fanatical Nazis. Although suffering from painful wounds which had rendered his left arm useless, he advanced on this strongly defended house and, after blasting out a wall with bazooka fire, charged through a hail of bullets. Wedging his sub-machine gun under his uninjured arm, he rushed into the house through the hole torn by his rockets, killed five of the enemy and forced the remaining twelve to surrender. As he emerged to continue his fearless attack, he was hit again and critically wounded. In agony and with one eye pierced by a shell fragment, he shouted for his men to follow him to the next house. He was determined to stay in the fighting and did remain at the head of his platoon until forcibly evacuated..."

Company G met the same fanatical resistance in the south part of the city but cleared its section shortly before Company L.

Late that night the town was completely cleared of Germans and the 15th Infantry had captured another hundred prisoners. The regimental I and R platoons, under 1st Lt. Robert Wann, were attached to 3rd battalion for the battle, and distinguished themselves in combat.

The Way It Was

The convent fell to Company K early the following morning after an all-night siege. The monastery gave up fifty more prisoners, in addition to about 150 civilians hiding in the basement.

While the remainder of the regiment was concentrating on the Sigolsheim attack, Company E, commanded by Capt. Charles Adams, cleared the enemy from the area north of the Weiss River, which was the right boundary of the regiment. This mission in itself resulted in many firefights in which the enemy used mortars, machine guns, and Flakwagons. More than twenty Germans were killed in one of these engagements.

In this area, however, the enemy proved himself particularly obstinate. His infiltration back into the area along the Weiss became a nightly process, and it was necessary to work the vicinity over again and again, since the Weiss was easily forded.

A nasty surprise awaited our troops on Hill 216. Previously reported clear of enemy, the enemy soon proved in occupation of the crest (which was east of the road leading south from Bennwihr) in sizable strength and determined to hold.

Throughout 15th Infantry's occupation of the Bennwihr-Sigolsheim area, and 30th Infantry's subsequent control of the sector, Hill 216 with its sizable, determined forces of enemy defenders, was a salient into our lines. The western side was cleared only after a series of small attacks by 15th and 30th Infantry, but the enemy remained in control of the east side up until the full-scale Division attack which commenced January 22, when the 254th Infantry drove him from it. The crest was no-man's land.

In addition to capturing Bennwihr and Sigolsheim, the 15th Infantry had annihilated the *Zeiher* Battle Group and the SS Battle Group *Braun,* taking nearly 500 prisoners during the last ten days of December.

Following clearance of the 15th Infantry sector to the Fecht River on the east, the Division began regrouping, and received as an attachment the 254th Infantry of the 63rd Infantry Division to assist in defending the Division front, which had been broadened by the removal of the 3rd Algerian Division, the unit that occupied our right flank during the Sigolsheim-Bennwihr offensive. The purpose of attaching the 254th was to add to the Division's strength and to give the regiment combat seasoning.

Charles R. Castellaw

On New Year's day the Division sector in the Vosges Mountains covered a frontage of approximately fifteen miles between Chatenois (west of Selestat) and Orbey, which is just south of La Poutroie.

The 15th Infantry held the longest front, its line running from Chatenois, through Bennwihr, to a point west of Alspach. The 7th Infantry's line began at Alspach and terminated at Orbey.

There were numerous adjustments to the Division boundary during the first three weeks of January, chief of which was the extension of the Division front about six miles west into high Vosges.

These were the days of the "great scare." Even though the enemy had by now been definitely stopped in the Ardennes and the Bulge was being slowly whittled away, although the Seventh Army had temporarily halted with considerable loss the renewed offensive toward the south, the enemy still held the initiative in most areas of the front. A decision to move administrative elements out of Strasbourg, pending the necessity of withdrawing tactical troops to the Vosges, precipitated a panic in the Alsatian Capital. A large number of loyal Frenchmen were fleeing the city in terror of their lives should the Germans return. United States and French flags disappeared from the windows, to be replaced in some instances with the swastika. Two men from the Strasbourg staff of the *Stars and Stripes* and three members of the 3rd Division's *Front Line* staff formed the only U.S. administrative establishment remaining in the city. (The command post and some troops of 42nd Infantry Division, in tactical control of the area, remained in Strasbourg throughout this period.) The two newspaper groups worked together in producing a *Stars and Stripes* with a special, boxed daily column in French for the benefit of the panic-stricken population. It and the daily presence of Americans did much to dispel many of the Alsatians' fears. The *Front Line* likewise continued to make its regular weekly appearance.

Division Order of Battle personnel had some difficulty in piecing together some of the rag, tag and bobtail which opposed the Division on its long front. Upon moving into the sector, we inherited from the 36th Division the following Battle Groups (each of about battalion size): *Ayrer, Bermann, Backe, Braun, SS Dietrichs, Eberle, Fischer; Fuhrguth, Geiser; Herbrechtsmeier, Hock, Huth, Krebs, Landeberger; Lang, Probst, Reimers, Remmes, Schaefer, Scheck, Schweitzer, Waliner, Wasser, Zeihter,* and *Winter.*

The Way It Was

As the Division took its own prisoners, however, these elements shook down and sorted themselves generally into members of regular divisions, principal of which were the 198th Infantry Division, 708th *Volksgrenadier* Division, 16th and 189th Infantry Divisions. Toward the end of December, two battalions of the 40th *Panzer Grenadier* Replacement Training Battalion made their appearance. Also known to be on the bridgehead and against some of which the 3rd Infantry Division later fought were: 269th VG Division, 159th VG Division and 338th Infantry Division.

The 254th Infantry, attached to the 3rd, was assigned a defensive sector during the adjustments and the 290th Engineer Combat Battalion, a unit with no previous battle experience, was attached for use as infantry. A French parachute battalion was also attached.

Winter weather was present with all its mountain fury with the coming of January and frostbite cases were added to the trench foot casualties brought by cool, rainy days the previous three months.

Generally speaking, the situation in the first three weeks was characterized by defensive actions and patrolling on both sides, with the east slopes of Hill 216 occupying the most important role.

It was a snowy and cold New Year's Eve and the 10th Engineer Battalion was busy all night keeping roads passable. Company A, commanded by Capt. Albert H. Cook, spread cinders and sand on the road from Kaysersberg. Company B, under Capt. Daniel A. Raymond, de-iced and drained the Riquewihr-Kientzheim road, while Company C, commanded by 1st Lt. Robert L. Bangert, continued the never-ending task of erecting triple concertina wire around and in front of our positions.

By the end of December 1944, the battle to reduce the Colmar Pocket had reached a stalemate. The fury of the battle had resulted in heavy casualties to both enemy and our own forces. While French forces were being readjusted to either continue the attack or to meet a German attack to retake the Vosges Mountains and Strasbourg, the Regiment was extended thinly over a wide front with the mission of holding an MLR extending 2000 meters East of Sigolsheim to the heart of the forest of Bois Communal de Kaysersberg. For this purpose, the 1st Battalion and the AT Company of the 254th Infantry Regiment were attached. At the close of the period, the 1st Battalion was to be relieved by the 1st Battalion, 254th Infantry Regiment.

221

Charles R. Castellaw

Meanwhile defensive organization was being steadily improved, mines and booby traps were being installed, and extensive tactical and protective wire was being laid. Aggressive patrolling to harass and probe the enemy positions was being conducted nightly.

While in the Strasbourg sector we found the enemy air to be more active than usual. He flew several strafing and bombing missions, but our successful AA defense brought a good number of his planes down.

At the middle of the period we were taken from our reserve position and moved south to the Kaysersberg sector to attack and clear enemy from the Kaysersberg hills. Our attack carried us over the same sort of rugged terrain we had grown to accept as typical of the Vosges Mountains, dense forests, steep mountains and deep narrow valleys and draws. The enemy occupied strong points of resistance that had to be reduced one by one. Of unusual strength was the resistance met on the high ground just North of Kaysersberg. There the enemy was in the strength of one small battalion, and in a position to avail themselves of some World War I fortifications. These old fortifications consisted of badly eroded trenches and concrete bunkers, both so well overgrown with brush that it was practically impossible to detect them until fire disclosed these positions.

One of our battalions made a sneak stream-crossing of the Weiss River during the hours of darkness, and was able to drive the enemy from the nose of high ground south of the town. Another battalion, after sharp patrol clashes, was able to enter and occupy most of Kaysersberg proper against moderate resistance.

We did not have long to remain in these positions before the enemy started his counterattacks. That the enemy considered our newly won sector to be one of great importance is proven by the ferocity of his counterattacks. He first hit our 1st Battalion on the high ground South of Kaysersberg. Striking from the south, east and northeast with a series of counterattacks ranging in size from platoons to two battalions, the enemy stormed our positions with a fanatical fury that broke against our hastily prepared defenses and left his dead literally in stacks. For all his efforts in this sector, the enemy's attacks were of limited short-lived success. He did succeed in forcing our B Company back from hill 409 on the Eastern end of the hill mass but our counterattacks of the following day restored this position.

The Way It Was

In Kaysersberg, the enemy launched a counterattack of about one battalion plus units that had previously occupied the town. Attacking under a blanket of artillery and supported by at least five tanks and SP's, the enemy succeeded in occupying about one half of the town. This fighting was of a bitter house-to-house and room-by-room type with every bit of the town bitterly contested. When the French armored force attacked through us, they were successful in driving the enemy from Kaysersberg and pushing on to take Ammerschwihr and Kientzheim.

We occupied Kaysersberg, Kientzheim, Ammerschwihr, and the high ground north and south of Kaysersberg. Immediately we started a program of aggressive patrols to probe the enemy positions and keep him worried about his own security. These patrols had been able to work deep into enemy territory by locating gaps in his lines. Many of our patrols carried radios and were able to adjust fire on located enemy positions. On his side, the enemy attempted many patrols, but most of these were beaten off by mortar fire before they reached our positions. In several instances, our patrols were in a position to shoot up the enemy patrols before he could clear his front lines.

After Sigolsheim was taken and we occupied it, the enemy attempted several counterattacks of company size or larger. In most cases the attacks were located and beaten off by artillery, mortar and Cannon Company fire. The few elements that reached our lines were promptly driven back.

Enemy artillery for the latter half of this period may be classified as heavy. He employed tanks, SP's, heavy mortars and all classes of artillery to harass our positions in and around the towns.

Many units were identified in our sector. Most interesting of these were the school troop battalions, consisting of groups of OCS, NCO, and various technical schools assembled and used as Infantry. All troops of this class demonstrated a most aggressive spirit and generally high individual fighting qualities. SS troops were employed as ordinary Infantry, especially in defensive positions of importance.

We were troubled by activities of enemy agents all through our present sector. Several radio transmitters were located, one with a map showing our positions in Kaysersberg. Some cases of mines and booby traps in our lines were located before they did any harm.

Charles R. Castellaw

In general, the enemy bitterly contested our occupation of our present sector with strong counterattacks, artillery and fifth column activities. His losses were extremely heavy, especially in his counterattacks. At the close of the period, the enemy continued his patrols and use of artillery but generally seemed satisfied to remain on the defensive.

Late one night Company E of the 30th Infantry, commanded by 1st Lt. Douglas W. Chambers, engaged a strong enemy patrol in a small arms fight in the woods north of the Weiss River and another German patrol overran the outposts of Company F, commanded by 1st Lt. Richard N. Hagelin. These outposts, located south of Hill 216, were reestablished before daylight, however.

At about midnight of January 2, Companies E and F of the 15th Infantry attacked south along the eastern slopes of Hill 216, intent on clearing the hill and the area south to the Weiss River. The 30th Infantry assisted the attack by sending out three strong combat patrols with artillery support.

Company E of the 15th met heavy resistance at a road curve northeast of the hill and suffered heavy casualties when the enemy set up a searing defense with machine guns, *Panzerfaust,* small arms, mortars, and hand grenades. The attack, originally scheduled as a strong raid supported by tanks, quickly turned into a bloody full-scale pitched engagement. Two of the supporting tanks were almost immediately destroyed by either *Panzerfaust* or antitank fire as they crossed the rise of the crest, and the company commander, Capt. Charles E. Adams, went forward to supervise his men personally. While he was moving forward he stepped into a hole in which there was an enemy soldier, who immediately shot and killed him. The company was disorganized and forced to fall back.

Company F, commanded by Capt. Hugh H. Bruner, proceeded will down the forward slopes of the hill but was hit by a strong enemy counterattack early in the morning. A heavy firefight ensued but Company F held its ground. A short time later, the Germans launched another counterattack supported by tanks and Captain Bruner's five men fell back to the road leading to Bennwihr. The two companies took sixteen prisoners in the attack. The enemy's reluctance to abandon any of the terrain under his control was proving costly to

The Way It Was

both forces and the pocket of resistance of Hill 216 developed into a bloody battlefield.

Enemy patrols, clad in white garments as camouflage in the snow, were little less aggressive than our own, and continuous clashes between them took place during the next several days. Our own troops, without camouflage clothing, improvised by using mattress covers.

On January 4 the Division sector was extended on the right to include Le Rudlin and abandoned on the left to exclude Zellenberg and Ostheim. The 15th Infantry, which had occupied the extreme left of the Division front, moved to the extreme right, putting our troops deeper into the heights of the Vosges.

A strong German counterattack against the 1st French Motorized Infantry Division, on the Division's left flank, was launched January 7 and resulted in the extension of the 3rd Division's zone farther north, and the 254th Infantry was regrouped to take over the newly acquired sector in the vicinity of Ribeauville.

Assisted by diversionary fire by the 7th Infantry's field artillery, chemical, tank, tank-destroyer, and anti-aircraft attachments, the 30th Infantry staged two attacks on January 8, the purpose being to divert the enemy's attention from the fact that an Allied division was being replaced in another sector of the perimeter surrounding the enemy Colmar bridgehead.

Company A, commanded by 1st Lt. Willard C. Johnson, moved through Company C at 1430, under cover of smoke from 4.2 chemical mortars and 81mm mortars, and reached the crest of Hill 216 after overcoming resistance from dug-in infantry using small arms and machine guns. After killing and capturing a number of Germans, Company C, commanded by 1st Lt. Charles P. Murray, Jr, relieved Company A in its new positions.

Simultaneously Company I, under 1st Lt. Darwyn E. Walker, attacked south from Ammerschwihr toward Hill 616, which lies just west of Katzenthal. Company C of the 756th Tank Battalion, commanded by Capt. John W. Heard, was in close support of the attackers.

After a difficult 45-minute climb through the heavy snow, the company came under enemy fire from German positions halfway up the hill and about eighty-five yards to the front. A Flakwagon on a hill

Charles R. Castellaw

500 yards southwest of Hill 616 poured extremely accurate fire on Lieutenant Walker's men and they were forced back to cover in a clump of trees. A second attack ended in the same manner and the company swung around the hill out of range of the Flakwagon and attacked for the third time.

It was here that S/Sgt. Russell E. Dunham, acting platoon sergeant of the 3rd platoon and commonly known to his buddies as "The Arsenal," performed the actions that earned him the Congressional Medal of Honor.

Dunham carried a dozen hand grenades that hung from his suspenders, from the buttonholes in his clothes and from his belt. And he had eleven full magazines of carbine ammunition, four in pouches, seven more in his pockets.

The enemy machine guns had a clear, snow-covered field of fire from solidly built emplacements covered with logs hidden by recent heavy snows. Two-man foxholes protected the machine-gun position from all sides.

Dunham's platoon moved forward, with the sergeant far out in front, crawling from small bush to tree stump into the very face of the German fire. A machine gun on the left of his platoon front received first attention and Dunham edged his way toward it until he reached a point about ten yards away. Jumping to his feet, he charged the position, throwing hand grenades, firing his carbine from the hip and yelling as he went. A second machine gun on the right fired a full clip at him and Dunham fell, a 10-inch gash ripped across his back.

The doughty sergeant rolled fifteen feet down the hill, arose, and charged again as his mattress-cover uniform turned red with blood. An enemy egg grenade fell at his feet, was quickly kicked aside and exploded in the snow several yards away. Dunham continued to fire, killed the machine gunner and his assistant, and yanked a third German from the emplacement when his carbine was empty.

Refusing evacuation by the medics, Dunham led the advance on the second machine gun some seventy-five yards up the hill. Again, he was the lone figure out in front, leaving a crimson trail in the snow as he crept toward the blazing gun. Rifle fire and rifle grenades raked his path. Dunham got within throwing range and tossed a grenade that bounced off a tree a little to the right of the machine gun

The Way It Was

emplacement. His next heave was a bull's eye that killed the entire gun crew.

Two Germans raised their heads from a nearby foxhole to take a bead on Dunham. The sergeant promptly killed one and wounded the other, winging a third who tried to escape.

The mattress cover was rosy as Sergeant Dunham briefed his platoon for the attack on a third machine gun hidden about a hundred yards up on the side of the hill. Again, he was the platoon's "advance element" as he sneaked to the kill.

This time he was favored with a deserving stroke of luck when a German fired point blank at him and missed after Dunham had just tossed a grenade that neutralized the gun. The poor-shooting rifleman fell dead from a Dunham bullet. Another shouted *"Kamerad"* and gave up.

Dunham continued his maniacal attack on enemy foxholes, killed one more German, shot five others as they attempted to flee, and took another prisoner.

Dunham's total was three enemy machine guns destroyed, nine dead Germans, seven wounded, and two prisoners. He had fired 175 rounds of ammunition and tossed eleven of his twelve hand grenades.

Praise was later heaped upon Dunham by Lieutenant Walker, his company commander, and by 2nd Lt. Glenn A. Black who had been Dunham's first sergeant on the day of the attack, prior to receiving a battlefield promotion.

The next few days featured the normal firefights that come with vigorous patrolling and in addition, some of the bitterest give-and-take small engagements the Division ever had encountered. Frequent efforts were made by the enemy to infiltrate our positions to obtain information concerning the shifts that were being made in the front lines of the 3rd Division.

The nights were moonless and bitterly cold; the days chilly and misty and both forces were using houses scattered throughout the area in "no-man's land" as outposts. The Division Operations Report rarely failed to record an account of an attack on one or more of them, either by our patrols or by the enemy.

Preceded by an artillery and mortar barrage, a strong enemy patrol staged a midnight raid January 9 on a platoon command post near La

Charles R. Castellaw

Baroche and took one officer and seven men, retiring under cover of artillery fire.

A patrol leader of Company L, 7th Infantry, S/Sgt. Herman F. Nevers, reported the same night that he had been seized and taken to a house in the La Baroche vicinity and effected an escape while he was being questioned when he drew a small non-functioning pistol that he had concealed in one of his boots. He held the surprised Germans at bay and backed out of the building into the darkness.

A 254th Infantry outpost was also attacked that night by a patrol of superior force and had to withdraw from its position until the next morning.

An enemy propaganda truck, interspersing subversive words with popular American "hillbilly" music, turned its loud speakers toward the 7th Infantry sector while the men were sweating "chow" on the night of January 10. Our artillery answered with well-placed fire that silenced the music.

Our artillery also stopped a sizable attack by an infiltrating group that reached a point west of Ammerschwihr on January 15. A similar attack on an outpost near Ostheim was staged the next morning and the Germans took thirteen prisoners. This latter attack, however, was overshadowed by a highly successful raid conducted the same morning by the 3rd battalion of the 7th Infantry, commanded by Lt. Col. Lloyd B. Ramsey.

Company L, commanded by Capt. Phillip T. Perry, crossed its line of departure at 0630 and immediately encountered heavy enemy mortar and small-arms fire near La Baroche, and a concentration of eight German machine guns north of this point held up the company's advance.

A house that contained about thirty enemy was blown up when one of Captain Perry's men placed a satchel charge in it. Three enemy machine guns also were silenced before the raiders withdrew.

Companies I and K, under Captains Edward J. Brink and Francis J. Kret, respectively, attacked south at a point east of Company L's effort. Company I headed toward the little village of Braderhau, neutralized a machine gun, and captured a few prisoners en route. A heavy firefight ensued when a strong enemy force was encountered just north of Braderhau. Four more German machine guns were destroyed in this battle.

The Way It Was

Company K also silenced four enemy machine guns, killed a large number of Germans, and forced the foe to desert his positions in the area.

The regimental Battle Patrol assisted the 3rd battalion's raid with a diversionary attack on Hill 806, near La Rochette. This raid, which was started and ended before daylight, brought several casualties to the Patrol when it came under heavy artillery fire. The Patrol closed on the Germans, however, and inflicted severe losses on them before withdrawing just prior to dawn.

The raiding companies all withdrew early in the morning. All had accomplished their mission of locating enemy strongholds and measuring their strength.

The tacit understanding which had existed among officers and men of the Division that the defensive was not our style, well though the 3rd had performed that role (Cf. Anzio— February) when assigned to it, was sometimes expressed by a shrug, a grimace, and the unanswerable question, "How long before...?" To an outsider these cryptic signs would have meant nothing. To veterans indoctrinated in the 3rd Infantry Division this restlessness when confronted with stalemate spoke volumes, but translated might be stated very simply: "How long before we start another attack? How long before they shove us in to knock out this damn pocket?"

By the same token, the restlessness could not be interpreted as eagerness. Such an assumption would have been foolish. The cold, bone-chilling winds, the quality and spirit of the German defenders as evidenced during the grim fights for Kaysersberg, Sigolsheim and Bennwihr, the day-and-night bitterly-fought patrol clashes, the trench foot and the frostbite, all precluded any tendency toward individual desire to tangle again full-scale with the enemy. But the restlessness persisted. "We'll have to be at it soon." The feeling pervaded every platoon and squad.

"As long as there's a war and as long as there's a 3rd Division, the 3rd Division will be in that war." Variations on this same theme were repeated many times by nearly every wearer of the blue-and-white patch. The knowledge was omnipresent. In nearly every case there was a matter-of-fact acceptance of the fact that soon we would return to the offensive. Coupled with this was the feeling of surety, born of

Charles R. Castellaw

success in battle, that the 3rd would accomplish successfully any task given it. And that is the feeling that wins battles.

Preparing to Push Ahead

Withdrawal from the lines in preparation for an offensive began with the 7th Infantry during the night of January 17-18. The 3rd battalion, 254th Infantry, moved from Ribeauville to the vicinity of Kaysersberg and during the hours of darkness relieved the 1st Battalion, 7th, on positions, to become attached to the 7th Infantry. This relief was completed by 02:00, and 1st Battalion moved into Alspach. The 290 Combat Engineer Battalion moved from St. Croix to the vicinity of Hachimette and relieved 2nd battalion and Antitank Company, 7th Infantry, likewise coming under the command of 7th Infantry. By 0450, this relief was complete and the 2nd battalion, with AT Company, assembled in La Poutroie. The battalion moved to Kaysersberg by motor during the morning.

The 28th Infantry Division, after participating in the initial stages of the Ardennes counteroffensive and suffering great losses, had been relieved from attachment to Twenty-first Army Group and sent south to join Sixth Army Group, which in turn assigned the division to assist, in a minor role, in the attack against the north flank of the Colmar Pocket. As the 3rd shifted and regrouped in preparation for withdrawing the bulk of its striking force to the east, in the general vicinity of Guemar, elements of the 28th slipped into position on the right of the 254th Infantry, which held down the 3rd's right flank.

There was no time to lose in preparing for the coming operation. On the same day that relief of the 3rd was completed by the 28th, January 20, French I Corps launched its drive against the south side of the Pocket from long-held positions immediately to the north of Mulhouse. We had learned at Anzio of the invaluable need for coordination between the Cassino and beachhead forces. If the German defenders of the Colmar Pocket were to be kept from shifting their strength from one dangerous sector to another, repelling individual attacks in sequence, our attack must get away on time. The date was already set—January 22.

Individual units had begun conducting as much training as was practical under the circumstances, upon their separate reliefs from the

The Way It Was

line. All armor and all combat vehicles were painted white. Mattress covers, sheets, pillowcases, everything available in the way of white cloth—was set upon and redesigned into "spook suits" for camouflage in the snow. The infantry regiments also undertook limited training programs in small-unit problems, speed marches, weapons training, field firing, night problems, river crossing technique, and use of the German *Panzerfaust.*

The 10th Engineer Battalion assembled bridging materials for the operation.

The narrow zone that we faced was characterized by a front line that followed for the greater part the Fecht River. This stream splits the town of Ostheim and forms the southeast boundary of Guemar. The primary move, therefore, was a crossing of its flooded, icy waters. Although the Division's "target" was not announced to any but important commanders until the latest possible date in the interests of security, regimental and smaller-unit intelligence officers had long concentrated on gathering information relative to the width, depth, steepness of banks, and conditions and swiftness of water of all streams which lay along a possible future zone of advance. The Fecht had been thoroughly "cased" in preparation for the unnamed eventuality, as had the Weiss. Information was also sought from left-flank French elements as to the same conditions prevailing with respect to the Ill River. Possible marshy areas had also come under the same critical scrutiny: "Is it frozen? How deep is the water? Is it possible to go around it without going too far out of the way?"

In addition to the all-important terrain study, of course, there was the never-ending quest for enemy dispositions and order of battle. The best information available prior to the attack placed the 748th *VG* Regiment of the 708th *VG* Division, and a battalion of the 760th *VG* Regiment, from the same division, to our front. An additional battalion of the 760th and elements of the 728th *VG* Regiment, same division, were suspected but lacked definite confirmation.

The enemy's counteroffensive possibilities were well summed up in the January 17 Division G-2 Report: "While the new Russian offensive in Poland may seem to be a long way from our front-line infantry platoon positions, it is bound to have an immediate and profound effect on the enemy capabilities in the Alsace pocket.

Charles R. Castellaw

"This effect stems directly from the priorities on reinforcements (both men and material) which will have to be reshuffled among the various fronts. Heretofore top priority has gone to the Belgium front, with the Upper Rhine not far behind. Now, however, Poland is bound to absorb everything the Germans can throw into it, at least until the Russian drives are well stopped. The result should be a decline in enemy ability to send important reinforcements, especially for offensive purposes, into the Colmar Bridgehead. Under pressure, the enemy will always be able to find scratch units to try to keep us from reaching important objectives, but fresh divisions are a luxury he can hardly afford in a sector like this when he needs them for fire-fighting purposes in other parts of his household..."

Substantially, that was the picture of the enemy's *offensive* capabilities. His defensive capabilities, however, were to prove an entirely different story. For, in telling the story of the Colmar Pocket, it must be emphasized that terrain and weather were the equal of the worst any unit ever contended with anywhere. From Guemar to Neuf-Brisach there was hardly a depression in the ground worthy of the name, with the exception of a few stream beds (the Fecht, the Ill, the Colmar, and Rhone-Rhine Canals), the basements of houses in the captured towns and old Maginot Line emplacements—from all of which the enemy had to be driven—and finally a few bomb and shell holes, the impressions of which were much less deep than could normally be expected, due to the frozen solidity of the ground.

The mercury in thermometers constantly stood at minus 10 degrees C. (14° F) which was about the highest point reached during the day. In the late afternoon, early morning and during each night the temperature dropped lower and stayed there. This may not seem extremely cold weather to inhabitants of the northern and eastern parts of the United States, but it must be remembered that men were fighting, attempting to sleep, fording streams, and dying in constant exposure to these temperatures. To experience a few seconds' exposure of nose and ears to the icy gusts of wind which constantly swept down from the high Vosges was almost unbearable.

The overall plan of the Division attack was as follows: To attack on D-day, H-hour, force crossings of the Fecht and Ill Rivers in the Guemar-Ostheim area; to pivot to the south, force crossings over the Colmar Canal in the Wickerschwihr area, block to the southwest in

The Way It Was

the area southwest of Houssen, and *isolate* Colmar on the east. (It was known that the capture of Colmar was assured once it became isolated from the main road feeding it with supplies and reinforcements via the two bridges over the Rhine near Neuf-Brisach.)

Upon completion of this action, the Division was to group the bulk of its infantry in the Holtzwihr-Riedwihr area, and the bulk of its attached Armored Combat Command in the Horbourg-Bischwihr-Andolsheim area, prepared to:

One: Capture Colmar and block the Fecht Valley immediately west of Turckheim, or

Two: Assist 5 DB (5th French Armored Division) in the capture of Neuf-Brisach.

Separate missions of the regiments were:

30th Infantry (Attached: Company C, 756 Tank Battalion; Company C, 601st Tank Destroyer Battalion; Company B, 99th Chemical Battalion; Reconnaissance Company, 601st Tank Destroyer Battalion; 3rd Reconnaissance Troop and Division Battle Patrol; 3rd platoon, Company D, 756th Tank Battalion; three sections, 441st AAA AW Battalion (SP)):

To force a crossing of the Fecht River in its zone, advance with all possible speed to clear the east-west road in its zone through Colmar Forest *(Foret Communale de Colmar),* and seize objectives indicated on the Ill River.

To force a crossing of the Ill River at the earliest possible moment and continue the advance to seize objectives indicated (along a line running east from the Ill River south of Maison Rouge Bridge).

To extend south to another phase line, blocking to the east.

On Division order, to be prepared to regroup in the Horbourg-Bennwihr area, prepared to execute Maneuver I and capture Colmar from the east, or to pass to Division reserve.

In addition, 30th Infantry was to protect its own left throughout the advance south along the east side of the Ill; to protect the Division left; to maintain contact with 1 DM1 and 5 DB on the left flank, and to reinforce its supporting engineers with one rifle company from the regiment's reserve battalion for the purpose of carrying an infantry footbridge from the Fecht River to the Ill.

7th Infantry (Attached: Company A, 756th Tank Battalion; Company A, 601st Tank Destroyer Battalion; Company C, 99th

Charles R. Castellaw

Chemical Mortar Battalion—one platoon; Company D, 756th Tank Battalion—two platoons and three sections of the 441st AAA):

To force a crossing of the Fecht in its zone; advance with all possible speed to seize objectives in a line to the west of 30th Infantry's first phase line across the Ill.

To clear the east-west road in its zone through the Colmar Forest and the road running east from Ostheim in its zone.

To extend its line further south, seizing and holding the objectives taken within the boundary defined.

To push strong combat patrols to the southwest in the direction of Ingersheim and to the south in the direction of Colmar.

On Division order to assemble on last line gained, and to be prepared:

To attack toward Neuf-Brisach and objectives in that vicinity.

To execute Maneuver I and capture Colmar, or

To execute Maneuver 2, isolate Colmar on the south, capture Wintzenheim and Turckheim, and block to the southwest as indicated.

254th Infantry (Attached: one platoon, Company B, 756th; one platoon, Company B 601st; one platoon, Company A, 99th Chemical; two sections, 441st AAA Battalion):

Attack through 28th Infantry Division north of Hill 216 at daylight of D+1, isolate and capture Hill 216, seize Line A-B (extension of 30th and 7th first phase line, to the west), in zone, and seize and hold bridge over the Fecht River immediately west of its junction with the Weiss River.

Push strong combat patrols to the south on Ingersheim.

On Division order following the forcing of the Fecht River, assemble 2nd battalion in the Beblenheim area under regimental control.

On Division order, undergo relief of positions on line A-B, relieve elements of 7tb Infantry on line C-D (second phase line) between the Fecht and Ill Rivers, prevent enemy movement northeast of this line, and patrol vigorously to the south on Colmar and to the southwest in Ingersheim.

Protect Division right.

Maintain contact with 28th Infantry Division on right.

Coordinate directly with commanding officer of regiment on right in reference to passage and assistance.

The Way It Was

15th Infantry was assigned the mission of crossing the Fecht immediately behind 30th Infantry to assemble in Division reserve, or

On Division order from present assembly area or the Colmar Forest, be prepared to assume the mission of either the 7th or 30th Infantry Regiments.

The remainder of the order pertaining to 15th Infantry specified several alternatives, duplicating those found in orders for the 7th and 30th, providing the 15th took over for either of them.

French II Corps Artillery was to support the 3rd Infantry Division attack by reinforcing direct-support fires, and by supplementing interdiction, counterbattery, and harassing fires of the Division Artillery.

In addition a powerful air program was to be conducted in support of the Division attack in conjunction with an over-all air program in the entire First French Army zone.

CC4 of the French 5th Armored Division (5 DB) was attached to 3rd Infantry Division for the attack.

Attacking on our left at daylight of D-plus-1 was 1st *Division Motonse' Infanterie.*

The attack was scheduled to begin three hours after darkness on January 22, the first anniversary of the landing of the Division below Nettuno. During the morning of January 22 units began moving to the forward assembly areas, and footbridges and heavy bridging material were moved to proposed crossing sites at Guemar and Ostheim during the night. Company A, 10th Engineers, under the command of 1st Lt. Robert K. Fleet, hid a preconstructed 84-foot span in a cemetery north of Guemar.

The 7th and 30th Infantry Regiments, commanded by Lt. Col. John A. Heintges and Col. Lionel C. McGarr, respectively, began their crossing of the Fecht River by stealth at Guemar at 2100, on a front measuring less than 1000 yards in width. It was a repetition of the Meurthe stunt, and it worked. In the 7th zone two platoons crossed just prior to H-Hour and seized bridgeheads. Artillery fell on both bridges of the 7th, and enemy heavy mortar fire fell on 1st Battalion, 30th Infantry, but enemy infantry resistance was negligible.

The 3rd battalion, 7th Infantry, commanded by Lt. Col. Lloyd B. Ramsey, after crossing the river swung southeast and encountered enemy small-arms and machine-gun fire in the *Bois Communale de*

Charles R. Castellaw

Guemar. After overcoming this resistance the battalion, with Company I on the right and Company L on the left, moved swiftly across the east-west road which runs along the northern edge of the *Foret Communale de Colmar.*

Clearing the woods as they advanced, Colonel Ramsey's men continued past Ostheim and to a small wooded area, Brunnwald, where they beat off an enemy counterattack consisting of tanks and infantry which came from the east. Our artillery and mortar fire played an important part in stopping the German counter-thrust while elements of Lt. Col. Glenn F. Rogers' 756th Tank Battalion supported the battalion all along the route of advance. Company A, under Capt. Orlando A. Richardson, Jr., and elements of Company D, commanded by Capt. Robert F. Kramer, were attached throughout the 7th Infantry.

Maj. Kenneth W. Wallace's 1st Battalion turned directly south after crossing the river and suffered some casualties as the troops moved through a wooded area filled with wire obstacles and mines. The battalion entered Ostheim from the north at 0400 and engaged the Germans in a heavy small arms and machine-gun battle that lasted for five hours.

The enemy continued to resist fiercely in the southern part of the town, where every window was a potential sniper's nest. By 1730, however, the last vestige of resistance had ended and the battalion was in full possession of the city.

The 2nd battalion, which had followed in the wake of the assault battalions, moved rapidly south to the Bois dit de Rothleible after engaging in a hot firefight en route.

The 30th Infantry crossed the Fecht with the 1st Battalion, under the command of Lt. Col. Mackenzie E. Porter, on the left and 3rd battalion, commanded by Maj. Robert B. Pridgen, on the right.

Meeting little opposition, 1st Battalion continued through the *Foret Communale de Colmar* to the east and had elements across the Ill River by daybreak. By 0900 the entire battalion had crossed the Ill and moved south along the east bank of the stream, heading for the Mai son Rouge Bridge, at the southeast corner of the forest.

The 3rd battalion, 30th cut southeast through the forest, and encountered a *schu*minefield and two enemy strongpoints during its advance. A brisk firefight was staged at Niederwald, a crossroad

The Way It Was

settlement in the *Foret Communale,* but the doughboys soon eliminated this obstacle.

<u>Serious Miscalculations</u>

Closing in on the Maison Rouge Bridge, Major Pridgen's battalion had it, intact, by 1155.

That little wooden bridge figured greatly in the 30th Infantry's plans, and around it revolved one of the most fateful moments of the regiment or Division in the entire war.

Foreseeing the possibility of capturing the bridge, Division engineers had ordered reinforcing treadway to be delivered as soon as possible to the bridge site once it was captured in order to get armor across in the minimum possible time. Traffic along the roads to the rear was heavy. The engineers, having already allocated most of the available treadway to other bridge projects, sent forward all the remaining treadway to the Maison Rouge site. When they had a chance to look the bridge over and measure it, the amount was just fifteen feet short.

Traffic over the roads to the rear was heavy. The time required to obtain an extra fifteen feet might be prohibitive. After a certain number of tactical vehicles of the 30th had passed over the bridge, it was closed to traffic and the treadway was laid on either side. A 15-foot gap remained in the center.

The order had been given: "Get armor across the Ill with all possible speed." The engineer officer in charge was dubious, but did not want to delay the armor. One tank started across. The bridge shook a bit, but that was nothing unusual. The driver stopped. Engineers, watching tensely, decided the bridge was stable. They waved the tank on. The full weight of the tank passed on to the non-reinforced section of the bridge. There was a rending crash and the bridge collapsed to the level of the river, the tank staying just above water. The crew clambered out. A few minutes passed. A truck, bearing an amount of treadway sufficient to have bridged the gap arrived on the scene.

While the 7th and 30th Infantry regiments were attacking their objectives, the 254th Infantry assaulted Hill 216 at daylight. This long-time salient in our lines proved as difficult as ever, with one important

Charles R. Castellaw

difference. It was no longer the sole point of attack, but only one of many. By noon, the 254th had routed the Germans from well dug-in positions on the eastern slopes, which were protected by schumines and booby traps, plus the fire of machine guns, small arms, and Panzerfaust. This clearing of the enemy from the far side of Hill 216 eliminated a strongpoint that jeopardized the flank of our attacking units and deprived the Germans of an extraordinary observation post.

Following the capture of Hill 216, 254th Infantry continued its mission of clearing the area south to the Weiss River, and of capturing a bridge across the Fecht River, in conjunction with joining the 7th Infantry in that area, once the enemy had been cleared from the lower Fecht stream bank near its juncture with the Weiss.

Heavy fighting here carried into the following day. The 1st Battalion, leading the attack, became stalled and the 3rd battalion was committed around its right flank. Troops of the 254th were forced virtually to ferret out the Germans of their dug-in positions in a yard-by-yard advance that was bitterly contested all the way.

The Germans had nearly recovered from the initial shock of the surprise attack. The enemy was marshalling every tank and automatic weapon at his command to stem the tide of our advance. The battle of armor and infantry that was waged in and around the wooded areas in the vicinity of Houssen, Riedwihr, Holtzwihr, and Wickerschwihr will be remembered as one of the most bitterly fought engagements, and without doubt one of the most important, that the 3rd Division ever encountered.

During the afternoon of the 23rd, 30th Infantry forward elements reached the outskirts of Riedwihr and Holtzwihr and held the clump of woods known as Bois de Riedwihr.

Companies I and K had moved into the northern edge of Holtzwihr. The position of the 1st and 3rd battalions at this time was like a finger sticking deep into enemy territory. Opposition had been so light up to this point that the 30th had lanced ahead and was completely exposed on the left flank, resistance against the French having prevented them from advancing rapidly, and ahead of 7th Infantry on the right, which was also encountering very tenacious resistance.

At 1650 the first blow struck. Companies I and K of the 30 under 1st Lts. Darwyn E. Walker and Ross H. Calvert, respectively, without

The Way It Was

armor, advanced into Holtzwihr. Ten enemy tanks and tank destroyers accompanied by at least a hundred foot troops moved into and beyond Holtzwihr from the southeast. The tanks broke up into groups of two's and three's and sliced the 30th's positions into several pockets. Tank machine-gun fire whipped along the snow-covered ground in murderous grazing fire and the tanks and tank destroyers fired as they came.

The 3rd battalion had just completed a rapid move and even had the men had time to dig in they would have been completely frustrated. The ground was frozen solid. It would have taken TNT charges to blow holes in it. And it was perfectly flat. There was not a vestige of cover as 3rd battalion, struck from three sides and without even one tank or tank destroyer to shoot at the oncoming assortment of power, vainly tried to repel the counterattack. Also important was the fact that artillery FOs with the 30th had not yet established radio communication.

The result was a foregone conclusion. 3rd battalion, badly disorganized, was forced to make its way back toward the Ill and the protection afforded by its banks.

At 1720, as the 1st Battalion was about to reach Riedwihr, the blow fell on it as it had on the 3rd. The enemy hit with all he had. Men sought in vain for cover. Bands of grazing machine-gun fire criss-crossed in vicious, cracking streams. As in the case of 3rd battalion, 1st Battalion had nowhere to go but to the rear—if possible—nothing with which to combat the thick-sided enemy tanks and the *Jagdpanzer* tank destroyers, and above all no holes from which to fight.

During the withdrawals, handfuls of brave men in each company braved almost certain death or capture to stick it out on the hopeless positions. Despite open flanks on the right and left, small, bitter and last-ditch actions were fought by isolated groups, such as those led by 1st Lts. Darwyn E. Walker and Ross H. Calvert, who were last seen on that day entering a patch of woods from which two enemy tanks shortly thereafter emerged. In the Orchbach stream bed, east of the Ill by several hundred yards, a group of 30th Infantry men was still in position the next day when a counterattack was launched and the ground was regained!

Charles R. Castellaw

At the Maison Rouge Bridge site, bystanders gazed ruefully at a Sherman tank sitting in the center of the Ill River, icy waves lapping at the base of its turret.

The 2nd battalion, 30th, under Maj. Fames L. Osgard, had crossed the Ill at the southeast corner of the Colmar Forest, but had hardly had time to get reorganized before it, too, was counterattacked by enemy tanks and infantry and was forced back across the river, where it set up temporary positions in the Colmar woods. Approximately 350 men, most of whom were captured, were lost by the 30th in this counterattack. However, during the withdrawal machine-gun sections from H and D Companies and small groups of infantrymen, chiefly from Companies A, B, C and E held on the east side of the Ill and covered the remainder of the battalion.

As night drew on, the enemy was completely in possession of the east bank of the Ill, with this important exception. Lt. Colonel MacKenzie Porter and Capt. William F. Stucky organized a group and stuck it out on the east side, north of Maison Rouge. It was the 3rd Infantry Division's sole bridgehead during that dark night of January 23-24.

The 30th Infantry was in a bad way. A hurry-up call went out for pyramidal tents, blankets, clothes, and hot coffee and food. Regimental supply personnel scoured their stocks and brought these items forward. Division G-4 also got an urgent call: "Send us dry clothes, rifles, and machine guns." A good proportion of the entire regiment was nearly frozen from its terrible exposure to the Ill River and the icy blasts of wind that greeted the men as they clambered from the water.

Straggler posts were set up along all possible routes to the rear, to direct the men back into the line. Although terribly chilled, the offensive spirit was still present in many of them. When collected by the officers they moved up into defensive positions west of the Ill supported by their massed armor and covered by their riflemen and machine guns east of the river. The attitude of some of the men was expressed by several who were wringing out their wet clothes, their weapons at their sides: "Yes sir, we can hold! No goddamn kraut is going to kick the hell out of us and get by with it! We'll be here in the morning."

The Way It Was

The tenure of 7th Infantry troops in Ostheim was even threatened for a time when the enemy organized for a strong counterattack from Houssen but our artillery massed heavy concentrations on the enemy force and broke up the attack at its inception.

The 15th Infantry was also very busy during the night of January 23-24. The attack must be pushed at all costs. It was obvious that 30th Infantry would need some time in which to reorganize. The 3rd battalion, 15th Infantry, was chosen to cross the Ill first, to seize a bridgehead around Maison Rouge to enable the engineers to get the all-important bridge in. Enemy tanks had ranged to within as close as a quarter-mile, firing direct fire on the bridge site.

The 3rd battalion jumped off at 0300, with Company I on the left and Company K on the right. The attack made good progress east of the Ill until Company I was counterattacked by four tanks and large numbers of enemy infantry. Again, still lacking armor pending a suitable bridge across the Ill, Company I was forced back in much the same manner as had been 30th Infantry the previous day. Three tanks supporting the 15th Infantry from the west bank of the river were neutralized in a few minutes. The 1st Battalion, 15th Infantry, moving up to the line of departure by 1000, was about to attack in conjunction with 3rd battalion when the counterattack hit the latter.

The 1st Battalion was temporarily held up, but by noon was ready to deliver its attack. The advance rapidly moved through 3rd battalion at Maison Rouge Bridge, to the woods northeast of Riedwihr. Here, however, enemy tanks and infantry were encountered and forced 1st Battalion—without armor as had been its predecessors—to withdraw from the woods. At any rate, we now held a bridgehead, and the engineers went forward with all possible speed, completing the bridge. It was more than obvious that the attack east of the Ill would get nowhere if supporting armor was not in close support of our infantry troops.

The enemy taunted us with a special propaganda leaflet sent over by enemy artillery, claiming that over one hundred members of Company I, 30th Infantry, including 1st Lt. Darwyn E. Walker—whom the leaflet named—had been captured on May 23. (In Walker's case, at least, it was true. Both he and 1st Lt. Ross H. Calvert, Company K commander, were later liberated by United States troops in Germany. Walker was liberated by his own Division.)

Charles R. Castellaw

After completing the clearance of Ostheim, the 1st Battalion of the 7th Infantry, commanded by Maj. Kenneth W. Wallace, had attacked shortly after midnight of January 24 toward Chateau de Schoppenwihr. A strong counterattack consisting of enemy infantry and six tanks came at daybreak. Three of the tanks were destroyed, but the fighting continued all day. It was not until 1830 that night that the Germans were finally driven from their positions in the Chateau area and in the woods between the railroad tracks and west to the Fecht River. Company C, 99th Chemical Battalion, laid down a heavy smoke screen while the fight was at its height, thus enabling Company A, 7th, to rejoin its battalion by crossing the open under cover of smoke at Bois dit de Rothleible. The additional strength was both timely and necessary.

The 3rd battalion, 7th Infantry, had a fierce fight in the Brunnwald woods, where the enemy had infiltrated while the struggle for the Chateau was in progress. The infiltration was followed by reinforcements after dark and when the 3rd raided the positions at about midnight the enemy was prepared to resist with great strength. Mortars, machine guns and small arms provided stiff opposition to the raiders.

Company L, commanded by 1st Lt. Orville L. Dilley, moved around the tip of the woods and ran into German machine guns and Flakwagons. Company A, 756th Tank Battalion, under Capt. Orlando A. Richardson, Jr., and Company A of the 601st TD Battalion, with Capt. Francis X. Lambert commanding, were supporting the 7th in the attack and our armor fought the enemy tanks and tank destroyers to a standstill.

Concealed German bozookamen, mechanized and horse-drawn antitank guns, mark IV and Mark V tanks, were strewn throughout the area. Our casualties also were high and included six or seven pieces of armor.

At the end of the first forty-eight hours, an important identification among enemy units had been made. As suspected, the two battalions of the 760 VG regiment opposed us, as well as elements of 748th, 225th, 308th, and 728th VG regiments. An additional unit, the 602nd Mobile Battalion, was almost wiped out during the period. The new identification, however, was that of the enemy 67th Reconnaissance Battalion from the 2nd Mountain Division, previously

The Way It Was

identified in Norway. This was combined with the recognition of another element of the same division, the 137th Mountain Regiment, in the I French Corps zone. It provided an indication that the enemy was not going to let the Colmar Pocket be eliminated without a determined effort to prevent it. The 2nd Mountain Division actually was earmarked for the pocket to replace the 269th Infantry Division, which previously had been sneaked out and sent to the Russian front. The enemy vainly hoped the switch could be completed before any Allied offensive could be started against the pocket.

Also known to be opposing our advance were Battle Group *Diemer* and 235th Engineer Battalion. Suspected were elements of the 40th PG *(Panzer Grenadier)* Replacement Battalion in the 254th Infantry zone and a possible addition of elements of the 137th Mountain Regiment opposing the 7th Infantry.

By 2010 of the night of January 24, the 254th Infantry's 3rd battalion, which had been committed around the right flank of 1st Battalion in the regiment's attack south toward the Weiss River from Hill 216, reached the Weiss. The regiment thus held the river line east to its juncture with the Fecht, although north of that point, along the Fecht stream line, the area was not completely clear of enemy.

Company K, 7th Infantry, commanded by Capt. Francis J. Kret, was still in close contact with the enemy in the woods when the 7th struck south in an all-out attack, with three battalions abreast, at daybreak, January 25. Company I, under 1st Lt. William D. Anthone, was left to contain the enemy in the forest while the bulk of the regiment made the attack, which began after a heavy artillery and mortar concentration had been placed on Houssen and the surrounding area.

Meanwhile, across the Ill, the 2nd and 3rd battalions, 15th Infantry, took up the fight at 0300 the morning of January 25. They encountered enemy small arms, machine-gun, 20mm, tank, and mortar fire about 300 yards northwest of Riedwihr. Two tanks and a tank destroyer with the 2nd battalion (a bridge strong enough for armor had finally been put in several hundred yards north of Maison Rouge) became stuck, and the battalion withdrew about 700 yards. The men were not in the confusion that our elements had been the previous two days, however, when there was no supporting armor whatsoever. The battalion was quickly reorganized. Maj. John O'Connell's 3rd

Charles R. Castellaw

battalion, with Companies K and L in the assault, encountered enemy in the vicinity of a road junction northeast of Riedwihr. Company K was disorganized and forced to withdraw. Company L succeeded in driving the enemy from some buildings there, and by noon the 3rd battalion was awaiting relief by elements of the French CC4, preparatory to attacking Riedwihr.

The very relentlessness of the Division attacks slowly wore the Germans down and the towns of Riedwihr, Rosenkranz, and Houssen fell during the torrid fighting of January 25-26.

The 7th Infantry inflicted terrific losses on the enemy when the Germans launched a strong counterattack during the afternoon of January 25. The 1st Battalion, beating back the onslaught, turned the counterattack into an enemy rout and drove along the east-west road into Rosenkranz while 3rd battalion was holding firm against strong enemy armor and infantry pressure.

During the night of January 25 near Rosenkranz, Pfc. Jose F. Valdez gave his life in sacrifice. He was on outpost duty with five other soldiers when the enemy counterattacked with overwhelming strength. From his position near some woods about five hundred yards beyond his lines, he observed a hostile tank about 75 yards away and raked it with automatic-rifle fire until it withdrew. Soon afterwards, he saw three enemy stealthily approaching through the woods. At thirty yards' distance, he engaged in a firefight with them until he had killed all three. The enemy quickly launched an attack with two full companies of infantrymen, blasting the patrol with murderous concentrations of automatic and rifle fire and beginning an encircling movement that forced the patrol leader to order a withdrawal. Private Valdez volunteered to cover the maneuver, and as the patrol, one by one, plunged through the enemy fire toward their own lines, Private Valdez fired burst after burst into the swarming enemy. The citation of his Medal of Honor award reads in part:

"...he was struck by a bullet which entered his stomach, and, passing through his body, emerged from the back. Overcoming agonizing pain, he regained control of himself and resumed his firing position, delivering a protective screen of bullets until all others of the patrol were safe. By field telephone, he called for artillery and mortar fire on the Germans and corrected the range until he had shells falling within fifty yards of his position. For fifteen minutes, he refused to be

The Way It Was

dislodged by more than two hundred of the enemy, then seeing that the barrage had broken the counterattack, he dragged himself back to his own lines. He later died as a result of his wounds..."

Final mopping-up of Houssen was done the same day by the 2nd and 3rd battalions.

Colonel Heintges' regiment took 166 prisoners, including three officers, and killed and wounded a great number of Germans during the 24-hour period beginning at noon, January 25. The 67th Reconnaissance Battalion of the German 2nd Mountain Division, being fed into the line as it moved down from Norway, was caught by several stray artillery TOT's fired into Houssen prior to the attack, and was completely disorganized. Although this battalion contained 700 men, it was no opposition for the 7th's attack.

The 1st Battalion of the 15th, commanded by Maj. Kenneth B. Potter, with the 2nd battalion, under Lt. Col. Eugene F. Salet, on its flank, advanced into the woods west of Riedwihr during the afternoon of the 25th and actually fought until its ammunition ran out after they had penetrated some 600 yards into the forest against tree-to-tree resistance. Major Potter stopped the advance of his battalion until ammunition could be brought up and the attack was resumed at 0200 in the morning.

The 2nd battalion, 15th Infantry, moving from positions northwest of Riedwihr, also expended all its ammunition late that night and after being resupplied continued the advance and reached its objective on the south edge of the woods at 0930 the next morning.

The 3rd battalion fought its way to the outer edge of Riedwihr at about midnight and within an hour had cleared the Germans out of the city and had patrols out toward Wickerschwihr to the south.

While the 7th and 15th attacked their objectives, the 254th had been relieved by the 28th Division's 112th Infantry by 0700 of January 25 on the Division right. After coordinating with 7th Infantry in cleaning out the Fecht River bed, the 254th was committed on the Division left, to attack Jebsheim. The end of its first day's fighting found the regiment temporarily stopped by bitter resistance, and temporary defensive preparations were made along an intermittent stream that ran just west of Jebsheim. An old mill on the stream was a landmark of the area.

Charles R. Castellaw

Another Act of Bravery: Audie Murphy

The 1st and 2nd battalions of the 15th were holding a line along the south edges of Le Schmalholtz and Brunnwald woods on the afternoon of the 26th, and occupied the Bois de Riedwihr on the north. Enemy infantry, reinforced by armor, struck the 1st Battalion positions on the west side of the woods. An enemy 88mm gun caught one of our tank destroyers flush in the middle, and a swarm of German armor overran the positions of Company B, thus threatening the Division's control of the forest which dominated the German stronghold of Holtzwihr, to the south.

It was here that 1st Lt. Audie L. Murphy stopped an attack practically single-handedly.

Lt. Col. Keith L. Ware, 15th Infantry Executive Officer, said later: "Control (of the Bois de Riedwihr) had been wrested from the enemy at a heavy cost in blood. Its possession was of cardinal importance.

"Accordingly, on the afternoon of January 26, the enemy launched a determined counterattack, hurling two companies and six heavy tanks at Company B's position in an effort to retake the woods at any cost."

1st Lt. Walter W. Weispfenning, a Field Artillery forward observer, said, "The woods were sparse and there was practically no underbrush. I could see everything that happened. The kraut tanks rumbled past Murphy's position, passing within fifty yards of him and firing at him as they went by. They did not want to close in for the kill because they wanted to give our tank destroyer, which was burning but not in flames, as wide a berth as possible.

"While we tried to hold off the tanks with directed artillery fire and bazooka rockets, the German infantry line, consisting of two full-strength companies of 125 men each, surged across the open meadow in a wide arc. They fired at Murphy with machine pistols and rifles as they advanced.

"Then I saw Lieutenant Murphy do the bravest thing that I had ever seen a man do in combat. With the Germans only a hundred yards away and still moving up on him, he climbed into the slowly burning tank destroyer and began firing the .50-caliber machine gun at the krauts. He was completely exposed and silhouetted against the background of bare trees and snow, with a fire under him that

The Way It Was

threatened to blow the destroyer to bits if it reached the gasoline and ammunition. Eighty-eight millimeter shells, machine-gun, machine pistol and rifle fire crashed all about him.

"Standing on top of the tank destroyer, Murphy raked the approaching enemy force with machine-gun fire. Twelve Germans, stealing up a ditch to flank him from his right were killed in the gully at 50-yard range by concentrated fire from his machine gun. Twice the tank destroyer he was standing on was hit by artillery fire and the Lieutenant was enveloped in clouds of smoke and spurts of flame. His clothing was torn and riddled by flying shell fragments and bits of rock. Bullets ricocheted off the tank destroyer as the enemy concentrated the full fury of his fire on this one-man strongpoint."

Sgt. Elmer C. Brawley added: "The enemy tanks, meanwhile, returned because lieutenant Murphy had held up the supporting infantry and they were apparently loathe to advance further without infantry support. These tanks added their murderous fire to that of the kraut artillery and small-arms fire that showered the Lieutenant's position without stopping.

"The German infantrymen got within ten yards of the Lieutenant, who killed them in the draws, in the meadows, in the woods—wherever he saw them. Though wounded and covered with soot and dirt that must have obscured his vision at times, he held the enemy at bay, killing and wounding at least thirty-five during the next hour.

"Lieutenant Murphy, worn out and bleeding profusely, then limped forward through a continuing hail of fire and brought the company forward. Refusing to be evacuated, he led us in a strong attack against the enemy, dislodging the Germans from the whole area. When the fight was over, he allowed his wound to be treated on the field."

Pfc. Anthony V. Abramski, a member of Company B, added that the company was ordered to withdraw to prepared positions inside the woods when an enemy artillery concentration that preceded the attack began.

"Lieutenant Murphy remained at his command post under a tree so that he could direct artillery fire on the advancing tanks," Abramski said. "Together with a tank destroyer, which was across the main road through the woods and about ten yards to his right rear, he held that rear-guard position under raking fire from the German tanks.

Charles R. Castellaw

"From my position in the woods, I saw a direct hit on our tank destroyer from a *Jagdpanther* carrying an 88mm gun. The crew piled out as fast as they could and withdrew toward the company position in the forest. And that is when Lieutenant Murphy took over," concluded Abramski. For his action, Lieutenant Murphy later was awarded the Congressional Medal of Honor.

Simultaneously with the smash against 1st Battalion, 15th Infantry, the enemy, attacking north from Holtzwihr, struck at 2nd battalion positions on the south rim of the forest. Our artillery, however, laid some excellent concentrations on the advancing Germans and marked the area with smoke for friendly fighter-bombers that strafed the enemy forces and attacked their assembly areas in Holtzwihr. The attack came as though planned by a scenario writer. All day the skies had been cloudy. A few minutes before the German counterattack began, the area over the woods became clear enough for our fighter-bombers to strike, causing many casualties and proving instrumental in forcing a complete German withdrawal. Then the clouds closed in once more.

During the struggle a number of enemy entered the woods from the east and got behind 2nd battalion positions. A hurriedly gathered task force of doughboys, with a Flakwagon in support, was organized, and the enemy was put to flight after a stiff engagement.

The 254th Infantry jumped off at 1630 in resumption of its attack toward Jebsheim; 1st Battalion was on the right, 2nd battalion on the left. The 1st Battalion encountered strong enemy resistance from a pillbox 500 yards north of Jebsheim, which was seven feet high and manned by twelve men. Following its reduction, the advance continued. The 2nd battalion entered Jebsheim at 2355, following a 15-minute artillery barrage, and 1st Battalion followed. Stiff house-to-house fighting lasted through the night and into the morning.

The 3rd battalion, 254th Infantry attacked at 1750, January 26, with the mission of advancing southeast and clearing the Bois de Jebsheim from the south. Prepared enemy positions were encountered along a stream line and the advance was slow, likewise continuing throughout the night into the next day.

The 7th Infantry's 1st and 2nd battalions made local attacks during the afternoon of the 26th to improve their positions preparatory to relief. The 3rd battalion, following artillery preparation, attacked south

The Way It Was

from Brunnwald woods at 1300, with the Battle Patrol attacking east of Houssen. This got away at 1300 with the purpose of clearing some enemy who were well entrenched between a dike and the Ill River on the left flank. Company I was particularly successful in its mission, although it was a very bloody small attack. During the night, 28th Division's 109th Infantry elements relieved 7th Infantry, which went into Division reserve after having attacked continuously since the night of January 22.

The morning of January 27th saw a reorganized, vengeful 30th Infantry in the fight again. The 2nd battalion left its assembly area at 0445 in an attack toward the Colmar Canal, which was coordinated with French units on its flank. The 1st Battalion moved out, crossing its line of departure and clearing across the road leading southwest from Riedwihr to an area in the vicinity of west of Wicherschwihr by 0510. The 3rd battalion blocked east of the Ill River. By 0845, Company E reported the east side of Holtzwihr clear. Company F, after losing a tank to enemy bazooka fire, withdrew to its line of departure to reorganize, and attacked again, to report the remainder of Holtzwihr clear by 0950. The 1st Battalion cleaned out Wickerschwihr by noon.

We had dug in and it was time to set up the outpost. We had located a house with a half basement for the outpost. I thought it would be much better staying in a basement than in a foxhole. The foxhole was cold and wet. I said, "I will take one of the men and man the outpost tonight." We operated by one man standing guard and lookout while the other slept. I was taking my turn sleeping when the lookout ran in and woke me, telling me that a German patrol was outside. I pulled him down to the floor and told him to be quiet. The patrol came to the door and started ordering us to come out. We got as close to the floor as we could with our M-Is ready and I told him not to fire until I gave the orders.

After a few minutes the enemy opened fire, sprayed the walls of the basement, and then withdrew. Lucky for us, all bullets went over us.

The Division Commander later praised the 30th Infantry for its rapid reorganization and resumption of the offensive. In his own words: "It took a fighting regiment to make the gains you made on January 22-23, but it took a great regiment to come back after the

Charles R. Castellaw

reverses you suffered and kick hell out of the kraut at Holtzwihr and Wickerschwihr."

By noon of the 27[th,] all but the southern tip of Jebsheim was reported clear by the 254th Infantry. Elements of 5 DB moved in to take charge of the southern part of the town, and strong German elements infiltrated back in. The task of clearing them out the French then handed back to the 254th because of their lack of infantry. Fierce fighting continued in that small tip for two more days and it was nearly midnight of January 29th before the 254th Infantry could finally and authoritatively report Jebsheim free of Germans. The regiment, new to combat prior to joining the 3rd in the Colmar Pocket, acquitted itself with distinction, first in clearing troublesome Hill 216 and then mopping up in Jebsheim, taking a total of nearly 1,000 prisoners in three days. (The importance of Jebsheim was that it was one of a string of fortified towns on the enemy's main north-south communication artery.)

The Colmar Pocket Falls

It now remained for the 15th and 30th Infantry regiments to clear out a few scattered German elements north of the Colmar Canal and the next large phase of the operation was ready to be initiated. During that two-day period, thorough preparations were made to slam across the canal in force, and to move far and fast. This time there was to be no repetition of the grinding battle of attrition that had characterized the fighting so far.

Patrols to the Canal reported that it was about fifty feet wide and five feet deep, its steep banks being some twelve feet high and about eight feet wide at the top and fifteen at the bottom. The water was slow moving, but not frozen.

At 2100, January 28, the 3rd Infantry Division passed from control of II French Corps to control of XXI American Corps, which was commanded by Maj. Gen. F. W. Milburn.

Reconnaissance along the north bank of the Colmar Canal was continuous during the hours of darkness January 28-29. Huge trucks hauling engineer bridging equipment clogged the roads behind the forward areas.

The Way It Was

The entire French 5 DB was attached to the 3rd Division as of 1635, January 29.

That evening, with the coming of darkness, 7th and 15th Infantry Regiments stole to the edges of the Colmar Canal with engineer rubber boats, and waited.

Heavy concentrations of preparatory fire of all weapons broke loose just preceding the crossing. During a 24-hour period beginning at 1800, the artillery battalions fired 16,438 rounds of ammunition, most of which was fired at the beginning of the attack, while the 441st AAA Battalion, under command of Lt. Col. Thomas H. Leary, fired 22,300 rounds of .50-caliber ammunition during the first three hours of the attack. The antiaircraft gunners sent a continuous hail of shells into enemy positions across the canal and into the towns of Bischwihr, Fortschwihr, and Muntzenheim.

Operation "Krautbuster" was initiated at 2100. Behind the furious screen of preparatory shells, leading elements of the 7th Infantry moved down the steep banks of the canal and paddled across. Enemy resistance was surprisingly light. The 1st and 3rd battalions of the 7th were completely across by 2205; the 15th Infantry had its bridging supplies held up by heavy traffic, but began crossing at 2145 with the 2nd and 3rd battalions in the lead. By midnight the 7th and 15th were completely across.

Company B, 7th Infantry, engaged some enemy in a firefight while the remainder of 1st Battalion moved into Bischwihr at 2245. The 3rd battalion on the right, also attacking Bischwihr, encountered some resistance in the town but reported the town clear at 2400.

No less speedy was the 15th Infantry's rapid attack upon Muntzenheim. The 2nd and 3rd battalions reorganized after the canal crossing, with 1st Battalion crossing behind them. The 2nd and 3rd then attacked Muntzenheim from the west with 3rd battalion on the left. Company K was reported on its objective by 0110 and the first elements of the 2nd battalion were reported in the town at 0130.

After Muntzenheim was cleared, the 3rd battalion remained in the town and the 2nd battalion attacked Fortschwihr from the northeast in conjunction with 1st Battalion (less certain elements) which attacked south to the town from assembly areas. The town was cleared in short order. During the attack on the two villages approximately 200

Charles R. Castellaw

prisoners were taken; a 105mm gun with crew, an 88mm gun with crew and two 120mm mortars were captured intact.

The 2nd battalion, 7th Infantry now did some broken-field running. Having crossed the canal on footbridges at 2330, the battalion moved rapidly toward Wihr-en-Plaine, and was approaching it by 0130 in the face of tank fire and some small-arms resistance. Companies F and G entered the town at 0205 as two enemy tank destroyers penetrated between the two companies and the battalion OP group, a member of which was Maj. Jack M. Duncan, the battalion commander. A phenomenal 500-foot bazooka shot by Pfc. Joseph L. Bale destroyed one of the tank destroyers, setting it on fire. The other fled, as did the accompanying enemy infantry.

By 0315, the battalion was meeting scattered resistance in Wihr-en-Plaine. At 0630, there was a strong counterattack of enemy armor and infantry. Fierce fighting ensued. By noon the battalion controlled the northern half of the town and was fighting in the southern portion.

During this time, 254th Infantry had launched an attack south from Jebsheim to the Colmar Canal and east toward the Rhone-Rhine Canal. At the time 7th Infantry began its crossing of the Colmar Canal, all resistance in Jebsheim had ceased. 575 prisoners were taken there the last day of fighting.

The bitter fight in Wihr-en-Plaine conducted by 2nd battalion, 7th Infantry with Company L attached continued on through the 30th of January. After repulsing a second counterattack early in the afternoon, 2nd battalion and Company L attacked south at 1430, with the 7th Infantry Battle Patrol also participating. Some more of Wihr-en-Plaine was cleared after a hard, close-in fight, and another counterattack at 1830 was repelled. The artillery placed a TOT on Horbourg, adjoining. The 2nd battalion jumped off to attack Wihren-Plaine's southwest edge at 2230 followed by elements of CC 4, which were to pass through the battalion and enter Colmar providing a bridge were seized.

The 1st Battalion, 15th Infantry, assembled east of captured Fortschwihr at 1640, January 30, and attacked the woods to the southeast. The battalion encountered little or no enemy resistance. Company B was reported on its objective at 1830, Company A on its objective by 1835.

The Way It Was

The 1st Battalion remained in position until noon the following day. The 2nd battalion, minus Company F, which was guarding a bridge across the Canal, remained in Fortschwihr.

Elements of the French CC 5 attacked Urschenheim from Muntzenheim at 1700. After an extremely stiff fight the town was reported clear at 2000 and Company I, 15th Infantry was ordered to take it over, which it did at 2200.

The 30th Infantry held and cleared the south bank of the Colmar Canal, blocking to the east and west. It was shot at from the south where enemy groups still held out. The 28th Division had not yet attacked south into Colmar, leaving the regiment's right flank open.

The 1st Battalion, 30th Infantry remained in blocking positions to the east in Wickerschwihr, with Company A outposting bridges. Company A was relieved of these positions early on January 31 by elements of the 75th U.S. Infantry Division, which had been brought down from the northern Allied front and was in the process of being placed into position between the 3rd and 28th Divisions.

The 2nd battalion also remained in position for the January 30-31 period, as did 3rd battalion, although the latter, and especially Company L, was subjected to very heavy artillery, Flakwagon, machine-gun, and rifle fire in its mission of blocking and clearing. At 1500 an enemy group of about forty men began an attack toward Company L, but artillery and mortar fire stopped them.

The 1st Battalion, 7th Infantry moved south from Bischwihr at 1700 and entered the Niederwald woods. The battalion encountered only light resistance. At 0700 next morning a reported 200 enemy approaching the southern edge of the woods were taken under artillery fire and routed. An armored infantry force from CC 4 joined 1st Battalion. The 1st Battalion continued scouring Le Niederwald for isolated groups of enemy.

The 2nd battalion, 7th Infantry continued its fight throughout the night of January 30-31. At 0120 Companies E and L (attached) were 300 yards short of a key road junction in Wihr-en-Plaine, near Horbourg, encountering stiff enemy resistance. They had made only fifty yards and were held up by an antitank ditch at 0435. Company E received a counterattack at 0700 and repulsed it only after bitter fighting.

Charles R. Castellaw

The 3rd battalion (minus Company L) entered the woods northwest of 1st Battalion and encountered strong small arms resistance. Company I followed 3rd battalion and engaged the enemy in the woods in a firefight, killing many enemy and taking sixteen prisoners.

The 2nd battalion seized the road junction in Wihr-en-Plaine by noon and pushed on to Horbourg.

French CC S pushed on from Urschenheim to Durrenentzen, and engaged the enemy there in a hard fight. Before the town was taken the French lost nine tanks.

The 2nd battalion and Company L, 7th Infantry, together with CC 4 attacked Horbourg shortly after noon January 31. By 1435, they were in the town fighting a stubbornly resisting foe. By 1535 they held half the town and were fighting from house-to-house as the French armor drove on through. Artillery was directed on enemy withdrawing from the town. A TOT was placed on the west side of the Ill River and advance elements of the 2nd battalion reached the Ill at midnight, putting the town completely in our hands.

The attack was about to go into its final phase. The 15th and 30th Infantry Regiments concentrated on clearing out all enemy west of the Rhone-Rhine Canal which ran north from Neuf-Brisach. The 1st Battalion, 15th Infantry attacked east from Urschenheim to clear the woods and secure a bridge across the Rhone-Rhine Canal near Kunzheim. During the advance, which was led by Company B with armor, 1st Battalion destroyed two enemy tanks and damaged one. The 2nd battalion attacked at 0100, February 1, on the regimental left flank, and advanced to the east along the Colmar Canal, reaching a position from which it could cover the bridge with fire. The 3rd battalion prepared to make an attack to clear the woods between the 1st and 2nd battalions.

By the end of January, the battle to reduce the Colmar Pocket was at its peak. The fury of past battles and the coming of others presented the thought that the reduction of this pocket would not be an easy one. Now that the enemy knew of our intentions, he fought for every yard of ground, counterattacking repeatedly to regain positions that had been overrun by our troops. While the enemy suffered heavily from casualties and the loss of equipment, we too sustained losses not as much as he of course, but enough to be felt. At the close of the period the Regiment, after holding down a defensive position on the

The Way It Was

Northern edge of the Colmar Canal and the Eastern edge of the Ill River, was assembled in Division Reserve in the towns of Hoitzwihr and Wickerschwihr in preparation for the resumption of the attack to the Southeast.

During the period January 1 to January 16 the enemy, in our sector, held a line running generally from Katzenthal to the Weiss River then along the South side of the Weiss River Southeast to the Fecht River. This line consisted of foxholes 20 to 50 meters apart, dug-in MG and a few pillboxes with outposts out to front. Their positions were staggered to form a defensive line approximately 200 meters in depth.

The enemy frequently sent recon and combat patrols against our lines during the hours of darkness, and in the early morning fog. All during the period the enemy made good use of his prepared positions, occupying one position one night and changing to other positions the next night.

During the latter part of the period, the enemy began to send strong combat patrols against our positions and made several attempts to knockout or capture our outposts.

Unoccupied pillboxes were found in the vicinity of (705483). Our F Company took one of these pillboxes. This pillbox was very near the enemy positions and he made several attempts to retake it.

During the period, we ran several strong combat patrols and a company raid on an enemy position on Hill 616 (647601). The company raid was very successful. The enemy was taken by complete surprise; his defensive fires were called for too late and fell on our line of departure after the troops had crossed it. Company I completely overran the enemy positions on the forward slope of the hill, killing a large number of enemy and taking a total of ten prisoners of war.

Enemy artillery for the period was moderate. During the first few days of the period enemy artillery was very heavy, with Kaysersberg, Ammerschwihr, Sigolsheim and Kientzheim his main targets. His principle targets, for the latter part of the period, were the towns and the road nets in the vicinity of the towns, with most of his fire falling during the hours of darkness. Although he used light artillery most of the time, 150mm and 170mm were used to interdict Kaysersberg and Aispach.

Charles R. Castellaw

The enemy made good use of his tanks and SP guns, using them for interdictory fire. Nebelwerfer fire was reported on two occasions, but was not confirmed. The enemy used 120mm mortar on our front lines and on the towns in the forward areas.

During the period 17 January through 21 January, the Regiment was relieved from the Kaysersberg sector and moved to St. Croix. While in the St. Croix area, patrols were operating in the Guemar sector gathering information for our attack of 22 January. Enemy patrols were also active in this sector and most of our patrols made contact with small enemy patrols or outposts.

Our attack during the night of 22 January was met with only light resistance. The enemy held the Colmar Forest with a series of strong points along the north and western edge of the woods, with a few strongpoints around the trail junctions in the woods. The enemy did not have prepared positions east of the L'Ill River to fall back to. Although our advance was very rapid, the enemy managed to bring in armor and Infantry with which he launched a counterattack against our troops in the vicinity of Holtzwihr. Our troops were without armor and were forced to withdraw to the L' Ill River. During the night of 22 January to the 23rd January, the enemy brought in elements of the 2nd Mt. Division and some armor from the east side of the Rhine River. He used these troops piecemeal in an effort to drive all our forces back across the L' Ill River, and to retain his MLR in the Colmar Forest.

The enemy made good use of his armor, which was supported by Infantry, during the first part of the attack, bringing it up to our line on the east side of the L' Ill River and firing across the river and on our bridge sites. The effectiveness of the enemy armor was due to the fact that we were not able to get our armor across the river to meet his attack.

The enemy continued to counterattack our positions and those of 15th Infantry during the 24th and 25th of January, with Infantry and armor. He used men from company trains and other rear installations for some of these attacks.

On the night of the 25th of January, our 1st and 2nd battalions moved into the woods to launch an attack to retake Holtzwihr, and to drive on to the Colmar Canal. The enemy launched a counterattack against our troops while they were moving to the line of departure.

The Way It Was

This counterattack was driven back and our attack jumped off with elements of CC 4. With his attack broken up, the enemy made an effort to hold the towns of Holtzwihr and Wickerschwihr but by morning was forced to retreat across the Colmar Canal. Although the enemy had heavy casualties, he managed to bring in more troops and armor in order to hold our forces on the north side of the Colmar Canal. He immediately began to send patrols across the canal, using tanks and SP and MG fire for support.

Although the enemy was cleared from the east side of the L'Ill River and the north side of the Colmar Canal, he was able to keep the southwest corner of our sector covered by fire. His positions across the river consisted of well-dug in MG positions, mortar, SP guns and light artillery. The enemy was very active in the northeast corner of the Colmar Canal.

During the period the enemy used mortar, tank, and SP guns for his defensive fires rather than artillery.

At the end of the period the enemy was falling back towards the Rhine River after suffering very heavy losses in personnel, armor and equipment.

The 1st Battalion, 30th Infantry, moved out at 0100, February 1, to clear a stretch east of the Rhone-Rhine Canal. Company A, in the lead, reached its objective at 0625 and fired on enemy vehicles with Cannon Company and artillery fires. At 0637, Companies B and C reached the west side of the canal. Company C crossed the canal on locks at 0717. At 0722, Company A repulsed a two-tank attack. The battalion took 124 prisoners in the twenty-four hours ending noon of February 1.

The 2nd battalion, 30th Infantry, continued clearing objectives west of the Rhone-Rhine Canal during the February 1-2 period. The 3rd battalion repulsed a 40-man, two-tank counterattack, shortly after noon of February 1.

The next play belonged to 7th Infantry. During the night of January 31-February 1, the regiment was relieved from its newly won positions by elements of the 75th Infantry Division and assembled in Urschenheim. From here the battalions moved to Wickerschwihr, and foot elements moved by marching to the Rhone-Rhine Canal.

Artzenheim, on the east side of the Rhone-Rhine Canal, had been taken by the French 1 DM1. The plan now was for 7th Infantry to

Charles R. Castellaw

attack south from Artzenheim in the direction of Neuf-Brisach, which lay close to the Rhine River and east of which were the two bridges over which the Germans had been supplying the bulk of their bridgehead forces for so long.

The attack got off at 0500, February 2, 2nd and 3rd battalions abreast. By 0615 Company I had penetrated to the northern edge of Kunzheim. The 2nd battalion became engaged in a small arms and machine gun fight for Baltzenheim at 0800, while 3rd battalion fought to clear Kunzheim. By 0900, both towns were cleared.

With Kunzheim taken, next step was Biesheim, then the final objective, Neuf-Brisach. Leading elements of the 30th Infantry were cleaning out the southern edges of the Schaeferwald woods, a southwestern projection of Bois de Biesheim directly east of Widensolen. To the south, athwart the 30th Infantry's path which was clearly outlined and guided by the converging lines of the Widensolen and Rhone-Rhine Canals, were the northern moats and city wall of Neuf-Brisach.

The 15th Infantry moved behind the 7th Infantry into Kunzheim, ready to follow the 7th then to continue branching out to the southeast, to clean out the enlarged zone of advance caused by the southeast bend of the Rhine in the vicinity of Fort Mortier.

At 0230, February 3, Col. Heintges' 2nd and 3rd battalions attacked, 3rd battalion on the right following the east bank of the Rhone-Rhine Canal. The 1st Battalion was in reserve, and followed at 0600.

The 2nd battalion passed through enemy in trenches north of Biesheim in the darkness, and entered Biesheim at 0400. The battalion's hardest fight was encountered in these trenches.

It was in the light of a waning moon that the advancing infantry was ambushed. Enemy forces outnumbering the Infantry point four to one poured withering artillery, mortar, machine-gun and small-arms fire into the stricken men from the flanks, forcing them to seek the cover of a ditch which they found already occupied by enemy foot troops. As the opposing infantrymen struggled in hand-to-hand combat, T/5 Forrest E. Peden, an artillery forward observer from Battery C, 10th Field Artillery Battalion, accompanying the Infantry, courageously went to the assistance of two wounded soldiers and rendered them first aid under heavy fire. With radio communications

The Way It Was

inoperative, he realized that the unit would be wiped out unless help could be secured from the rear. On his own initiative he ran eight hundred yards to the battalion command post through a hail of bullets, which pierced his jacket, and there secured two light tanks to go to the aid of his hard-pressed comrades. Knowing the terrible risk involved, he climbed upon the hull of the lead tank and guided it into battle. The tank lumbered on through a murderous concentration of fire until it reached the ditch. A direct hit struck the tank, just as it was about to go into action, turning it into a burning pyre and killing T/5 Peden. His death was not in vain. The remainder of the battalion was guided to the scene of action by the flames and relieved their embattled comrades. Peden was posthumously awarded the Medal of Honor.

The 3rd battalion, on the other hand, became involved with enemy along the canal, and initially only Company I succeeded in entering Biesheim. Enemy in the "Jewish Cemetery" also took Lt. Col. Lloyd B. Ramsey's assault elements under fire from their east flank. Maj. Kenneth W. Wallace's 1st Battalion, following the 2nd battalion under Maj. Jack M. Duncan, discovered when daylight came that the hardest enemy opposition had actually been by-passed and that a very determined group held out in the Jewish Cemetery and in pillboxes between that point and the Rhine. The 1st Battalion was involved in a stiff fight all day and half the night of February 3-4, when the cemetery and surrounding area finally were reported clear. At 0400, the battalion was ordered to return to Kunzheim, pending further action.

During most of February 3, the 3rd and 2nd battalions continued to work on Biesheim and it was cleared of Germans by 1700. The 3rd battalion captured 250 prisoners and 2nd battalion took about 150.

Meanwhile the 30th Infantry had attacked south along the west bank of the Rhone-Rhine Canal on February 3 and elements of the 1st Battalion, under Lt. Col. Mackenzie E. Porter, reached the canal bridge east of Biesheim, where enemy fire was received.

Maj. Kenneth B. Potter's 1st Battalion, 15th Infantry, attacked east during the early morning hours of February 4 to assist the 1st Battalion, 7th Infantry in clearing the cemetery area. A small task force from the battalion then moved north from Biesheim to clear up scattered enemy resistance elements along the Kunzheim-Biesheim

Charles R. Castellaw

road, and it was this that shortly thereafter enabled Major Wallace's Battalion to return to Kunzheim.

During the night of February 3-4 and February 4-5, 2nd battalion, 30th Infantry, commanded by Maj. James A. Osgard, sent patrols toward Neuf-Brisach, as did the 1st Battalion. Elements of the 1st Battalion encountered some enemy pillboxes at 1925, February 3, succeeded in eliminating two of them by 2100, and at 2340 sent a platoon from Company A to occupy the pillboxes.

At 0435 a five-man patrol from Company A went to a point approximately 500 meters north of Neuf-Brisach and succeeded in returning with twenty-four German prisoners. Major Osgard's 2nd battalion, and 3rd battalion, under Maj. Christopher W. Chaney, maintained aggressive combat patrols to the front and flanks during the 24-hour period beginning noon, February 3.

At 0015, February 5, 7th Infantry left the line of departure at Biesheim. The 1st Battalion's mission was to seize the crossroads north of Vogelsheim; 3rd battalion on the right had the mission of seizing the railroad station and sealing the northeast and east entrances to Neuf-Brisach. The 2nd battalion was then to pass through 3rd battalion and seize the hospital and factory area southeast of Neuf-Brisach.

The 15th Infantry already had moved to the southeast of Biesheim, where elements of 1st Battalion had seized a crossroads there. Maj. John O'Connell's 3rd battalion cleared the Boulay Woods along the banks of the Rhine and was then moved south to continue clearing the woods to the south. Lt. Col. Eugene Salet's 2nd battalion, 15th Infantry, also worked on the territory along the banks of the Rhine, operating south of the 3rd battalion.

The 7th Infantry succeeded in clearing Vogelsheim by 0630, February 5, and 2nd battalion moved through on schedule, clearing out the hospital and factory area with little trouble. During the night of February 5-6, a patrol from Company K, led by Sgt. Chester M. Owens, reconnoitered to the east and northeast of Neuf-Brisach, and succeeded in reaching the northeast wall without being fired upon.

The 15th Infantry encountered considerable trouble at Fort Mortier, southeast of Biesheim, on the afternoon of February 5, but the fort was cleared out by 2100. The 1st Battalion accomplished this mission. The 3rd battalion continued to move south. By 1730,

The Way It Was

Company K had cut the main highway bridge approach, and Company I had moved even further south and cut the railway bridge approach.

Neuf-Brisach was now nearly sealed off. During the night of February 6th, the enemy began evacuating the fortress city. Preparatory to this, however, there was a stiff fight north of the city. The 1st Battalion, 30th Infantry, during the night of February 4-5 assigned Company C the mission of ascertaining the condition of a bridge across the Widensolen Canal just east of Petite Hollande Ferme. At 0430, the four men of the point of 1st Lt. Louis J. Lombardi's 2nd Platoon were fired upon by machine guns in the vicinity of the bridge and from machine guns at the farm. The platoon thereupon withdrew slightly and dug in along the east bank of the canal.

Company B, 30th Infantry attacked through Company A along the west bank of the Rhone-Rhine Canal a few minutes after 1500, February 5, with predesignated phase lines. The attack was successful. The company "peeled off" to the right by platoons, with armor support, and took seventy-eight prisoners, wounded fourteen more, and killed four.

The company set up an outpost line between canals and shortly thereafter Company C, moving south along the Widensolen Canal, contacted Company B's right elements, and the two companies set up their defense.

That same night of February 5, 2nd battalion, 30th Infantry moved by marching to Biesheim and at 2030 the battalion attacked toward Vogelsheim in column of companies. The area east and south of Vogelsheim was interdicted by our artillery as the battalion advanced. Light opposition was encountered and the town of Vogelgrun was reported clear by 2315.

After the 2nd battalion's successful attack on Vogelgrun, the 3rd battalion launched an attack on Algolsheim. The enemy here was supported by at least three tanks, and intense artillery fire was received from enemy Flak guns east of the Rhine. Under the command of Lt. Col. Christopher W. Chaney, the battalion fought through the afternoon of February 6 and into the morning of February 7 to clear the town, beating off one enemy counterattack after the town was taken.

Charles R. Castellaw

Pfc. Kenneth E. LaRue of Company B led a patrol to the northeast wall of Neuf-Brisach during the night of February 5-6, with a mission of determining the condition of the railroad bridge in that vicinity. The men found strong demolition charges laid, but the bridge was intact. The patrol drew four or five rounds of sniper fire and observed about five men in a nearby grape vineyard. Company C personnel captured these the following morning.

At 0900, February 6, elements of the 2nd battalion, 7th Infantry reported heavy enemy traffic evacuating from the town on the southeast road leading from Neuf-Brisach. Major Duncan ordered artillery, tank, and infantry weapons fire laid on this traffic.

At 0800 Sgt. Elbert Tapley of Company C, 30th Infantry led a three-man patrol to the north wall of town and was fired on by an enemy machine gun. However, the patrol remained in wait and at about 1000 observed a white flag above the arch entrance way into the town. Sergeant Tapley returned to find his company moving one platoon down to the northwest wall.

At about 0930, a Company B platoon under S/Sgt. Richard B. Weiler moved south in column. As the men neared the railroad bridge, they observed a civilian who, after some persuasion, jumped down into the dry moat and led the platoon to a narrow, low-ceilinged 60-foot tunnel which led through the wall into the town.

The 3rd Platoon, Company C, under 1st Lt. Hennon Gilbert, however, had preceded the Company B Platoon. Led by Sergeant Tapley, the platoon approached a blown bridge on the northwest edge of town, and two young French children went down into the moat to guide them through the archway into town.

Since this platoon entered first, it took all the prisoners. In one building in the north part of town there were thirty-eight. The others drifted in, in groups of three and four, until a total of seventy-six had been accounted for. There was no fighting in the town.

By 1115, it was radioed that the town was clear of enemy.

The ending was as anti-climactic as the fighting which preceded it had been fierce. The fact that entry into the town was made easily did not detract from the work of the regiments in Neuf-Brisach's near vicinity.

Thus fell Neuf-Brisach, entered by 1st Battalion, 30th Infantry. Built in 1472, and first destroyed by the Germans in 1870, the town

The Way It Was

had been built to withstand a siege. The 3rd Infantry Division's chosen method of attack made direct assault unnecessary. The Division's work was done.

Maj. Gen. John W. O'Daniel, who had commanded 3rd Infantry Division since February 17, 1944—through the push to Rome, Southern France, and the Vosges Mountains—had this to say to the Division upon the completion of the 16-day attack against the Colmar Pocket:

"In crossing the Fecht and Ill Rivers, the Colmar and Rhone-Rhine Canals, and your attacks toward Neuf-Brisach, culminating in the routing of the Germans and the capture of the Neuf-Brisach area, you have participated in the *most outstanding* operation in the career of your Division.

"You drove on relentlessly day and night through the worst of weather. Your action not only enabled you to advance, but also made possible the advance of all other forces in the bridgehead and hastened the collapse and elimination of the German-held Colmar Pocket.

"As your commander, I congratulate you on your outstanding performance and am proud of the honor of being in command of such a superb group of fighting men."

Said Maj. Gen. F. W. Milburn, XXI Corps Commander: "The operations of the XXI Corps in the Colmar area have been successfully completed. Colmar has been liberated and the enemy has been driven to the east of the Rhine.

"The success of these operations has been due to the loyalty, the gallantry, and the unselfish devotion to duty of the many thousands of officers and enlisted men of the units that constitute the XXI Corps.

"*The 3rd Infantry Division was particularly outstanding in these operations.* It performed its assigned missions with great enthusiasm. It completed these missions successfully, contributing materially thereby to the great victory achieved by our units.

"I wish to commend you, the officers, and enlisted men of the 3rd Infantry Division for the superior manner in which they performed during these operations. Their actions were superb, and they reflect the finest traditions of the Armies of the United States."

"...This commendable operation," said Lt. Gen. Jacob Devers, Sixth Army Group Commander, "is in the best tradition of the 3rd

Charles R. Castellaw

Infantry Division and has added another glorious chapter to your outstanding record which includes almost 400 combat days and nineteen Medals of Honor. I congratulate each officer and man on this fine organization of which you should all be justly proud."

Bare statistics shed further light on the Colmar accomplishment. The 3rd Infantry Division, reinforced, during the 16-day period, captured twenty-two towns, over 4,200 prisoners, and killed an enemy total disproportionately high to the total number captured. It virtually destroyed the 708th VG and 2nd Mountain Divisions, badly mauled the 189th and 16th VG Divisions, and destroyed a great amount of all types of enemy material.

General Charles de Gaulle, head of the Provisional French Government, chose another way of saying "Thanks." On February 20, 1945, there was a notable ceremony in Colmar. The 1st Battalion, 30th Infantry represented the 3rd Division's infantry; a battery of the 41st FA Battalion, the artillery. The 3rd Reconnaissance Troop was also represented by a platoon.

General Jean de Lattre de Tassigny, commander of the First French Army, pinned the Order of the Croix de Guerre to the Division's colors. He then conferred the Legion D'Honneur, 3rd Degree, and the Croix de Guerre with Palm on the 3rd's Commanding General, John W. "Iron Mike" O'Daniel.

With the capture of Neuf-Brisach, the end of the Colmar Pocket was assured. The enemy was now unable to supply or reinforce his troops. As the 3rd Infantry Division inexorably closed on the two bridges over the Rhine east of Neuf-Brisach the enemy demolished them.

The United States 12th Armored Division raced south from Colmar and made contact with I French Corps elements at Houffach. The mop-up of the remaining elements of the German Nineteenth Army took only a few days. And again the 3rd took up its Watch on the Rhine.

Limited training was undertaken almost immediately as the Division outposted and patrolled, and made plans to deal with any German attempts to recross the river. The 7th and 30th Infantry Regiments handled this task, while 15th Infantry remained in reserve.

The Way It Was

The 254th Infantry was completely relieved on February 9 and reverted to control of its parent organization, the 63rd Infantry Division.

By February 10, a subparagraph in the G-2 Periodic Report noted that: "Organized enemy resistance west of the Rhine River between Strasbourg and the Swiss border is reported to have ceased."

The 99th Chemical Mortar Battalion remained in Division reserve, registering, firing on targets of opportunity, and firing smoke missions across the Rhine. The 168th Chemical Company continued smoke operations along the river, screening our movements from the enemy in Germany until the morning of February 12, when a detachment from the 21st Chemical Company relieved it.

Relieved

Commencing on February 16, elements of the 4th *Regiment Tirailleurs Marocain* of the 2nd *Division Infanterie Motorisé* reconnoitered 7th and 30th Infantry positions, preparatory to relief of the entire Division. "You're going back so far you'll be able to eat ice cream," a happy General Devers had promised the Division at the finish of the attack, and the 3rd was ready to take the Sixth Army Group Commander at his word.

The relief commenced on February 17 and at 1800, February 18, control of the sector passed from the Commanding General, 3rd Infantry Division, to the Commanding General of the 2nd DIM.

The 3rd assembled and made preparations to move to prearranged areas in Lorraine near Nancy, after 188 days of continuous contact with the enemy.

Pont-a-Mousson is almost exactly halfway between Nancy and Metz. There is a sign that reads "Nancy 27 km" and directly below it with an arrow pointing in the opposite direction the legend says, "Metz 28 km." It was here that the Division command post set up for business. The regiments disposed themselves in small towns all along the Nancy-Metz highway. The 7th Infantry's 1st Battalion was stationed in Belleville, the 2nd at Dieulouard, and the 3rd at Marbache, all between Pont-à-Mousson and Nancy. Near Pont-à-Mousson the 30th Infantry set up housekeeping: 1st Battalion near Eulmont, 2nd at Bouxieres, and 3rd battalion at Lay St. Christopher. The 15th Infantry

265

Charles R. Castellaw

bivouacked in towns north of Pont-à-Mousson, in the vicinity of Pagny.

The official status of the Division was now SHAEF reserve, but there were few who doubted that recommitment to combat would long be delayed. Meanwhile, rest, rehabilitation, and then, inevitably, training, were the order of the day. The infantry regiments began training new replacements, just as did the 601st Tank Destroyer Battalion and 756th Tank Battalion. The armored attachments had suffered heavier casualties in the Colmar attack than in any campaign since the push to Rome. New tanks, new tank destroyers, and reinforcements were received and absorbed into the framework of organizations. The 441st AAA AW Battalion's Battery C was immediately set to work providing antiaircraft protection for lines of communications, bivouac areas and bridges, while the other two lettered batteries underwent rehabilitation.

The 10th Engineer Battalion and 3rd Reconnaissance Troop likewise began rehabilitation and reception of reinforcements.

Along with the commencement of training, recreation was introduced to an organization that had known little recreation since its stay in Puzzle, near Naples, six months before. Pass trucks began making regular runs to Nancy, which by now was a large hospital and base-section strongpoint, and the locale of *beaucoup femmes*, always a subject of considerable interest to soldiers. Nancy, in many places virtually untouched by bombs and shells, was a sight for eyes weary of scarred, razed Alsatian villages.

More Fighting

But the war, as always, soon predominated and subordinated all other efforts. As February passed into March, the training program rounded off. This consisted of intensive practice in street fighting, the attack of permanent fortifications, weapons firing, intelligence, night operations, and the technique of river crossings.

The period opened with our troops moving to an assembly area near and in Urschenheim for an attack against the enemy in the Bois de Biesheim and Bois de Urschenheim. The enemy held these woods with a line of foxholes along its western edge and a few strongpoints

The Way It Was

near the trail crossings. The enemy had approximately 200 men in the sector and a few pieces of armor.

The enemy offered light resistance to our advance through the woods during the early morning of 1 February, '45. However, the resistance began to increase in the afternoon and the enemy launched several small counterattacks against our forward positions and along the canal.

An enemy strongpoint in the vicinity (833395) supported by at least one SP gun gave us quite a bit of trouble. The enemy did everything possible to hold this strongpoint and the Biesheim Bridge across the Rhine-Rhone Canal. He launched a counterattack supported by armor to keep our troops from the bridge site and later blew the bridge just as our troops reached it.

On one occasion, the enemy used barges to move in on one of our outposts along the canal. These barges were 150 feet in length and about 6 feet high. Machine guns were mounted on the barges and the enemy was armed with automatic weapons.

During the period, the enemy made use of every available man, using many from his trains, rear installations, and all the stragglers he could round up. These men were not well informed and were committed piecemeal with orders to hold at all costs.

After being driven from the woods, the enemy continued to hold a line about 1000 to 1200 yards north of Neuf-Brisach between the Widensolen and the Rhine-Rhone Canals. This line was held by at least 200 men and was his main defense for the city of Neuf-Brisach. The line consisted of communication trenches with pillboxes near the Rhine-Rhone Canal and a strongpoint of three houses near the center of the line.

The enemy allowed small recon patrols to pass through his lines on several occasions but fired on larger patrols.

A well-planned afternoon attack by the 1st Battalion cleared the area of enemy, capturing 75 prisoners of war, killing and wounding many others. This opened the way for the attack on Neuf-Brisach, which the enemy gave up with little resistance.

The enemy offered light resistance to our advance from Volgelsheim to the Rhine River with the exception of two pillboxes and a house two hundred meters east of Algolsheim.

Charles R. Castellaw

Enemy artillery during the first part of the period was heavy, especially in the Bois de Biesheim, along the Rhine-Rhone Canal and in the towns of Urschenheim and Widensolen. The enemy made good use of his dual-purpose 88's, firing as many as 16 guns at one time in one area. Heavy mortars and SP guns were also used to a great extent.

The towns of Volgelsheim and Algolsheim also received heavy artillery fire the first day they were taken by our troops.

Enemy aircraft were used against our forward positions. The town of Algolsheim was bombed three times by one or two jet-propelled planes.

During the latter part of the period the enemy artillery decreased to 20-30 rounds per day in our regimental sector as compared with 2000 rounds per day during the first part of the period.

The period closed with the enemy manning pillboxes along the eastern banks of the Rhine River, and trying to reorganize his forces.

The War is Over for Me

My feet had been giving me a lot of trouble from the wet, cold, freezing weather and had turned blue. We had received clean socks. As I pulled my boots and socks off to change, one of my fellow soldiers saw my feet. He told me if I wanted to keep my feet, I should go to the doctor. Also, he said that when I got back to the farm it would be hard for me to follow a pair of mules pulling a plow in a wheelchair.

I considered my options. First, I wanted to be in my Company when the war ended. Second, I wanted to receive the promotion that I had been promised and knew that if I went to the doctor he would send me to the hospital. This would end my chance of receiving the promotion. Third, if I stayed with my unit, I would be taking a chance of losing my feet and my life. My platoon had about a 300% turnover since I entered it.

For several months there had been no one left that was in my platoon when I entered. I considered the fact that my luck could run out anytime. I decided that I would play it safe and go to the doctor early the next morning. The doctor took one look at my feet and said, "I am sending you to the Field Hospital." I was transported to the hospital by jeep. When I arrived, I was given clean clothes and I took

The Way It Was

a hot shower. After showering and dressing, I reported to the kitchen. The cook served me two pancakes and as soon as I ate them, he served me two more. After I had eaten two servings, he asked me if I wanted more. I said, "I hate to ask you to keep cooking, but I could eat two more." He replied, "I will cook them as long as you eat them, even if it is all day." This was about mid-morning.

After eating I was led to a cot and told to go to bed. I went to sleep and did not wake up until the next morning. When the doctor came, he said he had been in to see me the evening before, but I was sleeping and he thought I needed sleep more than anything else so he did not wake me. After he examined my feet he said, "Your war is over, and I am sending you to an Evacuation Hospital at Southampton, England. From there you will be sent back to the States."

After a few days, I was sent to the Evacuation Hospital at Southampton, England, by hospital ship. I was checked in at the hospital and told that I would be sent back to the States as soon as transportation was available, which was a long wait.

Peace

On the night of May 8, 1945, Captain Clem met Marshal Kesselring on his private train, the "Brunswick," which had moved to the south of the lake. From that time on, communication was constant with the Allied high command, including General Eisenhower, and remained constant until the following day when representatives of Sixth Army Group headquarters appeared to receive the Marshal's final surrender. This historic act, involving the submission of more than one million enemy troops, took place in the "Brunswick" at the little town of Saalfelden. The last German force in Europe had surrendered.

At 0241, Monday, May 7, 1945 at Reims, France, General of the Army Eisenhower turned to his Deputy Commander British Marshal Tedder and said, "Thank you very much, Arthur." Then he held up two pens with which surrender had been signed and made a "V" for victory. Peace had officially come to Europe.

269

Charles R. Castellaw

Table of Casualties[15]
3rd Infantry Division, Germany
(March 15, 1945 through May 8, 1945)

Killed in Action	373
Wounded in Action	1744
Missing in Action	416
Total Battle Casualties	2533
Non-Battle Casualties	1909
Reinforcements Officers	56
Reinforcements E M	1970
Hospital Return-to-Unit Officers	63
Hospital Return-to- Unit E M	1278
Known Enemy Casualties	
Killed in Action	381
Wounded in Action	1020
Captured	101,201

Table of Casualties[16]
30th Regiment, 3rd Infantry Division
(From August 15, 1944 through May 8, 1945)
From Invasion of Southern France to the End of the War

	Officers	**E. M.**[2]
Beginning Strength	167	3419
Killed in Action	34	547
Wounded in Action	117	2419
Non Battle Casualties	136	3862
Total Casualties	253	6828
Missing in Action	10	1266
Died of Wounds	2	56
Replacements	142	3562
Reassigned and Joined	172	3814
Missing in Action to Duty	1	697
Duty to AWOL[1]	0	436

---

[15] Figures from A C or S, G-1, 3rd Infantry Division.
[16] Report of Operation, 30th U.S. Infantry, 3rd Division, National Archives and Records Administration.

AWOL[1] to Duty	0	409
Duty to Confinement	1	71
Ending Strength	124	2571

1. Absent without leave 2. Enlisted men

Even with two-thirds of the German Army engaged by Russia, it took every man the Nation saw fit to mobilize to do our part of the job in Europe and at the same time keep the Japanese enemy under control in the Pacific. What would have been the result had the Red Army been defeated and the British Islands invaded, we can only guess. The possibility is rather terrifying.

Toatl allied mobilization exceeded 62,000,000; total enemy mobilization, 30,000,000. Even with our overwhelming concentration of air power and fire power, this war has been the most costly of any in which the Nation has been engaged. The victory in Europe alone cost us 772,626 battle casualties of which 160,045 are dead. The price of victory in the Pacific was 170,596 including 41,322 dead. Army battle deaths since 7 December 1941, were greater than the combined losses, Union and Confederate, of the Civil War. I present the following comparisons of the battle deaths we have suffered in all our wars so that there can be no misunderstanding of the enormous cost of this conflict, for which we were so completely unprepared:

	Number of Months Duration	Total battle deaths
American Revolution	80	4,044
War of 1812	30	1,877
Mexican War	20	1,721
Civil War (Union Losses)	48	110,070
Civil War (Confederate Losses)	48	74,524
Spanish-American	4	345
World War I	19	50,510
World War II (1941-1945)	44	201,367
Korean (1950-1953)		54,246
Vietnam (1965-1973)		58,135

Charles R. Castellaw

In writing this book, my number one objective was to tell the story as and like it happened. In the part dealing with WW II, I gave a lot of credit to others because war battles are won by team effort. I was awarded the Bronze Star metal for for heroic action against the enemy in France but I did not consider Charles Ray Castellaw a war hero. I thought it was my duty to do what I did to stay alive and help win the war. When the 2nd battalion, 30th Regiment, 3rd Division was in combat from the time I entered the unit until I was sent to the hospital, I was there doing what I could to stay alive and help win the war.

The Way It Was

Section 3

On April 13, 1945, I was told to pack my belongings and be ready to board ship the next day. We would be on our way to the States. After a 14-day voyage, we arrived in the New York harbor on April 28th. Upon arrival, we were transported by train in a Pullman birth to Fort Carson Military Hospital in Colorado Springs, Colorado.

After I arrived with others from the same hospital in England, we were given an orientation program which did not answer our question, "When were we going home?" We were given several options of things to do, but the only thing we had to do was to make up our bed every morning. Also, we were told that as decisions were being made, we would receive our instructions.

On July 28, 1945, I received a medical discharge, a pair of special shoes, $300 in mustering out pay, and a train ticket for Bells, Tennessee. After arriving in Bells, I saw one of my neighbors, Arthur Pipkins. I asked him when he would be going home and would he give me a ride to my house. He said, "I am ready to go now and you can ride with me." I felt sure he really was not ready to go but wanted to take me home.

My family was surprised to see me because they were not expecting me. Word of my return traveled fast in the community. It was not long before several friends, neighbors, and relatives came to see me. I was glad to see each and every one of them but I felt uncomfortable in their presence. My thoughts were about Betty Jo and seeing her.

After having dinner with my family, I went to see Betty Jo. I was glad to see her but felt uncomfortable as we embraced. We spent a quiet evening together engaged in small talk. I left early with the excuse that I was tired and needed sleep.

I spent the next several weeks thinking about my situation but could not make any decisions. I had lost interest in farming and could not develop interest in another occupation. I was having a hard time sleeping as well. At night I would have dreams about being in combat, including specific traumatic episodes. At times I would dream of being in a situation where the enemy would be at an

Charles R. Castellaw

advantage and I would be suffering because my M-1 rifle would not work or the ammunition would be a dud.

I knew I could go to the Veterans Hospital at Memphis, Tennessee. I thought that if I did go, my problem would be diagnosed as "shell shock" or crazy. At times I did question my sanity, but I was determined that I would not discuss my problem with Betty Jo or my family.

When Betty Jo would try to discuss our future, I would change the subject. I could see that our relationship was falling apart, but I did not know what to do about it.

She had graduated from high school the past spring and was working at a beauty parlor. She said that she would go to beautician school and I could go to barber school. After that we would open a joint beauty parlor and barbershop. This did not appeal to me so I would not discuss it with her or make any suggestions.

Some of the things that would upset me were stories about individuals that got out of their military obligation. There was one story about Frank Sinatra getting his draft board to classify him as 4-F by claiming that he had a hearing problem. I could not understand that. If his claim was true, why did it not affect his musical performances? When I was in combat, there was a man about age 35 in my platoon with a hearing problem.

My mother told me about a lady coming in the church one Sunday, sitting beside her and remarking that she thought it was terrible that the draft board would not permit her son to go to school. He had a farm deferment. Mama told her that she would be happy just to know where her boys were. At that time my brother, Carl, was on a battleship in the Pacific, and I was in combat in Europe.

One night Betty Jo and I went to the show in Brownsville, Tennessee. The movie was a war story. The picture upset me to the extent that I had to leave the movie. Betty Jo saw how upset I was and apologized for going to see a war picture.

I had thought about how much I loved Betty Jo and wanted to marry her. Because of my fear and lack of confidence, I could not tell her how I felt.

Our relationship continued for about three months after I arrived home from the service. Then one night she seemed to be very cool toward me and told me that she was going to Memphis, Tennessee, to live. It was clear to me that she was telling me that it was all over between us. I got very little sleep that night. All I could think about was that I had lost her. I had let the war destroy what I wanted most out of life. The next day I decided that I would try to see her and tell her how I felt about her and how I wanted us to make plans for our future. With this in mind, I called her at the beauty parlor where she worked and told her that I was going to Jackson later that afternoon and asked her to go with me. She agreed. I met her when she got off work, and we drove to Jackson, Tennessee. We talked very little, mostly small talk. I was unable to tell her how I felt about her and what I wanted us to do. When I returned her to her house and said good-bye, I knew that it was all over between us and I probably would never see her again.

I spent the following year living with my parents. I worked part time with my father, but did not seek outside employment. My recurrent dreams of specific traumatic episodes of combat continued, but it seemed to me that I was learning to live with the problem. During that year, I did not develop a relationship with another woman.

Robert Castellaw in his old country store

Charles R. Castellaw

In September, 1946, under the GI Bill, I enrolled at the University of Tennessee, Knoxville, in the College of Agriculture. The first year was very difficult for me, as I could not concentrate. My mind would wander off into my memories of the war. For the next three years, I stayed very busy, which helped me adjust to a normal life style. I graduated in August, 1949.

Originally, I had planned a career in agriculture equipment sales. However, on the advice of one of my professors, I interviewed for a teaching position as vocational agriculture teacher in a secondary school in a small town, Sharon, in west Tennessee. The principal was a good salesman and convinced me to take the job. Since the school had never had a vocational agricultural program before, the position allowed me to design the building and curriculum myself. I thought this was the opportunity of a lifetime. I reported for work two days later. I also decided to become a full-time member of the community, joining the volunteer fire department and such. As the agriculture instructor, I visited local farmers to offer suggestions and help them as well. This helped me to become a member of the community even though I was an outsider.

After a while, some of the community wives developed a plan for me to meet one of the local single girls at a card party. Sarah Stoker was a first grade teacher. We hit it off the first night. We went together on a regular basis. The following year, 1951, we were married and set up in a rented house. Eventually we built our own home, doing most of the labor ourselves. It took seven years to complete.

I had been in Sharon for about two years when I walked into a local business. The owner came up to me and said, "We need a magistrate, and we've decided you should be it." I told him I didn't know anything about the job and wouldn't know what to do. He assured me it would be fine and they would handle the election. I was elected unopposed. For eighteen years, I was county magistrate, which also meant that I was a city court magistrate. This compares to the general session court of today. As a member of the county court, I was involved in several issues. One that stands out in my mind was a bond issue to update our schools and a countywide school construction plan. As chairman of that committee, I lost hours of sleep trying to figure out how to convince the rest of the court, fifty-four

The Way It Was

members, to pass the referendum. It was the largest bond ever issued in our county. I decided to present it to the court not in millions of dollars, but the average cost per person, per day. In doing this, I realized the cost could be converted into cigarettes per person per year. After my presentation, it was voted in unanimously. I was very pleased as well as surprised.

In the fifties, farmers were brought under the Social Security Act. Obviously, prior to this, they did not pay social security taxes. The IRS and Social Security Service provided training for agriculture teachers so they could help the farmers. I attended the training and as a result set up an adult farmer class in one of our communities in an old school building and offered classes to the farmers. I assisted them in filing their income taxes and social security reports.

After talking with the farmers, I realized they did not really keep records. I had to teach them record keeping. At that time, the John Deere Company was distributing farm record books. I secured enough of these to give to each of my students. I asked the farmers to bring in whatever information they had kept for the past year. Some would bring in slips of paper and receipts for fertilizer or feed and also copies of sales of cows or milk. I had one farmer bring in a calendar on which he had written a sale or purchase on the particular date. The first year was difficult because I had to take all of that information and put in the proper format. This was a tremendous amount of work and the only way I was able to accomplish it was to start at the end of every school day until dark. We were able to get all of our records straightened out and filed by April 15. The farmers should have had it turned in by February 15, but the school we attended worked out a deal to where any farmer that we helped could file a complete and correct income tax report by April 15 and would not be penalized. This gave us confidence in doing a job that we were dedicated to do.

Another part of this program that was very interesting was that there were several farmers already sixty-five years old at this time and old enough to draw social security. They could file back reports to cover a certain number of quarters to qualify them for social security. In a short period of time, we were able to get them their benefits. They had not expected to receive this money, and it came in very handy for many people who were in need.

Charles R. Castellaw

I enjoyed a successful career in education, twenty-three years as a teacher and nine years in administration. Sarah and I raised three boys, Michael Ray (July 29, 1952), Charles Robert (March 19, 1955), and John Neil (November 13, 1958).

We were very happy, spending family vacations every June in Gatlinburg, Tennessee. The untimely death of my first son, Mike, brought that idyllic life to an end. On April 14, 1974, Mike, his wife and another couple were boating on Kentucky Lake. They were staying at a cabin I had built in 1972, against my wife's wishes. Mike, a junior engineering student at the University of Tennessee, drowned in a boating accident. My wife, Sarah, never recovered from the loss. She blamed me for his death as I had built the cabin. This caused a terrible strain on our marriage. Finally in 1983, I could stand no more and we were separated. We signed a mutually agreed upon financial settlement and were divorced. We kept in touch, and I would visit her at her flower and gift shop. This continued until her death on December 1, 1990. On February 9, 1993, our third son, John Neil, had a seizure and drowned in a bathtub in Memphis, Tennessee. This was obviously a great shock. I was vacationing in Florida at the time.

Our son, Charles Robert, has spent several years searching for his place in life. Formerly a lawyer, he has changed from job to job without establishing a permanent place in society.

The Way It Was

I Returned To France

After I returned home from WW II, I often thought about the woman that I met in the basement of the Saales Sanitarium and her twin girls. A few years later, I decided that I would return to Saales, France and visit her and her family. I wanted to meet her husband who served in the German Army. He was young and like me, he served a cause created by political leaders. I was unable to make the trip until after I retired from work.

On April 16, 1997, I wrote a letter addressed to the Mayor of Saales, France and in this letter I explained what took place in the Sanitarium basement on November 23, 1944. I had dinner with the woman that I met at the Sanitarium, her twin girls (13 months old) and her father and mother. I stated that I wanted to make contact with her but did not remember her name. I wanted to visit her and some of the places where I had been during WWII.

I received a letter from Jean Vogel, Mayor, City of Saales. He stated that he transmitted my letter to Mr. Gobinet, former Mayor and Historian of Sales. Mr. Gobinet made researches in order to find people who were in the basement when I entered it. He stated that this was an unforgettable event which remains in memories and still today almost everybody in Saales knows the story about a large part of the population who took refuge in the basement of the Sanitarium, while my army unit was engaged with the German Army in the forest over-looking the Sanitarium. Nobody could tell who was the woman with twin girls. A decision was made to print my letter in the local newspaper. In answer to my letter, a lady called in and said, "I am one of those twins listed in his letter".

My case was turned over to Luc Heinrich who lived in Mutzig. He was a young man that could speak and write English and had developed a strong interest in WWII history. Luc wrote me a letter and we developed a plan for my trip.

On Monday, Septermber 8, 1997, at 1:53 PM, I boarded an American Airlines plane in Nashville, Tennessee airport for Chicago Ohare airport. About two hours after arriving, I boarded an American Airlines plane for Paris, France. On the plane, I met a lady who was going to Paris to see a friend. I told her about my trip and that I was

279

taking a train from Paris to Strasbourg so I could see the country. She said that her friend would be in his car and that they would take me to the train station. We arrived in Paris on Tuesday, the 9th of September at 8:00 AM. Her friend was waiting for her. When we pulled out of the airport onto the street, I saw a big McDonalds sign.

I had about a one hour layover at the train station. At the train station and the airport I was surprised to see Army Soldiers patrolling with sub-machine guns. I used the delay time to look around and talk to some of the people. Those who could speak English seemed to be very anxious to talk to me. It may have been my American southern accent.

At Fort Mutzig

The train trip from Paris to Strasbourg was very enjoyable. I learned that countries with fast electric trains were much advanced over the United States in transportation. I believe that over the years the American oil companies had something to do with this. I traveled by bus from Strasbourg to Mutzig. When I arrived at my hotel in Mutzig, I was ready for a shower and bed.

The next day, Luc met me at my hotel and we spent the day seeing the sights in Mutzig. I saw a plaque honoring the first American soldier killed in Mutzig. We visited several places, including the museum. Later that week, with one of Luc friends, we visit the (Mutzig) Maginot Line fort.

Luc Heinrich on the left and his friend on the right, Louis Meyer

The decision to construct the fort was made in January of 1893 by Emperor William II of Germany. The first work began in April, 1893 and construction took 21 years. Total cost: 15 million gold marks. It

The Way It Was

would house 6500 men and was self-sufficient, including a modern hospital. The fort is open for visitors. The trip is two hours and 3 KM long, of which about half is under ground with numerous staircases. The interior temperature is approximately 11°C in all seasons. Numerous original equipment is on display, including kitchens, machine rooms, bakery, wells, generators, machine gun chest (1914), infantry shelters (1899-1910, 1914), two artillery observation post (1905), etc.

One day we went to Saales to visit what was a Sanitarum when I was there in 1944. It had been converted into a modern hospital. I was disappointed because I thought I would recognize it. I had not been told that it had been changed into a modern hospital. As we toured the hospital, I did not recognize anything until we were in the basement and the tour guide stopped and pointed to some old steps and said, "During WWII an American soldier came down those steps and stood here and told the people in the basement that he was an American soldier. I looked at him and said, "That soldier was me." He looked at me as if to say, "It cannot be."

While I was in Mutzig, I had some free time to visit. I visited a school and other places of interest. I visited the mountains. They were beautiful, covered with green trees and other vegetation. This scene was quite different from the scene of dead looking trees, snow, ice and cold weather that we encountered in the fall of 1944, which was the coldest winter that they had had in several years. As I looked at the terrain, I had visions of those wounded and killed. The sight of body parts scattered over the battle field was terrible, but to me the worse sight was the look on a dying soldier's face as I stepped over him in order to move on. My thoughts were, what can I say about those young foot soldiers who had paid the supreme price for a cause that should had never happened. I believe Louis Adamic said it best when he said, "There is a certain blend of courage, integrity, character and principle which has no satisfactory dictionary name but has been called different things at different times in different countries. Our American name for it is, 'GUTS'.

While I was in France, the Mayor of Mutzig awarded me the Mutzig City Medal. When I visited Rasheem, the Mayor there awarded me their City Medal.

Luc gave me a date on which he said he had planned a trip for us but did not say where and what it was about. On that date we went to Saales and were greeted by Mayor Jean Vogel and several others in a crowd in front of City Hall. The Schlapach twins, Edith and Elise, the twins of Lucie Schlapach, the lady that I met in the Sanatorum, were there. After a brief ceremony, we went into City Hall which was flying the American flag. As we entered a room in City Hall, I saw tables draped with white table cloths and covered with food. A man walked up to me and asked, "Do you drink wine?" I said, "Yes." Then bottles of wine were placed on the tables. After a few speeches, we sat down and ate.

Left to right

The Way It Was

Front row – Elsie Colombo, Jean Vogal (Mayor), Charles Castellaw, Edith Schlapach.
Back row – Robert Meltz, Rene Benoit, Louis Colombo, Andie Gass

When the inside activity was over, we walked outside. A man walked up to me and said, "I want you to go with me to my truck. I have something I want to show you." At the truck he pulled out an American WWII helmet. He said that he was sixteen and in the basement when I entered it and when he went outside, he found the helmet and if I wanted it, I could have it. I accepted the helmet and thanked him. During the battle for the Sanitarium one of my friends was hit and I believe the helmet was his. I do not remember his name but I have tried to locate him or his family.

I enjoyed talking to Edith and Elise. I learned from them that their mother had died two years earlier and their father had died ten years before our meeting. I had the honor of having dinner with them and other family members in one of their homes. The next day I packed up and checked out of the hotel and began my trip to Germany to visit the village of Metzals. My mother's grandparents came to the United States from Metzals. After a two day visit, I went to Frankfurt, Germany and on September 22, 1997, I boarded a plane for home.

Charles R. Castellaw

The Way It Was

Epilogue

Seven years after my wife's death, I learned that Betty Jo's husband had died fourteen years earlier. I made arrangements, through one of Betty Jo's sisters, to visit her at her home in Memphis, Tennessee.

It had been fifty-three years since we had seen each other. After entering her house I looked at her and said, "You got away from me once but you are not going to get away from me again." After my first visit, I asked her to dinner. I went by Houston's, one of Memphis's premier restaurants and enlisted the aid of the hostess. I told her that I wanted to really impress my date that evening, as I had not seen her in 53 years. She agreed to help me.

When we walked into Houston's that night, it was very crowded. I walked right up to the hostess and said, "I'm Charles Castellaw." She said, "Follow me, Mr. Castellaw." We were led to a table on a raised platform with candles burning. Dinner was wonderful. I was old-fashioned and did not try to kiss Betty Jo goodnight.

During our brief courtship, I would drive approximately 150 miles each time to take her out. I would stay with a good friend. I remember one occasion when I tested the waters to see how I was doing. We talked about the Lonely Hearts Club and various singles groups. I told her I thought she should get into circulation, meet some nice man and start dating. She looked at me and said, "I want to go out with you and you alone." I knew I was headed in the right direction.

That Christmas Betty Jo spent the holiday with her youngest daughter in Virginia. I met her upon her return to Memphis. At the door I handed her a rather large gift-wrapped box. Inside she found a second box, then a third. Inside the third box was a diamond ring. To this point, we had not discussed marriage. As she looked at the ring, she asked when we were getting married. I said since it was already 4:30 on a Saturday afternoon, Monday would be soon enough. We set the date in March the 13th. She wondered how to tell her children. She had told them about me prior.

At that time, the phone rang and it was her oldest daughter. Betty Jo told her about our plans. Her daughter gave her blessing, as did her

Charles R. Castellaw

son. I felt her youngest daughter did not quite approve of the arrangements.

The Way It Was

On March 13, 1999, we were married in the First Evangelical Church in Memphis, Tennessee with family members and many friends attending. Afterwards we went to my home on the Kentucky Lake and spent a week together. For our honeymoon, we went on a cruise. Upon returning to Tennessee, we have resided in my home. The past three and a half years have been very happy. We have traveled quite a bit, two cruises, a twenty-one day European tour, and many trips throughout the States. Most of our time is spent on the lake, but we also stay at Betty Jo's home in Memphis at times. We plan to continue traveling as long as we are able.

Charles and Betty Jo Castellaw, February 13, 1998

Charles R. Castellaw

The Way It Was

Readings and Other Information

Charles Ray Castellw's personal experiences and experiences of others.

General Marshall's Victory Report, Biennial Report of the Chief of Staff of the U.S. Army 1943-45 to the Secretary of War.

Operations Report of the 30th Infantry Regiment from D-Day, Southern France to the end of the war in Europe.

U.S. Census Report, 1920.

The American Legion Magazines.

World War II Magazines.

Disable American Veterans Magazines.

History of the 30th Infantry Regiment WW II

Society of the 3rd Infantry Division

Center of Military History U.S. Army

National Infantry Museum, Fort Benning, Georgia.

Records Office, Haywood County Courthouse, Brownsville, Tennessee

Holly Grove, Jones Station and Wellwood Historicalture Society, Elma Ross Public Library, Brownsville, Tennessee

Air Force Historical Research Agency, Maxwell AFB, Montgomery, Ala.

United States Army in World War II, pub. 12-2&3, Center of Military History, United States Army

History of the Third Infantry Division in World War II

Printed in the United States
21801LVS00002B/45-110